W9-ACJ-612

Endless Things

Endless Things

Endless Things

Endless Things

a part of

ÆGYPT

John Crowley

Small Beer Press
Northampton, MA

This is a work of fiction. All characters and events portrayed in this book are either fictitious or used fictitiously.

Small Beer Press
176 Prospect Avenue
Northampton, MA 01060
www.smallbeerpress.com
info@smallbeerpress.com

Distributed to the trade by Consortium.

Library of Congress Cataloging-in-Publication Data

Crowley, John, 1942-
Endless things : a novel / John Crowley. -- 1st ed.
p. cm.
"Being the fourth part of Aegypt."
ISBN-13: 978-1-931520-22-5 (alk. paper)
ISBN-10: 1-931520-22-4 (alk. paper)
I. Title.

PS3553.R597E53 2007
813'.54--dc22

2006102023

First edition 1 2 3 4 5 6 7 8 9 0

Printed on Recycled Paper by Hamilton Printing in Rensselaer, New York.
Text set in Centaur MT 12.

"But then," I said, feeling a bit bemused, "would we have to eat again from the Tree of Knowledge, in order to fall back into the state of innocence?"

"Of course," he answered. "That is the final chapter of the history of the world."

—Heinrich von Kleist
"On the Marionette Theatre"

I
REGNUM

1

Y-tag was the designation that Hitler and the German high command gave to the day—it was September 2, 1939—on which they had determined to send their forces across the border into Poland. I don't know if this was the strategists' usual way of naming such a day, or was only invented for this day of this year. *Y-tag:* a juncture, a crossroads that could not ever afterward be returned to.

The weather was beautiful in that season of that year, endless hot golden stasis of possibility and sweetness: everyone remembers. In New York City the World's Fair was open, "Building the World of Tomorrow," and Axel Moffett went out with Winnie Oliphant in late September, along with Winnie's brother Sam and Sam's new wife, Opal. There was a special subway train that took them out from Grand Central, an express that stopped at its own brand-new station right at the Fair's gate. Tickets to the Fair cost seventy-five cents, but Axel noted that you could spend as much as five dollars for a book of tickets to all the big shows and a lunch too. "Let's just get in," said Sam.

Sam and Opal, living in Kentucky, hadn't met Axel Moffett before; he had been courting Winnie for some time, and she had been writing funny little disparaging notes about him to Sam in Kentucky, who said to Opal that he thought maybe the lady doth protest too much. Axel lived in Greenwich Village, and had met Winnie in Union Square, near where he worked and she was trying business school. They both liked to get a frank from a cart for lunch on nice days. Sam and Opal had come north in Sam's old Buick so Opal could meet the Oliphant family. Opal was pregnant already. "I hope it's a girl," she said when Winnie touched the dove gray gabardine over her stomach.

Axel bought a guidebook, whose cover showed the Trylon and Perisphere, and a white city, and crossing searchlights illuminating little airplanes. He searched in its pages, falling behind the others and then hurrying to catch up on his oddly small and well-shod feet. They came to the center, the Theme Center. "The only all-white buildings at the Fair," Axel read, and they looked up and up, shading their eyes, at the impossibly slim, impossibly aspiring thing. Inside the great white sphere there was a model city of the time to come, a small World of Tomorrow inside the big one. The line of people who had come from all over the country and the world to see it wound up the white ramps and bridges and stairs in their hundreds to the little door that gave into the sphere. "Too long," said Sam.

"We came on too nice a day," Opal said. "We should have come in the rain." They all laughed, because rain seemed so unlikely here; here the sky would always be this azure.

"Well, it is the Theme Exhibit," Axel said wistfully. He read from the guidebook: "'Here in the "Democracity" exhibit we are introduced to the tools and techniques necessary to live full lives in the world to come.'"

"We'll just have to take our chances, I guess," Sam said. "Where now?"

"I'd like to see the Kentucky exhibit," Opal said loyally.

"I don't think there is one," Axel said. "Not every state has one."

Everywhere they wandered they saw things vastly oversized, as though brought back from some titanic elsewhere by explorers, like King Kong. The cash register that counted the visitors to the Fair, as big as a cottage; an auto piston, working away obscenely; the world's largest typewriter; a giant bank vault door; the worker with his flame held aloft atop the tower of Russia's building. "USSR," said Sam. "Not Russia."

"So what do you think?" Opal asked Sam, taking his arm and glancing back at Winnie and Axel coming along behind.

"Well," said Sam. "I don't think he's the marrying kind."

"Oh Sam."

"I don't think so," Sam said, smiling.

"She's taller than he is," Opal said. Axel had stopped to light Winnie's Old Gold, though he didn't take one himself; he shook out the match with care. "That's always a little tough."

"Is that so?" said Sam, still smiling.

It was the cleanest public place they had ever been in. The thousands of well-dressed people walked or rode in little teardrop-shaped cars or took pictures of one another in front of gleaming buildings of white and pale pink and citron. Best dressed of all were the Negroes, in groups or couples, bright frocks and spectator shoes and wide hats like flowers. Opal took Sam's hand and glanced up at him (she was small, he was tall) and they were both thinking (not in words) that there really was going to be a new world, and maybe it wouldn't be possible to stay and raise a child—children—in the Cumberland highlands of Kentucky where nothing changed, or seemed only to get worse. No matter the pity and commitment you felt.

"Where now?" said Sam.

There were a hundred maps of the World of Tomorrow, all of them a little different. Some showed the buildings standing up in perspective, the spire and sphere, the strange streamlined shapes. Others showed the plan of colors, how each sector had its special color, which grew deeper the farther you got from the white center, so you always knew where you were. There were maps engraved on stone and maps on the paper place mats of the restaurant, blotted by the circles of their frosted glasses.

"Maybe Axel and I should head over to the Congress of Beauties," said Sam, who had taken Axel's guidebook and bent back the cover as though it were a *Reader's Digest.* "'A tribute to the body beautiful,'" he read. "'In a formal garden and woodland, there is room for several thousand people to view the devotees of health through sunshine.'"

"Sam," said Opal.

"It's okay," he said, grinning at Axel. "I'm a doctor. I'd be there if you fainted, too."

In the AT&T Building they took a hearing test and tried the Voice Mirror that let them hear their voices as others heard them; they sounded thin and squeaky in their own ears, even Axel's, which was studiedly rich and low. In the Demonstration Call Room, Opal was chosen by lot to be one of those allowed to make a telephone call to anywhere in the United States, no part of it unreachable any longer.

"Oh, that's too funny," Winnie said. Opal stepped up to the operator in uniform and headphone and gave her the number of the county clerk of Breshy County, Kentucky, who lived in the town of Bondieu. The operator turned to her switchboard and put through the call. Everyone in the Demonstration Call Room could hear the call make its way through the national web, from operator to operator, as lights lit up on a great map of America.

Central, said the operator in Bondieu, and the people in the Demonstration Call Room in Long Island made a small sound of awe.

The World's Fair operator gave her the number of the county clerk.

Oh, he ain't home, said Central. (Her name was Ivy. Opal felt a stab of homesickness.)

"Please put the call through," they heard the operator say.

I can tell you he ain't home, said Central. *I just now seen him out the winder, on his way to the drugstore.*

Now people in the Demonstration Call Room were starting to laugh.

"This call is coming from the New York World's Fair," the operator said, as primly, as mechanically as she could. "Please connect."

Well, all right, said Ivy. *But y'all gone get no satisfaction.*

Everyone but the operator was laughing now, listening to the phone ring in the empty house far away; laughing not in an unkind way, but only to show they knew that the World of Tomorrow might be a little farther off than it seemed to be here, which was no surprise really, and reflected badly on no one, not the backward little town or the flustered uniformed lady in her swivel chair. It was just time, time passing at different rates everywhere over the world, faster or more slowly. It was said that in that very moment the Polish cavalry officers were riding into battle on their horses against the German tanks, their swords lifted.

Before Poland's building at the Fair, tall and steely, almost hard to look up at in the noon sun, there was a statue of a Polish king on horseback, his two swords lifted and crossed in an X as though to bar entrance. "Ladislaus Jagiello," said Axel, not reading from the guidebook, where this king was unmentioned. "It must be."

"Well, sure," Sam said.

"Yes. Who defeated the Teutonic Knights. Yes." And he touched his straw fedora, to tip it back, or to salute.

They had come into the Court of the Nations, having lost the main way, so many forking paths. Axel kept stopping to pick up things on the ground, study them, discard them in the trash bins: helping to keep the place pristine, Sam said to Opal. There were flowers everywhere, banks and carpets and reaching spires, the same now as they had always been, always would be. "I love hydrangeas," Opal said, and cupped tenderly a round blue bloom as big as a baby's head.

It seemed that among these orgulous or clean-limbed buildings with their muscleman statues and ranked flags an argument was being conducted, claims put forward or refuted, that Americans like them were supposed to hear, if they could. "The Jewish Palestine pavilion," Axel read, somewhat asweat, unable to stop reading to the others even when they didn't listen. "A series of dioramas depicts the Holy Land of Yesterday and Tomorrow. Various displays portray the work of reclamation accomplished by Jewish settlers—the irrigation of desert wastes, the cultivation of farmlands. An answer to the charge of unproductiveness leveled at the Jew."

"Maybe it's time for lunch," said Sam.

Without noticing where they walked, they had come before the Czech pavilion. There was no longer a Czechoslovakia, and yet the pavilion was not closed, a plain smallish place like a new clinic or grade school. They walked around it but didn't go in, as though they might intrude on a private grief. They remembered hearing on the radio, the Red and the Blue Networks: the German army coming into Prague, the distant noise like the sea's roar that was the engines of the trucks and tanks or the sound of people cheering, for there were some who cheered.

"Where will they go now, what will become of them?" Winnie asked. She meant the stranded Czech workers inside.

"They can go home. I think they can."

"I think I wouldn't, even if I could."

"'An exhibition is devoted to the country's history and civilization,'" Axel read. "'A colorfully arranged travel exhibit illustrates scenic attractions within the recently revised borders.'"

"Bastards," said Sam.

There were letters running along the top of the building, carved in the stone, or made to look so. "What does it say?" Winnie asked.

"'When the wrath of the nations is passed,'" Axel and Sam read together, pointing up, "'the rule of thy country shall return to thee, O Czech people.'"

"Oh my God."

"It means the founding of the republic, after the war," Sam said. "It was meant to suggest that, I'd guess. Means something else now."

"Who said it? Whose name is it there?"

"Comenius," Sam read, and shrugged to indicate the name meant nothing to him, and turned away.

"Comenius," said Axel loudly, standing forth and seeming to glare at Sam, as though finally he had had enough, but of what? "John Comenius.

The Bohemian educator and thinker. Sixteen hundreds. The founder of education, of modern education, educational methods, yes right. A man of peace, exiled, roamed the world looking for help. From every king and ruler. Every king and ruler."

He snatched his hat from his head, and pressed it to his bosom. "Yes. Yes. The Thirty Years' War. The wrath of the nations. He fled. Fled the invading Hapsburg army. Wandered the world for years, never to return."

They all looked at him, for they hadn't heard anyone say *never to return* like that and mean it.

Never to return. To many Fair visitors in that month, not just to those four, there would come a moment like this one, when they knew what way the world would take, indeed had already set out on. Sam and Opal, Winnie and Axel: even though almost two years followed in their lives that seemed not so different from other years, when people got married and had children and died and were buried and the world of tomorrow both arrived and came no closer, everything at last did take that way, which no one wanted and everyone expected.

Pierce Moffett, Axel and Winnie's son, would come to know this story well: he would make his mother tell it over to him before he could really understand it, for it contained the mystery of his origins. How his mother- and father-to-be rode out to the Fair side by side in the subway, and said not a shy word to each other; how his aunt Opal put in a call to the little town in Kentucky, and everyone laughed. How Axel then took Winnie to spaghetti restaurants in the Village, museums uptown; how they got their marriage license at City Hall, amid the soldiers and sailors and the girls they'd soon be parted from. And how in the middle of the war he, Pierce, came to be; how glad they were, how much they loved him.

The day after Pearl Harbor, Sam Oliphant went down to the recruiting center, and within weeks he was uniformed and in command of a medical unit. Doctors were badly needed. He came home on leave for a week and kissed his children and his wife farewell and flew out to Hawaii, and then he was sent farther and farther into the great Western sea. Winnie watched the gray battleships cut the brilliant water in the newsreels, the flotillas of planes cut the foamy clouds, planes whose crews Sam attended. Opal sent on to her the flimsy sheets of V-mail that Sam wrote, jokey and sweet and scary. Often he couldn't name the places he was, but sometimes he could, and Axel and she would look at the atlas and try to find them. *Adagios of islands,* Axel said.

Axel was not called up: something, some weakness or problem, kept him out. He did war work alongside people with exemptions or disabilities that were often a lot more obvious than his. He had a lapel button to wear, and moved it carefully each night from blue suit to gray. Before Winnie too could find something to do, she learned she was pregnant.

On hot nights in that summer, when she could no longer bear to sit in their apartment by the fan, legs splayed like a fat person and mouth open, Axel took her on the Staten Island Ferry to get a breeze. Some days when he was at work, she went to the air-conditioned movies. Or she went over to Manhattan and uptown to the Metropolitan Museum, cool and huge, or the Museum of Natural History, not walking far within but finding a gallery or room she liked and sitting, placid as a houseplant in the dimness.

Natural history: the words soothed and calmed her all by themselves, not merely different from corrosive human history but its antidote. A nightmare from which I am trying to awaken: that's what Axel said history was. That was only another quotation, though; Axel didn't mind history, he loved it actually, and seemed not to see that it led to this, to people's brothers and husbands being sundered from them and sent far away for remote causes, for vengeance or conquest or to stop wrongdoing, whatever history's reasons were.

She walked in the room of Asian fauna, where animals and birds from the Pacific were mounted and put behind glass in spaces that reproduced the lands they came from, far islands whose names she read with a shock, for they were the very ones that were now in the papers and in Sam's letters, where the terrible fighting was going on; they appeared in the newsreels blasted and smoky and gray, but here they were green and altogether still. New Guinea. Samoa. The Solomons. Fabulous birds in a thousand colors who had lived there unobserved for centuries, for all time. The diorama of Samoa was set high on a cliff above the sea, looking down through the leaves and vines to an empty beach; it took you a while to see, perched at the end of a twisted limb, a small brilliant bird.

Empty. Before humans. Winnie after the months of fear—months of thinking about those soldiers and their fear when they had to go ashore on such beaches against the Jap machine guns and then pour fire into their holes to burn them out—was tempted to wish men or Man had never gone to those places, never found them and put them at risk so thoughtlessly. For there were no birds there now, she bet, no blossoms. Which led to the thought that it would be better if men hadn't come to be at all, the peace and endlessness without them: and she drew away from that thought in a little awe.

Sam returned unhurt. Coming down whole and hale (a little fatter, even) from the great brown plane almost before its props stopped turning, one of so many in their billed or cloth caps, brown leather jackets, brown ties tucked into their shirts. A major: they had told him that if he stayed in he'd be made a colonel in two years. Winnie and Axel and their son Pierce on the tarmac behind the fence, with Opal and Sam's son and daughter, and all the other wives and children.

Winnie thought later that it must be Pierce's first memory, and he came to believe that it might be, that the little brown pictures Opal took—of Sam holding his son Joe aloft, Sam grinning cheek to cheek with his sister—were things he had seen and stored away. The small flag he was given to wave. How he cried when Sam bent to dandle him, cried and cried till Sam took off the scary phallic cap.

It was in any case the first time he ever saw the man under whose roof and rule he would live for ten years.

You remember the reason for that: how Winnie learned what kind of man Axel was, not the marrying kind (it was Axel himself who told her, in tears, late in the night or early in the morning of a day in Pierce's tenth year, Pierce asleep in the far room); what things he had done before his marriage, maybe even after it, the felony arrest long ago that had made him undraftable, she stopped her ears at that point. *The way I'm made,* he said.

When she packed her bags and took her son to live in Kentucky with her newly widowed brother (for it was Opal, beautiful, wise Opal, who didn't live long, and Sam who was left to mourn), it was as though her own life bent backward just at that awful juncture, returned to take instead a way that she had projected for herself when she was a child; as though Axel's sin or sickness had been the necessary condition by which she took her rightful place beside her brother, in his kitchen and on the distaff side of his fireplace, in her chair just smaller than his. It seemed—not in the first flush of horror and amazement, but not very long after—so clear a case of benevolent or at least right-thinking Destiny in action that she really held nothing against Axel, and even let Pierce spend days with him now and then in Brooklyn when the family came north.

She never could bring herself to touch him again, though.

The way Pierce pleased his father when they were together (and he did want to please him, mostly) was to listen to him talk, as Winnie had done, and which Pierce did then and ever after. Axel was one of those people who seem to have been born without a filter between brain-thought and tongue-thought: to be with him was to be set afloat or submerged in his tumbling stream of consciousness, where floated odd learning, famous names, the movie version of his own life and adventures, fragments of verse and song, injunctions, dreads, self-pity, antique piety, the catchphrases of a thousand years. *With how sad steps O Moon thou climb'st the skies,* he would say; *rum, sodomy, and the lash; inter fæces et urinam nascimur,* plangently in altar-boy pronunciation; *Count Alucard? Why I don't believe that's a Transylvanian name. . . .* He could often seem like other people when in public, but alone with you he overflowed those banks, and you fled or you followed: whether borne along as Winnie had been, trailing one hand, or poling as fast as you could down the same thousand-branching streams and through its bogs and backwaters, as Pierce felt he must. He could weary of Axel, but he never despised him, because he was never taught that what Axel possessed wasn't worth possessing, and also because he was afraid to: afraid that if he hurt his father he would hurt him mortally, and so lose the last of something that he had already lost nearly all of, without which he would cease to exist.

Anyway he liked knowing things. From his earliest years he gathered things to know like grain, and never forget them afterward. He learned what Axel knew, and then later he learned where Axel had learned those things; he came to know many things Axel would never learn. When Axel was on TV—an unbelievable overturning of the natural course of things, that he should be there, looking like himself but smaller and smoother: a doll of himself, answering questions on a famous quiz show for big money—Pierce knew the answer to the question that finally stopped him. You could only miss one, and then you left, shaking the hand of the host and the other guy, who looked like Arnold Stang and sounded like somebody else entirely.

The question that stopped Axel was *What is the Samian letter, and after whom is it named?*

Pierce Moffett was a junior at St. Guinefort's Academy then, watching TV in the crowded student lounge—you may not remember that, but maybe you remember the tick-tock music that played while Axel stared like a damned soul, everybody who heard it played week after week remembers it. And Pierce knew: he knew what the Samian letter was, and after whom it was named, and his father didn't.

2

Y.

It stood at the head of the tall double-columned page, above and precedent to all things that only begin with Y, Yaasriel and Yalkut and Yggdrasil and Yoga and Yoruba: both a signum and its initial, which is what had attracted Pierce's attention to it. Only A and O and X were accorded the same status in this book, which was called *A Dictionary of the Devils, Dæmons, and Deities of Mankind,* by Alexis Payne de St.-Phalle.

The twenty-fifth letter of the English alphabet, the book told him, *it is also the tenth of the Hebrew—the Yod. Its numerical equivalent is Ten, the perfect number. In the Hebrew Cabala it is the* membrum virile *and is expressed by the hand with bent forefinger. The Y, or upsilon, is the* litera Pythagoræ, *and was long believed to have been first constructed by the Samian philosopher himself (it was often called the "Samian letter") and its mystic significance is Choice: the two branches signify the paths of Virtue and Vice respectively, the narrow right way leading to virtue, the wider left to vice.*

Pierce didn't know then why ten was the perfect number, but he guessed what a *membrum virile* might be (bent his forefinger to resemble his own). After some searching he found the Samian philosopher too: avoider of beans, reincarnationist, man-god.

A sign for human life, its form taken from crossroads and tree forks and the springing of arches. Lydgate will have it that the stem stands for the years of youth, before the hard choices of maturity are made. In Christian thought its branches separate Salvation and Damnation, the horns of the tree of life, the Cross. Nor does this exhaust its significations: a more secret dogma is supposed to be expressed in it, one that certain Rosicrucians pretended to be on the point of disclosing, before that sect spoke no more.

At the age he was when he first read this—ten or eleven—Pierce had no sense of how much time or space separated these characters, Samians and Hebrews and Rosicrucians; somehow they all existed together in the root of time, back before the choice of a way was made. Gathered together in this book they seemed gathered in a world of their own, openable and closable, discrete, though containing many things his own world also did. Later on he would wonder if certain pages of it hadn't become entangled with his growing brain, so that he wouldn't always know what he had taken from it and what he had conceived himself. He could be haunted for days by a not-quite-recoverable image—a blackened obelisk, with palms and elephant; or find himself saying over and over to himself like a charm or a madman's rant a word that he seemed to have made up but surely hadn't (*Yggdrasil, Adocentyn*), and he would, sometimes, guess that that book was the source. Sometimes it was.

Pierce never revealed that he'd known the answer to the question that defeated Axel.

So he had had his own secrets and unsayable things, things out of which a double life is made, as his father's and his mother's lives were made of them. Sometimes laid deep like mines or bombs (he thought you'd have to explain this to young people nowadays, who didn't live such lives, probably) so that you had to proceed with care along your way, not come upon them unexpectedly or at the wrong time, at a juncture, and have them explode.

Homo, viator in bivio, the Latin Church declared, offering to help. Man, voyager on forking paths. There's no provision, though, for going *back,* is there, back over the thrown Y switches of our lives, the ones that shot our little handcar off its straight way and onto the way we took instead, as in the silent comedies that Axel loved: no way to go back and fix the thing broken, or break the silence that later exploded. An infinite number of junctures lies between us and that crisis or crux, and passing back again across each one would generate by itself a further juncture, a double infinity, an infinitesimal calculus; you'd never get back to there, and if you could you'd never return again to here where you started from: and why would you need to go back in the first place except to learn how to go on from right here, to go on along the way you have to go?

And yet we want always, always to go back. What if we could, we think, what if we could. We want to make our way back along those tracks, over every switch, to the single, consequential divide: there where we can see ourselves still standing, indecisive and hesitant, or cocksure and about to step off firmly in the wrong direction. We want to appear before ourselves—shockingly old, in strange clothes (though not so strange as we then imagined we would by now be wearing)—and clothed too in the authority of the uncanny. We want to take ourselves aside, in the single brief moment that would be allotted us, and give ourselves the one piece of advice, the one warning, the one straight steer that will put us on the correct road, the road we should take, the road we have a *right* to take, for it is truly ours.

Then to make our way forward again, through all the new branching ways, to where we left from, which will *not* be the same place, but instead will be the place we ought to be, the course of our real lives.

We plot and plan how we might help ourselves out of every little pitfall and pothole—*not the checked suit, you dope; lose the checked suit*—no that's idle, not worth the investment of longing, of rewriting. But oh if we could decide on just the one moment, the one *critical* moment, and we can; and if we could reduce the time asked for to the barest minimum, no big discourse but only the few minatory words that would change everything, the words that we could not have thought or said then. *Marry her. Don't marry her.* Surely if the time required were so little, and only the one instance asked for, and the need so obvious.

When we come to cease fretting in this way, if we ever do cease, then at the same time we come to know, for sure, that we will die.

Pierce Moffett had known times (more than one, each one canceling all the former ones) when his need to go and knock on his own door had been so great, the bleak longing for things not to have turned out as they had so intense, that he was able to believe for a second or two that an exception to a universal one-way rule might be made just for him, since it was so clear what he ought to have done: not panic or dither or comically misunderstand or fall into mind-clouding passions, but to be temperate, fair, and wise. Of course and always, this involved not being himself as he had once been, but himself as he had later become, had become because of the very vicissitudes through which he had passed, on the very roads he had chosen or been forced along, suffering what he there suffered, learning what he learned.

Now he was older than his father had been when he blew the question about the Samian letter on network television; he had long ago wished his last desperate with-all-his-heart wish. He did know very well that he would die, and he knew what was still left for him to do so that he might earn that death. He wouldn't go back if he could. And yet he was still one who spent or wasted much mental time in reviewing past choices and chances, even without that irritable striving toward correcting them. He did it with events in history, he did it with the lives of his parents, with his own life too: tugging on the infinite lines, to see what he might have caught instead. And the place he now was—the place he had come to—was the right place to ponder: the things he once did that he should not have done, the things he should have done and did not do. Years could be spent here in the contemplation.

Pierce lifted his eyes from his endless copy work, and fetched breath. It was spring, and opalescent buds were visible on the twig tips of the espaliered shrubs that branched and rebranched across the walls of the walled garden outside his door, a garden no bigger than the little room he sat in.

Go back, go back. This is how you climb Mount Purgatory, by going on and back at once. And it gets easier (they all say) the farther up you get.

The low bells rang for Terce, calling the brothers from field and cell and workshop to their prayers.

3

Years before, Pierce set out from the little house he then had in the Faraway Hills, going by bus to New York City, where he had lived before that, thence to travel by air to the Old World. He was bound by a spell he had mistakenly cast on his own soul, and a number of small devils had attached themselves to him; they rose away like blackbirds from a cornfield when he shook himself hard enough spiritually, but settled again as soon as his attention was turned. He wasn't the first traveler to hope that if he moved fast enough they might fall behind.

The Rasmussen Foundation—Boney Rasmussen himself, in fact—had commissioned the trip, though Boney was now dead and what he wanted Pierce to accomplish abroad was perhaps therefore made moot. The Rasmussen Foundation had chosen Pierce because he had discovered, in the home of the late novelist Fellowes Kraft, an unfinished historical epic or fantasia of Kraft's that Boney Rasmussen had been sure was a map or a plan or a guide or a masque or an allegory of some kind that he, Pierce, was uniquely equipped to explicate. Pierce had with him a couple of just-pressed credit cards, the bills for which would be going to the Rasmussen Foundation's accountant ("Don't you lose them," Rosie Rasmussen, the foundation's new director, told him as she tugged straight the lapels of his overcoat), and a pocketful of cash as well, in the form of azure Peregrine's Cheques, each with the familiar little etched cartouche containing St. James with staff and shell.

Also, he had a new red notebook, made in China; an old guidebook, also red, once the property of Fellowes Kraft, annotated by him in ghostly pencil; and Kraft's autobiography, *Sit Down, Sorrow,* a limited edition probably not meant for a vade mecum and looking to fall apart before the journey was done.

From those two books, and from some letters of Kraft's to Boney and other remains, Pierce and Rosie had worked out an itinerary. Modeled on Kraft's last trip to Europe in 1968, ten years before and more, it was basically a running line connecting certain map names, some of them very well known and some not: cities and towns, empty plains, fortresses, rooms in high castles, views from promontories. It was arranged west to east, for convenience; it ought maybe to have been more roundabout, narratively, but still it had a shape as laid out that wasn't untrue to the logic of his pursuit, logic being mostly all it had. It would bear him beyond the Iron Curtain if he followed it to the end, a prospect he found absurdly unsettling: to high mountains where ancient medicinal baths bubbled and stank, and in summer porcine party leaders (crowned heads, once) lay sunk in warm mud. From such a spa Kraft had years before sent home a telegram to Boney Rasmussen: *Have what we sought for, packed w/ troubles in old kit bag.*

At last to the marvelous caves, high up and down deep, that were marked with two stars in the red guidebook (Pierce was studying it again as his bus pulled into Port Authority station in New York City): one a printed star and the other drawn by Kraft in pencil, the quick star we make with a single running line. *Crossing a narrow trestle bridge over a cascade that falls to the valley of the Elbe, we pass for 10 km along the Polish-Czech frontier, and then we join again the road from Joachimsbad. A short but stiff climb takes us up to the cavern entrance, from where guided tours descend several times daily to the wonders below the earth.*

Despite this prolepsis, Pierce wasn't sure in what his pilgrimage would issue, if in anything. Certainly it was for no discoveries that she supposed he would make that Rosie Rasmussen had sent Pierce off; it was more for his own sake, as she sent her daughter off on some task—to gather flowers, or water them—when the griefs of life came too close, and threatened to engulf her. Pierce was supposed to have a book of his own to finish, too, that he was to do research for in the libraries of England and Europe; but what he hadn't told Rosie, sure that if she knew she would withdraw the foundation's offer, was that there was no book; he had ceased trying to write it.

These nesting negatives—the thing Fellowes Kraft had not really brought home, or Boney had not got from him; the book he hadn't finished, and the one Pierce couldn't write; Rosie's unbelief, and the untruths of the ages that in her opinion had fed Boney's unwillingness to see life, and death, as they are—ought to have added up to only a bigger nothing, but descending from the bus at Port Authority Pierce didn't feel foolish or imposed upon, or even as wretched as he had long been feeling. The air—his own, not the city's—seemed terribly clear for once, the world somber and chastened, emptied somehow but real: as it can seem the day after a dreadful storm-driven argument with a loved one, in which things long unsaid are said or shouted, and then can never be withdrawn. What now? you think on such a day. What now?

He climbed from the bus at the central station and went out into the streets. It was February, and the stirred pudding of snow and filth was thick; the year was an abyssal one in the life of his old city, all former hopes seemingly defeated and the new wealth, though coming on, not yet apparent or even able to be conceived of, by Pierce anyway.

First he had to go twenty blocks south, to where his agent had her office, not different from her apartment, a place he'd never seen before. Julie Rosengarten had shared his own apartment in another part of town, another world-age than this one. He had a tale to tell her, heavier to carry than the bags he lugged, about how he would not be writing the book that she had, on the basis of a few pages of mystification, sold for him to a great and impatient publisher. He was embarrassed at his failure, but more embarrassed at the thing itself that he had conceived of, and as glad to be free of it as a man who has lost a gangrened limb: the rest of him was all the sounder. It was a dumb idea, transcendently, flagrantly dumb, a cheap trick if it had worked and it would not have worked. If ever he wanted to achieve something in history or scholarship, he had to drown those kittens, and never tell.

But passing down through the metropolis, he thought why these scruples, why had his feet grown cold, didn't he see which side his bread was buttered on? If there wasn't this to do, what the hell would there be? And what big crime was the metaphysical trick his proposed book was to play when weighed against the other things now jostling one another onto the best-seller lists (Pierce still kept tabs on these lists)—the sequel, for instance, to *Phæton's Car*, all about alien visitations in ancient times, by an author once held up to Pierce as an example of how far he might go and not be scorned; another, about Jesus faking his own execution and escaping to England, himself his own Grail, thence to Spain where he founded a royal line, his heirs still traceable today. Or *You Can Profit from the Coming Last Days*, twenty weeks on the list. Or—everyone was reading it, Pierce saw its glossy black covers everywhere—a long tract about fairies, and their world inside this one, and an endless winter they will turn at last to spring.

And yet:

"I can't write it," he said to Julie. "I'm not going to."

"Oh for God's sake, Pierce."

"No, really."

"Writers hit these blocks. I know. Believe me."

Subtly plumper, and richer in more ways than one, Julie had otherwise remained the same: her face a direct descendant of the one he'd known, her place her place, and recognizable as such the moment he looked around.

"Tell me," she said.

"I just," he said. "I just can't go on pretending that I believe these things are possible."

"What things?"

"All the things. More than one history of the world. Magic. Cosmic crossroads, world-ages, an altered physics. The possibilities."

"Possibilities are always possible," Julie said.

"Tell me what'll happen when I inform them I can't do the book. I've sort of spent all the money."

"Pierce, listen."

"I could offer them something else instead. I don't know what." Around him on her high shelves, on her desk and on her bed, were other possibilities: mystery, horror, romance, true crime, sex advice, pathos. All of those he had suffered.

"Just show me what you have."

"I didn't bring it. I left it behind."

She regarded him in some disgust. "Okay, what happens," she said, "is that we say nothing to them. When your deadline comes we say nothing. When they ask about it we say you've run into some difficulties and are hard at work on them, and we get another deadline; we don't ask for the next installment on the advance. Time passes."

"Uh huh."

"Meanwhile lots of things could happen. You could change your mind, and you will, or if you don't you could change the book. The publisher could change his mind, decide he doesn't want the book, return you the rights. The publisher could go out of business."

"The horse could learn to talk."

"Anyway what you don't do is give the money back. For sure not yet."

"My father owns a house in Brooklyn," Pierce said. "I'm not sure what its situation is, but I thought maybe I could borrow against it."

Her look of disgust had softened to a kind of amusement, with something long-suffering in it; for just a moment she resembled his mother. "Pierce," she said.

"All right, all right."

"So who's paying for this trip you're taking?" she asked. "And isn't it part of the same mission? The same, I mean, project?"

"Yes, in a way."

"Are you going to give them back their money?"

"Well, theirs is a grant," he said. "It's sort of exploratory. I mean nothing necessarily has to come of it. Nothing has to be produced." He smiled and shrugged: *that's all I know*. For a time they regarded each other, not yet thinking of the long-ago life they had shared, but not thinking anything else either.

"You okay?" she said then.

"I don't know."

"Then that's not okay."

"You know when all this started?" he said.

"All what?"

"This thing I'm doing. Or actually not doing. It was a night on Tenth Street. The night of the student takeover at Barnabas College. Remember?"

"I remember that day," she said. "Listen. Will you send me what you've got? Maybe I can think about it."

"Ægypt," he said. "That was the day, or the night, I remembered. You were in bed. It was hot. I stood at the window."

Come to bed she had said to him, stoned and sleepy; he wasn't sleepy, though the short night was all but gone. Earlier that day the little college where he taught had been taken over by young people (some not so young) demanding Paradise now, and other things; faculty, including Pierce, locked themselves in their offices till the students were ejected by police. Pierce, released and having returned to his railroad flat downtown, thought he could still taste tear gas in the midnight air. Anyway the neighborhood around was all alive and murmuring, as though on its way, a caravan drawn on toward the future from the past, going by him where he stood. And he knew that of course you had to be on their side, you had to be, but that he himself must go back, if he could, and he knew that he could. While the others went on, he would go back, to the city in the farthest east of that old land, the city Adocentyn.

Dawn winds rising as night turned pale. It was there that it started; and if it wasn't there it was somewhere else, near there or far off, where? If it had no starting place, it could have no ending.

"I'll do what I can," he said.

He got off the train again in Brooklyn, at Prospect Park, to walk the rest of the way; to see the arch at Grand Army Plaza, walk west to Park Slope past the Montauk Club, where his father used to point to the Venetian arches and brickwork, talk about Ruskin, and show him the frieze that displays the history of the Montauk Indians in terra-cotta. Terra-cotta. Pietre-dure. Gutta-percha. Cass Gilbert, the architect who designed the Woolworth Building, once lived in that pleasant brownstone, built by himself. He had stopped to greet Axel one day, one day long ago, an aged, aged man; Pierce was a boy in a gabardine suit with short pants, and was given a nickel with a bison on one side and an Indian, not a Montauk, on the other.

Was it so? He had been plagued lately by false memories suddenly occurring to him, more vivid and sudden than the real thing, unless they *were* the real thing, rushing in to supplant the old memories, themselves now become false.

His own old house. All through his childhood he had carried a key to this door, his latchkey (the only one he had ever referred to so). And then somewhere he had lost it and never replaced it. He went to press the bell's cracked black nipple—beside it the little typewritten card yellowed and faint with his own last name on it, the selfsame as ever—and then he noticed that the door was not fully shut.

He pushed it open and stepped in. On the entranceway floor a mosaic of two dolphins chasing each other's tails. A thousand Brooklyn buildings had one like it; it had made Axel talk of Etruscans and Pompeii and the Baths of Caracalla, and Gravely the super had used to wash it and wax it often. It could hardly be seen now. Gravely was dead: the last time Pierce spoke to Axel, Axel had told him that. Pierce when he was a child had always been told to call him Mr. Gravely, as though the world probably wouldn't readily grant him that honor and Pierce must remember to.

The door of Axel's apartment on the second floor stood open too.

Hearing laughter inside, Pierce looked in, and the laughter ceased. Three guys, stretched at their ease on his father's ancient furniture, looked upon him; they certainly seemed at home, booted feet on the coffee table and beer bottles close at hand on the floor.

"Hi," Pierce said.

"Looking for somebody?"

"Axel. Axel Moffett."

From the bathroom in the hall there came then, as though summoned by Pierce's request, another man, barefoot, plucking at the front of his sweatpants. By their looks the three on the couch referred Pierce to him.

"Yeah?"

He had a gold cross in the V of his shirt, a broken nose like a thug in the funny papers, and a watchcap on his grizzled head.

"Where's Axel?" Pierce asked.

"Who wants to know?"

"I'm his son."

"You're kidding."

"No."

"Well, for Christ's sake." He scratched his head, rubbing the rough cap back and forth with a forefinger, and regarded Pierce's bags. "You come to stay?"

"No actually."

"There's room."

"No. I'm only here one night. I'm flying to Europe tomorrow."

"No shit." The man seemed unimpressed, maybe unconvinced, and went on regarding Pierce with what seemed a hostile, reptilian scrutiny, unblinking. "Axel know that?"

"I came to tell him."

Two of the three on the couch now laughed, as though they found this comically inadequate, which it was. The older man looked their way, and they stopped.

"So anyway you came," he said to Pierce. "That's something." He came close to Pierce and put out a large and knob-knuckled hand, unsmiling still. "Pierce."

"Yes." The grip was iron.

"Good."

"Where is he now, can you tell me?" Pierce asked. "Do you know?"

"I got some ideas. Some of the guys started the celebration early." Knowing laughter from the boys on the couch. "He's with them. The usual places."

"Celebration."

"Don't worry. It'll cycle back here. Or we can go hunt 'em up. You won't miss a thing."

For a time the two looked at each other as, with gradual certainty, Pierce came to understand.

"His birthday," he said.

"Sixty-three," said the watchcap. And of course it was, noble, benevolent Aquarius. He knew that. And now he knew the man before him too. This was the Chief, of whom Axel had told him: the Navy man (retired) who managed a team of young working men, who earned extra money and got away from their families on weekends by doing reclamation in Brooklyn buildings. Axel was accountant and factotum. Pierce didn't know they had moved in, apparently to stay.

"Europe," the Chief said, whose unwavering gaze was unsettling, and intended no doubt to be so. Pierce wondered what they had done to Axel. Or taken from him. There were so many disasters Axel could let himself in for, his misapprehensions and his grandeurs. "Whatcha want over there?"

"It's sort of a research trip," Pierce said. "Historical research." He turned away then, as though this answer were sufficient, to study the battered apartment, the building materials stacked against the wall, the rolled rug in the corner. A battered birdcage lay in pieces, the bird flown or dead; gone.

"Yeah, we're working on the place," said the Chief. "The whole building. We got the tenants out and we're upgrading. What we're doing for Axel. I'll show you around."

There was a pounding of feet on the stair, past the door, on upward to the third floor, leaving a mephitic trail of cheerful obscenities as it went up. The three men on Axel's couch arose as one to follow, calling out as they left. *A. A.*

"You know he really shouldn't drink a lot," Pierce said.

"So you'll be staying tonight," the Chief said. "He'll be glad. You know he always expects you. See, your bed's made."

It was. The old chenille bedspread it had always worn, a new slough in its middle, though.

"Sixty-three," said the Chief, observing the bed with Pierce as though there were someone in it. "So you would have been born 1942 or so?"

"Um yes."

"I was in the Pacific then."

"Aha."

"Axel missed the big one. Never mind." He scratched his head again, a habit. "You want coffee? A beer?"

"No neither," Pierce said. "Actually I may not be able to stay. I thought I'd get out toward the airport, you know, get a motel room out there, so I'd be close in the morning. My flight's early." None of this was true.

"Naw," said the Chief.

"And in fact," Pierce said, "I have to go back to Manhattan for a while tonight. This evening. Shortly."

The Chief was still shaking his head. "You'll leave the bags here," he said, his voice harsh from a lifetime of barking orders. "You'll come back tonight. Axel will be here, you'll have a drink with us, in the morning we'll take you out to Idlewild in the truck."

"JFK," said Pierce.

"Listen," said the Chief, advancing. "I'll tell you something. There is nothing you could want that can't be found right here. In Brooklyn. In the five boroughs at the *most*."

Somewhere in the building something heavy fell or was thrown down the stairs, while men laughed.

"I guess that must be true," Pierce said.

"You're not shittn me," said the Chief. Pierce now noticed that the man's right finger and thumb ticked rhythmically together. Effects of drink, or a palsy. "You know he needs somebody. If it's not you it's got to be somebody."

Pierce said nothing.

"The man's a genius," the Chief said. "What he knows." He tapped a temple with his forefinger. "Maybe you take after him."

Nothing.

"A good man too. He knows something about loyalty. Actually a lot."

Pierce was uncertain how long he could stand up under these implied reproaches. He managed to nod, slightly and solemnly. On the floor above, the roughhouse (as Axel would surely call it) worsened. A fight, maybe a mock fight, punches thrown, thud of boots. *Fawken A. Fawken assho.*

"So," said Pierce. "Okay."

From an ashtray on the mantelpiece the Chief took a business card. "You probably know the number here," he said, and Pierce did, even the old letter exchange that had once named his neighborhood, its bounds mysterious. Only by means of the dial plates of phones could you discover what places were within it and what places were outside it; the candy store nearby was in, so was the branch library blocks away, but the movie theater on the avenue wasn't. "There's another number too. We got a warehouse space in Greenpoint."

Pierce looked at the card, which bore their numbers, and a cartoon crown, chosen from a printer's catalog.

Park Reclamation and Renovation
Warehousing *Fulfillment*

He thought: What if it's all all right, and they will be kind to him, and cherish him; keep him from harm, and not fall into fools' errors, make bad decisions; will think of him and his unworldliness when they dream up their schemes? What is fulfillment, and how do they do it?

"Okay," he said again, and took the Chief's hand. Outside the naked windows (what had become of their lifelong brown drapes?) a short day was closing, the black skyline and the sky too familiar. "I gotta go."

She lived up on the Upper East Side, almost under the shadow of the Queensborough Bridge, in a five-story building that was once also shadowed by the rattling El. It was ready now for the renovators and reclaimers, to turn its railroad apartments into expensive studios, but that hadn't happened so far.

The front door was open, maybe stood open always—Pierce hadn't ever been here before, had only heard about it from her on the phone, those rare times she called. He went up. They didn't know, his neighbors up in the country, the feel of these banisters thick with a hundred coats of cheap enamel, these worn rubber treads. He had lived for years going up and down stairs like these, streets like these. And then he had left at last, impelled by her to take another way.

He had used to call her Sphinx, softly in her ear in bed, and then later to himself when he thought of her. Not for her silence, she was a Chatty Cathy most of the time, but for her fine-boned cat's body and the gloss of her thick fur and the alien eyes in her human face. And for the riddle she posed maybe, for she was a Gypsy, or her mother was: *gitana*, race of Egypt once though no more. Her name had been Diamond Solitaire when she toured with a ragtag theater company of trannies and egotists, still her friends, doing improv and performance pieces in shifting venues. But back before that, when she was unfolding in her unmarried mother's womb, she needed a name (her mother thought) that such a girl as she growing up would want and need to have, a name sturdy and lusterless but not plain or gray; and so she got the name that nuns and her stepfather and unemployment offices would all call her, if no one else. Her mother believed she'd made the name up herself, and in a sense she had, though it wasn't her daughter alone who bore it.

This was her door. On it was a big decal, the red oval of the Holmes Security Agency, an armed Athena and a sunset or sunrise. Premises Protected. He doubted that; a piece of city irony. He listened at the door to what he might hear within (nothing) and then he knocked, and found that so far from being locked it wasn't even shut.

"Charis," he said. "Hey."

The door opened at his push and he saw her rising from a sofa, or a mattress clothed in figured stuffs, a stricken look for a moment on her face that cut him as the same face could in dreams. Then that passed, and simple delight replaced it.

"Oh my God! Pierce!"

He opened his arms, hands displayed, here I am, as I am. She opened her arms too and they embraced lightly, tentatively.

"Pierce," she said. "My god. Back in the big city."

"Just for a day."

"Then home to the country?"

"No. I'm going to Europe."

"Gee, wow," she said. "Europe. How fun. You'll love it."

They stood together in the doorway a long moment, uncertain. Then she pulled him into the apartment.

It was as he imagined it might be, just as. Here were the ad hoc furnishings made from street finds, the walls of alligatored tenement paint disguised in hangings, like a khan's tent. Here were the things she now made her living buying and selling, gathered on her daily hunts through junk shops and rummage sales and the Salvation Army store. She'd once told him that when she was young she thought the Salvation Army had been formed for just this, the salvation of your old stuff from eternal discarding: your hats and coats and sunsuits and stopped clocks and three-legged chairs.

She took a seat, her seat, on the pillowed mattress on the floor, folding up with an easeful practiced motion, like a cat. "So hey," she said; she looked at him, and laughed, as if he'd prompted a funny memory of their life together, though he'd done nothing.

He sat on a low velvet hassock.

"You going alone?" she asked. "All by your lonesome?"

"Yep." He nodded, nodded, no help for it.

"I'd go," she said.

"Hey," he answered, and opened his hands again, ready when you are, any time; and he felt a long impossible future come to be and then burn out.

"So you didn't get married, out there in the country," she said to him.

"No. Nope."

"Nobody good enough for you."

"Right."

"You're a good guy," she said. "You deserve somebody good."

"Don't say that," he said.

She picked up from the cluttered low table beside her—it was a wooden cable spool, he guessed, covered in scarves—a cigarette holder, jade.

"How's your mother?" he asked.

"Aw. The same."

He thought of her mother's apartment, a big old-fashioned place on the other side of town, where at Christmas once an old Gypsy woman had told his fortune. An old, old Gypsy; and her mother; and her.

"And you?" he asked. "Steady guy?"

"Two," she said, and laughed. "Yeah. I sort of got them spelling each other, you know?"

"Do they know about each other?"

"Actually no. One of them works way downtown, days, and I see him at night. The other is up around here, and works nights. So."

"Cox and Box," said Pierce.

"You're not kidding," she said. "Anyway it's fun." She turned the cigarette holder in her small smooth hands. "So come on," she said. "Tell me how you've been. You know you don't look all that hot. I don't know about the beard."

He had just begun to grow it. He rubbed it now, a scratchy sound. "Not all that hot, no."

"No?"

He clutched his brow, and she came closer to where he sat, and, smiling, put a hand on his knee. "I'll tell you something," he said. "When I moved out of the city. After you . . . well. The day I moved out. I made myself a promise. That I'd give up on love."

Still smiling, she shook her head: don't get it.

"I thought I'd had enough," he said. "After you. I mean enough in both senses. Enough to last me; and as much as I could take."

"Wow," she said. "Dumb idea."

He nodded. But it was true: he had thought that all that had happened between the two of them was enough to fill a soul to overflowing, and if time ever emptied his, new wine could not, surely should not, be poured in.

"So, what," she said. "You were going to join a monastery?"

"No no," he said. "I wasn't going that far. I'm not the monastic type. I was just going to. To keep my fancy free."

"Really."

"Really."

"Don't tell me," she said, profoundly tickled. "It didn't work out."

He hung his head.

"Jeez, Pierce," she said. "You never go to the movies? Read a book? Don't you know what happens to people who make promises like that?"

He did, he had known very well, but those were only stories after all, and because they were, the end or final capitulation to Love in effect came first in them; the initial vow of abnegation was just a means to it, and all the chastening errors and humiliations that lay in between were nothing, nothing at all, the confusions of a night, everybody already knew, even the suffering fool himself seemed to know from the beginning, because he was after all in a story: so you laughed, for him and with him.

"So who was she," Charis asked with a sigh: let's get started.

"Her name was Rose."

"Huh." She seemed not quite to believe this. "And what was she like?"

What was she like. Pierce for a moment couldn't answer. He had been lately experiencing a sort of intermittent catatonia, a division of consciousness when certain questions were put to him, wherein lengthy explanations or ponderings occurred within him even as his mouth opened and his jaw lifted and dropped saying things other than the things he thought, or nothing. What was she like? She was like him: he had once in bed told her that, though he didn't really believe it. He had told her that he knew what it was like to be her, her on the inside; but he never knew if she believed him. Really, nothing that he knew about her or that she had said about herself accounted for her, just as it might be said to him, Here is a night-blooming orchid that awakens only once a year and smells of flesh—all that could be said about it was that if it didn't, then there would be no such bloom. The same for Rose.

"And so what happened?"

He stopped again, chin wagging for a moment like a ventriloquist's dummy whose partner has fallen silent. He thought to say he had got lost in a haunted wood, because he thought he saw her go that way, or simply because he lost the right way. The thorn trees there bled when he cut them with his sword. He had met himself—right hand raised, in strange clothes, coming toward him, about to speak a warning, ask an unanswerable question. But he turned away, and went on. He was tricked into binding and whipping his beloved, and only discovered his mistake (that it wasn't his beloved, or his blows weren't kisses) too late.

"Ooh. She liked that stuff?"

"She did."

"Do you?"

"I did. Because she did."

She waited.

"It was," Pierce said. "It was um. It was actually a lot of fun. I have to admit." He saw reflected in her face the whiskery skull-grin he was making, and ceased.

"Nobody's ever gonna hit *me*," she said.

"No," he said, sure of it.

"I mean sometimes a little spank," she said. "On the behind. Sometimes it feels good. Right on that hole."

Her level cool eyes. Never complain, never explain: her motto, she always said. In dreams he had seen her too sometimes, Charis, on the path ahead, turning to look back, with just those eyes. Or maybe it wasn't her, or Rose either, or anyone.

"But listen," she said, cross-legged now on her divan, a little idol. "Weren't you afraid you might go too far with her? That's what I always wonder. Like how were you supposed to know if she. You know. Didn't want to."

"Oh she could tell me," Pierce said, and ground his hands together. "Even if I wouldn't listen when she said no. Wasn't supposed to listen."

"Then how did she tell you?"

"She could say: I tell you three times."

"'I tell you three times.' That's it?"

He lowered his head, bare and ashamed.

"Okay," Charis said cautiously but not judgmentally, calm counselor or therapist. "So go on."

So go on. *Iter in antiquam silvam, stabula alta ferarum.* They had gone on, into the forest primeval, where the beasts den in the deep dark. How far in did they go? Only halfway: then, of course, they began to come out again, though he at least didn't know that. He told about the cutting of her hair, how deeply that got her too, another set of wires crossed; how he had been able to overmaster her simply by showing her the scissors (*territio realis*) and taking her hair in handfuls, gentle but firm, and not to be refused. And other things.

"So let me see if I get this," Charis said. Her black brows knitted. "You've got this woman who likes stuff. *Needs* stuff. She has to have stuff, but she can't say she wants it. So you get her somehow so that she can't get away, strap her up real good, and then while she's that way you do the stuff to her she wants you to do. The stuff she needs. While she says, No no, please no, and you don't listen."

He nodded.

"You figured out what she wants, and you gave it to her. Without her asking. Or even admitting. Which she couldn't do."

He nodded still.

"Well. Jeez. A person can't ask for more than that, Pierce. Isn't that just love? To do that for somebody? Isn't that what it means?"

Could it be that her eyes regarding him were soft? He turned away, feeling a great heaving in his chest as though the hurt heart there were making a break for it; clapped a hand over his mouth to keep it in. It had only been a month or so since he had broken for good with Rose. Not long, not long at all. Real love: if it was, would Charis know, someone like her? Maybe she alone.

"So where is she now?" Charis asked softly. "Are you still . . . ?"

"No. No no. She's gone."

"Gone? Like vanished?"

"To Peru." He searched his coat pockets for something he didn't find. "Last I heard."

"Peru."

"She became a Christian," Pierce said. "A sort of Christian. She joined a cult, actually."

"A Peruvian cult?"

"They have some sort of connection there," he said. "A mission."

"Like converting people?"

"Bringing them the message. The Word. They're a tiny group, but they pretend to be international. The Powerhouse International."

"The what house?"

"Powerhouse. The Bible is the powerhouse." To say anything about them, to use the fraught words they used, was to him like touching dead flesh, or being spat on by strangers, why? For how long?

Charis shook her head in wonderment. "So when she got converted, that was the end of that stuff, huh? You and her. The things you did."

"Well," he said. "No. Not right away."

"Oh no?" she said. "No?" She laughed greatly, as though some simple truth about humanity, or women, or life on earth had been confirmed. "Uh-huh. So then how did it end? Between you?"

"Well, her faith," he said. "So-called. After a while it just got insupportable."

"Really."

"Really." Insupportable, that was the word, he couldn't support it, for our support is reason, and what our reason will not support we let fall, we walk away from it, everybody does, except those people; it was all he had done, all that he needed to admit he had done. Insupportable. "God," he said. "Old Nobadaddy. Guy in the sky. I mean, come on."

"Hey," she said. "You know I believe in God."

"You do?"

"Sure. Don't look so amazed. I could never have got through the stuff I had to get through. *Never.* I couldn't go on." She laughed a little, at herself, at what his face showed. "I mean I don't go to like *church,* I'm not, you know, *good.* But still. Yeah. Never could have made it. Without him. Who can."

For just a moment, a vast moment, Pierce knew what that would be like: the ground of being your own friend and helper, a pour of power out of elsewhere into your heart, without judgment, asking nothing, giving all that was needed, the last resort. For a moment it was so: everything was unchanged, no different and yet all different. Then it was gone.

He stood. Winter light was citron in the windows now, and Pierce thought he knew why she didn't light lights—she had no power, no bill to pay. He hadn't removed his coat. "Okay," he said.

"Pierce," she said softly. "Don't go."

She got up herself, and took his arm. She poured him liqueur in a tiny glass of many colors. For a long time they sat together, and he listened to her story of her own life, and felt the gnaw of boredom it's not uncommon to feel in the presence of one you love and have long ago lost and can't have. She gave him a tour of her apartment, bedroom kitchen front room all in a row, like the apartment he was living in when they first met, the same he had lived in with Julie Rosengarten before: an Old Law apartment. The refrigerator, unused, was covered in a glamorous fringed shawl on which embroidered beasts and birds cavorted in Eden. Outside on the windowsill a bottle of juice and a loaf of bread and some plastic containers kept cool.

"You ever going to get electricity?"

"It means signing up for stuff. I sublet, Pierce. I pay my bills in cash. I'm invisible."

The bedroom, offered to him with the same gesture that his own bedroom had been offered to him by the Chief. More full of more things, this strange art form or indulgence she spent her time and thought on, arrangement of miniature stage sets, marionette tableaus, dioramas no one would ever see but her and her friends and lovers. He thought about her growing old, and turned away.

"Aren't these valuable?" he asked, pointing to a cluster of miniature women gathered like a coven on the refrigerator's top, a mermaid, a Barbie, a Betty Boop, and a Betty Crocker. The one he had noticed was an ivory Chinese figurine, nude and marked with fine blue dashed lines: the kind that, he understood, women once used when consulting doctors, pointing out their pains on its bare body rather than uncovering their own.

"Dunno," she said. She lifted it from among the others. "You think so?"

"I think they are."

"You need it," she said.

"I do?"

"You do," she said, and, taking his hand, she put the little lady into it. "You do."

He could close his fist around it, and hide it completely: almost. Charis named a figure, less than it was worth surely, but still a good sum. He'd thought, of course, that she meant it as a gift, and tried not to let it show that he'd thought so. He only nodded sagely, studying the thing; then he gave it to her to hold while he got out money. Money of the foundation's, meant, he told her, for his trip.

"Well, sure," she said. "And here's your first souvenir."

"Okay."

She offered to find something to wrap it in, but he took it and put it bare in his overcoat pocket. "She'll be all right," he said.

"Okay." She slipped her arm in his, walked the few steps to her door. "People learn things about themselves, you know, Pierce. They do, finally. Sometimes what they don't want to know."

"Yes."

"Me, I've learned that I don't really have a warm heart. I mean it doesn't warm up by itself." She tapped it lightly, the place where it was hidden. "I need to be loved. Somebody's gotta love me like nuts. And if they do, then . . ." She made a two-handed catch-fire gesture and a sound. "You know?"

"Yes. I do."

"You have a warm heart," she said. "A real little steam engine in there. I always thought."

"Oh," he said. "Well. I don't know. I just feel that I failed her. She went over to them because she was in trouble, in real trouble. *Fatal* trouble almost, really. Yes, I think so. There was a night, a night on the hill, in her car, when she. Well. Never mind. But I couldn't see, couldn't admit that she was in such trouble, and do something for her. Something. I couldn't."

Charis listened, saying nothing.

"So how can I call it love? When I did nothing?"

"Hey," Charis said softly. "It's not like she was counting on you." She studied him. "Was she?"

"No."

"There was no deal, was there?" She crossed her thin arms before her, cold in her doorway. "There's got to be a deal made. You guys never had a deal like that, did you?"

"No."

"See?"

He must have looked unconvinced, because she took his lapel, looking up, her golden eyes. "You're a good guy," she said. "You ought to get somebody good. But Pierce." She waited till he looked at her. "You got to make a deal, and make it stick. You and her. You got to know what deal you've made, and it's got to have something for you, and something for her. You got to deal. Even I know that."

She tugged his high head down toward hers to kiss his cheek. He thought of the last time he and she had parted, when money had changed hands too. And a kiss and an embrace that was like having all your lost treasure returned to you at once, and at once taken away again; and then the door closed and locked.

A deal. He had certainly never struck a deal with Charis, though possibly he had assumed she had issued terms, terms that he thought he had accepted: that wasn't the same thing as a deal, he guessed.

He hadn't told Charis that he had asked Rose to marry him, one night, one endless night. It was all he could think of to do, and it was not in order to rescue her, but himself: if she could say yes, then her soul would not be theirs, she would not be their captive forever and his own soul die. That was the deal he offered. She didn't take it.

It turns out—he'd read the literature, actually—that such affairs as theirs was don't often flourish or last long, because at bottom what the two *folles* in the *folie à deux* want from each other is impossible to have, indeed what each one needs makes it impossible to give what the other wants. For A wants B to place herself—say *her* just for instance—entirely in his power, willingly, in each instance: to say Yes with all her being and desire. But B needs A to *deprive* her of her will, take away her power of assent or dissent, so that what is done is not done by her at all.

So what they do, A and B, is to pretend, for each other's sake, on each other's behalf: A pretends to unfeeling cruelty, B to resistance and ultimate capitulation. And, sly game players that they often are, they can go on long pretending, but the farther they press the game, the closer comes the moment when the contradiction becomes clear to each of them, not always the same moment for both unfortunately. That's why it's so often A who in the end is on his knees, and saying Please please, and B whose eyes are cold and turned away, wondering why she's there.

Poor A, poor B.

In the street it smelled of snow coming. He turned toward the subway, closing his coat with his right hand, pocketing his left. The little figurine—he had already forgotten it was there—slipped into his fingers, and the sudden touch of her ivory flesh was mild and pacifying. For the next months she lay there, he felt her placid curves amid the loose pence and marks and lire, the maps and subway tickets; when his trip was done and he hung the old coat on a hook, she remained. The winter after that he got a new coat, a wadded parka like everyone else's, and not until the old coat was gathered up one day with other things for the Salvation Army did another hand reach in and find her there amid the long-ago litter, unremoved.

He returned to Brooklyn and Park Slope, and to his father's house. Axel was still not there, and neither was the Chief; the young men who came and went and lay around gave him beer to drink and a spot on the couch before the big TV that had come to inhabit the corner. The Ayatollah's face and pisshole eyes, that seemed to hang on the screen like Emmanuel Goldstein's for a full two minutes' hate.

He got away as soon as he could to his old room, and to his bed, which felt as though it had been slept in by many, one at a time at least, he hoped. He slept, startled awake by the comings and goings of Renovators and Reclaimers; he dreamed that he had a dream about his father, who was lost and sick and in trouble, dead maybe and in Purgatory, asking for help, but Pierce couldn't answer somehow, nor ask what was the matter; and when he woke up he found himself on a cold hillside, the house and all Park Slope gone. Then he woke up.

There was silence in the house so deep it might have been empty. Pierce scribbled a note for Axel (one of the silent sleepers must be him) and went carefully out through the darkened rooms. He collected his dreadful bags and carried them bumping the walls down to the street. Snow was falling thickly. It was nearly an hour before he could attract the attention of a gypsy cab, and still he stepped out at the airport way too early, unshowered, unbreakfasted, afraid.

4

The abbey bells rang Sext, the sixth hour of the day, high noon. Pierce lifted his head to listen. What is the meaning of the sixth hour, on what then do we meditate? At this hour Adam was made, at this hour he sinned; at the sixth hour Noah went in to the Ark and at the sixth hour came out again. At the sixth hour Christ was crucified, reversing Adam's sin. Every hour of the monk's day contains a part of the day-shaped history of the world.

Through the universe, the human world, and the year, the stories recapitulate, reverse, return. Every Mass is the story of the making, loss, damnation, redemption, and remaking of the world, the Sacrifice at its center. Adam was born or conceived on the hill that would later be named Golgotha, the center of the world, beneath the Y of the Tree of the Knowledge of Good and Evil, from whose wood the Cross would in time be made; and the letters of his name ADAM name the four directions in Greek: North, South, East and West. He was born on the Equinox, the same day the coming of Jesus was announced to Mary: *Ave,* said the angel to Mary that spring morning, reversing the damnation that sprang from *Eva.*

Blessed circularity, never done. Even the End of the World was able to be repeated in the course of every turn of the heavens around earth—or rather of earth's spin around the sun, a shift of perspective that made no difference on earth really, though it had seemed once to be an utter upset of that same circularity. Of course the Christian story at its first appearance had been not an embodiment but an enemy of circularity, a one-way street from Creation through Cross to Conclusion, and for millions (he supposed it must be millions) it still was. For Pierce and others (millions too, he was sure, though maybe a vertical millions reaching back toward prehistory, rather than the horizontal millions going to church and mosque today) the simple straight story was uniquely repellent, repellent in a way no other could be; for him and his like, the whole history of the church (his church, this church) was nothing but a process by which its original one-way progression was tamed, and turned around like the Worm to bite its own tail or tale, which would otherwise be *insupportable,* impossible to assert or believe. On Good Friday in the abbey church, the perpetual light above the altar, always burning night and day, would be put out: God would die, the world grow cold. Everything would be over. On Easter Sunday it would be lit again, never to go out: God lives again. The next Holy Days, the same. We live in a story with a Beginning, a Middle, and an End, but within that story is another, the same, and within that one, also another, and each is bigger and longer than the previous one, and of *that* there is no beginning and no end.

It was like Adam and his navel.

He thought this, in just these words—*like Adam and his navel*—and without his willing it (in fact he was surprised, his attention caught, as though he'd felt a tug just then on Ariadne's thread) he remembered several things at once.

He remembered the great book wherein the Y and a thousand other mysteries had been explained or set for him to ponder, and the entry on ADAM.

He remembered the day when he had first arrived in the Faraway Hills, and how at a Full Moon Party by the Blackbury River he had suddenly known he would abandon his calling as a teacher of history, and try to make a living elsewhere by other means; maybe (he'd thought in the sweetness of liberation) he'd set up shop, and for a buck apiece wrangle hard questions people had that history could answer. Like the question of how, when we get to Heaven, we will know which man there is father Adam. Not a minute later a tall barefoot woman in a glowing sundress had passed him by, and he heard someone call to her. *Hi, Rose.*

And he also remembered how, near the bitter end of what began at that party with that motion of his soul or head, he lay in his small house beside the same river, and Rose Ryder was with him. The hour must have been Matins, he thought: the hour of Judgment, and the hour of the perishing of the world. They were not sleeping but talking, and the subject was biblical inerrancy. Pierce had for some weeks been spending a lot of his actually pretty substantial erudition, wide if shallow, in resolving for her sake a few of the chasms between the Word and the world, at the same time as he tried to tease her into laughing off the whole stupid thing and returning into his orbit once again, and she did laugh, often enough, at his act. So this night she had said something (this was delicate archaeology, recreating that ancient black predawn, from here where he now sat in the sun) something about evolution and the evidence for it, which he said was of course indisputable, please. And she had, what, she had demurred, or said it wasn't the point anyway. And he said Don't worry, the question could be easily resolved and nothing lost, not God's omnipotence or the Bible story or the millions of years of bones and fossils, and he knew how.

How?

Well, he'd said, it's like Adam's navel.

An old trick question, very old, medieval maybe. When we get to Heaven how will we be able to know which man there is Adam? We will because *he'll be the one without a navel.* Because he was never attached to an umbilical cord. He had no mother, came from no womb, had no history. So there it was. But no, of course he *did* have a history: his own grown body was a history, and so were the plants and the animals around him, the slow-forming stars he saw in the sky. The answer is (Pierce with raised forefinger explicated this) that there is no time for God, no past-present-future, he can bring the universe into existence *at any moment of its history*: the universe comes to be at the moment when God wills it to be, with all its previous millennia intact. Do you see? he'd said to Rose. It never existed before that moment, and after that moment it always did. And on the sixth day he makes a man of dust, and breathes life into him: and hair has already grown on his head, and teeth in his mouth, and a beard on his face, and he has a navel on his stomach, from his nonexistent life as a fetus, his ontogeny that never happened recapitulating a phylogeny ditto.

See how useful, how neat? That whole evolution problem rendered moot, do you see? It's all okay; it's not Mere Chance. If God chose, he could take six days to do it all in, which is what the Bible says, what Rose in the bed beside him then was committed to believing. But of course, if you like, you can think he chose to create it all, all its starry depths in all their cosmic evolution, in a single moment: say, just in that moment when Adam opens his eyes to perceive it.

She was impressed. He thought she was. He remembered that she had been. He'd left aside the question of who, just at that moment when the lamp was lit in Adam's head, was creating whom. But he couldn't refrain from pointing out that if you didn't accept the Bible chronology, and had none in particular to replace it with, then you had no way of saying what moment God would choose in which to bring the universe into being. It could be any one; a billion years ago, or just now. Right now, this moment, he'd said, and he sat up and stretched out his arms and closed his eyes: just now, as I open my eyes. All time and history, all my own history too, right up to the very memory I have of just now closing my eyes—it all never existed before, and would all, right now, come into being.

Now. And he opened his eyes on her.

She was on her elbow, looking at him, bare, lost to him; and his cold bedroom was around them; and a huge grief or pity (but for whom?) had seized his throat; and he had begun helplessly to weep, sobbing as she looked on in amazement.

Pierce felt in his body the bell claps of noon, each one stepping upon the trailing tail of the previous one, until no more came, and the twelfth sang alone and died away.

He thought how, in one way if only in one way, Rose and Charis were alike. He thought that neither had ever loved any man, not in the times when he had known them, nor before. Charis had surely known this; but like a person color-blind from birth she probably hadn't regretted it very much, and had gone on (still went on, maybe) secretly believing that others had fooled themselves into thinking a valuable and useful facet of the world—color, love (or Love)—supposedly existed but didn't really. Emperor's new clothes. He hadn't seen her or heard of Charis for a dozen years or more, and wondered sometimes what deal she had struck, if she had, for what she needed, whatever it was.

Sometimes, though, he could perceive Rose, not as she had been, as he had known her, but as she might be now. He would sometimes see with startling suddenness, as in a showstone or a confirming dream, how she lived with them still, her Bible cult, the Powerhouse; getting along, dealing with its hierarchies and its powers as she had always dealt with the world—by indirection, conditional assent, abstraction of her spirit from things she couldn't get her body out of, willingness too to try to live up to others' standards, at least until she saw no path there for herself and her nature. It must be the case that, in any cult not murderous or psychotic, life eventually settles down and becomes like life anywhere, livings still to get, dishes to wash, rubs and hurts to assuage or nurse in secret. Self-regard to maintain by cunning or other means. Lies to tell. Of course.

It was likely she had never been truly subject to them even back then. The

God or godliness she wanted to get for herself was only a new good offered to her to pursue, not really different from health or wealth. It was only he who thought she had laid a way out of the world; only he who ever really believed or feared there was such a way. Following the path that he had made or found through her body he had come himself to be within their unreal heaven and hell, under the rule of their god and his prophets, an enchantment he had not known could happen to a human of his time and place, though common enough (he knew by report) in other times and places. It was there, in that false world, that his spirit had resided while his body walked the Old World searching for the thing lost, in his bad shoes and his overcoat from which the lining had begun to droop. Under his arm that mad guidebook of Kraft's, and the new little red notebook, made in China—still with him here, its pages foxed with London rain and Roman wine—and an umbrella for the endless drizzle, one of a series of umbrellas that he bought and lost as he went, one at almost every *pensione,* on every train.

Boney Rasmussen was already dead when Pierce set out that winter to find the Elixir to make him better. So there was no one on whose behalf he could have sought it but his own. In fact, as he knew very well even then, there is no other living person for whom it can be sought: though it can only be found, if it's found, for everyone.

What he hadn't known, and would never learn later, was that by then the thing lost had already been found. It had been found by him and others, and redeemed from the place where it was hidden and at threat, and restored to the place it should possess; and this event had stopped the decline of the whole world toward dissolution, toward frozen inanition and repetition such as Pierce had experienced in the cold halls and hot rooms of Rose. The world—"the world," all this, day and night, self and others, things and other things, inside and out—had been coasting to a stop, and just in time had been put back in a forward gear again. And then it could continue, and would, until all traces of that moment of redemption were erased from all hearts and memories (But you remember it, don't you? Night, and the woods, and the lights put out, and one light restored?). New-wakened Adam would then open his eyes again, the beautiful circle would close, and roll on forever into the future and the past at once.

5

So:

The snow had continued to fall, and grown steadily fiercer, till the airport, great-winged white bird, was wrapped in it. Outside the wide windows, airplanes were ghostly, moving to their assigned runways with lights burning. Then not moving. Pierce, ticket in hand, heard that his flight was to be delayed. Then further delayed. Then canceled. New arrangements to make for the night flight, if there was to be one.

At evening, Pierce and his fellows arrayed themselves on hard benches designed only for a brief alighting in passage, not for the comfort of the benighted and delayed; there was no way Pierce could twist his big frame into more than a moment's repose. He gazed in envy at men and women and children who had tucked up nearby with their coats up to their chins or their heads under their wings, breathing softly as though enchanted. The short day turned toward darkness.

Maybe he wouldn't go, after all. He thought this, and grew still. Maybe he'd sit here as the snow flew and covered the world, sit for days, for months; he'd sleep and dream, fill his new red journal with what he might have done but finally did not do, and go farther inward than he would ever dare to go outward.

And just then in the limbo-like procession of snowbound souls through the great space, a figure attracted his attention, and at the same moment the figure seemed to notice him: a man not large but somehow big around, in a jaunty feathered fedora and a fur-collared coat, a leather document case tucked under his arm and a small suitcase on a little trundle he pulled along.

It was Frank Walker Barr, once Pierce's professor and advisor at Noate University. His eyebrows rose, and he stepped or rolled toward Pierce with an air that seemed to suggest he was conscious of illustrating the ancient wisdom about coincidences—that if you run into someone you haven't seen in years, it's certain you will very soon run into him again, and then a third charmed time. For Pierce had, not two months before, walked and talked with Barr in an obscure resort in Florida, and been told truths, and tried to listen. This after he had not seen his old mentor for a decade.

"Hello again," Frank Walker Barr said to him. The plump coat over his tweeds made him a Humpty Dumpty, the same chummy, threatening smile cleaving his great face almost in two, hand held out to shake. "You're traveling?"

"Yes."

"Abroad?"

"Well, yes. Britain, then Europe. Italy. Germany."

"Research."

"Um in part. And you?"

"I hadn't been planning on it, but yes. In part," Barr said, regarding him with interest, "because of the conversation we had in Florida."

"Oh?"

"Your book."

"Oh."

"Soon after we got home. I decided to go to meet some colleagues instead of resting at home."

"Colleagues where?"

"Taffy worried, because she couldn't come. Family matters. She worries too much. She thinks she needs to be near me at all times. To take down my last worlds maybe. I mean words."

"Aha."

"Egypt," Barr said. "A small conference of paleographers."

"And you're delayed as well?"

"Oh hours. We'd better have a drink. Come along."

"I think they closed the bar."

"The Olympic Club. For frequent flyers. Just down here," Barr said.

An awesome refusal broached in Pierce's soul. He already suspected that he had entered into one of those chain narratives where an innocent is handed on from one garrulous interlocutor to another, follows fingerboards to the next who points him to the next. Until he refuses to play anymore. And so wins. *You're nothing but a pack of cards.*

After a moment, though, he gathered up his shabby impedimenta and followed his former teacher, who had begun to roll away purposefully through the crowd.

~

It was his mother whom Pierce had gone to Florida to visit, on the first leg (as he would come to see it) of this his way away: the little motel where she and her friend Doris now lived and made a living, where she had gone after Sam Oliphant was dead. Pierce came to make her speak, to answer him at last, to explain why it was that everything that happened to him or ever could happen to him seemed to have been fixed by his twelfth year, why he could somehow never go onward but only turn back: a fate like one of those diagrams in the Boy Scout manual he had once cherished, bowline on a bight maybe, a rope following minute arrows, inward, around, out but always back in again, strong and un-undoable.

For instance, there in that little Florida resort town, on the esplanade, he'd met Barr. He'd first read a book of Barr's in his twelfth year. Barr had afterward been his advisor at Noate University, and had used his long pull to get Pierce his first teaching job, at Barnabas College. There was apparently no life passage he could make without Barr standing there, or nearby, amused and foresighted.

"Now tell me all about it," Barr had asked him, there in the sun-warmed Florida evening. "Your concept."

He had brought Pierce to his own little condo on the beach, to have a drink with him and his wife, Taffy. *Second* wife. Over the last dozen years Taffy had been appearing more and more prominently in the forematter of Barr's books, moving up from the Acknowledgments page (where she had first appeared under her own last name), to a Dedication, to a line beneath Barr's own on the title page (though in smaller type), lastly to full partner, not in smaller type. By Frank Walker Barr and Taffy B. Barr. The books themselves seemed unchanged.

"Well," Pierce said, sun through their window impaling the promised drink in his hand. "It was something you said. Once when we met in New York."

"Ah yes."

"You talked about how someone might do history even if there weren't universities and tenure. How you could go to work answering questions, questions about the past that people have."

"Ah yes," Barr said again, though Pierce was unconvinced he actually remembered this exchange, in a dark hotel bar so long ago.

"As an example," Pierce said, "you asked why so many people believe that

Gypsies are able to tell fortunes. Prophesy. Do magic. Where they get these supposed powers."

Taffy, who was years younger and a couple of inches taller than her husband, watched and listened as she made a cold supper in the condo's tiny galley. Pink shrimp and avocado and bright tomatoes. Her coloring was what Pierce thought was called *roan* in horses; she had that strong and slightly desiccated look of women who were cute early on and are going to make it through to handsome age, but just barely.

"That's where it began," Pierce said.

"It," said Barr.

"Yes, I found out," Pierce said.

"Simple enough," Barr said.

"You said," Pierce said, and swallowed—this was hard to recount, because *it* was Pierce's book, which he had been compelled by Barr's question to set out on, and which he already suspected would never be completed. "You said that there is more than one history of the world. More than one. One for each of us, you said."

"Yes."

"I thought what would happen if you took that as true. Literally true, not metaphorically or."

"Not just more than one history of the world," Barr said. "More than one world?"

"It seemed to me a case could really sort of be made." He knew he was saying too much, and couldn't stop, as though here before these beings, regarding him kindly enough but with a shaming wisdom in their tolerant smiles—so lucky, too, unlike him, lucky in each other—he had perforce to unburden himself of this, this. "So then I'd consider how such other worlds are made, or were made," he said. "How does one world turn into another, become the next. How are they, you know, cast."

"*Cosmopœia*," said Barr. "World-making."

"Um yes."

"That *pœia* being the root of our word poetry, of course. Poets being makers. Makers of poems, and of the worlds in them." He sipped the martini he held. "So I'd guess you're embarked on a piece of poetry too. And that your taking this metaphor literally is itself a species of metaphor."

Pierce said nothing in response to this, tried to smile inscrutably, knowing he could not himself have thought of that formula, and wondering if it was so.

Taffy was now stripping the skin from tiny blood oranges and dropping the sections in a cut-glass bowl. "I'd need an example," she said. "An instance."

"That's what I mean," Pierce said. "I mean that's where the question led me. To Egypt, which is where Gypsies come from, and where magic was invented, and the gods first worshipped."

"Oh?"

"Only of course they don't," Pierce said. "They were *believed* to come from there. But the place they were believed to come from wasn't the Egypt we know. It was another Egypt."

"Ah yes," said Frank Walker Barr.

"Another Egypt," said his wife. "Well, now."

Pierce began to explain about the ancient writings ascribed to Hermes Trismegistus, priest and king of Egypt, and the error that Renaissance thinkers had made, to suppose that these late-antique Greek metaphysical vaporings were authentic Egyptian beliefs; and Barr put in that at that time hieroglyphics of course couldn't be read, and were interpreted as mystic signs when mystic signs were all the rage; and Taffy went on working, raising her eyes now and then to one or the other of them; and Pierce had the impression that she actually knew all this already, and that Barr knew she knew it, and they were both at work eliciting it from him, Pierce, like cops at an interrogation, or parents listening to a child's story, not news to them.

"Ægypt," he said. "A land that never existed. Where Hermes was king, where magic worked; and the memory of it descends to us to this day, and we can remember it even though the land ceased to exist, and now never existed. We made a new one to replace it. Egypt."

"'When I was a king in Egypt,'" Taffy declaimed, "'and you were a Christian slave.'"

"Babylon," said her husband.

"I'm not babbling," she said. "It's a poem."

She had enough oranges now in her bowl, it seemed, and to them she added a bag of tiny marshmallows. She noticed Pierce watching her preparations.

"Ambrosia," she said. She poured honey over it from a jar. Sue Bee. "That's what it's called. I don't know why. Frank loves it."

Frank smiled, in fact he beamed, and the beam fell upon Pierce. "Want some?" he asked.

"Oh no," Pierce said. "Oh no. None for me, thanks. None for me."

That wasn't all that befell Pierce there in the Sunshine State that week. It was then that he discovered something he had once promised he could find but had never actually believed existed, a thing he had told Julie Rosengarten would be disclosed in the last pages of his book, a thing—maybe the only thing—that had survived from a former age when things were not as they are now but worked in a different way, something that really still worked that way, the way things once did. He found it in the place where he should have known it was, but had not before been able to see into; down a different passage, in the deep dark, and yet not far away at all. That's all been told; the story's still there to be discovered in at least a few libraries and in those blessed stores that keep unwanted books until their time at last comes around, if it does, or at least until they catch someone's eye or stir someone's heart, unless their paper yellows and crumbles into illegibility first: the whole story of how Pierce found the thing that he had sought for, right in his own backyard. Not that it mattered then, really, materially, since Pierce was never going to write that book nor any other like it; and this he confessed to Barr in the Olympic Club at JFK.

"That's too bad," Barr said. "Too bad. Because of course there's been some remarkable new thinking on the subject lately. Egypt and Greek wisdom. You must have been following. Major controversy."

Pierce nodded cautiously. He hadn't been following.

"I'm guessing," Barr said, "that you got your grounding in this matter largely from Frances Yates. *Dame* Frances Yates."

Pierce was vaguely shocked, hearing the name said aloud, a cloudlet of actuality emitted on the stale false air. A sort of category error. No one should speak that name but him, in his heart.

"Wonderful woman. *Giordano Bruno and the Hermetic Tradition.* It's where we all got it, isn't it? You're going to London? You should look her up. She's at the Warburg Institute, you know."

"Yes."

"Wonderful woman. Major influence. Give her my regards when you see her. She could be wrong, though."

"Wrong in what way?"

"Well, centrally, her thesis—it's hardly hers alone—is that the Renaissance made this colossal mistake in the dating of the pseudo-Egyptian manuscripts that they attributed to a single author, this semidivine Hermes Trismegistus; that what they had were in fact Hellenistic writings that had been given a false provenance by their author, or authors, as was so common in that time. So the wonderful mystical Egyptian world they depicted was in fact post-Plato, even post-Christian. A dream."

"Yes."

"That's the consensus view. All the scholars. But what if they're wrong? They were the latest word when you were at school, but that was some time ago." Twinkle. "I think a case can be made—well, it *is* being made—that those writings, the so-called Hermetic Corpus, go back well before Christianity."

"Really?"

"Half a millennium before. Not all of them, of course, maybe not even all of any one, but large parts of them. It may be that some of them date to a time when the temples of Egypt were still standing, the priesthood still functioning."

"But everybody says. Not just Yates. Everybody agrees."

"Well, of course there's good philological evidence that the writings *as we have them* are late Greek. But that doesn't mean they don't contain older materials. Much older." He drank. "Anyway, everybody *doesn't* agree. Flinders Petrie didn't agree."

That impossible name, a name for an archæologist in a comic book, breaker of stones, studier of fragments, Flinders Petrie. Pierce had got Petrie's books from the State Library in Kentucky, back when he had himself first set out for those realms. In childhood: that long ago. The sand-colored photographs, sand-colored man in pith helmet and wrinkled shorts.

"Petrie thought that the writings, the core writings, dated to the fifth century BCE. And because the Egyptian religion was so insular—remember, the Greeks held the Egyptians in high regard, but the Egyptians didn't have much regard for the Greeks—you could at that date still have found remote temples in Upper Egypt where the scribes were writing in hieroglyphics, copying magical and theological papyri, 'writings of Thoth,' as some are described in Greek. Kom Ombo. The Temple of Isis at Philæ. And the Hermetic manuscripts we know, even if they were written in Greek and collected in the first centuries AD, might have been based on what was still a living tradition. Might well."

"But don't they incorporate a lot of Platonic philosophy? Or stuff that sounds like Plato, or even the Gospel of John?"

"Sure. And scholars have assumed that the Egyptians had no such metaphysics, only ritual and myth, and so the metaphysics of the Hermetica must derive from Plato, and not the other way around."

"Even though Plato said it *was* the other way around, that he owed Egypt."

"Yes. That's the new view. That Plato—and Thucydides and Herodotus and Pliny—knew what they were talking about when they said that their knowledge of the gods and the cosmos derived from Egypt. Their laws even. Certainly their writing. The historian's rule being this: that if a people's culture retains lots of stories about their history or origins that are not particularly to their credit, they ought to be taken seriously as likely to have some factual basis."

"So maybe they aren't wrong."

"They? Which they?"

"The Hermeticists. The Renaissance Egyptophiles. Bruno and Fludd and Kircher. The Rosicrucians and the Masons, who think they all come from Egypt, because of the Hermetic stuff."

"There is," said Barr, "that possibility. Yes."

Gentle voices had been speaking while the two men conversed, like spirit informants, telling of the world and the air, planes landing from Africa, Asia, Europe, and now they were told that Barr's to Athens, Cairo, and Delhi was ready for boarding. Barr looked at his watch and stood up.

"Maybe I'll learn more," he said. "It's all very controversial. A lot of people don't like this downgrading of the Greeks and Greek originality in favor of Africans. When new Hermetic manuscripts were found among the Dead Sea Scrolls, Father Festugière, the great student of Hermeticism, said he was sure not much could be learned from *une jarre d'Egypt.*"

"But you do think so," Pierce said. "That it might be so. As the Renaissance thought. At least a little."

"Well, it's a new age," Barr said. He yanked out the handle of his nifty trundle and turned to go, lifting a parting hand. "All that stuff is coming back."

No word yet from out of the air for Pierce, and (though uncertain it was permitted him) he sat in the Olympic Club while the ice in his drink turned to water, listening still to Barr's words and feeling the strangest feeling as he repeated them, the feeling of something healed, or knitted, or resealed, within him but not only within him: a thing that had once been one, and was then divided, becoming one again.

He'd thought that if you went back, went back through the centuries far enough, at a certain point the way to Egypt—to the Egypt of archæology, the long-lived culture of the dead, the hard-headed small brown people with their revolting rituals of mummification and their gods ever multiplying as in a children's game—that way would part from the way that led to a land he called Ægypt: a name he'd found in that dictionary of the old or other world, the alphabetic world within the world. Ægypt: dream country of philosophers and healers, speaking statues, teachers of Plato and Pythagoras. But what if—like the Nile—this Y was actually right side up, and he alone had got it upside down; what if it had all always been one country, and only divided in two as it came close to the present, and you could reach it again by going back from here along either horn?

It, the real country. Not Ægypt but Egypt.

Maybe there was indeed something of Egypt—the place where actual men and women had lived and died and prayed and thought for centuries—preserved in the *conversazione* of Florentine Platonists, in the rituals and costumes of Freemasons. Not all that they *thought* there was, of course, but more than the scholars he'd been reading would allow. The real arcana of the real priests of Thoth and Asclæpius might have lived on, a slight, slim thread but never broken, tangled up in Hermes, passing down to Bruno and to Mozart and George Washington and the French Revolution, down to the Thursday night rituals in the halls of midwestern cities, the bankers and businessmen with their trowels and embroidered aprons, their eyeglasses and dentures.

Another thing Barr had once said to him. Strange, he'd said, strange how the past continually enlarges, rather than shrinking with distance.

Maybe that's because we actually move toward it rather than away. There is no world of tomorrow, no such thing: we move always toward what we were, to know it again. He did, anyway.

What about that for an ending to his nonexistent book, the revelation that sober historians of the new age had made old Ægypt real again, and proved mad Bruno right. And they had done that because the making of new ages—in past as well as future—is what we do with the dark backward and abysm of time. *Cosmopœia.* If he were a historian, he thought, a real historian, that's what he'd do, or help to do.

Meanwhile Frank Walker Barr went down along the wide stream of travelers, thinking too: thinking of the basements of the library at Noate, a day a couple of months before when he'd sat at one of the long scarred wooden tables there, with a box open before him, one of the boxes that the Noate library used to store fragile and ephemeral things, worth it or otherwise, always worth it if you happened to be in search of one such, as Barr on that day was.

He'd been reading those new polemical accounts of Egyptian and Greek history, which exposed the old standard histories as having a bias toward the North and the light-skinned peoples, against the South and the dark-skinned. Understandable but long unchallenged. He, Barr, though always glad to see the past reimagined, and older visions brought forward again in the course of time, hadn't himself made up his mind on the issues; but a note referring to a surprising source had struck him. W. M. F. Petrie, "Historical References in the Hermetic Writings," *Transactions of the Third International Congress of the History of Religions* (1908), pp. 196–225.

The library didn't have that volume, but it had, here in the basement, the same paper in pamphlet form, from a time when intellectual and political controversy was carried on by means of publications like these, gray cheap paper not meant to last, salvos or squibs. Ancient smell as of tomb dust or cerements. Petrie's argument for an early date for the so-called Hermetica was based on the fact that the Greek conquerors, or inheritors, of Pharaonic Egypt were demonstrably fascinated by the Egyptian past, and restored many temples and religious sites, and collected codices. He thought that the Hermetica were simply a small part of the copying of ancient Egyptian sacred manuscripts that the Greeks did. Most of those manuscripts were then lost, and the Greek copies lost too, lost with so much of everything. But not these. Found and not lost; not all.

Barr had put down the pamphlet then, captured by the sudden unfolding of an inward image: desert, and a buried temple uncovered. A familiar image, an image he had been profoundly gratified and thrilled by once, as he was gratified by it now. From where had he acquired it to store it away untasted for so long? From the movies, of course, but which one? Movie sand, wind-disturbed, moving away to show the tips of pillars, then the heads of idols: so, the ground we stand on is not the floor of earth, there are floors beneath us. Look, now it's coming clear as the wind, what a wind, pushes the sand away: it's a door, like a cellar door, a black block, and in its center a ring to grasp and pull it up by. Barr knew that when it was lifted there would be stairs that led down, and those stairs would lead somewhere we can't help but go.

A little later that day, in Barr's house up on the heights of the Morningside Hills, where many famed scholars and teachers live backyard to backyard, Taffy B. Barr stood before her open refrigerator, one arm akimbo. On the counter by her lay a heap of tomatoes, a brain-shaped cauliflower, a cantaloupe and a clutch of beets with spreading red-veined greens. She had forgotten why she had opened the refrigerator and was pondering or pausing to see if the reason would return to her when the phone rang. She shut the great vault (the light within winking off and plunging the foodstuffs within again into darkness) and answered. It was Frank, calling from his office, with a plan to announce.

"Frank, let's talk," she said when he paused.

"We're talking."

"At dinner."

"I need to find my passport," he said. "I move it from place to place in order to remember where I put it, but it associates logically with nothing else. It's sui generis."

"Frank. It's a bad idea."

"It's a good idea. My best in months."

"Okay. We'll talk."

"Love you."

"Love you too."

Taffy hung up the phone; she looked up at the clock on the wall (a

Regulator) and down at the vegetables on her counter, and remembered: aioli.

She'd tried, his good wife, at dinner that night and at the breakfast and lunch that followed, to talk him out of it, and failed. And so (Frank Barr in Kennedy Airport said to himself) the youth arose, and took a plane. No youth any longer, but still hale; he patted ritually the pocket where his pills were kept.

He would stop in Athens and be met there by an old—no, better say a *former*—graduate student of his, a woman dark and sloe-eyed enough to be Greek but in fact a Jewess from Schenectady. Zoe. *Zoe mu sas agapo.* Thence to Egypt, from where the gods of Greece had come at first, where the Greek wise men used to go to consult with the priests of Isis and Osiris, to sleep in the temples of Asclæpius and there dream a good dream. His colleagues had written that they might leave the conference for a day or two, rent a Land Rover, hire a guide. Make an expedition up the Nile to the temple island of Philæ. Would Frank like to come? He would. And may he (Frank Walker Barr prayed, to no particular god or goddess) dream there a good dream of his own.

6

Rosie—I am going on the train today to meet Frances Yates, Dame Frances Yates, you've heard me talk about her. If anybody can tell me what I'm supposed to do next, she can. She lives with her sister and her dogs and cats an hour from London, and we're to have tea. I can't explain here how it happened. Excuse the postcard. Pierce

"Now tell me where you've been," she said, clasping her hands before her as though in supplication. "And where you mean to go."

Everyone who's seen her says she looked just like Margaret Rutherford, but in her shabby overcoat buttoned one button wrong (she'd just come in from the potting shed) and her hair coming loose from its great pins, she was the White Queen more exactly.

"Well," Pierce said, "I've been to Glastonbury, and . . ."

"You've bean to Glostonbrie?" Her mobile eyebrows rose. "Why, you might be in search of the Grail."

He had gone to Glastonbury, the first of all his memory places, or Kraft's, starred in the guide, and site of more than one scene in Kraft's last novel. The Isle of Avalon. He would enter many churches in the coming months, very many, and of them all it was this ruined one alone that didn't inspire in him an awful trepidation: guilt, threat, pity. Its nave and transept frozen grass, its lead roof the leaden English sky. Nice. He had imagined, without thinking it through, that the places he was to go to would be somehow lost in remoteness, fallen and neglected, like ziggurats in Yucatán. This was so mown and tidied, so worked up and mapped and labeled and furnished with souvenirs, that what mystery it might once have had could not reach him, and for that he was grateful. In Kraft's old guidebook, he read about Joseph of Arimathea, Aldhelm and Dunstan, Arthur and Guinevere. He walked the ruins, the vanished cloister, fratery, library. He went out to Chalice Hill and the Holy Well. *The masonry of the Well has been the cause of much discussion. Possibly it is connected with the Druids, associated with ancient rituals of sun and water. Certainly it is orientated, as has been proved by measurements on Midsummer Day. The stones are placed in wedge formation, as in the Pyramids. Sir Flinders Petrie was of the opinion that the Well might have been rock hewn by Egyptian colonists in about the year 200 BC.*

Well, okay. He let the icy bloodred waters flow over his hand (*chalybeate, radioactive, neverfailing*) and then went up the bare Tor on a spiral track (*the ascent from Chilkwell Street is easy*) toward the tower on top. Soon the air was sharp as knives in his throat.

"You didn't quite reach it," said the Dame. She let her folded hands fall in her lap, his own spirit or lame body dropping from the unscaled height. "Well. A shame. You have such a view from there. That's the reward."

"Panoramic," her sister said. In all her books, Dame Frances credits her sister, indispensable helper and friend. It was she, lean and sharp faced as the Red Queen, who brought the tea, then sat, picked up her knitting. "Your friend Dr. John Dee knew that spot well, of course."

"*Our* friend Dr. Dee," said Frances, and they both smiled at Pierce.

From the top of the Tor John Dee could have seen all the way to Wales, from where his people came. In Kraft's last unfinished book, he can also see from there a great ring of landscape giants, signs of the Zodiac marked out for miles around in the earth of Somerset by churchyards, knolls, river bends, rock outcroppings. Later Pierce found this supposed zodiac and its giants described where Kraft had doubtless found it too—in the pages of the *Dictionary of Deities, Devils, and Dæmons of Mankind,* by Alexis Payne de St.-Phalle.

When Dee at the end of his life returns to the well and the Tor, the Zodiac in the earth is gone, can't be seen any longer from the hill's height. In Kraft's story. Just earth after all.

"But," the Red Queen asked the White Queen, "how would he," indicating Pierce in the chair opposite, "have come to know of John Dee atole? It seems quite unlikely."

"Well, of course John Dee has a history in America," said the White Queen. "He went to America." She bent her head to Pierce. "With the group you there call the Pilgrims."

He could only regard her, goggling probably, trying to remember Dee's death date—1609? Not later, surely.

"Not the man himself," she said, buttering toast. "But his thought, and his mark. Oh yes. John Winthrop was a devotee of Dee and his learning—you weren't aware? He brought a whole alchemical library with him to the New World, and he used Dee's Monas as his personal sign." She bit into her toast with large strong teeth, lifting her eyebrows merrily at him. He began to suspect that she knew very well she was being unsettling. "Think what its adventures might have bean, thereafter."

"Yes." Among them his own chapter of the Invisible College, in the mountains of eastern Kentucky twenty-five years before; himself, his cousins, his heroes.

"And where do you go next?" she asked. "On your quest."

"I'm going next to Germany," Pierce said. "Heidelberg."

At this name she and her sister turned slowly to look on one another with unreadable expressions, unreadable to him, British expressions of alarm, or astonishment, or amusement, or all of those and more. As one their looks returned to him, and both at once said, "Ah: the Winter King."

"Excuse me?"

"You are in pursuit of the Winter King," said the Dame.

"The winter king?"

"You know of him."

"No. Well, yes. There was a novel of Kraft's. That novelist who."

"Ah, he."

"*The Winter King*. I read it. I must have. I don't remember it."

"No? You will want to know the tale. The whole tale."

"Oh?" He thought that in British English *want* meant *need*, or had once.

"It's quite a tragic one," her sister said. "Best to hear it before you go."

He said nothing, unable to refuse. Dame Frances clapped her hands before her like a concert singer about to begin. "King James I, who feared so many things, who wanted to secure everyone's good opinion, was angling for a Spanish marriage for his son, Henry, to protect him from the Catholic powers. Then Henry, whom everyone loved and admired, parfit gentil knight, died suddenly."

"A fever," said her sister. "From sweating after a game of tennis. So they said."

"And so then James married his eldest daughter, Elizabeth, to the German prince palatine, Frederick, who was—or was likely to be when he was a bit more secure—the leader of the Protestant powers in Europe. A very suitable match. Two young people, quite attractive, it's said, certainly energetic and with a great deal of dash—actually they seem to me a very Shakespearean couple—they are married with great pomp in the winter of 1613, and go back to Frederick's capital, Heidelberg. Which is extensively modernized and beautified with gardens, grottoes, statues. They seem a sublimely fortunate pair.

"Then." She lowered her chin, looking at him above her glasses, mouth solemnly pursed. "The Holy Roman emperor, an aged nonentity named Matthias, dies. He was not only emperor but also the Catholic king of a largely Protestant Bohemia. The crown of Bohemia is, theoretically at least, elective, and when the archduke of Austria—a devout activist Catholic who is certain to be elected the next emperor—wins the Bohemian crown for himself as well, a group of Protestant nobles in Prague revolt. From a high window in Prague castle the archduke's surrogates are thrown . . ."

"The Defenestration of Prague," Pierce said. Long, long ago they had asked Axel on television: *By what name do we know the event that took place in Prague in 1618 and began the Thirty Years' War, and what does the word mean?* Defenestration: throwing-out-of-the-window. "For heaven's sake."

"The Bohemians then turn to Frederick and elect him their king instead. And he accepts. And for a single winter, while the imperial armies gather force and the German Protestant princes waver and argue, and James in London offers no help atole, the two of them, Frederick and Elizabeth, reign in Prague castle. Then, in one sharp, quick battle, the emperor's forces defeat him utterly. Utterly. He barely escapes, his reign is over, he and his queen flee into exile, and all is as though it had not bean. Soon his home country is devastated. Thirty years of war begin, the first European world war.

"And the question is: why did he do it? Why did he think he could? And why did anyone else think so? Answer that, and it will lead you back to that sign, and poor John Dee."

She said it as though she herself knew the answer very well, and her sister too, who now lowered her knitting and said—like a character in a play, filling in an audience by telling another character what both of them know very well—"Why, was it not poor Alexis who first put this question to you? And challenged *you* to answer it?"

"Alexis," said the Dame, putting a finger to her chin in thought. "In service of his Dictionary. Do you think so?"

"Yes." The thing she knitted had grown noticeably longer.

"So long ago," said the Dame, regarding Pierce. "I knew so little."

"You don't mean," Pierce said at last, "an author, a sort of author, named St.-Phalle? Alexis Payne de St.-Phalle?"

Dame Frances blinked. "Oh, did you know him?"

"Well, no. I mean I didn't know *him*."

Dame Frances bent inquiringly to her sister, who said loudly, "He didn't know him."

"Poor old dear," said Frances. "I knew him, oh not well, but for quite a long time. Yes. You mean this fellow." She went again to her shelves, and drew out a large book, bound in imitation leather, that bore on its spine the sign of the Monas.

"He used often to come to the institute," she said dreamily, opening the book. "When he was in good health, in the days I first began to work there. Always busily collecting references and making memoranda. For his books. Though this may have bean his only one, in fact."

Pierce had in his life seen three copies of that book. This one of hers; before that, the one in the Blackbury Jambs Free Library, that Fellowes Kraft had so often taken out; and before that, the one sent to his house, unasked for, by the state librarian in Lexington, Kentucky, a woman surely of the Yates type, a chain to her glasses.

"But you see he wasn't a scholar atole, really," she said. "He was a sort of antiquarian, a jackdaw, collecting shiny bits of this and that, whatever caught his fancy. Indeed he looked rather like a jackdaw. That was how he seemed to me then, at any rate. I was very young."

Pierce stood, unable to stay seated, and came closer as she turned the pages of the Dictionary she held. Soon she would come upon the entry for the Invisible College.

"I imagine he took a bit of a fancy to you," her sister said, resuming her knitting. "So many of the older ones did."

Frances closed her eyes, so as not to hear this, and went on. "We did rather stay in touch. He ceased to come round, later on, and I learned where he kept himself, a couple of rooms in Notting Hill. Now and then if convenient I'd look in. Bring him some beef tea. Fetch him a book. For his researches." She smiled: a gentle, a wholly gentle and knowing smile.

"Notes," said her sister. Her scarf was long enough to strangle her with.

"He'd write me little notes. Peculiar little notes pointing out small things. Only when I found them recently in a box, all clipped together—you see I am of the jackdaw clan myself—they seemed to make a kind of story or narrative, like the clues of a scavenger hunt."

She shut the book, not perhaps noticing Pierce's index pointing to the entry, the picture, his mouth open; and she replaced it, not in the place from which she had drawn it. "I have bean," she said to him confidentially, as though she might be overheard, or as though she said something that might be thought unkind, "so embarrassed by the sort of person one can encounter, when doing the work that I do. Those who believe that age-old conspiracies are still afoot, reaching back to the Pyramids; that the Rosicrucians are now about, and working on our behalf; that there is a story ongoing. I supposed him to be one such. But he was something different, I think. He *was* a Rosicrucian, you see; he believed himself to be one. But he also knew the secret to being a Rosicrucian: that you can only strive and hope and wish to be one. That is what a Rosicrucian is; it is all that one is."

Two Siamese cats had come into the room, and now wound themselves around the Dame's thick legs, looking at Pierce as though they too were in on the joke.

"The great genealogy of knowledge," Dame Frances said, sighing. "The transmission of occult understanding from master to master. All of them longed to be part of it, you see. To be tapped, to be taken in, taught the secret language. The Invisible College. But there were no masters, no brothers. It was never anything but a chain of books; all that it ever was. Books and their readers. And Plato said: We think, when we read a book, that we hear the voice of a person; but if we try to question a book, it can't answer."

She thrust her fists into the pockets of her ancient cardigan, and regarded Pierce with what, unmistakably, was compassion. "Of course we forgive them, we must. As we would forgive our own family. Because, you know, that is what they are."

No: he hadn't really sat like Alice between her and her sister, to be pointed on his way; never even left London once he'd come back from Glastonbury. He *saw* her—he really did see her, round little figure in the lobby of the Warburg Institute, tugging on a mac and hefting a plump belted briefcase while speaking in atrociously accented French to a tall gent who bent to hear. It had to be her. Maybe if she'd been alone he'd have spoken to her—he really did have Barr's regards to deliver—and who knows what might have developed then; but surely the first question she'd have asked him would have been about that albatross around his neck, and he grew shy or sad or ashamed and said nothing, only nodded at her as she nodded inquiringly at him.

He did find, in a tomblike mystic bookstore, a copy of her newest book, *The Rosicrucian Enlightenment,* and bought it, and from out of it she did keep speaking to him, though she would not answer his questions. She said that the Rosicrucian movement arose from what she called "Dee's Bohemian mission"—even though Dee had gone back to England, and was dead some years when the Rosicrucian rumors started to run, still there must have been something. Something that he did or left behind there, something that he saw or learned or preached, something that people remembered. In Kraft's story, whose plot Pierce was following here—which was like trying to get around Lake Superior with the help of a copy of "Hiawatha"—the thing left behind in Prague wasn't a lesson or an achievement but a claim, or a promise: that he could make the Stone for the Emperor Rudolph. That, and the body of Edward Kelley, out of which Dee's gold had come, and his angels, and everything.

Whatever it was, maybe young Frederick had to find it if he was to go on being king, and had reason to think he could. And he never found it. Not in our story of the history of the world.

The frontispiece of her book—which is what started Pierce's mental journey to the suburbs and Dame Frances's villa and the book he imagined to be standing on her bookshelf—was the same picture that in the *Dictionary of Deities, Devils, and Dæmons of Mankind* had illustrated the entry on the Invisible College. The picture, a surreal wood engraving, came originally, it said here, from a book or tract called *Speculum sophicum rhodo-stauroticum.* "Speculum sophicum rhodo-stauroticum," Pierce said aloud, reading this on the Tube, then again out on the street; he would find himself saying these dactyls over to himself aloud or silently all winter as he walked the continent, like someone repeating the name of the thing he's mislaid as he searches for it. *Spec*ulum *Soph*icum *Rhodo*-staur *Ot*icum. The picture showed—you remember—the Invisible College of the Rose-Cross brothers, a ludicrous high wagon that is a house or mansion, crowded with the Brothers at their work, the house mounted on inadequate wheels but really powered by wide saillike wings: if he'd been asked to draw the thing from memory, Pierce would actually have given it not wings but sails.

As Fellowes Kraft had done, in his last unfinished book. In which this winged wagon appeared as John Dee's own wagon, sailing over high Germany with Dee and his wife and children aboard. And also a werewolf, an angel in a jar, and a fortune in fairy gold.

Rosie—I think the unfinished parts of Kraft's book were going to be about the Rosicrucians, and about a marriage. A prince and a princess. The sites are marked in the guidebook, and I think I know now how to follow them, or at least I can go the same way they went. There is a jukebox in this pub, I wouldn't have thought that was allowed, it's playing a loud country version of "Rose in Spanish Harlem" and I'm not thinking straight. The guidebook will guide me. By the way forget that last card; it was a joke sort of.

The coldest winter since the Little Ice Age of the Jacobean period, said the television mounted above the bar in this actually rather squalid saloon he had wandered into. The queen herself had been stuck in the snow on her way to Scotland, and had to get off her train, and be taken in by her subjects, given warming drink. A gill of Scotch, called whisky, was in the bottom of Pierce's glass; he swallowed it, took out his guidebook, his gloves, and his map of the Underground: down into which he now he must go.

We emerge from Charing Cross Station to view, at the head of Whitehall, the **statue of Charles I** now so weathered and decayed. Opposite the gate into the **Horse Guards Parade** stands the magnificent Palladian **Banqueting House,** designed by Inigo Jones with the ceiling by Rubens (1630), glorifying the House of Stuart and in particular King James I. Today it houses the **United Services Museum**; visitors may view among other exhibits the skeleton of one of Napoleon's chargers.

Now on either side the broad expanse of **Whitehall** is lined by the great buildings of government. Once upon a time, one entered upon Whitehall Palace precincts at this point through a magnificent towered **gate** wrongly called "Holbein's Gate." Going forward through that gate, you would find yourself walking by a tall brick wall on the left, which was the wall of the old Whitehall Palace

but if you stepped *backward* instead, backward through the Holbein Gate, to pass along that high brick wall, which is now on your right side, then beyond it would lie the Privy Garden, all knots and neat geometries, where the lords and ladies may frequently be seen awhispering; and across from it, the ball courts where court tennis and featherball and on rainy days even bowls are played. Here young Prince Henry fenced and played tennis daylong, and here after a hot sweat on a cool day he contracted his last fever. West of the bowls-house is the cockpit, which is a theatre as well, and adjacent are the Cockpit Lodgings, where Princess Elizabeth, who loves plays and players, awaits her husband to be. On your left will be the shabby and inadequate Banqueting House, not yet replaced by Inigo Jones's creation; it has been in use since Cardinal Wolsey's day. Thereby opens the great Court Gate that leads to the Palace proper, where there was wont to be a continual throng, either of Gallants standing to ravish themselves with the sight of Ladies handsome Legs and Insteps as they tooke Coache; Or of the tribe of liveries, by whom you could scarce passe without a jeare or a saucy answer to your question.

Leave the Great Court if you have the *entrée* and go up the flight of stone stairs to the Guard Chamber, where his Majesties great Beefe-eaters are in attendance, which is nothing but to tell Tales, devoure the beverage, keepe a great fire, and carry up Dishes, wherein their fingers would bee sometimes before they come to the king's Table.

Leaving thence we come out upon the Terrace, a cloister that runs round the open square known as the Preaching Place and connects the Royal Quarters with The Banqueting House, and which is now so rotten and ill repaired that it will collapse in a year and nearly kill the Spanish Ambassador, and where on a December night, a Masque being presented at court, one woman among the rest lost her honesty, for which she was carried to the porters lodge, being surprized at her busines on the top of the Taras.

At Christmas along this Terrace or Taras, in furs and holly crowns, snow hissing in the cressets, the Court passes, newly come out of mourning for Prince Henry. There are to be plays and music, for this is the day of the betrothal of Frederick and Elizabeth, two handsome and personable young people who are actually in love, who fell in love at first sight; theirs will be the preeminent dynastic coupling of Protestant Europe, though it is whisperd hee is much too young and small timbred to undertake such a taske.

Among the entertainments tonight the King's Men will perform a play of Shakespeare's, *The Tempest*, not a new play but newly mounted and with a Masque just composed and inserted by the author in honor of the royal match.

The author happening in that cold winter of the Wedding to be in London, buying property near the Blackfriars Theater. Not having walked those streets then for years; no, not since 1610, when he came to make complaint to Thorpe for his printing of the sonnets, the which Thorpe got from that thieving rascal W.H., no 'twere best he think not on't. On that visit, two years and more ago, he had gone up the river too, for to call upon old Dr. Dee in his Mortlake house, old friend and teacher of players and stage carpenters, to consult with him upon the pains and weakness in his legs; to find that the doctor had died a twelvemonth. Standing in the great room wherefrom the books, glasses, stones, staves, globes, maps, and all had been sold or lost or taken. Dead: dead after years of silence. His daughter there alone, who had nursed him as best she could. I knew him long ago, he said to her; I came here as a boy; I loved him and I honor him. And he had gone thence back downriver, a sharp wind blowing, blow away vanitie; and he bethought him, how a wise man, great doctor, midwife of nature's wonders, untrammeled in his powers, charger of spirits, might be driven to silence, retirement, abnegation. No, not driven neither: his powers unlost, but only put away; the spirits at length released that he had commanded. *Ile burn my books.* No, not that, not burned; poor Kit, not burned.

Shipwreck. His mind harping on shipwreck those years, no marvel. A story of three realms—one of politic working, lords and plots and the world's business; one of magic such as Dr. Dee had talked of, had worked in too it may be, benign and fearsome, graves oped, noontime sun bedimmed; and one the realm of nature, plain, longed-for, impossible to restore.

A year after that, *The Tempest* was at Blackfriars, Burbage giving fire to the rattling thunder, the kettles beaten in the cellarage, the isle full of noyses. And now this year, at Christmas, at court, the marvels and wonders it called for would be the more marvelous and wonderful, since Mr. In-I-go Jones of the jesting name would be the master carpenter. Disappearing banquets and flitting spirits and transformations to music. And Burbage had asked the author for a new little Masque too, a demi-Masque, for the betrothal of Elizabeth and her German.

It was easily done. Waiting upon his lawyer in his chambers, he called for a pen and some paper. Nuptial blessings were certainly proper to the play,

Ferdinand having passed all the tests set him by Prospero, including a solemn vow not to break Miranda's virgin knot before the wedding.

I must
Bestow vpon the eyes of this yong couple
Some vanity of mine Art. It is my promise,
And they expect it of me.

Cold airs from the lawyer's window corner; coldest winter in years. *Ile break my staff.* John Dee's was long broken now. His own was merely the stick he leaned on in these London streets, where the younglings hurried laughing by. He scribbled. Not many more short lines like these left to make, and very likely he would not finish all that he had begun; but that he could not finish was not reason he should not go on.

Now come my Ariell, bring a Corolary,
Rather then want a Spirit; appear, & pertly.
No tongue: all eyes: be silent. [Soft musick.]

Later that month in the torchlit hall behind Inigo Jones's cloudie skies, all blue canvas and lath, three court ladies in dresses of their own designing take a deep breath, touch their bosoms, smile at one another. Three goddesses: Iris, Ceres, Juno. They descend, to applause, they step forth.

Honor, riches, marriage, blessing,
Long continuance, and encreasing,
Hourely ioyes, be still vpon you,
Iuno sings her blessings on you.
Earths increase, foyzon plentie,
Barnes, and Garners, neuer empty.
Vines, with clustring bunches growing,
Plants, with goodly burthen bowing:
Spring come to you at the farthest,
In the very end of Haruest.
Scarcity and want shall shun you,
Ceres blessing so is on you.

Then enter certaine Reapers (properly habited:) they ioyne with the Nimphes, in a gracefull dance, towards the end whereof, Prospero starts sodainly and speakes.

I had forgot that foule conspiracy
Of the beast Calliban, and his confederates
Against my life. The minute of their plot is almost come:
Well done, auoid: no more.

After which to a strange hollow and confused noyse, they heauily vanish.

They vanish. Heavily, which is sadly or sorrowfully. Blown away in the midst of.

Pierce, standing in the street before the Banqueting Hall—the new Banqueting Hall (1630) and not the old one, which has long been subsumed into the basements of the Ministry of Defence—said suddenly aloud, in grief and wonder, "He knew."

The Banqueting Hall was Closed for Renovations. Blue plastic tarpaulins clothed it, ballooning softly in the cold smoky air, as though the building were under sail. Cloud of traffic around him moving up and down. "He knew," Pierce said again. "It's as though he knew."

It's as though he knew. As though Prospero knew, and therefore Shakespeare knew; as though he knew what he couldn't possibly have known.

Pierce wrote this in his red journal in a Lyons tea shop, its windows steamed with winter, clatter of mugs, and smell of bacon and toast. He had the Puffin paperback of *The Tempest*, just acquired at a WH Smith stall, open to Act IV.

Prospero remembers the conspiracy and crime afoot, and immediately he spoils his show, orders all of it away, even though he's just said to the children, Hush and be mute, or else our spell is marred. Which means the spell is marred. And when his new son-in-law Frederick, I mean Ferdinand, looks in movéd sort as if he was dismayed, then Prospero tells him that the revels now are ended; he says that the actors that blessed them were all spirits, not goddesses of love and plenty at all, and are vanished into air. Not only that but all his son-in-law's hopes and ambitions, and all the towers and palaces and temples, and the whole world—the great Globe itself, and all which it inherit—are no more substantial, and we are all such stuff as dreams are made on. How can he say that, what did he mean, didn't Shakespeare think who was listening just then? Was he talking to himself, or to them, and how could he know how that marriage and its hopes and plans would all end? That like this insubstantial pageant faded, it would leave not a rack behind.

It's probably only that thing that Shakespeare does, how he infuses the most standard dramatic necessities with so much feeling, too much feeling for what's required. Maybe all he meant to do, dramatically speaking, was to get the story back on track after this new masque; maybe in his day Prospero at this moment was played as a standard absentminded wizard, just catching up with his own plots. But that's not how it feels. No. It feels like the end of all blessing.

Aboard the North Sea ferry, bound for the Hook of Holland and the Continent, cold ocean not far below his bed, his three cabinmates gently snoring, Pierce with his own tiny lamp lit, reading then writing.

Why does Prospero abjure his magic?

Wouldn't great magic like his have been a big help back in Milan, where he's headed? To build a better world, a new world? Is everything that he knows applicable only to this story on this island, and useless everywhere else? Nowhere does the play say so. What did Shakespeare know, and to whom was his warning issued?

Gongs and bells and the low thudding of the diesels.

Why is magic to be laid aside when the world's real work is taken up? Is that what I have to learn? Is it only that a story of magic can't end until magic is given up?

From the Hook of Holland he went to the Hague aboard a local train or trolley; it passed magically from the city into the countryside, past tiny tidy farms damp brown and gray, stopping at crossroads for people dressed in brown and gray to get on and off. He got off where his directions told him, a gray suburb where up a street was a consular office of the People's Republic of Czechoslovakia. An undistinguished building that might have been a small clinic or even a private house. Inside just two young men in open shirts and leather jackets, universal young men, one bearded, who welcomed him without ceremony, and helped him fill out the forms he needed for his visa. Czech flag on the wall with hammer and sickle. They copied the numbers from his passport, they photographed him and asked an array of personal questions that had no relation to one another or to anything else, as though randomly selected to test his memory—or his truthfulness, maybe, he thought with a comic stab of paranoia. And they gave him his visa, with pleasure it seemed. His photograph within it, dark turtleneck, tousled hair, black piratical beard, glower—would it help or hurt? Troublemaker or fellow traveler? Did it matter? It was a sort of handsome fellow, though not himself maybe. The other riders on the tiny train into the city watched him study it.

In the morning, sore and rattled from a night in a student hostel busy nightlong with comers and goers (no more of those, he vowed), he boarded a long sleek international train bound for Köln, which was Cologne, and the Rhine journey to Heidelberg.

Absurd, but I am continually surprised that the Europeans celebrate their own historic sites, not only the big ones but the littlest and least, places I've known about only as I got their names and map coordinates from esoteric works. Come to find out that they and their legends are well known, they are advertised, you pay money to enter them, and you get pamphlets that explain them all. At Heidelberg you're told every rooming house Goethe stayed in, what moonlight walks to take up onto the castle ramparts, just where Goethe stood when he famously observed, etc.; stationery, souvenir plates, beer mugs, with the same pictures engraved on them. Why did I think it would all lie neglected, only waiting for me? Because I didn't really believe it existed?

He hadn't; even as he walked it, it seemed to him that his own presence summoned this Old World into existence in all its solidity and fullness, a fullness at once expressive and as mute as stone, which a lot of it was, stone: churches and pavements and castle walls and apartment buildings where whoever lived: more mute and obdurate than he could have imagined in advance. He put out a hand and touched speechless stone and so caused it to come to be. It was unsettling. He couldn't make it stop. He got used to it.

Far famed, **Schloss Heidelberg** is part ruin, part restoration. The restored parts are largely without interest, resembling a combination of a Swiss *Stübli*

> and the smoking room of a Dutch ocean liner. Be sure to engage a *Führer* (official guide) if you wish to go through the maze of passages, rooms, belvederes, towers, and corridors, or you may never find a way out.

He might have liked to see what the smoking room of a Dutch ocean liner, or something resembling one, looked like; but the interiors were *geschlossen* for the winter months and there was no *Führer*. He wandered in the Schlosshof, the castle yard. A silver fog hung over the river Neckar and the toy town far below. Pierce followed the obvious way, down the sloping walks and *the famed terraced gardens,* beneath a great arch—*the **Elizabeth-Pforte**, built as a birthday surprise (legend has it) in a single night by the besotted Frederick V for his English queen*—and into a broad bare terrace. Where were the famed gardens?

"Here," said Dame Frances Yates. "The designer was Salomon de Caus, a French Protestant and an extremely brilliant garden architect and hydraulic engineer. He was on intimate terms with Inigo Jones . . ."

Fine rain had begun to fall. She took from her bag a collapsible umbrella, pointed it like an épée, and pressed a button; the umbrella opened as it lengthened. Pierce held it over the two of them, for she hardly reached his shoulder. She told him how de Caus had blasted away the mountain with gunpowder to level it for his gardens, how he constructed grottoes where musical fountains played, and a water organ based on a design in Vitruvius, and a statue of Memnon that sang when the sun struck it, "as in the classical story," which Pierce couldn't remember.

Nothing of what she described—geometrical beds, obelisks, an airy palace, a maze, another maze—could now be seen; only a mossy and almost illegible river god at the entrance to a grotto. A cave. Empty. The dumpling-shaped tourist with umbrella and walking shoes who had reminded him of Dame Frances stared with him into the dark echoey silence, and withdrew.

It was a ruin, more even than a ruin, a quasi-natural object, vine grown and shapeless, devolving from its status as a work of hands and minds to a complex lump of stone, disorganizing every day a little further in the entropy of hope and desire, which proceeds only one way. What had destroyed it? Lightning, said the guidebook, striking not once but twice, and a dynastic dispute with a French king in the following century. But Dame Frances said it was the two of them, Frederick and his Elizabeth, the might-be-happy couple blessed by Shakespeare's ambivalent mage. The two who in 1619 reigned for a winter as king and queen of Bohemia, a reign as brief and illusory as a masque: and who brought down upon their magic kingdom on the Rhine the *tercios* and the pikemen and the musketeers and the sappers and the end of everything.

7

She called him Celadon, after the shepherd-knight in d'Urfé's *L'Astrée,* that vastly popular romance about the Golden Age and the return of Astræa, goddess of Justice and Peace, ears of corn wound in her hair. *Iam redit et Virgo, redeunt Saturnia regna.* He wrote his love letters to her in French; she never learned German. The marriage had been the work of the nobleman Christian of Anhalt, a ferocious little man with wild red hair, tireless bearer of a heavy destiny (so he believed), and the counselor closest to Frederick. Frederick called him *Mon père.*

Anhalt was there to receive the Princess Palatine when she first arrived at Oppenheim in the Palatinate, and he brought her to Heidelberg, her new seat, by means of a series of masques and processions designed by wise workers to assure her and her spouse's health, happiness, and success, drawing down upon them the best astral and divine influences by the right arrangement of signs, persons, geometries, and words. She passed through arches covered with roses, with images of Church Fathers, Ancestors, Deities. A pretty boy gave her a basket of fruit in the name of Flora and Pomona—Spring and then Autumn, flower and then fruit—for Fertility; and she ate hungrily, and everyone laughed and rejoiced in her. Her husband came out to meet her in a wagon made like Jason's ship, sailing with the Argonauts to recover the Golden Fleece. Music, in Venus's mode (the Hypolydian) and generous Jupiter's (the Lydian) and smiling Sol's (the Dorian), but not the melancholic Hypodorian; there would be time enough for Saturnine music later.

She brought with her a troupe of English actors, for she loved plays and shows and let's-pretend above all things. They performed old plays and new, *Love's Labour's Lost* and *Love's Labour's Won, The Merrie Divil of Edmonton, A Game at Chesse,* which mocked the Spanish. Her Celadon delighted to see her laugh, delighted to see her delighted, and if plays delighted her there would be plays. No matter that his family was not only Calvinist but fiercely Calvinist: his father had once held up a consecrated host before the congregation and ripped it into shreds: "Fine god *you* are! We'll see who's stronger!" From then on it was tough bread and wooden mugs at the infrequent communions in his whitewashed chapel.

Frederick and his Elizabeth were beings of a different order. Of course they stood for True Religion, of course they were Evangelical, but they were also Hope and Beauty and Conciliation and Possibility and Fructification and Peace; somehow this seemed obvious to all, all at least who came within range of the happy rays their persons emanated. There were two young men in the throngs when He and She first met beneath the Arch at Heidelberg: one was a peregrinating Lutheran pastor, Johann Valentin Andreæ, and the other a student at the university, a Moravian and a member of the Moravian Brethren, a gentle pietist sect—his name was Jan Komensky, which he latinized to Comenius. And both of them felt it: good stars in conjunction, the world going the right way after a long wandering, Saturnian cold hatred and Martian hot fury both abating. Sun and the scent of roses.

More than that even.

They both imagined, Jan and Valentin—they talked about it long in the halls of the university, in the thronged inns and the silences of the *Bibliotheca palatina* where the great Johannes Gruter was librarian—that a universal reformation of the whole wide world might be beginning, now, right now. What did it matter that the almanacs and prophecies had so far been wrong—the fateful year 1600 had brought no vast changes that they could see—that didn't mean the world wasn't in the throes of a transformation, one that remained invisible so far. Anyway it filled their own souls. How could they help to forward it? Smuggled out of the dungeons of the Inquisition came manuscripts of Tommaso Campanella, who taught that the earth was now growing closer to the sun, and the temperature of the cold north was warming, and Love was increasing. Campanella projected a great city, perfect city, City of the Sun, ruled by a philosopher hidden in a circular tower inside a square inside the cubic walls of the city. A universal hieroglyphic picture-dictionary would cover those walls, instructing all the citizens in virtue and wisdom by the immediacy and force of its magic images.

Magic. Theurgical, cabalistical, alchemical, hieroglyphical, historico-alchemical, cabalistico-theurgical, thaumaturgico-iatrochemico-astrological. As the alchemist recreates in his furnace the entire world, which thereupon grows gold as gold grows in the *matrix* of the earth, but faster; as the cabalist manipulates the letters of the words by which God commanded the world to be and to be fruitful, thus sharing in the divine creative power; in the same way couldn't the slow-advancing history of the world be accelerated, if only its events could be read right? In 1614—when the sacred couple had been two years in Heidelberg and the two friends had parted, Comenius returning to the Czech lands, Andreæ to Tübingen to be a Lutheran pastor—there came the outfolding, the sudden way opening, the cry of summoning and possibility.

Universal and General Reformation of the Whole Wide World; together with the Fama Fraternitatis *of the laudable Order of the Rosy Cross, written to all the Learned and Rulers of Europe.* It was a little gray pamphlet printed in Cassel, it was a manuscript read in Prague, it was a letter warmly responded to in Germany, the respondent thrown into the galleys by the Jesuits (so the pamphlet itself proclaimed). *This happy time, when there is discovered not only the other half of the world, which lay hidden from us before, but also many wonderful and never-before-seen works and creatures; and men reimbued with great wisdom, who might renew all arts, so that Man might understand his own nobleness and worth, and why he is called Microcosm, and how far his knowledge might reach into Nature.*

Impossible not to be moved by these huge certainties. Andreæ in Tübingen, Comenius in Moravia, scholars and Inquisitors in Bavaria and Saxony read and reread. Who were these Brothers? They had long been among us, it appeared, awaiting their hour. The wisest of them, C.R., had traveled the world and discoursed with the wise in every land. The realms of the Turk too, Fez, Damascus, Ægypt and Arabia Felix. And from C.R. the wisdom passes to R.C., his brother, and B., a painter, and G., and P.D., their secretary. Thence to A., and D., and to J.O. in England, master of Cabala, as his book H. shows. With the whole alphabet seemingly summoned, the pamphlet then tells how the Brothers went out into various lands, not only to communicate their *Axiomata* secretly to the learned but to heal the sick for free; and they vow to keep their brotherhood a secret for a hundred years. Why now have they broken their silence? Because the lost tomb of Brother R.C. (or C.R.C. as he apparently becomes) has at last been discovered, and the door opened. *As also there shall be opened a door to Europe, which has already begun to appear, and which many expect and long for.*

Johann Valentin Andreæ stayed up all night reading, walked the streets, unable to stay still. What was he being told to do? What was being asked of him? How could the universal reformation of the world be both at hand and impossible? In a later age, unimaginable then, you would say: the current of that work passes through him, and the resistance of his soul heats him to incandescence.

Then silence. *Silentium post clamores,* the little screed promised, a pause for the leaven to work in souls, nothing more needing to be said.

Then in the following year a new call, another *libellum,* this one in Latin:

> *A brief consideration of a More Secret Philosophy, written by Philip à Gabella, a student of philosophy, now published for the first time together with the Confession of the R.C. Fraternity. Printed at Cassel by Wilhelm Wessel, printer to the Most Illustrious Prince, in 1615.*

The more secret philosophy was a sign, one he seemed both to have always known and to be seeing for the first time:

The *Consideratio* of the sign was an arithmetic, or a mathesis; the sign itself was a *stella hieroglyphica*—so it said of itself. It began with a Pythagorean Y, and therefore it might be a story, the history of the universe described as a soul's journey, or maybe a soul's journey described as the universe. Johann Valentin Andreæ stared at the sign, which seemed to him to be something like a small human figure, and then he studied the paragraphs that followed, recounting the vicissitudes, divisions, and reassemblings through which that figure was put. The more he stared the more he understood and the less he knew. He shook his head, laughed, felt tricked, wondered; he cast it aside, he picked it up again. It was a joke, but a good joke. Or it was no joke: the old cold world was ending, and an influx of the truth, light, and glory that God had commanded should accompany poor Adam from Paradise and sweeten his misery was about to poured upon the world.

For the past year Johann Valentin had studied in secret the Great Art of transmutation, as the Fraternity was said to be doing in many places, as he was seemingly commanded to do if he wanted to be one of them, if there were really any of them at all: to see how far his knowledge might reach into

Nature. His own mother was a chymist and worker in *materia medica*; he had stood by her as she worked at her stills and her ovens when he was a boy, but alone now he was too timid to start a physical fire, and to mix physical *alchymia* in physical cucurbites, to torment actual *materia* and lay his athenor within an actual physical stove. That was not the only way to work in the Art, though, he was sure. The heart was a stove too, the brain an athenor. He thought that this figure, this *stella hieroglyphica* that he looked at, might itself be a *précis* or epitome of the whole Art. It was the mathematical bones of the homunculus, a stick figure to be clothed in flesh, and that clothing was the Work, and the Self that resulted was the object and goal.

But there was, in the numbered and lettered paragraphs of the *Consideratio*, finally no story told. And transformation (Andreæ thought) was above all a *story*, whether in the fire or in the heart. So if he wanted a story he'd have to write it himself.

He would have to write it himself. A transmutation painful and sweet occurred in his own heart as he thought it—he would have to write the story absent from these pages. A story in which every chapter would relate the tale of another piece of the disassembled man reassembled, until the necessary happy ending.

Nor would he be throwing whatever pearls he owned before the swine of ignorance: for his story of the Art's workings would not reveal those workings except to those who already knew them. To anyone else it would be merely a pleasantry, a funny story. It was said that Apuleius's wicked story of the Golden Ass was actually the story of the transmutation, told in a comic tale that no one needed to believe

Johann Valentin Andreæ, Lutheran pastor of Tübingen, with the *Consideratio* beside him to guide him, sat down to write a comedy or *ludibrium* ("in imitation of the English actors," he said later.) He put down its title: *The Chemical Wedding, by Christian Rosencreutz.* Brother C.R.C. is the hero and the author, and his name is now revealed: he is Christian Rosencreutz, an elderly fellow, but not yet a knight, and as Andreæ's play or *ludus* opens, he is preparing his heart in prayer for the Easter celebration when a wind, a strong wind, a terrible wind blows up:

> So strong a wind that I thought the hill on which my little house was built would fly apart; but since I had seen the Devil do such things as this before

(for the Devil had often tried to injure me) I took courage, and went on meditating, till I felt somebody touch me on the back.

This frightened me so utterly that I didn't dare turn. I tried to stay as brave and calm as a person could under the circumstances. Then I felt my coat tugged at, and tugged again, and at last I looked around. A woman, splendid and beautiful, stood there, in a sky-colored robe, a heavens covered with stars. She held a trumpet of beaten gold in her hand , and there was a name engraved on it, which I could easily read, but which I am still forbidden to tell. Under her left arm she had a bundle of letters, in all languages, which it was apparent she was going to deliver to all countries; she had large and beautiful wings too, full of eyes like a peacock's, that would certainly lift and carry her as fast as an eagle. I might have noticed other things about her too, but she was with me so short a time, and I was so amazed and afraid, that this was all I saw. In fact as soon as I turned around to see her, she started going through her letters, and pulled one out—a small one—and very gravely she laid it on my table; then without having said a word, she left. But as she rose into the air, she blew a blast on her trumpet so loud that the whole hill echoed with it, and for a quarter of an hour afterward I couldn't hear myself think.

All this was so unexpected that I had no idea what to tell myself about it, or what to tell myself to do next. So I fell to my knees, and begged my Creator not to let anything happen to me that would imperil my eternal happiness; and then, trembling, I went to pick up the little letter—which was heavy, as heavy as though it were solid gold, or heavier. As I was cautiously inspecting it, I found a small seal, with an odd sort of cross on it, and the inscription *In hoc signo vinces*, which made me feel a little better, as such a seal certainly wouldn't have been used by the Devil. I opened the letter tenderly; it was blue inside and on the blue in golden letters these verses were written:

On this day, this day, this
The Royal Wedding is!
If you are one who's born to see it,
And if God Himself decree it,
Then you must to the Mountain wend
Where three stately temples stand.

From there you'll know
Which way to go.
Be wise, take care,
Wash well, look fair,
Or else the Wedding cannot save you.
Leave right away,
Watch what you weigh—
Too little, and they will not have you!

Beneath this was drawn the Bride and Groom, *Sponsus* and *Sponsa.*

(Here Johann Valentin paused, dipped his pen again, and drew a figure, tongue between his teeth and pen held vertical, copying as best he could the hieroglyph of Philip à Gabella.)

I nearly fainted, having read this; my hair stood on end, and a cold sweat trickled down my side—for this must be the very wedding that I had learned about in a vision seven years before! I had thought about it constantly, and studied the stars and planets to determine the day, and here it was—and yet I couldn't have predicted that it would come at such a bad time. I always thought that I would be an acceptable and even welcome guest, and only needed to be ready to attend, but now it seemed God's providence was directing this, which I hadn't been certain about before, and the more I thought about myself, the more I found in my head nothing but confusion and blindness about the mysteries. I couldn't even understand things that lay under my own feet, which I encountered and dealt with every day; I didn't feel I was "born to see" the secrets of nature. I thought that nature could find a better disciple anywhere at all to entrust with her precious (though temporary and mutable) treasures than I could ever be. I certainly had not been wise, or taken care, or "washed well"—my inner physical life, and my social commitments, and my compassion toward my neighbors, all needed improvement. Life was always prodding me to get more; I was forever wanting to look good in the world's eyes and succeed, instead of working for the betterment of men. I was always plotting how I could make a quick profit by this or that scheme, build a big house, make a name for myself, and all that.

But those lines about the "three temples" worried me the most; I couldn't figure out what they meant at all. It occurred to me that maybe I wasn't supposed to know yet—for I wouldn't be worrying about any of this if it hadn't been thus revealed to me, maybe too soon. But I also thought that God had let me know that I really ought to be present at the wedding, and so like a little child I gave thanks to Him, and asked that he keep me always in awe of Him, and fill my heart every day with wisdom and understanding, and lead me (even though I didn't deserve it) to a happy ending at last.

So I got ready for the journey. I put on my white linen coat, fastened with a bloodred ribbon bound crossways over my shoulder. I stuck four red roses in my hat, so that I would be somewhat noticeable among the crowd. For food I took bread and salt, as a wise man had once told me to do in cases like this—I found it did me good. But before I set out, I got down on my knees in my wedding garment and asked God that, if what seemed to be about to happen really did happen, only good would come of it; and I made a vow, that if anything was revealed to me, I wouldn't use it for my own benefit or power in the world, but for the spreading of His Name and the service of my neighbor.

And with that vow, and in high hopes, I went out of my little room, and with joy I set out.

8

If all the world were made of letters and names, then a text out of nowhere could explode it, enter into its tissues like a germ or a seed, working both ways at once, toward foreword, toward epilogue, and remake its sense. That's what happened in Europe in 1615 when the Rosicrucian texts appeared, with their fantastic provenances and alphabetical prophets: or would have, if the world really were made of letters and names, and not the stuff it's made of. No one can account now for why these texts, unlike all the other wild prophecies, encoded romances, politico-chemical allegories, and religious polemics of the time, should have so taken the imagination. No one knows where either of the first two came from, who wrote them or why, what effect they were supposed then to have. The only name that can be identified for sure is that of the Lutheran pastor Johann Valentin Andreæ, who said he really did write the *Chemical Wedding*. Later he was sorry, and said he wished he hadn't written it.

Later.

Pierce in the little city below the ruins of Heidelberg castle read Dame Frances, who knew all about Christian Rosencreutz and Johann Valentin Andreæ and the *Chemical Wedding*, how it told of the founding of a Brotherhood of the Golden Stone, and of a wedding that takes place amid the magical gardens of a magical castle guarded by a lion. There are fountains described that are like Heidelberg's were. There is a knightly initiation, a little like the one whereby the real Frederick was really invested with the real Order of the Garter in actual Jacobean England. There is a play described in it that is like those the English actors really brought to Germany, and within that play a play. And look—the page was reprinted in Dame Frances's book—here in the *Chemical Wedding*, where the woman clothed as the sky and stars proffers her wedding invitation, right by the words *Sponsus* and *Sponsa*, there was (in the German) a crude mark that looks like, and in the English printings certainly becomes, the sign of the Monas, John Dee's own invention or discovery.

So she was right, and Johann Valentin's romance certainly does turn back to England, and the old English wizard, and that bright couple Shakespeare blessed, and their joined lions: the hopes the English placed in a smart dynastic coupling, the marriage of Thames and Rhine. But what if imagination could make it more? What if the hope then was that a *story* told about that wonderful and hopeful marriage might change its nature backward, and make it far more wonderful; what if language of the right kind, describing that more wonderful thing, could be powerful enough to change altogether what it described, even when what it described was something that had already happened? *Gematria*: the alteration of preexistent things by the alteration of the letters that constitute their true names, which first brought them into being.

And then to go on from there along the new way.

Pierce had come to think that magic, and stories intended to work magic, were made just opposite of the way stories in literature are made. In the stories of world literature, at least as he knew them in his own reading, one particular couple with a particular fate will stand for all couples in the toils of love and loss and struggle; Boy Meets Girl, Boy Loses Girl, Boy Gets Girl, or doesn't. But in magic, a general, universal couple—in alchemy the *Sponsus* and *Sponsa,* who near the end of the endless Work become pregnant with the Child who is the Stone—are at the same time each particular couple: they are Adam and Eve, Sun and Moon, Gold and Silver, Active and Passive, copper Venus and iron Mars, God and Mary, you and me, all of us at the work of generation. What they do is as though done by all, and the fruit of their union is for all to have, indeed all *do* have it just as soon as it's made. If it ever is.

So it would be no category error to identify one couple, one royal couple whom the whole world can see, with that general couple that is engendering the Stone. Because every couple can be so identified. That's what the *Chemical Wedding* did, and Frederick and Elizabeth were it, or It.

Beau Brachman once told him (whatever had become of Beau anyway, where was he now?) that there is no history. The world, he said, is like a hologram: break apart the photographic plate on which a hologram has been printed, and you can show that every part of it contains the whole image, if you look at it with laser light. Every part of every part, down to the smallest resolvable crumb. In the same way (Beau said) our original situation is present in every divisible moment of all succeeding situations, but (he said, and smiled that smile) you need a special light to see it.

If the Rose Cross was the *Monas hieroglyphica*, and the *Monas hieroglyphica* was the Golden Stone, and the Golden Stone was born of the coupling of the alchemical spouses, then (as in the best alchemical paradoxes) the Stone could only be generated by the action of the Stone, which, before it was generated, could not exist.

No wonder Andreæ called his work a comedy.

The culmination of the whole story, at the end of the Seventh Day, was the reception of the guests into the Order of the Golden Stone, after which they sailed away in their ships. So Yates said. Sailed away: either for the Fortunate Isles of the West to live happily ever after, or more likely to all the lands of men, to undertake the universal reformation of the whole wide world.

But what she didn't say is that Christian himself is left behind.

For on an earlier day of the story, Christian, roaming the wonderful castle to which his letter admitted him, went farther than he should. A mischievous young page told him that in a deep-down chamber Venus herself lay buried or asleep—did Christian want to see? He showed Christian a trapdoor of copper they could go down by. And Christian, trusting and terrified, followed him down.

> By the torch's light I saw a rich bed all made, hung with curious curtains. The page drew one aside, and there I saw the Lady Venus, stark naked—for he threw aside the coverlets too—lying there in such beauty, and somehow so astonishing, that I was almost beside myself. I could hardly say she wasn't a piece of marble carved, or a human corpse that lay there dead, for she was completely immobile, and yet I didn't dare touch her. The page covered her again, and drew the curtain, and yet she was still in my eyes, so to speak.
>
> My page put out the torch, and we climbed out again to the chamber above. Just then, in flew little Cupid, who at first was a little shy in our presence, considering what had been done to *him* the day before; but seeing us both looking more like the dead than the living, he couldn't help laughing, demanding to know what spirit had led me here. I answered, trembling, that I had lost my way in the castle, and just by chance happened to come here, and that the page had been looking everywhere for me, and at

last had found me here. I hoped, I said, that he wouldn't take it amiss.

"No, it's all right, my busy old grandpa," said Cupid, "but you might easily have played a nasty trick on me, if you had known about this door. I'd better fix that." And he put a strong lock on the copper door we had gone down by. I thanked God that he hadn't come upon us sooner! My page too was very glad that I had got him out of a tight spot.

Maybe Cupid believes him, maybe not, but the winged boy declares he has no choice but to punish Christian for coming so close to where his mother lies sleeping. He heats the tip of his golden dart in a candle flame and pricks Christian's right hand, laughing to see the blood well up. The mark will never vanish.

That naughty page. That cold goddess. That laughing boy.

The story of the wedding goes on from there. Guests are weighed and the lightweights expelled. The remaining guests travel to another, darker castle, where arduous labors of fire and water are undergone, plays are acted, boxes containing precious eggs are opened, and at last the dead king and queen are brought to life and the stone their son is manifested. Then the King (newmade, golden) brings the guests, all now sworn Brothers of the Golden Stone, back to the Wedding Castle. At the gate stands an aged porter—the very porter who once admitted Christian to these precincts, who was kind to him, who saw that he got safely inside. Long ago, the King tells the brothers, this porter came too as a guest to the castle, but after he was admitted he went wandering where he should not have gone, and spied prematurely on Mother Venus. For his sin he is condemned to stand here by the door, to let others in or keep them out, until the day when one comes who has done as he did, and who is willing to relieve him.

And—though *I hated myself and my tattling tongue that I couldn't keep quiet*—Christian must tell the King that he is, himself, that one. And he says that he will do what is required of him. *I said that if I could wish for anything at all right now, and have it come true, I would wish myself back home again. But I was told plainly that wishing did not stretch so far.*

His wish (the last wish, the wish to *undo*) can't be granted; he has to stay, and take the old porter's place. The next morning, he is told, the Knights will gather at the harbor, and board their red-sailed ships, and sail away; but Christian will have to remain alone at the castle, and take up his duties, until—perhaps—another appears, who has done what he has done, and is willing to replace him.

> Many gloomy thoughts were running around in my head, about what I was going to do, and how I would pass the time sitting at this gate for the rest of my life; and my final thought was that, old as I was, and in the nature of things not having many more years to live, this anguish and my sad life would quickly finish me off, and then my doorkeeping would be at an end. On the one hand it bothered me terribly that I had seen such gallant things, and must be robbed of them. On the other I was glad that at least I had been accepted and found worthy, and not forced to depart in shame.
>
> So after the king and his lords had bid each one good night, the brothers were conducted into their lodgings for the night. But I, wretched man, had nobody to show me where I was to go, and all I could do was to go on tormenting myself; and just so I would be always conscious of my function, I was made to put on the iron ring that the old porter had worn. Finally the King urged me, since this was the last time I was likely to see him as he was now, to remember that I should always behave myself in accordance with my place, and not act against the order. Upon which he took me in his arms, and kissed me, and by all this I understood for certain that in the morning I must in fact sit at my gate.

That's the end.

Except it isn't. The book doesn't, Pierce found, end. It has no ending; it stops, in midsentence, right there. There's nothing more but a brief statement not in Christian's own tale telling but in the book's own voice: *Here are missing about two leaves in quarto,* this note says, *and he—Christian, the author of this tale—though he supposed he must in the morning be a doorkeeper, returned home.*

What? Pierce stared at the page in astonishment.

Why was Christian allowed to go home? He should have gone on sitting by that door, from that day to this. Was the wrong that he had done not a wrong? Did his honesty in admitting what he'd done win him a pardon? If so, who pardoned him, who commuted his sentence? If the Golden King could not, who could? What other sinner came, and confessed, and took up the post in his stead? Did his author take pity on him? Or did Christian simply stand up, forgive himself, and walk away?

Like *The Tempest,* this so-called comedy—which started so much trouble in its time—had at its heart a dark spot, a contradiction, only made right by the assertion of a happy ending, the happy ending itself an abnegation. *Ile break my staff.*

Or maybe the desperate writer had only spun this twisted little sentence in order to tie the mystery up with it, shut the box he had himself left open; maybe he couldn't think how to end it, and just finished it up instead.

It seemed suddenly very important to Pierce that he know. He knew the story wasn't true. But he wanted to know what it meant. As though he had crossed the sea and come here only to learn.

De te fabula. Had he like Christian looked on Venus bare, too long or too soon, and now could never be a knight, be a brother, never find or make or effect any good thing? He looked at his palm. Was the best he could hope for just a chance to go home?

9

Rosie—I am writing this on the train from Heidelberg. I am going the wrong way, not south but north. We are going to be in Frankfurt in twenty minutes. Where G. Bruno wrote and published his last books, on atoms. There's a star next to Frankfurt in the guidebook, one of Kraft's. It was the book center of Europe

There in midsentence that postcard, of Heidelberg Castle by moonlight, was filled, and Pierce took out another to continue: *Frankfurt, the river Main.* Prewar, found in a train-station kiosk. He had a pocketful.

and still is. I will get off and go stand in the streets. I don't know how else to proceed. I don't understand how Giordano Bruno fits. By the time of the Winter King and the Bohemian thing he was 18 years dead and forgotten by everyone. No matter what Kraft thought. Weather is cold.

Snow fell in the streets of the Altstadt. Black Ys printed by Frankfurters' diverging footprint and tire-tread paths through the whitened lanes and streets. A huge red church of St. Bartholomew, where the electors once met to choose their emperor, and where the chosen emperors were crowned. Rudolf II sat for hours at his coronation listening to the reading of the Capitulation, an ancient volume detailing every free city's rights, every bishopric's standing, every duchy's ancient liberties, every crown's limits and traditions and exclusions (in Kraft, this was all in Kraft; Pierce knew nothing of it himself, he seemed to know less the farther from home he got) and in all those exclusions and freedoms and restrictions, which made his empire as ungovernable as life itself, the sad young man knew how dear and how complete his empire truly was: complete, and dear, because at its center sat his own person. Its center *was* his own person, still and empty. If he could only be calm, and keep his seat, and not try to do what could not be done, all would be well.

Fellowes Kraft liked empires that were so old, and grown so complex, that they could be named, and belonged to, and traveled in, but not controlled:

that had frontiers, but inside were limitless. Pierce thought he did, too.

Just at this early hour of the day the *Dom* was *geschlossen*. After a time Pierce returned in the gathering snow to the *Hauptbahnhof* to wait on a bench for the next train to the south. The cold was appalling, American cold, Minnesotan, Alaskan. In his bag, with the red guidebook and the new journal, was the only other reading matter he had, which was Kraft's memoir, *Sit Down, Sorrow.*

He had always known Kraft. So it seemed now. He knew Bruno because of a book Kraft had written about him, a book Pierce had at first thought was a novel too, but it wasn't. *Bruno's Journey,* Kraft's first, though Pierce in those days didn't notice that sort of thing either; books were books, all coevals in Bookland. Would he have been surprised if, in that year 1952, some agent of Y-shaped Time had come to tell him that he would be allied with Kraft in life and in death (Kraft's), repeating Kraft's journeys and his thoughts? He had not long ago marveled at the coincidence of his path and the older man's, and—anyway at the time—found in it a confirmation that the world held wonders: not that his own fate might be among those wonders, but that perhaps he actually *had* a fate, greatest wonder of all. Now he felt oftener that he rode an eternal bus, Kraft's life, which he could never get off.

In 1930 I closed my childhood like a book, and took ship for the world, Kraft's memoir began, and a closed book that childhood remained, though there were hints and phrases that revealed a little, hints that Pierce didn't think were accidental. He was without a father, had grown up alone with a weirdly feckless mother. Never married, of course, and without other relatives that he named; had never corresponded with others in the writing life, never formed literary friendships, or wasn't interested in detailing them; his best friend his dog, Scotty. There was no way to tell how he had come to write the books that he had written, why these anyway and not others; nor why they were the way they were. He did give an account of the growth of his erudition, and you could take that as an account of his heart too, maybe. Pierce, whether from pity, fear, or impatience, found it hard to read more than a page or two at a time; impatience, maybe, that the reason for his pity and fear were not being revealed, and would not be: not in here.

> I wanted warmth, and so I sailed to Naples: the silver Bay, the Grotta Azzura, golden stone warm in the sun. Only to find that the Mediterranean in winter was piercingly cold and damp, colder in effect than my far northern

land, for the citizenry seemed to have given no thought to the possibility—stunned into lassitude by the summer heat, maybe—and made no provision for chilling rains and the falling temperatures of rooms made of solid stone. Braziers and shutters, shawls and woolen socks, all rather ad lib. Maybe it won't last, they must think, summer will come back tomorrow. But it does last. And on the beach for weeks a sort of smelly thick seaweed was strewn each day, to be gathered for purposes I never learned, and replaced by more the next day: its sweetish rotten odor stayed with me for years. Never mind: I was Elsewhere! And the *napoletani* were as kind and importunate and brown and great-eyed and laughing, even as they shivered, as when the sun beat down. Which in the course of time it splendidly did again. But in that first winter, in the sweet loneliness of being truly adrift, I discovered the subject of a book, and the possibility within myself that I might write it. I discovered, in the Dominican abbey where it was his misfortune and his fate to have been immured, the philosopher and heretic Giordano Bruno (but he was a young man then, no more than a boy really, from the suburb of Nola). It was another solitary fellow, himself adrift, a scholar and antiquarian, who told me of Bruno and his story, and offered himself as guide to the Neapolitan places associated with him; it was he who showed me the cell where Bruno lived and thought, who took me to the church where he said his first mass, and the mountain beneath whose beetle he was born. Nor was that all I learned, and have learned later, from him. We were inseparable: an Anglo-French scholar, a young Nolan monk, and I; and we have continued to be, in shifting and altered ways, ever since.

Pierce looked to the bottom of the page, and to the back of the book, but the note that gave this Anglo-French, or imaginary, scholar's name—the note that Pierce only half believed he would find, really, the absolutely impossible last straw—wasn't there; and despite what was averred concerning him, the fellow vanished from the book in the very next paragraph: *When Bruno was summoned to Rome, never to return to Naples, I went as well, and our trio was dissolved.*

In Kraft's story it was his mastery of the Art of Memory, for which the Dominicans were well known, that first brought Bruno to Rome. Summoned thence by the Dominican cardinals around the pope to show off his powers.

That's certainly what he told the inquisitors in Venice. Whether or not he was ever really in Rome before he ran away, he was for sure here at the end, when for mad reasons of his own he came back, back from Protestant Frankfurt to Italy, apparently with plans to lay before the pope: a new ancient way of reforming and improving all human activity, and incidentally a new picture of the cosmos as well. Soon after he reached Venice he was arrested; after long interrogations, the Venetians turned him over (rather reluctantly) to Rome.

Frankfurt—Zurich—Milan—Genoa—Livorno—Rome. For a week Pierce wandered backward along the way that Bruno had at first taken fleeing from Rome and his order. In Kraft's story—not the book *Bruno's Journey*, but his big last unfinished novel—Bruno is warned by a young man who comes to him to tell him that proceedings in the Holy Office have begun against him. A young man who seems to know him seems also to know of a network of brothers who will take in the young runaway, keep him from the Inquisition, feed him and hide him and send him on to the next, a sort of heretics' Underground Railway that, for all Pierce knew, really existed, though this one of Kraft's seemed to come into existence only because Bruno himself proceeded along it: finding, at every stop, that sign that John Dee had made or discovered. He found it in books, on the signet rings of kindly helpers, in John Dee's own house in England, and in the center of Rudolf's palace in Prague, where Dee drew it with his staff on the stones of the floor. The center of the center of the empire at the center of the world. There for a moment the two stood together.

In Kraft's story.

But if Kraft could draw the young monk on, and give him shelter, refashion the world he went in, why did he then send him *back*, along the wrong ways, the fatal ways? Why couldn't he grant him the power to escape? What on earth was the point of writing a huge tragicomic epic full of powers and possibilities if it couldn't rescue him or anyone?

It was late afternoon when Pierce left the somewhat prisonlike *pensione* he had found in an anonymous part of town. His shoulders still felt the bags they had carried, but he didn't feel he could eat, or sleep. He thought of his father, Axel, and how he had promised, when he was just a kid, to bring Axel here one day, when he was grown up; here where Western Civilization lay cradled. He set out to find the Church of Santa Maria sopra Minerva, first stop on his list, double starred in Kraft's guidebook. It seemed to be not far away.

Before long he didn't know where he was exactly. European street names (he had only at length learned this, probably you were supposed to be born knowing) were not put up on posts on the street but stuck to the corner buildings' walls. Ill lit and ancient, most of them. He opened the guidebook in the streetlight, and tried to make sense of the finely printed little tissue-paper maps, tangled spaghetti of ancient streets stamped with coffin-shaped or cross-shaped churches. He turned, turned back. That vast dark-domed bulk there, an obelisk rising before it: surely that should be a landmark, even in a city made of them. He should try to find the Pantheon, right around here somewhere, and from there he might follow these instructions backward to the place he sought.

> Leaving the **Piazza de Rotonda** we follow the **Via dei Cestari** along the west side of the **Piazza della Minerva**. We will stop there to study the grand **Bernini monument**, which legend has it was inspired by a pair of ponderous pachyderms that visited Rome with a circus, where they attracted the attention of the greatest of all Baroque sculptors, Giovanni Lorenzo Bernini. In a neighborhood rich in obelisks—the obelisk of Psametticus, which we passed in the Piazza de Montecitorio; the obelisk of Rameses II, rising before the Pantheon—the one borne on an elephant's back in the Piazza della Minerva is the most beloved.

It had already begun to grow dark; the frantic crowds of careening vehicles in the streets, though oblivious of foot traffic or signals, had turned on their lights; Pierce was, he recalled, still in the Northern Hemisphere, in fact at about the same latitude as the Faraway Hills from which he had come, where it was also darkening now to a winter night. He walked on. There was no piazza, no elephant, no Via dei Cestari. He went into a café. It was apparently not the hour for coffee; the beautiful bright bar was empty. With its cellophane-wrapped boxes of chocolates and biscotti, its alchemist's row of colored bottles, its shiny steel counter and great angel-surmounted shrine-like machine, it was exactly like the hundreds of others he passed or drank in, one on almost every corner, enough for every Roman in the streets to rush into at once when necessary, to toss down a miniature coffee and be off again. He asked for a whisky. *Sit Down, Sorrow* was in his bag, and he fished it out.

> The idea that Bernini was inspired to make an elephant by an actual famous elephant, a sort of Roman Jumbo, is inadequate. The absurd but compelling idea of an elephant that bears on his back a granite obelisk actually derives from Francesco Colonna's 1499 novel *Hypnerotomachia Poliphili.* As Colonna's eponymous hero Poliphilus wanders in a *hortus conclusus,* fast asleep and in search of love, he comes upon a great marble elephant with an obelisk on his back. Within the hollow elephant (Poliphilus finds a door to go in by) lie the corpses or images of a naked man and woman, *Sponsus* and *Sponsa,* Matter and Form. The Rosicrucians would later make much of these weird allegories.

Pierce had found a folio edition of the *Hypnerotomachia Poliphili* on Kraft's own bookshelf, though he had read it first in college. The same edition even.

> Bernini must have liked this conception; he first designed an elephant cum obelisk for the gardens of Pope Alexander VII, where it would have been better suited than the Piazza Minerva. But no, it is here, midtown, somewhat lumpish and graceless as nothing else of Bernini's ever was, with no insides of course, or only imaginable ones. The obelisk is a real one, Roman booty; the famed Egyptologist Father Athanasius Kircher was called in to try to decode the hieroglyphics. The pope himself wrote the inscription for the base, which speaks of what great strength it requires to bear the wisdom of Egypt. Stand at its backside and you face the Dominican Church of Santa Maria sopra Minerva, built over an ancient temple site; in its abbey next door Giordano Bruno was arraigned, condemned, defrocked, stripped, and sent to his death. Wisdom's great weight!
>
> But after all it was almost seven decades after Bruno's death when the little wrinkled marble animal went up in the piazza. It was all unimportant then, Egypt, mere decoration, artifice, no harm in it; it was all over, gone, put away, annulled, no force in it any longer; Bruno's ashes scattered, unrecoverable; the world's page turned.

Out again into the evening. If Pierce could just know where he stood, which way was north, or east. Maybe he'd taken the wrong turn, a right not a left, at that Via Arco della Ciambella.

> If we have in error taken a right rather than a left at the Via Arco della Ciambella, we will soon enter the small **Piazza della Pigna**, where the famed great bronze **pinecone** of Rome again adorns the lost, the fallen but not forgotten Temple of Isis, yes her sacred *pigna* once stolen by the gloating triumphant popes for their own Temple of Peter over the river

No, no, he could no longer make out words. He turned, entered not a small piazza with or without a pinecone but a great boulevard, the Corso, traffic streaming beneath high dark palaces but the sidewalks empty, night come on now, his feet leaden but still able to feel pain; he had utterly lost his way and walked on anyway, nothing else to do. Turning away from the blinding headlights, he went only farther into the wrong Rome, until at last—near tears for more reasons than he could name—he surrendered, and seeing a rank of taxis, he took one to his *pensione.* Tomorrow, tomorrow. *Cras, cras,* the old Romans said. But Pierce was never to go that way again; and when he left Rome he still had not seen the elephant.

> If I chose Bruno by chance, I came to love him profoundly; he is one of those historical figures who is at once instantly accessible and yet permanently mysterious—just like our living friends and lovers, you see. When I came to read his works in Italian, I encountered a writer who was less a philosopher, it often seems, than a playwright, or even a novelist. His cosmologies are all dialogues; everybody gets to talk, himself or his stand-in only one among them. Some of the speakers we know to be fools, but others are merely in disagreement, and make some good points. The character who represents Bruno's thoughts is often only reporting what "the Nolan" believes or was heard to say; he may or may not be getting it entirely right, and there's no one to say for sure. We are reading Hamlet's story as reported by Horatio, as Hamlet might write it.

Another morning, and Pierce read on the bus. He was going the wrong way along the Via de Lungara, aiming for the Vatican and St. Peter's, but soon he would lift his eyes and sense something was wrong; get off, and set off on foot.

> I found it impossible not to take the man's side. He could be hugely Promethean—he was, after all, out to overthrow the entire religious

> conception of the universe, not only of its shape, like Copernicus, but of its structure, meaning, and reason for being—and at the same time a rude comedian, who wouldn't shut up and sit down no matter what heckling he got; who wrote a titanic epic of the Reformation of the Heavens by the Græco-Roman pantheon that ends up as a satire on reform, on men, on gods, on the heavens themselves. No one ever after understood it, maybe because its ironies are too enthusiastic, or because Bruno keeps taking everybody's side in turn almost too fast to follow. And when they had him at last in prison, at the Castel St. Angelo (you can see the room today, or could when I was there), he kept on asking to see the Pope, and explain everything: and there's no way to know if this was anything but one last impossible joke.

Pierce lowered the book. Why couldn't *he* take Bruno's side? He had once, hadn't he? What he felt compelled to do now was to counsel the man to sit down and shut up, he almost wanted to take the side of the authorities *against* him just in order to protect him. Pick a small universe, and go there and hide. Tell them you're sorry, that you didn't really mean it, that you'll take your medicine. Don't tease them, don't quibble, don't die.

He stood now at the end of a bridge, a great round tower over the river ahead, which the guidebook now reluctantly identified for him:

> If we have refreshed ourselves with a light lunch, we are now prepared to visit the **Castel St. Angelo**, which will take nearly all the afternoon. The emperor **Hadrian** began his mausoleum here in 135 AD. Square base, circular tower covered in earth, as was the Roman custom; atop that was put the great bronze **pinecone** that is now in the Vatican. A tomb for only a few decades, it has been most famously a fortress, the popes' stronghold for a thousand years.

The fun way to get into the Castel St. Angelo, the guidebook promised, was to go from the Vatican Palace, way over there, down into a narrow corridor that tunneled right through a wall, the popes' own bolt-hole. Narrow. Pierce's throat seized at the thought. In dreams he was invited into such places, or needed to enter them, and they grew smaller and tighter as he went, until panic woke him. No. He approached the *castello* instead sensibly over this bridge, the Ponte St. Angelo, past the lineup of Bernini's wind-tossed angels.

Great glowering shapeless mound. Its classical columns and decorations gone for centuries. A group was just then entering, led by a guide speaking in a language Pierce couldn't identify; he followed along with his book open. *We find ourselves first in an open courtyard; from here steps descend into the burial chamber of Hadrian.* And on the wall of the chamber, empty now—Pierce almost passed by it without noticing—was a stone plaque, carved with Hadrian's own little verse, his address to his own soul at parting.

Animula vagula blandula
Hospes comesque corporis
Quæ nunc abibis in loca
Pallidula rigida nudula
Nec ut soles dabis iocos

Pierce felt a shudder of pity. How could you ever translate those lines, so gently chilling, so un-Roman, so mild. Probably it couldn't be done. *Animula vagula blandula:* sweet little wandering spirit, little spirit wanderer, his soul like a child, like his own baby son. *Hospes* was the Latin word for stranger, and also for the shelter offered such a one: a word that ends up as both guest and ghost, host rather. Somewhere deep in Indo-European history, or in the heart, they had all the same root.

Sweet little spiritlet wanderer
My body's ghost-guest and companion
Where will you go now, what will become of you?
Pale little bare little shiverer
No more now the games you liked to play.

He had the sensation as he stood there of a hand slipping into his, and felt the world turn colorless and silent—it *was* colorless and silent here in this tomb, but now another world became so too; he cast no shadow there. *Won't you call me back at last?* He was not asked that, he heard that not, no. But he stood there as devastated as though he had been asked.

Why was he what he was, and not better? Was there still time? He had come to nothing. Why? Why had he not done what he should or could?

There wasn't an answer, only that hand slipping away again. A right hand, which had taken Pierce's left. A hot thread ran from there to where his heart had been. And Pierce thought: *I can't fill myself with only myself.*

The dull echo of shod feet on stone and far voices returned, and Pierce seemed to shrink, or expand, or both at once: to become small in a great world or huge enough to contain a small one. Only a moment had passed, it seemed. His group had gone on, and Pierce followed after. The guide pointed out a grille set into the floor, a dark deep hole below, and the crowd looked down in as they passed and made small sounds of awe and horror. *Prigione di San Marocco.* An oubliette, the only one Pierce had ever seen or would ever see, only excepting the ones within himself. And down there Casanova or Cagliostro or Benvenuto Cellini was briefly thrown, if he understood the guide.

Upward farther. They seemed to be climbing up around the funerary mound or mountain from within. Small doors led off the path to rooms named for various popes who hid there, or rested there; one a bathroom, with marble bath, painted grotesques. And then they came out onto the tower's top, where once the symbolic earth of the original Roman tomb had been laid, deep enough to grow trees; now all stone and a Renaissance fountain. Pleasant for the popes to wander in, refresh themselves. But around the courtyard, just below ground level, cells for celebrity prisoners: the guide showed them the stone air shafts rising here. For the Pope walking in the garden here to contemplate? Historic. *Prigione storiche,* the crowd whispered. Beatrice Cenci, who killed her father. Cardinal Carafa, strangled in his cell. Giordano Bruno. That one.

There was a way to go down into it.

Small. The thick door open, eternally now. In a sort of alcove was a stone shelf where his mat would have been laid. He must have had a table at least, and a stool. A bucket. A crucifix. It was said he was allowed no books except those that related directly to his defense, but that could have been thousands, a library. Not as large as the fluid living library in his head or heart. Hungry, though, maybe: the feeding of a prisoner was the responsibility of his family, and Bruno had none.

Pierce sat down on the stone bed. He touched the rough-smooth walls. He lifted his eyes to the square of sun at the top of the air shaft. Had Bruno suffered from heat in summer, cold in winter? Had they allowed him candles on long winter nights?

He wondered if it was really possible to be certain that this cell had been the one Bruno had been kept in. Had the knowledge somehow actually come down through the years, passed on from keeper to keeper, then archivist to archivist, guide to guide? And was it unchanged since then? It seemed that it could not have altered much: its stone walls, warm Roman stone, almost appealing, feet thick no doubt. He looked for incised initials, like Byron's at Chillon, but there were none, none now. No other mark either of the thousand he might have made.

The record of Bruno's trial before the Inquisition is lost: Pierce knew that. All that exists is a *sommario* of the proceedings prepared by the famed Jesuit cardinal and doctor of the church, Roberto Bellarmino, sainted in 1936, a big figure therefore in Pierce's childhood. Bellarmine apparently talked long with Bruno over the last year of his imprisonment. Winning heretics back to the church was a passion with the gentle ugly cardinal; he engaged in a long theologico-ecclesiastical dispute with King James I of England, father of Elizabeth, the Winter Queen. Getting Bruno to see his errors would have been a coup. With his powers Bruno could have become one of their stars, like Gaspar Schopp, the young Protestant scholar and thinker who turned Catholic, and who was there in the Campo dei Fiori at the end to watch Bruno burn.

Would His Eminence have come here to question Bruno, or would Bruno have been taken to him? His horn-rimmed spectacles, red silks sweeping this floor; a little stool for him set by a servant. Wearied maybe. Bruno never grew tired of talking.

Shall we go on, Fra' Giordano, from where we broke off: of things, and what causes them to come to be?

Your Eminence, by speaking of things we cause them to come to be: or to be tempted to come to be, or recognize in themselves the power to come to be. Why shouldn't it be so? We see ourselves in the mirror of the world, placed before us by the infinite creativity of divine intelligence; and that universe is as alive as we are ourselves; so it may see itself in the mirror of our intelligence, and think to refashion itself.

But it hasn't. It never has done that, refashioned as you say.

No?

No. It was fashioned by God in the beginning, and has remained as it was built. The foundations of the earth.

Oh? For how long then was the world flat, like a plate or a cowpat, and the sun went down at its western edge, and traveled through the Austral waters to rise again at its eastern?

It never was so. It was only our lack of understanding that described it in this way. It was always as it is now, a globe. In the center of the universe, around which the stars and planets go.

No edge? No Austral waters?

No. Of course not.

Ah. Well then. Maybe when we have described the earth long enough as traveling with the other planets around the sun, in an infinite universe of suns, then that too will always have been so.

But you couldn't know, really. Galileo hadn't yet been condemned, then; Bellarmino was himself a proponent of the New Learning. It was easy to imagine him trying hard to win Bruno over, probe for the places where his old faith might hook him again; explaining just what Bruno had to assent to, what minimum, in exchange for safety. All over Europe there were people doing it, in the lands of one confession or another. He, Pierce, had done it most of his life. He had thought, in the winter of this very year, in the middle of some very bad nights, that he might do it again: thought he might return, under threat of deracination and dissolution or out of a desperate hope of peace, to the safety of Mother Church. If only Mother Church had stayed put to return to.

But not Bruno.

How can I be as brave as you were? Pierce asked. If I can't go back and can't go forward, what can I do here?

It had begun to grow dim in the chamber. Pierce could no longer hear small sounds, feet striking stone, the grinding of a hinge. It might be that the hours of daylight when the prisons and the tomb itself could be visited were over, and he should have continued with his group of Belgians or whoever they had been; the doors he had passed through to reach this chamber might even now be shutting, one by one, all down or up the way that led to here, and he not be able to come out again till dawn.

10

Why is there anything and not rather nothing? Tell me. Why does a universe come to be?

—It comes to be because it can. No other reason.

And why is everything the way it is, and not some different way instead?

—It is the way it is because it chooses to be. It is always choosing, and thus changes how it is, within the limits of its nature.

But why should the things that are have these limits that they have, and not different ones?

—Because this is the age we inhabit, and not a different one.

And you—do you choose to be here, or are you constrained to be here?

—Who are you that you should ask me this?

A countryman of yours.

—Allow me to doubt that.

Why? What country do you say is yours?

—Who are you?

Have you forgotten me?

—"Forget" is not a power allotted to me.

Then you remember. In this city long years ago we met at first, in the library of the Vatican. Ever since then you have been my ally, my messenger—the messenger of a messenger! More too.

He did remember. Remembered how he was brought to Rome and permitted to sit in that library and read the works of Hermes Ægyptiacus. And he remembered the one who came to him there, and warned him as the angel warned the Holy Family, but to flee from, not to, Ægypt. Remembered the terrible gay eyes, the pitiless smile, the kind hand upon him to throw him out into the world, into the safety of no safety. Now he seemed a sadder, older fellow, in a plain gown of black stuff, than he had been when he had first come before Bruno, in the library of the Vatican next door. He crossed his slim legs, and took his knee in both his hands.

We will continue from where we broke off, he said. *Of what nature are the things of this world, this universe, that they are capable of continuous change, without falling into chaos?*

—The universe is infinite in all directions, without center or limit. In itself it has no qualities, it cannot even be said to have extension, because it is infinite, which is beyond size. It is a vacuum, or *æther*, or nothing, and that nothing is filled with an infinite number of *minima* or atoms, though these are not the tiny hard grains or balls of Lucretius, but invisible infinitesimal centers whose circumferences touch one another everywhere. The infinite universe is compressed within each infinite atom of the infinite number of atoms of which it is composed.

An infinity inside another infinity?

—An infinite number of infinities. Nothing, in fact, is finite except as it is perceived by the limiting categories of the mind. Indeed we keep coming upon things that disrupt those categories, like certain stones that have seemingly impossible properties of attraction, or animals that combine the qualities of sea and earth, or persons neither dead nor alive. The infinity contained within atoms is soul, that is, divine intelligence; all soul is the same, and only varies because of the disposition and nature of the atoms that compose it.

A sad fate to be made of agglomerations of atoms, and not by processes of Justice, Worth, Providence; to be a heap, rather than a self-based subject.

—All beings, including us human beings, are formed not by a process of casual agglomeration but by an internal principle of unity belonging to the atoms, their energy, their creative soul. Thus instead of a chaos they make the ranks and systems of things in all their specific and endless multiplicity, as the conjoined letters of the alphabet make the words of the language. The words of the world begin with the irreducible atoms, which have their rules of association and attraction, their passions and repulsions, demanding and forbidding certain combinations, permitting or discouraging others. Still the sentences they make are endless in number, and go on being made forever.

And how many categories and kinds of atoms are there? An infinite number too?

I don't know how many categories. I ponder how many would be necessary to account for a limitless number of combinations. I think of the words of a tongue, or of a tongue that has no limit, as perhaps the human tongue was before the fall of Babel. If there were no limit on how long the words could be, or how often the same word might appear in the whole, then a limited number of letters could create an infinite number of words. I think that a mere twenty-four letters, as in our alphabet, would be enough. That would suffice to spell the universe, and if we could come to understand them, name them, recognize them, we would know how.

Only a divine mind, a nous, could spell the infinite world with the letters you describe. How is your mere human mind to encompass them?

—The vicissitudes of nature are endless but not unlimited. There are reasons why some atoms are drawn to some others, to join with them, creating particular compounds, which in turn create bodies that persist as themselves through time. Those Reasons are like lamps lit within the things of which the world is composed, lamps that cast shadows of the things in the perceiving mind. By means of certain living images, the mind can grasp the Reasons and their working. For instance the reasons may be called gods, and the vicissitudes of nature may be truly reflected in stories of the gods. Thus the infinite number of things reflected in the mind is ordered into ranks and kinds, special and general, under all its varied aspects, which can be called Jupiter, Hera, Venus, Pallas, Minerva, Silenus, Pan.

So the gods are but stories.

—As the stories that we men read and write are but letters. Not the less true for that.

Very well, he said, after a moment's wavering between presence and absence, offended possibly. *Continue. How are these images for the Reasons cast?*

—We discover them. We have them within us, we have them inside, actually further inside than we are in ourselves. They are as much a part of nature as the atoms themselves, the numbers of Pythagoras, the figures of Euclid, the letters of the alphabet, the intentions of the spirit, the persons of the gods.

Why then do not all men agree on how the world and the things are to be conceived? Numbers and geometries are fixed, and describe many things under a few terms, but images may have as many forms as there are things, and what use is that?

—The images change because the world changes. It is a work that it undertakes itself, that goes on continuously. Merely my standing still changes the names around me. Every age must find its own figures for the things that are, to correspond to a changed reality. As in the practice of *alchymia,* where one thing can be seen under many figures, so that Mercurius is called a dragon, a serpent, a mermaid, a whore, tears, rain, dew, bee, Cupid, or lion, without error or ambiguity, because Mercurius is continually changed in the work.

His interlocutor smiled and perhaps slightly bent his head, as though he had noted the compliment paid his name and nature.

So they, I mean those compound bodies, made of those cohering atoms, do not remain stable.

—They do not. All compounds—ourselves and our bodies too—disintegrate over time. The bonds are merely bonds, however strong the attraction, and impermanent. Yet neither the corporeal substances, nor the atoms, nor their souls, can ever disappear. The atoms and the reasons that they bear inside themselves wander through the vicissitudes of matter, in search of other groups of *minima* that they recognize as compatible, and into which they insert themselves as into a new skin.

Are the minima *so wise as that?*

—The atom or *minimum* contains more energy than any corporeal mass of which it is a part, no matter how powerful—a sun, a star. The energy contained in and expressed by the minimum is *soul,* and that infinity is what makes us and all beings immortal, merely passing from being to being. If the process of that dissolution and agglomeration could be controlled, our beings, our selves, might pass intact to other beings. The Ægyptian priests inveigled the souls of stars into speaking statues of gods and beasts. We might—as those wise workers do who cast codes and ciphers—respell the words the atoms make, and therefore make of them other words, that is, other things.

So words are things?

—Better to say: things are words. This is the secret of the Cabala of the rabbis, which says that all things are made of the words of God, and to rearrange their letters must be to create new things.

This then is the principle of transubstantiation. Jesus's most brilliant trick—the minima *of his being, containing his infinite soul, passed unchanged into the circle of bread. Is that correct?*

—You have said it.

The gods too—their endless transformations into things, Jupiter into swans, showers of gold, bulls; others into other things, Venus into a cat, everyone knows.

—Everyone knows.

But of course such power of transubstantiation or metensomatosis *is impossible for those not gods or the sons of God. It may be that a clever man may have the power to make himself a simulacrum of another thing, and so fool the unwary.*

—It is possible. It is also possible for one living thing to become another, and thereby cease to be what it has been.

Possible!

—Unless we teach ourselves by our thoughts to act, there is no point in thinking. Every philosopher has attempted to describe the world, but the point is to contain it.

So the wise man may do what the immortals have done.

—Given enough years, a wise man might accomplish it.

Years, dearest friend, son and brother, are what you have.

With that, the messenger bent his head, smiling confidentially toward the immured philosopher. Around them the stone walls of his cell and the thicker ones of the *castello*; around the *castello* the Papal City all in its ranks and the battlements of the Holy Roman Empire around that.

I have a plan, he said.

II
BENEFACTA

1

When he came at length to believe that he was too sick to finish his last book—that he would himself be finished before it was—then the novelist Fellowes Kraft experienced contradictory impulses.

On the one hand, he thought to put it aside and think no more of it, while with the little time left him he put his (few, pitiful) affairs in order. On the other hand he wanted to do nothing but work at it, to be found at the end (facedown on his pages, like Proust) to have escaped or at least exited into it. He spent the mornings making long notes to himself about further chapters and scenes, further volumes even, expanding an already immense project into unrealizable grandeur (since he was to be freed, he supposed, from having to execute it) and then when the horrid lassitude returned at day's end, would push away the mess of alien handled paper feeling ashen and sad. Then he would find himself thinking, for no reason or for many reasons, of his mother.

In the course of, or more exactly instead of, settling his life's business he had been collecting from his files the letters his mother had written him over the years, most of which he had saved but never looked at again after first opening them (saved in their envelopes, whose faint addresses charted his own old restlessness, chasing him from house to apartment to *pensione* as the stamps in the corner rose in cost). There were fewer than he recalled.

"Son," she began, she always began, in pencil vanishing now but that would never vanish away. Son. What was he attempting to pack up, or unpack for good, that was in them? How could their envelopes, when he pressed open their torn mouths, exhale the familiar mildew of the house on Mechanic Street, after so long in his own house? It was the smell of the gnomes' entrance into the basement apartment, the crumbling linoleum of the hall; the smell of the damp-soft wooden stair that stepped up to the door to the alley: and it certified to him, as mere memory could not, that his own life had in fact begun and continued there, and so could not have done so anywhere else.

"Son, I forget whether I told you that Mrs. Auster in the front has died. So just for a moment there is no one in the house." This one from five years ago, just before the letters ceased to come anymore, before her final illness. "Now Baxter is worried that the next people to come and take the apartment will be negroes, because there are so many of them on Mechanic and all around. He's terribly worried, I don't know why."

Baxter. He should do something about Baxter, make sure he gets the house (though for sure now all filled with Negroes) for himself, blessing or curse or only destiny, amazing how few the choices we have, how strait the way. Baxter found asleep in the entranceway of the house on a December night in the Depression, taken in, still there tonight.

"Well it's odd," Ma had written, starting a fresh paragraph. "Baxter says that negroes care for nothing but sex. He says when they have their lodge meetings or preach or dance or have a rent party or perform in a jazz band they're only *playing* at those things, and what they're really doing is trying to get sex. I tell him I don't think that's different from anyone. People are always being blamed for doing things just to get sex, aren't they? It was always said when I was younger that whatever men say, they're only thinking about *one thing*, and this was always said in a very censorious way, as though the men were selfish hypocrites. No one ever considered that the poor men were to be pitied after all for even trying to think about anything else at all, trying to be politicians or preachers or banjo players or generals—because isn't it actually *Sex* that's selfish, Sex that twists every ambition and desire into only itself? Here a poor fellow wants to be a poet or a bandit and all he's allowed to make of his desires is babies."

Well it's odd. How often had he heard his mother say it, with her small smile of satisfaction, having hit on another flaw in the fabric (as it seemed to her), another mismatch of the soul and the earth.

Odd: all his friends who over the years had sobbed into their drinks about how they'd broken their mothers' hearts by not marrying, not making babies, and his own mother quite satisfied to learn of *her* son's constitution, even proud of him, as though it had been a sly choice of his, a way of defeating if not the enslaving itch itself then at least the usual outcome of it: embarrassingly curious as to how he had managed this coup against the world, and awarding some credit to herself too for taking his side in the matter.

Except for the iceman there had been no Negroes at all on Mechanic

Street when he was a boy, or much of anywhere else in the city beyond the confines of the Sunset district, which at the age of three or four he had named Browntown when he and his mother passed through it on the streetcar. With the other kids on his block he had followed the old long-armed hugely strong iceman in his wagon, waiting for the chunks of hard white-veined ice he would sometimes toss out to them. The cruel tongs with which he clamped the blocks and threw them onto his rubber-caped back. The dripping wagon advertised Coal and Ice, and he used to ponder that, why it was appropriate for one place to sell both, the fiery and the cold, the dirty and the clean.

He pocketed the letter in its envelope, disheartened suddenly, having glimpsed that eager receptive kid, and missing him: lost to him now, he alone left inside his flesh. Wonderful and terrible, how children love the world, and swallow it down daylong in spite of everything, everything.

There could hardly have been a street in the city less appropriate than Mechanic for his mother's house, though she hardly noticed: satisfied to be inappropriate everywhere, walking to market past the battling Polish housewives and the kids (heads cropped close for lice) who played tipcat and rolled smokes in the alleys: she in the remains of some ancient æsthetic costume, of which she had many, and her hair coming down. Buying a frightful yellow newspaper and a tin of Turkish cigarettes at the corner store and then making a telephone call that the whole store overheard, a call perhaps to the school principal to explain her son's absence from class: he standing beside her meanwhile (not as good as she was at assuming invisibility, at believing or pretending to believe that people neither notice nor care much about you) and staring fixedly at his shoes.

Back in their basement, when she lay on the musty divan and smoked her aromatic cigarette and read to him out of the newspaper (atrocious crimes and bizarre fatalities) he found it easier to be on her side against the world. They weren't the only ones on the street (she let him know) who lived without a husband or a father; they were simply the only ones too proud to lie, as the others did, who called themselves Mrs. and claimed to have husbands traveling the world or dead in the war. He wasn't, in fact, too proud to lie, and did lie, at school and on the street; but he was proud of her pride, and took it for his own.

For a long time he believed his mother didn't sleep at night, because she would now and then come into his room in the depths of darkness, wearing the clothes she had worn in the day, and wake him, to give him an orange section or a vegetable pill, or to rub camphorated oil into the wings of his nostrils. Often she was lying on the divan in the same clothes when he got out of bed in the morning. He could tell she had worked late into the night, because on her long table would be the piles of silk flowers she had made. Some of them went for hats; some were for restaurant tables; most were for deathless funeral wreaths. She who was so unhandy otherwise, who rarely even tried to master manual tasks, was magically good at her craft, the miniature blossoms realer than real coming to be within her nearly unmoving fingers as though she conjured them like an illusionist from her palm. Many years later, when he saw a "time-lapse" film of a flower sprouting, growing, putting forth petals and pistils, bowing its heavy head, all in a few seconds, he was made to think in wonder not of Mother Nature but of his own mother at work in the night, her pile of poppies and roses, oxeye daisies, lilies and blue lupines.

On an autumn morning when he was eight, nine perhaps, she woke him in the predawn. Instead of dosing him, she urged him gently out of bed and into his chilly knickerbockers. They were going somewhere. Where? To see an old friend of hers, who wanted to talk with him. No, not someone he knew. No, not a doctor. She gave him tea in the kitchen, whose windows were only just blooming gray, then pushed his cap on his head and went out with him into the silent alley.

How had she chosen that morning to begin his education? For sure there was nothing special about the date or the year or the day. He had not just reached the age of reason like the tough Polish boys who went together all on a day to communion, crossing into religious maturity, dressed fatuously in white and lace. Maybe (he thought later) she had picked the day just for being no day in particular. And yet the unguessable workings of his mother's spirit had been in a way the same as a flair for drama: plucking him out of bed without warning for what he intuited was a journey of initiation, a day unlike other days, a door opening in the wall of diurnality.

(That was how it had been too when one day he came home from school, and she met him at the door, and said to him mildly, *Guess who's here?* And then held open the kitchen door for him to see sitting at the table a pink-cheeked man with a kind smile and hurt eyes. His father, owner of his home, looking like Herbert Hoover in his tight suit and hard collar, and holding in his lap a big box of blocks. Was it that she thought her son needed no explanation, or couldn't grasp one? Was it that she had none to give, not to herself any more than to him? Or was it that she believed there was something salutary in the shock of sudden knowing? It had imparted to him a lifelong expectation of surprise, a conviction that everything important will come suddenly, leaping on the unwatched back like a predator, and nothing the same afterward: an expectation—he thought, now, this night, in helpless grief—that had caused him to neglect and not notice the very most important things, the things that had been alongside all the while, right in plain sight, his humble and now failing organs for a single instance; no matter, too late, too late.)

He had been surprised to see lamplight in the kitchens along the alley, and women inside making breakfast; he hadn't known life began so early. They had walked out to Mechanic Street and out and up the town.

Above the Mechanic district the climbing streets were filled with houses of decorated red stone or brick, with arches and steps and peaked roofs like those that had come in his box of blocks. He passed one after another of these ramifying places, following his mother in her tatty cloak, abashed by strangeness but not unwilling to miss school. The houses were mostly dark but for the areaways where maids and deliverymen went in and out. One or two of them (it would be the eventual fate of all, as the Heights district slid metaphorically downhill) had been divided up inside into warrens of rooms and apartments, though looking the same outside, and into one of these his mother took him, holding his shoulder now and steering him up stairs and down high-ceilinged corridors to a door she chose.

She knocked, perfunctorily, then opened, and looked within: lamplight from inside fell on her face, and just for a moment she reminded him of an illustration in a novel, peeking around the door of the room wherein the author has laid her fate; then she took him within.

The room (absurdly high-ceilinged, for it had been split off from a bigger room of proper proportions by a blank wall) could be read instantly, like a page: the single chair was by the window, its green velvet seat concave from being sat on; the lamp was on the table, and the book beneath the lamp, and the stool before the book; the towel hung above the washstand, the scrap of rug lay under. Coal smoldered in the grate; more filled the scuttle. The person who as it were projected all this around himself stood in the center of the carpet in a wadded dressing gown and a fez, hardly taller than the boy he looked at.

"This is Dr. Pons," his mother said, and that was all. Dr. Pons seemed to have a board jammed into the back of his dressing gown; soon his visitor would determine it was the man's own spine, severely twisted out of true. It gave a sort of spiral motion to his walk that was at once painful and fascinating to watch, a walk that Kraft had later on assigned to more than one character without ever (he thought) quite communicating its effect.

On that first day, his mother stayed there with him and the doctor (of what? Kraft had never asked) and listened; she drank pale tea that the doctor made on a gas ring, and so did the boy. On other days she would only take him to the door, or to the bottom of the street; at length he was left to make his way to this place himself.

How did his instruction begin, when it began? Going up to the Heights was a duty he did because she told him to, and he made little effort to remember the days or the hours. Was he told stories, or was he first asked questions? Was there a text, pages to turn and touch with a pencil tip; or did they only talk together, about his days and his life, his life on this earth; a lesson pointed up, a moral drawn?

Whatever it was, it couldn't have been really news, nor would he have been surprised or appalled by what Dr. Pons had to reveal to him. He knew about religion. There were churches at each end of his block on Mechanic Street: Precious Blood on the south, Reformed E.U.B. on the north, and his mother had explained to him their function; and at Christmas when on the steps of the Catholic church was set forth the little tableau, the chipped plaster figures of sheep and shepherd, camel and king and babe, she told him the story: how the son of a far-off invisible king came to be lost in a wide dark winter world; how he came to learn who he was and how he had come to be there, what task he had come to do, and who his real father was. The Christmas Story.

And now and then, at no fixed interval, a little group had used to gather at his mother's house and tell that story in other forms, or tell other stories with the same form, for it was thought to require many iterations, until one or another telling awakened the selfsame story lying coiled and unsuspected in the hearer's own heart.

The story, he would come to learn, was the one that Dr. Pons had to tell, and it was from Dr. Pons they had learned it, if they had not learned it from Dr. Pons's own teachers. When they told it in the house on Mechanic Street, the parts were acted out by abstract nouns that behaved like personages: Wisdom. Light. Truth. Darkness. Silence. *Wisdom fell outside the Limit that was Spirit, and in her fall the Darkness came into being; so she was the Light caught by the Darkness. And she wept: and her tears became the world we live in.* If he listened—which usually he did not—the big words would flicker into life in his mind for a moment as they were spoken of, only to go out again, like the terms in a physics lecture, Velocity, Force, Mass, Inertia, featureless balls and blocks colliding in no-space and not-time, which are yet supposed to contain the answer to the hardest question, or the second-hardest actually: *why is everything the way it is, and not some different way instead?*

They were a funny-looking bunch, Kraft remembered, most of them a little off-kilter or oddly shaped, hairless or wooly, with round soft stomachs or asymmetrical eyes or lumpy brows; they stuttered and fidgeted and sat without ease: as though their spirits had long lived uncomfortably within their swollen or shriveled bodies, which showed the signs of the struggle for dominance, still undecided. Some of them he would come to know pretty well, for they were later his mother's tenants, taking the two upper apartments briefly, living and sometimes dying up there, visited in their extremity by some—not all—of the others. They all seemed to die young of unlikely diseases or live to terrible old ages, burdened with bodily needs that they, and his mother, were contemptuous of but patient with. Mrs. Angustes has to go, son. Silently laboring toward the purgatorial john on his arm. How is it (he would come to wonder) that the adherents of a cult can elect to have, out of the common life we all must undergo, just those experiences that confirm them in their exclusive vision; how do they make themselves into people such as their cult believes all people to be?

For it was a cult he had grown up in, as he later understood, as he had understood in the simplest terms of specialness and exclusivity even when he was a kid: a small, a practically infinitesimal cult, but an old one, he was amazed when he learned how old, a thin but unbreakable dark thread unwound through the world for ages. The complex equations of suffering and scheming abstractions that his mother's friends talked of, and which Dr. Pons would in his serene whisper school him in, were an ancient answer to the truly hardest question of all: *why is there anything at all, and not just nothing?*

Once, before the beginning of anything, a number of great beings, angels with limitless, inconceivable powers, gathered together, driven by restless dissatisfaction that they could not account for. To distract themselves, they began to play a game of their own invention. They divided themselves into the various players, constructed parts and appendages for themselves by which they might play.

Though it never wholly assuaged their profound boredom, they became caught up in the game they had invented. The rules, continually elaborated to make the play more interesting, entangled them in limitless possibilities. They played on, forgetting why they played, forgetting themselves, their origins, forgetting finally that they played a game. They came to take their own idle construction—which we call Time and Space—for actuality; they forgot they had themselves devised the rules, and came to assume they had always been subject to them.

So the game has gone on being played, Dr. Pons said, from that time-before-time down to this; except that now and then some subdivided entity, some mirror fragment or mask piece of the original players, a pawn in the game, will stop in his tracks, seized by a restless dissatisfaction he can't account for: longing, boredom, and a certainty of belonging elsewhere. For those great beings who invented the game of time and space, the Archons: what they had done was simply to reduplicate themselves and their quandary over and over, dividing and redividing their infinite substances into all the things that are, animal vegetable mineral, and all the representations of those things, in an effort to fill their own emptiness.

That was to begin the story *in medias res,* but in fact there was nowhere else to begin except *in medias res.* For what was being told was not so much a story as a situation, a circumstance endlessly elaborating itself without ever unfolding any further, like an infinite carpet in which the central figure is surrounded by the same figure in a larger size, and that by the same figure in a still larger size, over and over.

And all those figures, Dr. Pons taught him, earthly and heavenly and above the heavens, are wrapped around a single infinitesimal spark of light at the center of being, like the layers and layers of pearl with which an oyster coats the grain of sand that irritates him so. That grain of light, irreducible, eternal, infinite even in being infinitesimal, is simply the centermost point of your heart.

Here Dr. Pons touched the corduroy above the boy's own heart.

And not until the last grim furious Archon remembers this, not until she surrenders her stake and tosses in her cards—and with them the hopeless delusion she has labored under (that she is ruler, that there is something to rule)—will that vast game board be folded up at last and put away, and the Players, knowing themselves to be incomplete, turn again toward the Pleroma, the Fullness, God: whose lack is all they really are.

God. Who is like a mother whose child has decided to run away from home, a child who packs his paper sack with lunch and his knapsack with things and then sets out never to return, and gets farther than he ever has before, the borders of lands so large and far he can't comprehend them; and thereupon forgets why he got so sad or angry or disgusted or impatient, and remembers his mother at home; and so he turns, and goes back, to find his mother in the kitchen, who only smiles at him and takes his hat from his head and tells him to wash up, unaware that he was ever gone, so long gone.

"We," Dr. Pons would say (and the boy he spoke to thought he meant *you and I,* and then later on he thought that Dr. Pons meant *we human persons,* and lastly he knew he meant *we few, our kind*): "We are the ones who remember. We are the latest and littlest of the replications of divine forgetfulness: and yet in our remembrance lies the salvation of all. For as we are the lowest and the last, farthest from the light, so we are also closest to the center, and the spark of light is near within us: the spark that, once awakened, we can fan into a flame."

Well. Kraft could recite the weird catechism still today, though he could only in the briefest moments (reminded by a smell of coal smoke, or the feel underfoot of cinders on ice) experience the drama Dr. Pons told of, and the limitless darkness in which as a boy he had always imagined it taking place.

His mother called it Knowing, but as he got older it seemed to him that it wasn't Knowing so much as it was Knowing Better, a kind of universal I-told-you-so that could be astonished by nothing. Mocking, cynical about human sentiment, except that what she mocked was not human pretensions but human humility: human trust in the goodness of life and the giver of life, human groveling before contemptible and shoddy nature. Ma always acted as though there were some metaphysical guarantee that a thing would do or be just what its name said it would do or be: if glue didn't stick two things together satisfactorily, she took it not as a sign that the things and the glue weren't suited or that the weather was damp; she saw (with mixed disgust and triumph) that the universe had (once more) failed to act on its promises, proving (once again) that it was not the place it purported to be. She was a tourist in a shoddy tourist cabin, only willing to put up with the inconvenience for the length of a brief vacation, and the weather turning wet.

"Son," she wrote to him, the year the Second War ended. "I read all the time now about the new Einstein bomb made out of atoms. They talk about how this terrible responsibility has fallen into our hands, that we can misuse this power, and blow up the world. And we will all have to control ourselves because of it. As though this bomb were the fault of people, when it isn't at all. The fault is in those atoms, isn't it. Going off in our faces like a trick cigar, or like that gimcrack Japanese jewelry box I had, that nipped my finger every time I opened it."

She no more credited human science with discoveries about the world than she would credit a man who fell down a well with having discovered it. She thought the duty of science was to provide us with a guidebook for getting safely around nature, a guidebook that could never be complete: there were always nasty surprises awaiting. Ma certainly had no conception of physics and assumed the rules could suddenly change in subtle ways, water at any time begin to flow uphill. He remembered how not long before she died, she had seen put up somewhere, inscribed on a pseudorustic board in comical lettering, what was called Murphy's Law: *If Something CAN Go Wrong, IT WILL!!!* How she had laughed, who hadn't laughed in a long year of sickness and pain. If something can go wrong, it will: the only law she would recognize in a lawless universe.

Somehow, despite her, he had himself grown up an optimist, expecting and even assuming the best would come to him, or at least a fair deal. He could remember a day lying, high up on a hill, looking over the city cleft by its busy waterway, whose distant reaches fought free of the city and wound far through autumn haze into pale imaginary hills: how he had understood that day for the first time that he loved the world, loved his own sensations of it, its weathers and its sights and tastes. He felt a deep pleasure in the discovery, and did not yet know that his consciousness of his pleasure in things was the beginning of his division from them. The pleasure could diminish, but the division, once begun, could never be healed.

Not such an optimist then after all, maybe possibly. Autumn too now outside his windows, outside his house from which he did not often venture. *Season of mists and mellow fruitfulness.* His mother couldn't abide Keats.

He hadn't often seen it at the time, but he came to see his mother's efforts to bring him up alone as a great heroism; strange and nearly mad as she was, she had apparently got up every day and willed herself to make a life for him that was not wholly unlike the lives lived by others, not so wholly unlike anyway that he would never find a place among them, and have only her. Clothes cleaned and pressed. Nourishing meals got up. Manners inculcated, cautions and reassurances made, his achievements and fears and hopes taken seriously if with some bafflement. He in turn had avoided, just barely, breaking her heart and emptying her life entirely in his struggle to climb up or down into the rooms and streets and public places where most of life was lived; even now, she dead many years, he could groan aloud or feel sweat break on his brow when (in the vacant middle of the night, reviewing his life, as he must now do) he thought how close he had come.

She had got him through high school—there he was in the class photograph in cap and gown; then she put on her hat and coat and was gone for a day, and returned haggard and proud, able to tell him that he would be able to go to the college that had accepted his smudgy application, she had got some concession out of Guess Who, and so if he worked and lived frugally. And he had gone, and stepped into Western Civilization as though it were the family firm, where a place had all along been waiting for him, which wasn't the case at all.

At college he turned to the past with hope and appetite, as though it were the future; and soon after he graduated he set out to make a living from it. The only residue left in him (he thought) from the peculiar childhood he had been subject to was the conviction, which only came to him rarely over the years but which was unrefusable when it came, that it is *not* unreasonable after all to believe that one's own subjectivity is bound up in the nature of things; that really we have no independent evidence of how the world is; that if our consciousness contributes to making the world, then our consciousness can alter it. Suddenly, in an Italian garden, on a winter day, knowing that it made perfect sense to think so, and feeling himself grow in an instant into a being inconceivably huge.

~

"Guess who's dead," Ma had written to him on September 1, 1930, here was the date, she usually dispensed with that. He knew by then a little more about his father and her relations with him: he was her mother's sister's husband, into whose house she had come as an orphaned girl of seventeen, to be something between adopted daughter and servant, and starting (by her sublime inattention partly, her son imagined, partly by her freedom) a foolish passion in her uncle's heart. Which he then thrust upon her apparently, repeatedly, taking dreadful chances, hand over her mouth in the pantry (so Kraft imagined it) and always reproachful of her afterward. Rich enough, though, to pay for the eventual consequence, which was a son, Kraft himself. Able too, it seemed, to bear a lifetime load of secret guilt, which, like fascination, she seemed to have generated in his heart by her almost inhuman indifference.

Poor man. She never felt sorry for him either.

The money he left his son, passed to him by discreet and disapproving lawyers, was enough to get Kraft to Europe and allow him to live in a kind of penurious luxury inconceivable at home, and spend something on treats for friends who were even poorer than he, in order to receive their gratitude—he would later learn better ways of winning them but still would never entirely trust his own charms. Before the money ran out he had written his first book, a life of Bruno.

Bruno, who really knew the world was made of one stuff everywhere, whether you called it Atoms or Soul or Meaning or Hylos; Bruno who proved there was no Down, no Up, no Inside, no Outside; whose gods were Lucianic bumblers, and the history of the universe the record of their crimes, follies, and misfortunes, and yet we love them, our love conquers them in its lover's welcome of every manifestation of their endless, pointless creativity. *The gods take pleasure in the multiform representation of multiform things, in the multiform fruits of all talents; for they have as great pleasure in all the things that are, and in all representations made of them, as in taking care that they be, and giving order and permission that they be made.*

Going down drunk to the Campo dei Fiori the July day he wrote the last pages of that book, where there stood a bronze statue of the man, incongruously robed in the Dominican habit he had long before discarded, hood shadowing his gaunt martyr's face. Buying roses from the flower sellers there to put before this effigy anyway, as the boys and girls courting and kidding on the fountain's lip watched him curiously.

The book—*Bruno's Journey*—was on his shelves now here, more than one edition, each though retaining the original's photograph of himself on the back. A pretty ephebe if he did say so himself, shock of pale golden hair and cheekbones bronzed by the Neapolitan sun, a look at once self-satisfied and sly. It was a young man's book, aphoristic and smart, not really wrong maybe but so insufficient it might as well have been.

The first man in Western history to have imagined that the universe is infinite, he wrote to his mother, sending her a copy from the city; and here was the letter that she had written back (he was never sure if she actually read the book). Her letter was mostly a quotation, copied from one of the slim and atrociously printed little tracts that passed for scripture in her sect, though actually rarely consulted: "Ialdabaoth desired to make a Creation like the Eternal and Infinite Pleroma, under the delusion that such a thing could be created, that he could copy Eternity by vast lengths of time ever lengthened, and Infinity by vast spaces continually multiplied. Thus he followed the Lie and the Darkness, proud in his unwisdom."

Well, didn't bomb-man Einstein agree, as far as Kraft could tell anyway, didn't he say that the universe was unbounded but not therefore infinite, and that a man setting out in a straight line from earth would never reach its frontiers, but would eventually, though still traveling his straight line, come back to the place from which he started?

As Fellowes Kraft had done too. Not to pretend that the findings of lofty science could be implicated in such a little human cycle. He had come back, at the end of his writing life, to where he stood at the beginning: to Rome, by Giordano Bruno's side. Having once again in his pages tried him, condemned him, put the tall dunce's hat on his head, tied him backward on the ass, the ass whipped from the prison through the streets past mocking and bloodthirsty or incurious crowds to the Campo dei Fiori where the stake has been erected. Ready but unable or unwilling to burn him again.

He put his hands on the sheets he had covered this day, not all of them with sense. *Endless things,* his mother had used to say, and write in her letters too: a little ejaculation or verbal sigh, the endless things of this world that trapped and pestered her or pleaded for her attention like unfed sheep. *Endless things,* he too had said, said to himself in those days when he had set out for the brand-new Old World in his twenties; *endless things,* his own small prayer and mantra as he stood on the boat deck or in the crowded and scented foreign street. To him it meant not the endless ghastly multiplication of things, as it did to her. It meant those things that roll on forever: travel, and the intoxications of thought and gaze and words, and possibility; sex, the sea, childhood and the view from there, the way ahead.

But of course (he thought now) it might also mean things without endings, without reprieve. Eternal return; limbo of the lost. Death. Bruno's journey to Hell, still going on, from that book to this.

Well, maybe there was a way, this time, to free him. Get him off.

The case clock in the far room whirred and then bonged once, as did his heart.

Yes: a way to free him that would change nothing, that would leave it all to happen just as it had done, as it must, only altogether otherwise. Kraft lifted the papers in his hands, and looked down at the words that his thumbs indicated.

Maybe, maybe there was.

2

Yes: that ass, the little ass that bore him.

Pierce Moffett in the middle of the *Magnificat* clapped his hand to his brow and made a haw of understanding and self-reproach that made the brothers around him turn to see. He was stunned not so much by the sudden insight arising in his mind as by his own obtuseness: that he could have been shuffling and reshuffling and considering those pages for so long and never noticed it.

But for Christ's sake: that little ass.

But then he thought no, he must be wrong, he was remembering the scene not as Kraft had left it in the manuscript but as he, Pierce, might have written it, or might write it now, because it was so right: he had a nearly uncontrollable impulse to get to his feet right now, in the midst of the prayer, clamber over the legs and laps of the brothers who filled the pew, like a playgoer who's had enough, and rush to his little room to find the pages.

Magnificat anima mea, the choristers sang, or should have sung. It was all in English now, the rare Latin plainsong falling on Pierce's soul like balm, in spite of everything; yes, all English, accompanied today by a brother on guitar. Pierce thought the older brothers must suffer from the change, but of course there was no way to ask them.

When Lauds was done and they had recessed from the cool church together, the brothers housing their meditating heads in their white *cuculli,* Pierce went back along the flagged halls to his room. Spring light still fell sweetly there. The furnishings were solid and plain, like school furniture: oak desk and chair, plain prie-dieu. A narrow bed, a crucifix at its head, Virgin at its foot. When Giordano Bruno was a young brother in the Dominican house in Naples, he had shocked his superiors by pitching out all the devotional clutter his cell had come to contain, all the statues of saints, the blessed palms and rosaries, the *memento mori,* leaving only a bare cross. So he could fill, perhaps, those bare spaces with pictures of his own.

On Pierce's desk was piled a photocopy of Kraft's last unfinished book, which for some years Pierce had thought himself free of. Brighter and cleaner in this form than it had been on shoddy goldenrod, but paler too, less distinct, speaking more softly. Seeing it at first was like seeing an old acquaintance after a like number of years, grown gray and strange to you but after a few moments the same. Almost the same.

Kraft's reputation as a novelist had, during those years, undergone an unexpected transformation. His books hadn't ever been as successful as other historical romances similar to his own, those fat but somehow lightweight confections that everyone read when they appeared and no one ever opened again. But—though Kraft certainly hadn't seen any reason to hope for it—his own readership had never entirely dried up; and though his books one by one went out of print, old copies were traded eagerly, and even began to fetch good prices; it became a sign of wide cultural sympathies to at least know about Kraft, as you knew about Erich Korngold or John Cowper Powys or Philip Dick: a never-populous archipelago you could imagine visiting one day, island-hopping through a large oeuvre and having fun.

So in time Kraft's copyright holders (the Rasmussen Foundation) opened negotiations with his old publisher, and though they didn't see prospects there, another house did, and the best known of the books began to come out in pretty "trade" paperbacks with striking covers, and newcomers found them and bought them, and so more were brought out: and then all of them, reissued in numbered volumes so that you could remember which ones you'd read and which were yet to go (they were admittedly pretty similar). It could be seen then that they told a single story, the main branch of them anyway, unfolding over time and populated by a large cast that migrated from book to book with the turning years. In chain bookstores Pierce Moffett with nameless feelings looked on the books that had measured out his childhood, *A Passage at Arms, Under Saturn, Bitten Apples, The Werewolf of Prague.*

The last remaining was this one, which the Rasmussen Foundation (Rosalind Rasmussen herself, actually, the executive director) asked Pierce to take up again: to edit, fix up and trim up and cap off so that it could be brought out too, finish the story, she said.

I don't think I can, Rosie, he'd told her (though here it was, piled beside the computer into which he was entering or keyboarding it, page after endless page); things, he said, had changed so much for him, she should get a real writer to do it, there were plenty. So Rosie said all right, she understood;

and then when a couple of days and sleepless nights had passed he wrote to her to say that well after all he would. He owed it to her, he said, for all that she had given him, all that he had left unfinished and unreturned. When he undid the wrappings and opened the box that contained the thing, though, he knew his reluctance hadn't been misplaced, the whole bad time in which it had figured so largely so long ago was in it, and he found he could hardly touch it for some time even in this clean new form, not the rotting corpse itself, just the bleached bones.

He marked now the place in it to which his transcribing (rewriting too, a bit) had reached, and dug down into the later, the latest, parts, and turned them out to read.

> At two in the morning on the 18th of February, brothers of the Headless John Society assembled at the Convent of St. Ursula in the depths of night, as was their habit, and processed to the fortress where Bruno was imprisoned, to awaken him, to "offer up the winter prayers" and give comfort and correction, maybe even snatch the man back from the abyss at the last instant. But no, he stayed up through the night with them talking and disputing, "setting his brain and mind to a thousand errors and vaingloryings" (But what were these really? What did he say at the last?) until the Servants of Justice came to take him.
>
> There was a little gray donkey tied up outside in the dawn light, where the crowds were being held back by the Servants.

A little gray donkey: yes. Whose common work this was, perhaps, a functionary himself in a way, employee of the Holy Office or of the secular arm, the Servants of Justice. How many condemned men had he borne on his back to the place of execution? Actually, though, there weren't that many, despite the Black Legend. Maybe none, then, none ever before.

> He was mounted backward on his steed to cheers of loathing, and a tall white paper hat put on his head, a fool as well as a devil.
>
> The crowds along the way were vast; it was a jubilee year, and all the City was being renewed, just as the Holy Catholic Church itself was. Fifty cardinals from all over Christendom were assembled here; there were processions, high masses, new churches dedicated daily. The little ceremony at

the square of the flower sellers was not even the best attended.

He was stripped naked after being tied to the stake. It's reported that a cross was held out to him at the last moment, but he turned away from it.

Pierce turned over the page. Yes: the man was going to get away, he was.

The little ass that had borne him stood by the scaffold; after the man had been dragged from his back the ass had been forgotten about, his rope not even tied. Jostled by those pushing forward to have a better look and those pushing back who had seen enough, the beast kicked once, and pranced away. No one stopped him, no one noticed him. He left the Campo dei Fiori (not pausing even at the unattended stalls where winter vegetables were sold, whose greens hung down temptingly) and entered the narrow streets beyond, Hat-makers' Street, Locksmiths' Street, Crossbow-makers' Street, Trunk-makers' Street, out beneath the high walls of palaces and churches, skirting the crowds that filled the Piazza Navona, finding another way, north, always north. Now and then boys or shopkeepers chased after him, housewives tried to snatch his lead, but he kicked out and brayed, and they laughed and fell behind; none could catch him. Some noticed the dark cross in the hair of his shaggy back, the cross that all asses still bear in honor of Our Lord, whom one of their kind once carried; but this cross was not the same, no not the same.

Pierce knew what cross it was, what complex figure rather, one that contained the cross of Christ and of the elements, and more: indeed everything, everything in one thing, a Monas, or rather the sign for it, the sign for its unimaginable unfigurable plenitude. No ass but this one ever bore it, and this one hadn't till this day. Giordano Bruno, though, had followed that sign since he had run away from Rome the first time, twenty years before, and now the sign was his, he was the sign, and it was he who was borne.

After many years had passed, the Vatican authorities would begin to claim that they hadn't burned Giordano Bruno at the stake at all, that what was burned that day on the square was a *simulacrum* or effigy. As all the papers relating to the trial and the execution had disappeared into deep and unbreachable archives, those who wished to believe this could. Something burned there in the Campo dei Fiori for sure, for a long time.

But not he. He was gone out of the city before those ashes were cold, on roads like those in Italian genre paintings: rural crossroads somnolent in the sun, a tavern, a guard with a pike, a broken arch from which saplings sprout and wash is hung. The high-piled ochre houses with their red roofs; a pot of basil in a window, and a woman daydreaming in another. Say, whose beast is that?

And from there, where? Kraft didn't say, hadn't written that, wasn't granted the time or the *compos mentis.*

Pierce put down the page.

A Y sprang from that scaffold on the Campo dei Fiori in Rome. One horn of it led to the one that led to the one that came eventually to here where Pierce sat, the world he lived in; but the narrow rightward horn went on just as far, growing ever farther from its broader mate, running into alternity forever, generating its own fartherness as it went.

Which Pierce could see, which Kraft surely always meant to write: that must be what some of the homeless and sometimes unnumbered pages were that constituted the typescript's end.

Which Pierce could write, almost, if he wanted or dared to, or were being asked to, as Boney Rasmussen had in fact once asked him to do in the year of his death. But no he was editor only, annotator and tidier of the other man's work.

For a long time Pierce sat at the desk, or lay on his bed, or stood in his walled garden, while that other farther story unfolded before or within him as plainly as though he could really read it there in the writings he possessed. He sat and stood and lay and laughed until the eternal bells called the brothers, once again, to prayer.

3

It was exceedingly odd, thought the Ass, to be thinking the thoughts he was thinking, or indeed to be thinking any thoughts at all, seeing as he had never done so in his life before, as far as he could remember; then again he had never before tried to remember anything either.

He, who had never considered himself to have a self, now found himself thinking that he was possessed of more than one, an old one and a new one, and that they didn't agree on how to go forward from here. They did not, or could not, agree on how to move at all. In his run for freedom he had given it no thought, but when he was far from the city crowds he stopped, weary yet exalted, to rest at last, foam on his lips and his flanks trembling; and then when he commanded himself to go on, he couldn't think exactly how it was done. Did he move the two feet on the left side of his body, then the two on the right? Or did he move the four of them each in turn, like four men shifting a heavy trunk? Or the right front leg and the back left together, then the other two?

Immobile in the roadway as he was, unable to make a choice among these methods, he was unaware of the peasant and his son who had come up behind him, though his protruding eyeballs should have warned him of them. The man took hold of his trailing rope, and at the same moment his son slipped a halter over his puzzled head. Then immediately he knew what to do, though it was too late: he planted his four hooves in the road and balked, and when the man pushed from behind he kicked out, and he turned his big lips inside out and brayed loud enough to bring the women to their doors to watch the contest. But at length the old man fetched a bunch of carrots, and the younger a stick, and the little ass remembered he had run for miles that day and not eaten. He tried to get his teeth into those carrots—but the peasant of course pulled them away, and then held them out again further on, tempting him to try again. And so between the *carrot* held out ahead and the blows of the *stick* behind, the Ass was at length brought to the man's dilapidated little farmstead and the manger where, amid the other incurious animals, he was shut in. Confused and horribly uncomfortable inside this rough skin, smelling still in his great nostrils the stench of his own burning, he could not know if he had escaped death only to be trapped forever in an even worse fate; and he lowered his great head, and wept.

There are kind masters and cruel masters but no good masters; what's good is to have no master. The Ass soon learned that there was no one in the world who was not his master, no one who did not have the right to strike him, goad him, insult him, injure him, withhold his rough feed, work him to exhaustion. His wit all went toward avoiding the worst, and it was easy to see what that was: in the clay yard a little mill stood, a *mola asinaria* (the Ass found he knew the Latin name), turned now by an old blind (or blinded) horse; a long bar was bound to his back and breast, and his hooves trod the circle, and the heavy stones ground together. The horse, swag bellied and otherwise thin as a bunch of sticks, seemed unlikely to continue in that labor for much longer. Each day the Ass observed him, to see if he might be faltering; each night he woke from horrid dreams to find that he himself was not, thank the gods, bound to the wheel after all—and to find, also, that he was still an ass.

So he scampered and kicked and tossed his big head like a frisky puppy, hoping to seem unsuited to the wheel; loaded with heavy panniers or heaped with fagots that pierced his hide, he tried to be patient and mild, for no burden could be greater than that blind journey to nowhere; he thought of the name Sisyphus but couldn't for a long time remember who that was.

He couldn't remember. His gigantic memory, the endless corridors and towers where who did what when to whom with what for what reason, on and on in ordered ranks, could simply not unfold into the small ass brain where it was now housed; the strong ass-heart could not fire it up or light its lengths and breadths. More than once in the first days of his escape, the Ass, unable to remember a thing or a name or a place or a picture that he had once needed only to raise a forefinger to find (he had no forefinger now), had thought of suicide: thought to fling himself down some ravine, leap into the river, eat poison—anything but fire, anything but that. There was no ravine along the way of his daily labors, though, and the river was far, and nothing he ate seemed even to disagree with him. What the Holy Office had not been able to do he would not be able to do for himself.

Days and months went by, seasons turned, he tried to keep an inward calendar, marking full moons with an imagined white stone, but when he went to look at it again he found the stones scattered. He put aside each night a wisp from his feed, but he trampled them inadvertently or ate them absentmindedly.

Thus a year passed, another, another. Once upon a time he had praised *asinitá*, the patience of asses, their willingness, their refusals and their truculence too; praised them as possessing a divine wisdom that ought to be enthroned in heaven. But that was a game, a play, a *ludus* or a *ludibrium*, written without this experience, which it seemed would last forever, until his poor soul was freed to feed at last upon the deathless grasses of Elysium. He began to pray that he might in the idiocy of daily labor forget that he was a man, or bore a man's spirit, and instead know nothing, nothing at all. Then, just as he was surrendering to despair, his fortunes altered.

The peasant who had first found him had fallen out with his son, and one day as the animals looked on in incomprehension (all but one of them) the two men, more bestial by far than those who observed them, went for each other with knives; son killed father, and then was taken away himself to be hanged. The lord of the manor pulled down the house and gave the land to the church, grisly ghosts and all; receivers came and put up for sale whatever of worth was movable. The Ass was driven with the other beasts to the fair and was there sold to a merchant to carry his goods.

Haberdashery, raw silks, the little ribbons or *zagarelle* that boys give to girls, gold and silver thread, combs, Spanish caps from Spanish Naples, the merchant carried his load from fair to fair: when one closed and its stalls were dismantled he knew of another one opening a day's walk away. He might acquire a large load of some commodity at one, cheeses or almonds or skins, taking a chance that he could make a profit on it at the next, and sometimes he bought a mule or two to carry it, and then sold them too. He was a busy round cheerful fretful man who could add and subtract and multiply on his fingers up to hundreds of *soldi*, and in his head turn the weights and measures of one region—of lead, silk cloth, pepper—into the measures of the next he came to.

His new little ass he kept, loading him to the withers and as high as his own head while whistling tunelessly and happily. And much as the Ass hated each morning, the new prospect, the new road, still he was not walking in a circle, and he could not despise his new master. When he stood to sleep beside him in the noontide, or alone in the innyard at night, he bent his mind to remember, remember; he worked his thick coarse tongue and the strong jaw that Samson had used for a weapon, so unsuited to what he needed it now to do. Walking the roads and highways from the fairs of Recanati and Sinigaglia in the Papal States across the mountains to the fairs authorized by the Republic of Venice at Bergamo and Brescia, he hawed and sighed and moaned in the back of his throat until his master struck him smartly in impatience, but it was quite suddenly and without forethought, on a rocky mountain road in a hurry to make town before nightfall, that at last he managed it:

—My load is unbalanced, he said. If you don't shift it you will lame me.

We are less surprised than perhaps we suppose we will be to hear our beasts talk. After all, they do in our dreams, and even awake we seem to hear their thoughts well enough. In scripture, when Balaam's little ass suddenly appealed to him, saying *What have I done unto thee, that thou hast smitten me these three times?* Balaam evinced no surprise at it. He simply answered: *Because you mocked me.*

So the merchant, after looking around himself a moment and realizing no one else could have spoken but the beast looking up at him in supplication, proceeded to repack the baggage on his back.

—Better? he asked then mockingly, as though daring the ass to speak again. But the Ass kept silent, amazed and suddenly cautious. The two of them went on.

That night, though, when the buying and selling were done, and the merchant had prepared his bed on the grounds where the fair had been held, as he sometimes did when the night was fine and warm and his goods were heavy, the Ass told him, or tried to tell him, how speech had become possible for him, without at the same time revealing that he hadn't always been what he now seemed, which might be dangerous.

For who was he, truly? To be called an Ass is simply to be recognized as an instance of the universal singularity, nothing but an example of a suffering and acting thing. Of which all other things are also perfect examples. "The ideal Ass is the productive, formative, and supranaturally perfecting principle of the asinine species, which, however much it is distinguished in the capacious bosom of nature from other species, nonetheless—and this is of the greatest importance—is, in the First Mind, not other than the type of all intelligences, dæmons, gods, worlds, and the universe; the type from which not only asses but men, stars, worlds, and beings all depend: in it there is no difference of subject or form, of thing or things; it is simple and one." He had written that, once. So the surprise was not (he told the merchant) that he could speak, but that so few other asses (or dogs or stars or stones or roses) ever did; at least not when human hearers were by.

Which in logic was actually an Equivocation, as he had been taught long ago, but the merchant only lay with his hands crossed over his breast and listened thoughtfully.

—Well, you are a true philosopher, he said then. I am only a man with a living to get. And hard as it may seem to require so well-spoken a creature as yourself to carry, the work still needs doing.

—Fair enough, said the Ass. If you will grant my poor self the general honor due to a being capable of speech, therefore reason, I will go on doing the work my shape suits me for. It's the best I could hope for, I suppose.

—That's fine then, said the merchant sleepily.

They didn't know their conversation was overheard.

Late in the night, before he could fully awaken and perceive what was happening to him, the Ass felt a bag slipped suddenly over his head.

—There is, said a voice, a pistol pointed at your head. It were best you be still.

And indeed the beast felt the prod of it behind his left ear.

—Come along, said the voice, and it will be to your advantage. Don't cry out.

The Ass understood immediately that the one, or ones, who were around him knew he was possessed not only of language but reason, if they could speak thus to him. He wondered if they also knew that his asinine nature wouldn't permit him to take even a step with his eyes blind. They must have, for after a moment the bag was drawn down enough for him to see; and—his heart huge to know his life and his adventure weren't to end, whether to grow worse or better—he went along with them. There were three, and they hurried him through the darkened grounds and the crowd of sleeping or unsleeping merchants, farmers, Gypsies, whores, out onto the highway, thence after a long walk (the Ass kept prudently silent) to the stable yard of a low inn, where more of their gang was gathered, who whistled and cheered softly to see their fellows bring in the prize, himself.

Who were they? Thieves? The pistol held to his head, he could perceive now, was only a stick of wood. What did they intend? And why, above all, did they speak to him, and to one another, in English?

—Masters, he said, in their own tongue—which caused a noise of delight or awe among them—masters, what do you want with me? Why have you abducted me?

—Because, said the largest of them, red cheeked and black whiskered and grinning with a set of cheerful gleaming white teeth, because you will make our fortune. And your own. We have, he said, a proposition.

They weren't thieves, or not usually thieves; they were a troupe of actors, traveling as the Ass and his (former) master did from fair to fair and town to town, as many English companies did. They weren't one of the great troupes with noble patrons that would entertain the Prince and Princess Palatine in Heidelberg, and then make progress through the courts and cities of Europe; they had a few bags filled with costumes, masks, crowns and foils, a set of moth-holed curtains, a drum, and a pipe. The six or eight of them played many parts in every play, changing behind the curtain from lord's cape and sword to swain's jerkin and bottle and rushing on stage again. They had been about to pack all their properties and go home again, no richer than they had come. Then this.

—Join our troop, they said. You'll never carry again, or carry no more than any of us. You'll be a comedian, you'll make us rich, and yourself as well, for we share and share alike, even the asses among us, ha ha.

It was an easy decision to make. The short summer night was past; dawn had come, and a ray of the all-giving sun now fell into that little stable yard. What *rich* might mean to one like himself he couldn't say, but if ease, and scope, and intellectual delight were all he got, it was more than the Ass he was could have aspired to, and ought to be enough for the man.

—What play shall we play? he said.

They laughed, they cheered, and their chief, or anyway the largest among them, pulled from his pack a greasy and leaf-curled book without a cover, and as everyone laughed some more, he proffered it and the Ass noticed, on the third finger of the man's hand, a ring: a ring cut with a curious figure that he was sure he remembered, or had once imagined, or in future might conceive. The player splayed open the pages and put the book before the Ass, who looked upon it, found he could read it, and trembled in amazement, for the story was his own:

> *Once as I grazed vpon the Lippe of steepe and stoney Rauine, conceiving the Desire to chew vpon a louely Cardoon or Thistle, growing some little way downe the Precipice, and Satisfyed that I coulde Stretch my longe Necke so farre without Perill, defying the pricks alike of Conscience and naturall Reason, I leaned out, and farther out, 'til I could no longer lean; and I fell from that Cliffy Height; and thereupon my Master knew, that he had bought mee but for Crow's-meate.*
>
> *Freed from the Prison of my Flesshe, I became a wandering Spirit, without Members; and I saw that, as to my Substance Spirituall, I was in no different case than all other Spirits, who vpon the dissoluing of their Animal or compound Bodies, begin straightaway to Transmigrate. For (as I saw) Fate not only remoueth all distinctioun (as regards their Corporality) between the Ass's flesshe and Man's, likewise between the Brute and the wholly Inanimate: also it remoueth all Distinctioun between the Asinine and the Human Soul, indeed betweene those souls and the soul that is found in all things.*

It was his own story, that is, his own work—it was the *Cabala del Caballo Pegaseo,* which he had written long years before, here translated from the Italian into English by his friend and follower Alexander Dicson, who missed him dreadfully after his departure from England, and who earned not a penny from the little book on whose title page his name stood beneath the author's, with his Oxford degree appended, and the date (1599). In surprise and pity the Ass studied the book, holding its pages down with an unhandy forefoot and tempted to eat the leaves rather than reading them. How had it come into the hands of this company? How was the Ass able to read it with his ass's poor eyes, and recognize it? How did Tom the grinning principal player come by the ring on his finger, just that ring with just that figure? And why did the Ass, as the players pointed out, bear the same figure on his own back, where all other asses bear the cross of Christ? How come? Because without these wonders, and all the others like them preceding and to come, there wouldn't be a story to tell, and without a story no one would come to hear—as every player knows.

~

For a year the company (they now called themselves I Giordanisti after the Ass had told them his tale, as much of it as he could remember) went up and down High Germany, playing the play of *The Transformations of Ass Onorius, the Cabalistical Steed,* partly in German, partly Italian, partly English, mostly in the universal language. In university towns they played the scenes of Onorius's metempsychosis into Aristotle, Pythagoras, a Grammarian, a Schoolman, as the students howled encouragement, an easy audience. They also played *Lucius, or the Life and Adventures of the Golden Ass,* from the book of Apuleius; performances might or might not, depending, include the scene of poor Lucius inveigled into the Matron's bed, but always included the final Transformation, of Lucius the Ass into Lucius the Man, by the sweet power of all-seeing Isis, clothed in the sky and the stars.

Their success was huge, and not so surprising; for after all the Ass, or his inhabiting spirit rather, had begun his writing life years ago with what? A play. A comedy in fact, *Il Candelaio.* And ever after he had set people to talking in his works, in his dialogues, and in his poems—fools, philosophers, pedants, gods, and goddesses.

Then the wind began to blow from another quarter. Maybe they should have been more cautious; maybe they should have avoided Apuleius, that infamous magician; maybe they shouldn't have become so far famed so quickly.

No no, they told the authorities who questioned them. No no, not magic, no none of that. Just ordinary stage tricks, sleight of hand, *Jahrmarktsgaukelei.* The Ass stood meekly silent before the tribunal as one of the company showed how the trick was done, *ventriloquia,* nothing forbidden about it. They were lucky to be only driven out of the parish and the town.

But it was hard for him to be silent. The more he wrote and spoke and thought, the more he seemed to himself the man who had once been, and the less the ass he was. For the first time he was ashamed of his nakedness. From patient he grew ill tempered, from gentle to surly, and at last became melancholy, would neither think nor write, finally not speak, not eat.

What to do? His fellows vowed to help him, do all they could, but there seemed only one possibility: he must hope for a further transformation, and somehow become a man entire. As Lucius Apuleius the Golden Ass does.

One certainty consoled me then in my darkest hour, says Lucius, *that the new year was here at last, and the wildflowers would soon be coming out to color the meadows; and in the gardens the rosebuds long imprisoned in their thorny stocks would appear, and open, and breathe out their indescribable odor; and I would eat and eat, and become once again myself.*

—But I *am* myself, said the Ass. I am an ass not figuratively, or platonically, or cabalistically, or in disguise or in effect, but actually. There is no rose for me to feed upon that will change me back; there is no way back at all.

—Ah, said the players, who pitied him, even though it would surely reduce their income if he were somehow made a man.

—I can't return, he said, to that Pythagorean way I chose to tread, and take the other way.

—No, said his fellows sadly, for neither could they.

—Very well then, said the Ass, and the players lifted their heads, for they heard a new note, as players are quick to do. We can't go back. No one can. What we were is not, but what we will be, we cannot know.

—Yes, said his companions.

—There is one place I could go, said the Ass after long thought. A city of wise workers, a city where transformation is not only possible but likely.

—What city?

—I was there. I was summoned to counsel the Emperor. I, I.

—Yes! said his companions. The little ass seemed in their eyes to grow in stature as he spoke, to a noble height, a proud determination.

—We'll go on, said the Ass. Go on by going back. To Prague.

—Prague! They rose as one, and looked on each other with gay resolve. Actors can do this, too: more than once they had got themselves in awful trouble by suddenly, and convincingly, pretending to grand emotions, a ringing curtain line. Eagle-browed Ass! Winged Ass! they sang. To Prague! they sang, and they set to, and packed their bags and their properties, and loaded them on the back of the Ass and into the bright new wagon that his mute cousin the mule pulled, and set out. Soon the road unrolled before them, running ever on. Over the hills and far away, sang the players.

Tom he was a piperes sonne
He stole a pipe and awaye he ronne
And the onlie tune that hee could play
Was Over the hills and farre away.

They all sang the chorus, and even the Ass hee-hawed like the famous ass musician of Bremen:

Over the hills and a grete way off
The wind shall blow my topknot off.

4

Behind the *gallimordium,* the old royal brothel, up a winding alley, were the gates of the great Jewish quarter of the city. Each evening those who had been out and about the city hurried within before the gates were shut, artisans and laborers and peddlers in their caftans marked with yellow circles and their tall pointed yellow hats with curious balls atop them, the richer men's caftans of silk, their hats brimmed with fur. The Ass and his two companions, Tom and another who best knew the German tongue, went in through the gates with them, looking neither right nor left, and into the crowded streets, some of the streets so narrow that the housewives could touch from window to window above the heads of those who passed or struggled to pass below. Other streets were closed above altogether, the buildings joined above them and turning them to caves or tunnels that went up and down stairs in the dark before debouching again into the day.

Up the little city past the Town Hall, whose clock was set out in Hebrew letters and whose hands ran backward like the eyes of Torah readers, past the synagogue called the New Synagogue that was as old as almost any church of the city (for the Jews, so the Jews asserted, had been in Prague from its founding): black and small it was, though, not great, and inside the walls were black too with a thousand years of candle smoke, the cantor ululating softly in the almemar as they went by.

Up farther, under another gallery, past a market now closing, cooped ducks, geese, and doves; a further tunnel of darkness, drip of cisterns, branching alleys to choose from, all different but indistinguishable; and at last to the house they sought, the most famous house of the quarter, before which a small crowd was as always gathered.

From surprise at their appearing there with the little ass beside them without lead or halter, the crowd let the players pass through, and go into the court within. Tom and his comrade went through an inner door and up a stairway, along a lightless corridor, Tom reaching before him with his hands to find the door; going first through a room of women and girls whose pale faces took light from the evening candles, who spoke and laughed among themselves as they passed, and then into a farther room, the *bet ha-midrash,* where the Great Rabbi taught, and men and boys listened and read.

He was Judah Loew ben Bezalel, the most famous of all the famous wise men of Prague. Jews from Rus and Damascus and Fez and Venice came to consult him. Doctor John Dee when he had lived here had heard of his wisdom, his *rabínská moudrost,* and had come here to learn with him. The Emperor Rudolf himself had been in awe of it, and once summoned the Rabbi to the Hradcany to question him; the Rabbi's son-in-law Isak Kohen wrote later that the Rabbi was brought to a small room, a curtain was pushed aside, the Emperor came in, asked the rabbi several questions, and then retired. What questions? What answers? Isak Kohen wrote: *what they talked of must, as is the imperial practice, not be revealed.*

Whatever the actors said to the rabbi, what craft of their own they exercised on the great still figure in the crowded room, it was enough to bring him down the stairs to the courtyard; there the little ass stood patiently, big head looking from side to side; and the rabbi sent away the other supplicants who waited there, and bent down, with his hands upon his knees, toward the Ass, and waited for it to tell its tale—as the two actors had said it would do, and all by itself.

And so it did, from beginning to end, supplemented by the human persons who had come with it. The rabbi, who considered it an affront to the endless invention of the Most High to be astonished by the speaking of an Ass, listened in silence to the end. Then he asked what it was the beast desired of him.

—I wish, said the Ass, to be transformed from the shape I now hold, and acquire a shape more suited to the spirit within me. For I can't go into the places of men in this form. I would be spurned, or burned for a devil. Burned again.

—And why is it, the rabbi said then (speaking in his own Jewish tongue, which an ancient secretary translated into German for the Ass and his companions) that you have come here to me? Why do you think I have a remedy for you?

His visitors looked at one another, each unwilling to be the first to speak, for they all knew why here, why him. He was the Maharal, not only wise but good, and able, out of his learning and holiness, to accomplish wonders. It was well known that he had once made a golem: a figure of earth, sculpted on the ground like a dead man or like the figure of dirt that God's fingers first made, which the rabbi then, by prayers and other rituals few know about and fewer would have dared repeat, caused to stir, awake, rise. To sit up groggily on his elbows, dropping clods, looking about himself in wonder (or was he an unthinking lump still, with no more consciousness than the Emperor's *Uhrwerk* figures, which seem to obey the Emperor's orders like courtiers and knights, but were only metal pins and springs—earth too?) and at length stand up on unsteady earthen legs, not very well formed but not the less amazing for that, and ready to obey the Maharal's instructions, until the wise rabbi drew from its muddy mouth (or ear, in other accounts) the *shem ha-meforash,* the capsule containing the Name, that had animated it, whereupon the big fellow broke apart into clods again. Or—in another story—until the rabbi erased one diacritical mark of the sacred word Truth, *emet,* that he had inscribed upon the creature's forehead, leaving the equally sacred word *met* or Death.

—Those are untrue stories, said the Maharal. Such things can be done by the cunning, but the truly learned refrain from them. To press light into darkness, to mix clean and unclean? Those who do so are brave perhaps and have great knowledge perhaps, but may the Holy One, blessed be he, protect me from imitating them.

—I don't ask that you do those things that are forbidden, said the Ass. Only that you help me to learn what I must, to do it for myself. I ask for what anyone ignorant may ask of you: instruction.

The rabbi regarded the beast before him. If it was not forbidden, it seemed to be required; it would be a mitzvah to help any being in the condition this one found itself in. The animal looked up at him with his great moist long-lashed eyes in supplication, and the rabbi had an irresistible impulse to scratch its head.

This too, then, would become one of the stories told of the Maharal, in some worlds at least; how he used to walk sometimes in the town with an ass by his side, without lead or halter, an ass that would stay obediently by him like a nobleman's dog, and look up with doglike attention to the Maharal, who seemed to speak to it confidentially, though surely (observers supposed) his words were for himself alone, or were for God's ear, for who else could hear?

—The Torah has six hundred thousand faces, the Maharal said to the Ass. One face for every Jew alive at the time *Moshe rebiana* revealed it. Some faces of the Torah are turned toward us, and some away; it is these turned-away faces we seek through *Hokhmath ha-Tseruf*, or, as it is said, *gematria*.

—This is the art by which form and substance may be transmuted, said the Ass.

When the rabbi said nothing in assent, the Ass added: So I have read in ancient authors.

—All the beings in the universe have come into existence through the work of the twenty-two letters, said the rabbi. By combining their different kinds, the twenty-two make, in all, 231 gates. Through these gates have come, in their troops and legions, all the things that have names, in all the three realms, that is, the World, the Year, and the Soul.

—Did they, then, precede the saying of the *Fiat lux*?

—Perhaps they did, said the rabbi. A midrash says that the Holy One, blessed be he, asked for workers to make the world, and the Torah replied: Take these twenty-two, of which I am made.

He spoke in simple terms, not only because he spoke in a language not his own, but also because he spoke to a famously simple beast, whose hooves clattered on the cobblestones beside him, whose long ears twitched and pointed as though in search of wisdom.

—Even so, the rabbi went on, it took several attempts to get a creation that would sustain itself at all: earlier creations preceded this one, coming to be and going out like the sparks thrown off by a smith's hammer as it strikes the iron on the anvil.

The Ass hee-hawed, for the idea of a Jove or Jehovah laboring over an infinite smithy, spoiling his work and beginning again, suited him very well: it was as though he'd thought of it himself.

The rabbi (not noticing the interruption) went on to explain that those first universes emanated entirely from his Power, his strict Justice; each was too difficult to maintain, and destroyed itself; only when balanced by the smile of his other aspect, Wisdom, Mother, and Spouse, was the world able to remain alive and persist in the place it had been summoned to.

—Yet even now the creation is not completed, said the rabbi. It is said that this world grows up through a succession of Years, or *shemitah*, each different in kind. The present *shemitah* emanates from the *sefira* Gevurah, judging Power: that is, the left hand of the Holy One. Anyone can see that this is so. And if this is so then the former age must have been that of the *sefira* Hesed, sweet Loving-kindness.

—And the age to come? asked the donkey.

—Rahamim: Beauty, Compassion, Mercy.

For a moment he paused, and lowered his head, and so did the beast beside him: as though to await that age, so long in dawning.

—Each Year, the rabbi then said, is seven thousand ordinary years long, and at the end of each, all things begin again, but differently.

—All things?

—Some say that in former *shemitah,* even the Torah did not contain the possibilities it contains now, and in the *shemitah* to come it will not contain them again, but will contain others it does not now. There are those who hold that there is a letter not present in the Torah in this age, a letter that the next age will reveal. A revelation that must of course change everything, however slightly.

—Ah, said the Ass; so it must.

—Others say that there are certain unfortunate souls formed in the last Year but still persisting in this one, where they wander in dissatisfaction, never at home, and not knowing why.

The Ass pondered this, and his own state.

—Perhaps, he said then, they are the greatest scholars, as well as the greatest fools. Searching for the sense that they remember, or expect, but that has changed forever.

The rabbi walked silently for a moment, as though testing against his inward understandings this remark, to see if it could be so.

—In any case, he said at last, those tales are false. There is but one age, one world, one Torah, one soul for each man.

The Ass didn't dispute the Great Rabbi, wise enough to know better, patient enough to wait. That he himself was the proof that a man could have more than one soul made for him in the bosom of Amphitrite he forbore to say. He only paused and parted his hind legs, and sent a stream of urine into the gutter, while the rabbi tactfully went on ahead, and paid no attention.

~

The work was long: the rabbi said it would be. The *Giordanisti* took rooms in a house in the castle district named after the Three Kings, *die Heilige drei Königen* (where one day in another world Franz Kafka would live, and dream about metamorphosis). To make their daily bread and board they put on plays once again, safer in this city than anywhere in the Empire. They acted, besides Onorius and Lucius, a new play of Johannes Faustus, like the ones the *Pragerei* loved—only in theirs the devil with whom Faust negotiates the sale of his soul was not a *schwarze Pudel* but a well-spoken Ass.

Meanwhile, every day if he could, the Ass traveled to the Jewish quarter, to the rabbi's house, to learn and hope.

He studied the nine chief methods of calculation or *gematria*, as Moses Cordovero lists them. Every letter by which the world was first called into being has a numeric equivalent, and gimetry is but the substitution of one name with another of the same numerological value—which value can however be calculated in an endless number of ways, for the letters of the names of the letters—the aleph of *aleph*, the beth of *beth*—have their own numerical values that can be drawn on too, and this being so no two numerically identical words are ever exactly identical, since their identity derives from different calculations.

He learned—indeed he already knew it, as he seemed already to have known everything he had learned as an ass, except how to sleep standing up and bear loads as large as himself—that all the names of the deity, the potent *semhamaphoræ*, which are the shadows of ideas, are all hidden in the letters that compose the scripture's tales and truths and laws. The whole of the Hebrew scripture is not other than the one Great Name, expressed in the quasi-endless vicissitudes of alphabetic calculation.

But for that to be so, then mustn't each of the stories that the scripture contains have been made to happen in the first place only so that it could be written down in certain words, having the value of certain numbers? If Samson had picked up not the jawbone of an ass but the thighbone of a tiger, one name of God would not be able to be read from the story.

—Are they all nothing but fables then? he asked the rabbi.

They sat (at least the rabbi and his secretary sat) studying in the inner court of the *bet ha-midrash*. The Ass, still an ass after many lessons, watched the rabbi's blunt quill dip in the inkhorn his secretary held, and make vermiform letters one after another.

—No, said the rabbi. Those events did occur, and they also have the hidden meanings that they have. The Almighty favored Abraham not because he was a good man, but because he was Abraham: and yet Abraham would not have been Abraham if he had not striven to be a good man. It is the same for all of us.

—The same for all of us, said the rabbi's secretary in Latin. *Idem ac omnibus.*

Was it, though, was it the same for all of us, the same as for Abraham? The Ass thought, as they studied, of his own story: a story he could not have imagined in advance of its coming to be, the story that had plucked him as a brand from the burning, marked him as the bearer of a knowledge he could no longer apprehend, brought him here to this land, to this city, to this crowded and odorous quarter. With how much farther to go, in what form, for what end.

We try to choose the good, he thought, and darkling and ignorant, to be wise: and in doing so we make the choices that will spell the stories, the stories that will body forth or contain or clothe the thousand- and ten-thousand-letter names of God. Those names—the skeleton of the made World, of the Year we inhabit, of the Soul we recognize within—all come to be in the stories we make. But the stories cannot be known before our labors make them; therefore neither can the names; therefore neither can the ending of the world we make.

—We are not required to complete the work, the rabbi said to the little beast. But neither are we free to desist from it.

A year passed before the Ass discovered the solution to his quandary, and when he did it was all on his own.

The stories that great Moses told, of the making of the world and the coming to be of men and beasts, angels and demons, fathers and heroes, sinners and journeys and judgments: they contained all the names of God in the permutations of the numbers of the letters of their words. So the rabbi said. But then, the Ass concluded, it must be that all those sacred histories could be exactly substituted by *other* stories about *other* journeys, judgments, heroes, *et cætera,* and—so long as they were told in words that had exactly the same numerical values—those stories would yield up the same names and numbers, indeed the same Great Name and Number. When he expressed this discovery to the rabbi, the rabbi at last sent him away, scandalized.

But it was so, and he knew it. And, finally and therefore, his own little name and its number, the number of his whole tale, could be reversed, construed, inverted, reduced, multiplied, and divided, and then made to spell out a new name, the name of a new being different from but exactly equivalent to the old, with a new tale, a tale both having been and still coming to be.

And into or onto that name and tale he could press or tack or strap or infuse or pour or discover his self and soul, as he had once before infused the same self and soul into the body and heart of an ass, and by similar means perhaps, only not numerological ones. (What ones, then? How had he done it? He couldn't remember.)

So he took the gold he had made as a comedian, and he caused to be made (by the same instrument maker then serving Johannes Kepler up in the castle on the hill) a vast set of interlocking brass wheels, which were etched and numbered like an astrolabe, or like the proportional compass of Fabricio Mordente, with the Hebrew letters, and the letters of Latin and Greek, and the lettered Divine Qualities of Raimundus Lullus for good measure. For the *signacula* of Moses were wonderful, and the hieroglyphs of Ægypt are wonderful, but all letters and the images made from them are finally just as wonderful and eternal, and are equally the world.

As the *Giordanisti* turned and turned these wheels at his instruction, he combined and transliterated and reflected the resulting nonsense in the mirror of his heart of hearts. His soul studied it in that mirror, where of course it appeared backward, upside down too like the reflection in a silver spoon's bowl; studied and read until it all ran backward again, that is forward, and so at last made sense, sweet sense, which raced through his fibers and his sinews and the macaroni of his veins and nerves, remaking him as it went.

He was a tabby kitten; then he was a stick of elmwood; a silvery trout with a rainbow belly wriggling in air; a live coal, shedding sparks; a gray pigeon, drop of ruby blood at its beak. For an infinitesimal instant he was an infinite number of things, and then for an endless moment he was one thing eternally.

Then he was a man. A small naked man, though not smaller or more naked than he had been in the Campo dei Fiori. His name was Philip à Gabella. Instead of hooves he had ten fingers—no, nine fingers, one *minimus* lost somewhere along the way or failing to be produced in metamorphosis. Big headed, exophthalmic, with large yellow teeth. A large *membrum virile* too: that and his loud and horripilating laugh being marks he would henceforward keep hidden, for he remembered how, long ago, they had frightened off the giants in their revolt against the gods—that is, the powers and the principalities. He remembered the tale, and the names of those gods and powers, and the names of the giants too. It was a well-known tale; its occurrence in many authors ancient and modern unrolled within him. The strong image of the ithyphallic Ass up on his hind legs displaying was one that he possessed; here it was.

And he laughed his terrible laugh then, right then, unable not to, laughed and laughed as the brothers covered their ears. Because he remembered.

He remembered. The great gates of the many-linked memory palaces he had built over the whole of his life before his death were flung open with a bang, for his new man's brain was large enough for them to unfold at last into, and they did unfold, they opened like the damp wings of butterflies just come from their cocoons, like folding game boards of a thousand inlaid panels, like cunts, like caves, like dreams suddenly remembered backward from their terminus at waking, *oh yes!* ever backward till their infinities can be glimpsed, distances where one day we will go, or might go.

He remembered all the writings he had written and all those that remained unwritten. He remembered the lands he had crossed, the languages he had mastered, the shoes he had worn out, the meals he had eaten or refused, the women he had coupled with, Venetian, Savoyard, Genevan, Picard, Walloon, English. He remembered the faces in all the crowds in all the squares of all the cities he had added to his own Memory City in the time he had walked the earth.

He remembered the prison in Rome where he had lain for so many years, and all the places he had traveled to while he lay there, on earth, under the earth, in the heavens: he remembered even the small window above, by which he had used to go out. He remembered all those he had summoned to sit with him there, and all the conversations he had had with them, the answers he had got from them. And also the questions they had asked, that he had answered. And lastly he remembered how he had learned from one of them, and from the instructions of his own soul, the means by which he had been able to run away, again.

Freed by his grandfather Hermes, who had told him the plan that he, Giordano, had already known before he was told it. Step by step. And who then said to him: *Now go, and free all men.*

And so he had gone from Rome and crossed the mountains and the plains and come to this golden city on four legs. Now again he had two, and a new or an old Work to accomplish, in consequence of all that he had been given; a Work he had been saved to do. And if he was not able to accomplish it all to the end, that was no reason not to begin.

—Let's begin, he said to the players gathered around him. He had clothed his nakedness in Faust's scholar's robe from their play, its hem somewhat cinder bitten from the squibs and firecrackers the demons threw on poor Faust at the play's ending. Tom tapped idly on the drum as they spoke. It was midnight in the *Heilige drei Königen.*

—What is it we are to begin?

—The unbinding of all men from their limits, said the Ass. Since we have begun with ourselves—with myself, I mean—let's continue.

Tap tap.

—And how are we to do such a thing as that?

—I have a plan, said the Ass, the former Ass.

Men can be freed from their bonds, he told them, but not from all bonds, for that would leave men beasts: it is in what binds them that they are men. To decide which of those bonds most leads to happiness is the goal of the *sapiens* who knows how binding is accomplished. He will give—or seem to give, in this matter there is no real difference, the sign is the thing—to every person what he or she most wants. *Unicuique suum,* to each his own: and to all as to each, for though every man and every woman is more or less different, the mass of men and women are more or less the same. And what do they want? Stories that end in happiness, weddings after adversity, triumphs of righteousness. Wonders and signs fulfilled. Then Adam returns refreshed and renewed; all is forgiven. Mercy, Pity, Peace. The Golden Age begins again, and lasts forever, until it ends.

—And how, said doubting Tom, are we to seem to give to all men what they most want? How are we to speak to the mass of men and women all at once, and yet give *unicuique suum?*

—How? said Philip à Gabella, the Ass made Man. We do it every day and twice on holidays. We will (here he lifted his new hands to them, his large gray eyes alight; it was hilarious and sad how they could still recognize in him their former companion), we will put on a play.

—A *play?*

—Let's, he said clapping, put on a play. A *ludibrium,* a show, a jest in all seriousness, a seriousness in all jest. Not in one place only but across the world, across this Europe at least. Such a play as has never in the history of the world been seen, a play that will force them all to *suspend their disbelief,* and not only watch and laugh and weep, but take part as well, and be themselves our actors.

—Who?

—Anyone who can hear. Kings, bishops, knights, magi, ploughmen, wives, nuns, wise men, fools, young, old, not yet born, already dead. All. The kingdom will be our stage, sun our lights, night our curtain.

—A kingdom for a stage! one player cried, and strutted and lifted his hand to raise the eyes and spirits of an imaginary audience. A kingdom for a stage, princes to act, and monarchs to behold the swelling scene!

—And what *bonds* will bring in our audience? asked grinning Thomas. What strengths seen to be ours alone will change the world before their eyes and ears?

—Love, Magic, Mathesis, said the Ass. And the greatest of these is Love.

—Religion, added a player piously. The will of Almighty God swayed by earnest prayer.

—Well said, the Ass proclaimed. Jesus was the greatest of the magicians, and the bond of religion is a strong one: let us decide which, of all religions, will best serve the mass of men now, and which will do the greatest harm. Promote the one, abjure the other. I myself (he added, to the astonishment of the players) prefer the Catholic religion. But the Lutheran is the more useful and commodious now.

—Then let's choose the more commodious and useful, the players said.

—We will be good Christians and Germans, said the Ass.

—*Ach du Lieber,* said Tom.

—We will condemn the Pope and the Sultan, and love Cabala and *prisca theologia* and Ægypt and the Jews. We will love the Emperor above all men. We will not blaspheme. We will speak with reverence of the Most High, and the life to come.

—Amen, they said.

—Will we be brothers? cried the Ass, Philip à Gabella, and held out his nine-fingered hands to them. Will we vow loyalty to one another, vow to do no hurt to men, to help, to heal, to make right?

—We will, said the others. We are Giordanisti. We are at your service.

—No more of that, or them, said Filippo: for there is no more Giordano. We are all brothers now. And we are the brothers of all those who have sought for us, dreamed of us, hoped that such ones as we might now live, or might one day come to be; all those who are *novatores,* and wish to make all new, and all those who long for the return of the *prisca theologia* of Orpheus, Ægypt, and Pythagoras. We will invite them all. For them the brothers will be both lure and lured, both the bait and the fisher.

—A sign, said the players. We must have a sign for our brotherhood.

The former Ass sat down, gathering his skirts from beneath him with a gesture he hadn't used in years. He put his new elbow on his new knee, and his new chin in his small hand, and drummed his fingers across his new soft cheek.

—A rose, he said at last. And a cross.

The players looked on one another, and nodded, considering. A rose and a cross: good.

—*Fraternitas Rosæ-Crucis,* he said. The players saw that there were tears in his large gray eyes. A rose, for the roses of many-named Isis that he had fed upon, after growing them in his own heart's hothouse. And a cross, not the Christian one but the cross of Ægypt that he had borne on his hairy back, the cross the players recognized, the Monad that the English doctor had rediscovered, which he had explicated for poor dead Giordano in the inmost room of the high castle above the very city where they now sat: the *crux ansata,* the little man with arms akimbo, the sign of himself.

—Now let us go, he said, rising, and ourselves bring this *cemittá* to an end, and usher in another, a better one, Mercy Beauty Peace, made by ourselves for all.

5

There was war in Heaven then.

Edward Kelley had first seen it *in chrystallo* in the city of Cracow long before: the angel bands issuing from their watchtowers at the four corners of the universe: *red as new-smitten blood,* he told John Dee, *lily white, green and garlic-bladed like a dragon's skin, black as raven hair or bilberry juice,* the four kinds of which the world is made, coming together in war: and not long until they met. In the lower heavens the souls of heroes, the great *dæmones,* the tutelary spirits, the angels of the nations, were thereupon set upon one another. They couldn't know that what was being fought over in Heaven was the shape of the world to come, in which none of them would figure. Yet since the lowest of the rulers of the air are coterminous or contiguous with the highest rulers of the earth, the states and nations, princes and churches, were agitated too, and thought they were plotted against, and had better preempt their enemies, and strike before they were struck.

In 1614 there began to appear those weird announcements of the Invisible Brothers among us, of the Universal Reformation of the Whole Wide World, starry messengers, and a More Secret Philosophy concerning a man-shaped cross (*stella hieroglyphica*), explicated by one Philip à Gabella, whom no one could find, to thank or to burn. And a hundred other brothers then made themselves known, all on their own, from England to Vienna: yes, I share in their plans and secrets; yes, I am a soldier of that unseen army of the wise and peaceable.

Then disaster: in June 1617, the Bohemian Estates met in Prague city and elected the Archduke Ferdinand of Austria to be their next king.

How could the estates have done it? Christian of Anhalt had urged and cajoled and begged them to elect Frederick, Prince Palatine, instead, a Protestant who would protect the rights of the Bohemian Protestant majority and all its churches, brotherhoods, congregations, a knight *sans peur et sans reproche* who was truly the one favored by all the powers of Heaven, whose father-in-law was King James of England, whose wife was named for their old English champion Elizabeth, the queen who confounded the Spanish fleet and sent it to the bottom. But no one else believed as yet in the pleasant young man or his wonderful fate. And as if in a dream where you can't help but do just what you mustn't, the baffled estates in the end voted for the Archduke Ferdinand, a rigid and ultra-Orthodox Catholic, a Hapsburg, a despot, and a very able and tenacious man, who was certain to be elected emperor soon as well.

It took a year of insults and punitive laws from the hand of this Catholic king-elect and his factors, but the Protestant nobles of Bohemia at length awakened, and revolted. On May 23, 1618, a deputation of great men, followed by a much larger crowd of citizens, went to the Hradschin, climbed the huge stair, took over the offices and rooms, herding the imperial officers like sheep before them, until the two imperial governors of the city were found in the last high chamber to which they had retreated. *Po staro . . . esku! Throw them out!*

The throwing-out-of-the-window of Prague. The elder governor, Martinic, went out first; Slavata, the other governor, begging for a confessor, clung to the jamb until his hand was struck with a dagger hilt and he went too. Their secretary, who was attempting to slip away quietly, was thrown out after them. None of the three was killed; they fell on a pyramid of dung below the window, which broke their fall, or maybe (as the Catholics claimed) they were aided by the Virgin Mary, who spread her sky blue cloak to catch them. Dung and the Virgin, and not much harm done: for this happened in Prague.

It was, for the time, a gentle revolution, a revolution made in the name of keeping all things as they were, as they had been under Rudolf, who never changed anything. A mob did invade the Jewish quarter, as a mob always did in upheavals of all kinds, but with less damage than was usual; Catholic churches were disestablished, but only those that had been recently built on land seized from Protestant congregations, and the Jesuits were expelled. And then the crown of Bohemia was offered to Frederick, the Elector Palatine.

This changed everything. Frederick was among few who were not surprised.

Should he accept? Did God truly want him to take up this cup? Or let it pass from him? He asked his wife. There would be hardships, he said. *I had rather eat cabbage as a queen than roast beef as a princess,* said Elizabeth.

He would be called a rebel against his emperor, an outlaw, he told her;

he would be at war against his sworn sovereign, God's anointed, whom he should respect above all. *Emperor Ferdinand has but one eye, and that one not good,* Elizabeth said.

Still he couldn't choose.

And at that moment there arrived at the gates of Heidelberg a troupe of actors, *Englische kömoedianten,* come with new plays, drum and tabor, beasts and tumblers, scattering rose petals and salt. Elizabeth clapped her hands. Oh, these are the best, said Anhalt, who knew everything, the best for tragedy, comedy, history, historical comedy, tragical history, pastoral tragical historical comical.

What were they playing? *A Game at Chess, showing the Wedding of the White Queen and the Red King, together with the infinite jests of Cupid, and the waking of his mother Venus; the Weighing up of those thought powerful and wise, and who is found wanting; the Solemn Vows taken of the Brothers of the Golden Stone to defend the King and Queen, their Son, their Daughter, and all persons of good will; Transformations and Wonders of earth, air, fire, and water, the joining of the Rose and Cross, and the return of all good things in the course of time.*

The play's the thing, whispered Tom to his fellows, by which we'll catch the conscience of the king.

And Frederick accepted the crown of Bohemia. In September 1619 he wrote to the Bohemian Estates: *It is a divine calling, and I must not refuse.* Next month the couple set out from Heidelberg, walking hand in hand beneath the Elizabeth-Pforte in dress of appropriate astrological colors, Venus's blue and white for her, Mars's gold and red for him. As though to reverse the music of loving-kindness that had played when Elizabeth had arrived from England, the drums and trumpets played in vehement Phrygian mode as they went out. Behind them came their soldiers, servants, lords, ladies, squires, pages—and their troupe of actors. Over the hills and far away.

It took them weeks to reach Prague. To transform the world as you pass through it takes a longer time than simply to cover ground. At every city and town of the Rhineland the people wept to see them go by, as though they took their homeland with them. On the other side of the border the towns and cities of Bohemia met them with joy and flung roses; then, as they climbed the mountains, there came at them out of the forest a crowd of harvestmen, Hussite farmers (or actors dressed as them) who made a roaring with their grain flails; their leader, a Hussite preacher, made a long speech of blessing and welcome. The land of Hus was safe beneath their rule.

And yet they were still just two happy people, young parents (one son already squalling in his crib, another in the oven), liable to offend their new subjects and tread on toes, but what could it really matter? In Prague city Elizabeth's gowns shocked the Calvinists, her breasts symbolic of course but also just breasts, and too exposed. The king swam naked in the Moldau, and she and her ladies watched from the bank: that upset the elders. Well, let them mutter, look at him rising from the waves like Leander, like a young river god. More people were shocked when she decided to take down an ancient corpus from his cross in the middle of the Caroline bridge. It had worked wonders for thousands, its nailed foot worn smooth by the kisses of the devout. *That naked swimmer,* said vengeful Elizabeth.

The former Giordanisti—unrecognizable to their old audiences, before whom they had once played the *Faustspiel* and the comic inventions of Onorio the ass—played now under the ægis of the king and his queen, before cloths of gold, in Prague's palaces and great houses, with music drawn from ancient sources, in dramas that were great Seals acted out by hypostases of Virtue and hilarious Vice, and the people laughed and wept and resolved to change their lives. They played *The Expulsion of the Triumphant Beast,* they played *The Wedding of Agent and Patient,* they played *The Apotheosis of Rudolf II in the Happy Isles.* Philip à Gabella and his troupe of actors took no part, though, in the celebratory Pageant of All the World Systems that was held in the streets, maybe prematurely, in honor of the royal couple—how could his infinite universe of suns and planets, forever continuing, be pictured?—but they could watch, and laugh. The scholars from the Carolinum presented the Ptolemaic world, replete with spheres and epicycles and green earth sheltered in God's arms, apple of his eye; Tycho Brahe's vision was produced by the artisans of the Imperial Observatory, with crane-flown acrobats as the circling, leaping planets around the gold-foil sun, but both sun and planets revolving together (the crowd cheered to see them fly) around the same green earth; and then there was Copernicus's great cart, drawn by thirty oxen, with the sun aboard, titanic lamp shining through a sun of glass, all the planets including little earth outflung. A face able to be seen glowing in the glass sun was said to be God Almighty, but some said it looked more like Galileo.

And next came Kepler's variant of this, a merry cart, the planetary orbits around the central sun expressed by the five geometric solids, and each of them producing an appropriate liquor, old beer for Saturn, white wine for Venus, golden Tokay for Jupiter—maybe it was these, dispensed too freely, but the pageant by degrees became disordered, pageant carts colliding, oxen and dray horses shunting one another, drivers unable to brake, and finally the World Systems themselves tilting and the flags and explanatory seals and spheres and *mappamundi* falling together, just plaster and lathe and paper after all, becoming finally inextricably mixed up, with priests, scholars, artisans, and partisans coming to blows, Copernicus's sun put out, the actors dressed as the planets tearing the finery from one another's persons to show the bare human within. So a good time was had by all, though some who witnessed it took it as an unsettling omen: the picture worlds colliding, and if they, why not the worlds they pictured?

Nevertheless the reign of King Frederick and Queen Elizabeth went on evolving. Hand in hand they walked through Rudolf's castle, nourished on Rudolf's jewels and stones, pulling out Rudolf's albums and turning over the gorgeous leaves; Frederick tried to brush away a gilded fly from one page, and found it was painted there! They laughed and laughed. And now what is this room? The ancient antiquary (he had served Rudolf, he was preserved like a *mummia* of Ægypt by handling precious things forever and ever) opened the tall narrow figured doors and let them into the tetradic chamber in the center of the castle, which was itself in the center of the world (as every true castle is). On the walls the Arcimboldo portraits, Summer Fall Winter Spring; Fire Water Earth Air; North South East West. They took hands.

In the center of the chamber, center of the floor's geometries, there was a humpbacked black ironbound trunk waiting to be opened.

Soon enough a Catholic mercenary army was on its way to Bohemia to suppress the rebellion of the Bohemian Estates and eject the so-called king they claimed to have anointed. The combined forces—Silesian, Austrian, Bavarian, Italian, Savoyard, Spanish, Flemish, French—advanced on Prague. As armies will, they left the country through which they passed a Brueghel hell: naked refugees, corpses of gutted cattle, dead children, the light of burning farmhouses. During the same weeks the Protestant forces of Europe gathered in

Prague, and their generals pledged their arms to the queen.

And there were other forces on the way to battle, unseen but perhaps felt by the Catholic combatants as they went—forces shadowing them, or leading them. Cherubim, seraphim, *nerozumim*. Earthlier forces too, passing through the Böhmerwald by night, through the high forest without misstep: long low four-footed shapes, red and brown, gray and black, eyes alight and long tongues panting. They were themselves—in their waking lives—Catholic, Utraquist, Protestant, Calvinist, Orthodox, but at night they all knew whose side they were on: the side that did not hate them, and would if they helped to win the victory accept their duty, forgive their crimes, and honor them as fighters for the world to come.

On the day of the battle little redheaded Christian of Anhalt commanded the king's forces on the summit of a white hill outside the city, flying the huge royal banner of green and yellow velvet, bearing the words *Diverti nescio*, I know no different way. No one could read the words, though, for a great dead calm prevailed, as still and clear as glass, here and elsewhere; in the light of dawn the opposing army seemed suddenly shockingly close to them, as though they saw themselves in an unexpected mirror at the turning of a corridor. A terrible clarity: those in the Protestant van could actually see (they never forgot it, those who survived) the teeth and tongues of the Catholic captains as they shouted the word of command.

The battle for the end of the world was long. From the heights of the castle, the ladies and the children gathered with their queen to watch its progress: for the two armies could be seen easily from this distance, toy armies suspended upside down in the middle of the air at the *foci* of Emperor Rudolf's great parabolic mirrors. The queen and the women wept for the hurt and the slain, cried out the names of their particular champions when they could be picked out from the heaving, thrashing throng. Other combatants seemed to wrestle in the disordered sky around them. And what or who was that now shambling out from the Bohemian rearguard, hugely tall? The ladies gathered at the mirror to see. Look what damage he does! A man? A beast? Ours? Whose?

It's the man made of earth the Great Rabbi has brought to life and released. The Maharal after long thought overcame his persistent doubts, and though he was certain that he could never be forgiven and would now go down in guilt into Sheol, he has asked himself: is it good for the Jews?

And it is. The city must not fall; if help is given to King Frederick, the secret promises of old Emperor Rudolf will be kept. If not, not; there will be no mercy for the Jews, no justice either.

Look, now it's lost a huge arm, struck and blown to dirt by a cannonball, but seems to be undeterred. Eyeless and noseless it sees and smells and does harm, treading heedlessly on corpses and wounded men; the Catholic forces fall back before it. Darkness comes at last, and then that other troop, those long-tailed ones that have dogged the Catholics through Bohemia, comes upon the field: and in the face of such a horror—a wolvish army—the Catholic army breaks. The battle is over. The dead lie scattered, but though night's ravens are already picking up the good scent of slaughter, these wolves will not feast: like lions, the noble bristle-backs will not touch a dead man. By dawn they are gone away, and the wagons come for the bodies, ours and theirs, dead and near-dead.

On that day, while the city rejoiced, in the Giant Mountains far from the battlefield there was carried with simple ceremony a great casket. Its attendants in black, the black wagon hung with faded roses and strewn with papery dry petals. A very large casket, because it contains a great corpse: Philip à Gabella, who despite his human form reached no farther than an ass's age, and who as death approached reverted, feature by feature, to the simple beast he had been. Speechless too finally as the brothers gathered in his byre to weep, and unable to give to them the last blessing they asked of him.

The cave is deep and cold where they inter him, in a cell no larger than the cell of his convent in Naples, his prison in Rome, but glittering with ten thousand carbuncles that have grown up in the still *matrix* of the earth and encrust the wrinkled walls: Andreas Boethius de Boodt, gem hunter to great Rudolf, discovered this place long years before, and told no one, knowing perhaps that one day a guest would arrive fit to lie in it.

No tears any longer. The brothers know that there is no death, that neither their friend Philip nor the little ass that embodied him nor great Bruno whose spirit found refuge in his body are passed away; the infinitesimals that composed them, in their transmigration across the infinite universe, will form other beings just as strange and plain and wonderful. He had only hoped—he even expected—that the atoms that composed his own soul might, in far centuries, be drawn again to one another, might seek for one another through the infinite spaces, and at length agglomerate somewhere, elsewhere, into another soul again, his own: and in their coming together know themselves as they had been. Somewhere, elsewhere, on this world or another, or this world when it would *be* another. Because you can't be born in the same world twice.

Te Deum and *Non Nobis* were sung that night in the Cathedral of St. Wenceslaus, the king and queen not in red and white any longer but in gold and silver, sun and moon, Apollo and Cynthia, resetting the clocks of creation to the first hour. A flight of *putti* filled the sanctuary during the service, their voices were heard, everyone saw: it seemed clear to all that this was a sign of God's blessing and congratulation upon them. (Really, though, the angels were only younglings, careless, passing through on their way elsewhere.)

Then to the golden city was summoned the brotherhood of the Monas, those who were not already resident there: men, women, and others, Jews, Italians, Dutchmen, priests, knights, gardeners, beggars, thieves. Those who knew how to handle angels, knew their tricksome and contrary natures; who knew the *Artes magnæ lucis et umbræ*, the great arts of light and shadow, which are greater even than the goldmakers' arts, though the goldmakers would be summoned too, and the shape-shifters and nightwalkers, and the daylight healers and the doctors of all sciences: all those who had sought for the Brothers of the Rose-Cross, or pretended to be among their number, or believed themselves to be, or knew they ought to be. They were summoned by a worldwide steganography that had long lain waiting to be sent out, an invisible inaudible Messenger, who came forth at just the right astral hour, and on great peacock-eyed wings, robed in blue and stars, bearing her packet of invitations, moved over the earth and the waters even as that Hour itself moved: and he, or is it she, is trumpeter and trumpet call in one, whisper-crying into each ear just the word that causes this heart to turn in the right direction: to go and pack with needful things a ragged bag, or an ironbound trunk, or a train of pack mules, and set out.

And there, in the tetradic chamber in the center of the castle in the center of the Golden City called Adocentyn, wouldn't they at last come together at the obvious hour of the obvious day? Wouldn't they at last put off their old garments, the garments they had worn so that they might go unremarked among all peoples in all places, the furred judge's robe, the armor and gauntlets, the motley, the threadbare scholar's gown, whore's finery, Gypsy bangles, cope and miter? *Brother,* they would say to one another; *brother,* and embrace, because at last they could. *You,* they would say, and laugh, or rejoice; I never thought to see *you* here. And others too, whom they could not see but could sense and delight in, beings come gently or wildly or somberly among them, agents and representatives of other realms, deep or high or far, come with blessing, warnings, gifts, challenges.

Then at last would be the Great Instauration, not all at once or without costs or sorrows, but at last everywhere: a backward revolution, a backflip of wonder performed to turn the progress of the world around like a galleon and head it again for the Age of Gold, which lies in the past, in the beginning, but which could now be sought for in the time to come, as Hermes Thrice-great in Ægypt so long ago predicted: *the restoration of all good things in the course of time by the will of God.* Or *by means of the gods,* as the Giordanisti would always say it; meaning by *gods* nothing other than the reasons of the world, the grammar of divine fecundity endless and ordered. The reasons that make all things to be as they are and yet make them always capable of transformation, the reasons that work and will go on working forever, just because they can: we call them gods because they are within us, because they made our bodies and our minds for us too, because we recognize their faces from long ago, because we love and need and fear them, every one.

And that is how the world came to be in which we would come to be. This world, our great wide wonderful beautiful world, and our benignant sun, Sol Apollo, since then grown even larger and more kind; and the great good beings who, like our Terra, circle him in love, those animals whom in time our æronauts will set out to visit, on winged ships that will be drawn up into the air and beyond the moon's sphere by Will and his cousin Eros. Our seas teeming with metamorphosis, the great gems growing in our caves, watched over by solitary dæmons; our walled and towered cities guarded too by their own *genii,* our famous colleges and abbeys where no sort of wisdom is forbidden and no error punished except by laughter. Our many well-loved monarchs, kings, and emperors holding their inoffensive dream empires together simply by sitting still at their centers like queen bees, to be fed on royal jelly by wise magi, who then can draw from those princes' fattened hearts the alphabet of all good things, Peace, Plenty, Justice, Delight, Wisdom, and Comfort. Mere signs, yes: but signs are food and nurture for us, they are in fact all the food and nurture that we need: all of us in here.

6

What happened next was that, twenty years earlier, Giordano Bruno chose not to escape from the papal prison in Rome and go wandering forgetful on four legs into the world.

—No, he said to his gray visitor, who seemed to have grown older as the years of their dialogue went on, older and yet no wiser. No.

Then you must sign the papers, revocations, confessions, admissions that they wish you to sign. Or they will burn you.

—No. I never will. Were I to do that, then their small world would go on existing for centuries more, for no philosopher would dare to speak out and tell them otherwise, and in his telling make it so. If I show they have power only over this aggregate of atoms, which they may render or discompose as they like or must, then another man may take heart. Finally they will cease. In time men will laugh at their strictures rules bulls anathemata.

It seems a slight chance, to go and be burned for.

Bruno didn't need to look upon his visitor to know that he meant this as a challenge, or a tease, or even an awed compliment. The gods are astonished by men, who can choose to do or say or seek what will bring them to destruction; and not even the gods who destroy them can always say they are mistaken to do it: though as often as not they are.

That long epic in verse that once upon a time Giordano Bruno wrote—*The Triumphant Beast Thrown Out,* the one that puzzled the inquisitors—told of a conference of all the gods in which, having themselves grown old and unlovely, they vow to reshape the heavens, and make all things new: a job they cannot, in the end, agree on how to accomplish. And—fortunately for us—they give it up.

Those men who wish to bring about the same universal reformation—the alteration of the whole wide world, with the end of making all men happy forever—should likewise give it up. It's not that it can't be done: perhaps no man, or men, or men and others, will ever be powerful enough to do it, but Bruno was sure there was no limit to the power that was available to the soul willing and able to forgo everything else to gain it—self, and ease, and peace, and complimentary love, and natural procreation. But it was not wisdom to try; ruin was far more likely than glory; give the great ball a kick and you can't know where it will rebound, or how far it will roll.

That's what he had learned from the thousand journeys he had made in thought, all the beings he had seen and been, in all the years he had sat in his cell on his bed of stone. Not escape or salvation: or rather, no other one but this one. The turnkey (and after he was gone his son) had looked in now and then through the small barred window to see him there, his eyes sometimes a little crossed and his mouth sometimes working as though he spoke, then listened, then spoke again; his hands moving in air, meaninglessly—the turnkey didn't perceive the pages of the books he turned—and sometimes shifting his cold hams on the stone; meanwhile Bruno had been sifting the days of his past, and walking the roads of this future and that one, to see where they would lead; in one, looking into the house of that Englishman, the empty house, and the man himself old and empty too it seemed, selling to a vile tradesman a gray glass wherein a spirit was surely contained, although he said there was none. Oh she was there, she was: she saw Bruno looking in to see her there, and he knew that she knew him, and would live forever. But the old man—a greater and better man than he had ever been, as his wisdom was greater than Bruno's knowledge—had surrendered his own magic, given it up, and by his own renunciation bade magic depart from the world. Because the time was past in which even the strongest spirit could be sure he would draw only goodness out of the future for man's aid.

So he would do that too. He would burn his books—or *they* would burn them, the books of which he was composed, the Book of Everything and Other Things that he contained, that he *was*. Giving up magic as that old Englishman did or one day would do. Silence and prayer at the end.

And perhaps he was wrong after all: perhaps no spirit was so strong as to refashion the earth, or even to choose to try. Maybe—it seemed to come to be so even as he thought it—maybe earth and time and the endless things were not to be ruled, for like cannot rule like. Was that another and opposite meaning of the tale of Actæon? *Actæon*: Why did the story seem to make a different sense to him now than it had made before?

If you won't bind the things of this world on men's behalf—as you have learned to do, and even to bind us gods on occasion—will you not stay to teach them to unbind themselves?

—To teach unbinding is only to bind further. Every man's bonds are his own: only that one who learns his unbinding from his own soul and the love of his neighbors and equals is truly unbound.

The reverend cardinals wish to teach the world that a free man can be destroyed as easily as a coward or a fool.

—That's not the lesson that the world will learn.

You must know that you renounce me in renouncing all that you have been and all that you have fashioned from the soul the gods gave you. I cannot aid you at the last.

—That soul was not mine to keep. It will go its own way. *Animula vagula blandula.* Let them catch it if they can.

Son.

The man Bruno crossed his arms before him, arms in his threadbare sleeves.

—Tell me only this, he said.

One last thing.

—Will it be you I see at the gates of Avernus? Conductor of souls, will it be you who guides me down?

But there was no answer, for there was no longer one who could answer. There was also no Avernus to go down to, there was no down, no up. With no further word, that *genius* or friend or master slapped his knees, rose, and departed: he would never in that age speak again to anyone, though many would think they heard him, and the images of him (finger to his lips and winged feet) would in those years vastly multiply. He went out, and up the dark passage into the sun. Then he took the few steps up to the doors of the papal apartment, to the Sala Paolina and its high frescoes—of the Archangel Michael sheathing his sword, the war in Heaven done; of the victories of Alexander the Great; the life of Saint Paul. *If I give up my body to be burned, and I have not love, it profiteth me nothing.* Having reached that room without being hindered, he opened a small door at the side, and put his foot upon a stair. Then he stopped—stood stock-still, as though he had thought of something, and if he could remember what it was, might turn and go back—but that wasn't it. It was that, with Bruno's refusal (whether *because* of it or merely *on the occasion* of it could not be known, and only Bruno himself could have thought adequately about the question), the gods, angels, monsters, powers, and principalities of that age began their retreat into the subsidiary realms where they reside today, harmless and unmoving, most of them anyway, for most of us most of the time. The bright god came to a stop there on his upward way, because the upward way just then ceased to be, and then the door that led to it ceased to be a door, and then he ceased to be himself, his head remaining half turned in wonder at what was coming over him. *What wind is that?* And there he is today, stopped in midstep, all in black, as flat and still as paint, unrecognizable even to those who most need to know him. Pierce Moffett, for instance, passing the same way nearly four centuries later, at a dark day's end climbing out from that prison too and reaching the same high still empty chamber, alone himself and grieving without reason: he turned his own head in that direction, where—according to his, that is Kraft's, guidebook—the chamber's decorator had painted a *trompe-l'oeil* door and staircase, apparently just to match a real one at the hall's far end. And on that imaginary stair was painted an imaginary young man in black, just going up, just turning to look back. *Legend claims this to be a portrait of Beatrice Cenci's advocate,* said that cunning heartless guidebook, *but if it is he, then he must have wandered backward fifty years from Beatrice's time to when these walls were painted; actually no one knows who he is, if indeed he is anyone at all.* And in the book's margin, beside the place, one of Kraft's little gray stars, nearly vanished.

So it was really Bruno, and not an eidolon or ghost or substitute or figment or illusion or spirit cognate made of thought, who burned to great acclaim and cries of loathing in the Campo dei Fiori in the Jubilee Year 1600. It was him, his flesh, his life, the books his mind was made of. The crowds were able to see the skin blister and blacken, the hair and beard combust, finally the body collapse into a shapeless mass like a burning building falling. Some said (later) that they saw his spirit rise up from the pyre and be snatched away by devils or angels, but people often say they see those things, and once having said them they begin to believe they really happened, and they never forget them.

Thereafter the rolling ball went that way and not the other way, to arrive again in the course of things at the year 1619, when a young man named René Descartes, a lawyer's son of no particular profession, went traveling in Germany, just as the Bohemians were making their stand against the Empire. He visited Heidelberg in its days of beauty, and later would remember the famed statues he saw there, moving solely from the force of water piped within them. Acis and Galatea. Echo and Narcissus. Apollo and the Muses.

Midas and the Singing Reeds. Was it perhaps in some similar way, René wondered, that the fleshly statues of our bodies also worked? When winter came he put up in a house in Neuburg, on the border of Bavaria. For weeks he stayed all alone in a room heated by a large ceramic stove—very warm—and thought. He was thinking of how a foundation for all knowledge might be discovered that had the certainty of the self-evident truths of mathematics, a philosophy free from the ambiguities and ambivalences of words. He had heard about the Rosicrucians, and of their promise of new and fruitful philosophies, and had thought of seeking them out; he even wrote out (but maybe it was just a joke) the elaborate title page of a book that would be dedicated to the Frères de la Rose-Croix, so famous in Germany.

We know how in that warm room, on the eve of St. Martin's Day, young René had a number of dreams, three in fact, which seemed to him of the utmost significance. He dreamed of a great deforming wind, and a school and a chapel that the wind propelled him toward; he dreamed of the gift of a sweet melon from another country; of an encyclopædia of all sciences, which became a book of poems. He tried to read the poems, but (as they do in dreams) they kept changing, the one he wanted to find gone. One by Ausonius began with what he recognized as Pythagoras's choice: *which way in life will I go?*

It's true, it's recorded. When he awoke from this dream he felt the world distorted, full of strange sparks or fires he could see in his room. When he slept and woke again, though, he felt certain that God had revealed truths to him that would take a lifetime to explicate, but would end at last in certainty. He thought the dreams had been sent to make him conscious of his sins, as well—sins no one knew about but he. And he thought of the Virgin, and vowed that, if he could, he would make a pilgrimage to her shrine at Loreto. Perhaps he was on his way there when he decided instead to join the Catholic forces marching to Prague for the battle against the Winter King and the Queen of Snow.

The battle for the end of the world was brief. At dawn René and the Imperial forces sang the *Salve Regina* and the attack began. The word of the day was "Sancta Maria." (For a long time—and the war beginning now would last thirty years—this would be a war between God and Mary.) And just as the mists lifted, revealing dimly each side to the other—heaving fields of creatures, like herds of haystacks or shaggy cattle on the move—a light wind sprang up.

A light wind, able to stir the yellow fog but not at first to disperse it. A wind young and inexperienced, learning its uses and its work, but so far aimless; a wind that had been borne along with the world's great slow-marching airs and atmospheres from west to east, from Albion to the Middle Sea and over the Bavarian mountains, wondering, wandering. As it blew more steadily over the White Mountain, the day grew clearer. Not the light of day: what the day *was* grew clearer, though not at once to everyone, and to some not at all.

A little wind. *The first wind bears in the time,* an angel said to John Dee, *and the second bears it away again.*

The Protestant soldiers on the heights felt it first, lifted their heads and noses to it, to see from which quarter it blew. The various unearthly powers standing behind them felt it too, and turned from the battle to the rearguard, to see who or what was coming through from behind. No zephyr they knew. They were astonished then to be picked up and swept away by it, one by one, as by a broom, right out of the to-be and back into the once-was forever. All in a moment those powers were gone, were nothing—for they had all along really been nothing, less than nothing, mere *signs,* mere *phantasmata,* and no help now to the human soldiers, left with only their human commanders, standing on an insignificant little hill outside a contested city in the middle of Europe at the start of another battle in another war. Their warm mammalian breath condensed on the damp cold air. They thought how short life is, and of how little worth is the promise of Heaven. On the other side the same, as in a mirror. Then the first wave of Catholic pikemen, crying out as though for their mothers, advanced against the Protestant left.

The Bohemians and their allies, though in the stronger position, broke quickly, evaporating, in effect, as though it had all been a show, and was now over. Anhalt, screaming hoarse with rage and panic, tried to hold the mob at sword's point, but couldn't. The soldiers and people inside the city locked the gates against them, left them to face the advancing enemy, and in the castle through that day and evening the king and his ministers disputed what to do next. There were reproaches; there were tears. The Bohemian leadership begged, demanded, shouted that the city had to be surrendered or it would be attacked and breached and put to the sword; the king berated them for cowardice—and was shocked to be berated in turn. He went on his knees to pray for guidance, but no one would kneel with him; he left the chamber, he fell into his wife's arms, she (terrified by how frightened he was, the deepest emotion she had ever seen pictured on his face, deeper than love, deeper than faith) could see that they had nothing left, nothing but flight. Anhalt in tears too said the same.

With only what they could push into a couple of coaches—someone thought to gather up the crown jewels, which would support them in exile for years—the Winter King and his Queen left Hradcany palace, nearly forgetting their baby son and heir—a nursemaid ran up at the last moment and thrust the little bundle into the queen's arms. Their people, servants, and followers, who knew what fate now awaited *them,* ran after the departing coaches, trying to climb aboard or hang on to the running boards, dropping away as the cavalcade careened downhill.

That little wind went away from the ghastly battlefield, growing just a little less little as it went, though few still could feel it. Nothing hindered it, perhaps because of its small size—it was no more than a breeze, really, a breath, the puff of air that comes in at the thick small windows of desert dwellings to touch a cheek and say that the simoom might be coming, or might not; hardly wind enough to cover with sands the tombs and temples that its mother had before uncovered. Yet it blew "far and wide"; there wouldn't be anywhere it didn't enter in, rattling the windows of the present and scattering the dealt cards of the past, pushing closed the doors of opened books and scrambling the sense of their indexes and *prolegomena.* Finally its baby breath, propelled by those fat cheeks, separated the *a* from the *e* in every word where they were joined, or suppressed one and left only the other, like conjoined twins that can't survive together, encyclopedias of aerial etheric demons in Egypt. Nobody noticed. And then with a little laugh it blew itself out, bowling up its own nonexistent fundament and drawing all of itself in after.

The imperial army entered Prague the next day without opposition. The soldiers were released on the city, as the phrase is, with the common results. One of those who entered was René Descartes, who wandered in the old town and up to the Carolinum; he had the idea that he would like to view the famous collection of Tycho Brahe's astronomical instruments that Johannes Kepler had left behind when he too left Prague precipitously. The young man had—would always have—an uncanny ability to pass single-mindedly through scenes that did not pertain to his own business, seeing in effect nothing. The instruments, unfortunately, had already been removed and dispersed, and René walked back again through the town, where snow was now beginning to fall, snow stained red in the squares and alleys. He was thinking again—of a way to reduce all kinds of physical problems to mathematical equations of the third and fourth degree, perhaps—and in his notebook that night he wrote: *On November 11, 1620, I began to conceive the foundation of an admirable discovery.*

In the coming weeks those of the Bohemian leadership who didn't escape abroad were methodically tried and executed by an imperial commission. One cheated them by committing suicide (another tower window, another leap) but his head and right hand were exhibited, nailed to the gallows. Eventually twenty-seven knights, counts, ministers and patriarchs, judges, scholars, and burghers were executed; lesser men were whipped, branded, or lost goods. That Hussite preacher who once led a parade of fellows dressed as sturdy Hussite peasants to welcome Elizabeth to Prague (what a noise they had made with their flails, those false harvestmen, flailing, flailing—what an ungodly noise!) and who had given tongue so long and loud to praise her—he had that tongue nailed to the gallows. Nothing was to be forgiven, or forgotten either.

Through the deepening snows Frederick and Elizabeth struggled toward home. Everyone says they were remarkably brave, clear eyed but calm, all happiness gone, everything lost, spoiled, and themselves to blame: especially Elizabeth. *Her mind,* said the English ambassador, *could not be brought under fortune.*

Home slipped out of reach. The Spanish general Spinola, the Spider, left Flanders with his army and moved toward the Rhine and the Palatinate. Soon Mainz had fallen to him (in stories of war, cities fall at the advance of generals, but it's not so; metonymy and synecdoche don't do the fighting and dying, the soldiers and the townspeople do, one at a time, and not in a sentence but for hours and days). Celadon, now with the Protestant forces trying to regroup, wrote to Elizabeth: *Voilà, my poor Heidelberg is taken. They have used all sorts of cruelties, pillaged the whole town, burnt all the suburbs, which were the chief beauty of the place.* The invaders seized the vast *Bibliotheca palatina,* which was sent off to Rome; the great librarian Gruter saw all his own lifetime's collection of books and papers thrown into the street and yard where horses were stabled, to be irremediably fouled. It always happens, a calculated insult, endlessly repeated: Protestant soldiery stable their horses in the chapels of saints, Catholics in the courtyards of schools or libraries. What was in poor Gruter's papers? *A whole world vanished here,* says Dame Yates. What story was lost in that street? None? This one?

There exist a number of broadsides mocking the runaway Winter King, political cartoons as dense with symbols as alchemical texts, let him who does not understand be silent, or learn. In many of them the king is shown with one stocking falling down—he has lost his garter, or Garter, which means his English father-in-law's support. And in one he stands uneasily, fearfully, upon a Y; the Y stands on a Z; the Z, on a wooden ball. Saturn with glass and wings and scythe looks on, old Kronos or Chronos, and he declares:

The wooden ball's this world of mine
Whereon the Bohemians wedded the Palatine.
They thought they'd teach the states anew,
Reform the schools, church, law courts too,
Return us to that blessed state
Before the apple Adam ate,
Or even Saturn's days of old
Which all men call my Age of Gold.
For this, those Rosicrucians yearn
The mountains into gold to turn.

So Y leads nowhere but to Z, the last letter, the end, the fall.

In Bohemia and Moravia the Czech Brethren were harshly suppressed; their chapels and houses despoiled, their ministers and bishops hunted down, driven away, hanged if they resisted. Their last bishop was Jan Andreas Comenius, who was driven from his home and his congregation with only what he could carry—papers, of course, mostly. He wrote then in despair or hope: *When the wrath of the nations has passed, the rule of thy country will return to thee, O Czech people.* It was not a time he himself would live to see; he would never see Moravia again. His wife and two of her children died of hardships on the way to shelter with a sympathetic lord in Brandeis; there he wrote *The Labyrinth of the World and the Paradise of the Heart.*

In that story—it would become a classic of Czech literature, until it became unreadable again—a pilgrim wanders in the dark maze of a city, which is divided into many quarters and streets, a multiplex of arches squares palaces and churches whereon he sees all arts and sciences laid out as in a Memory City. His foolish or obtuse companions insist on the wonder and worth of all that they see, though the pilgrim can only question. And a trumpet on high gathers all the seekers together, to the central square, where a robed brother offers Rosicrucian secrets for sale, in boxes with names like *Portae sapientae, Gymnasium universitatis, Bonum Micro-macro-cosmicon, Pyramis triumphalis.* They mustn't be opened, the hawker says, they will work by auto-penetration of the box, but some buyers do open them, to see the wondrous thing inside, and of course the boxes are empty, all empty, every one. Finally, despairing, the pilgrim hears a voice call to him: *Return whence you came, into the house of your heart, and close the doors.*

In Tübingen, Johann Valentin Andreae (Comenius's friend in a former age) opened his own old, old allegory, *The Chemical Wedding: by Christian Rosencreutz,* which he wanted no one any longer to read. But there was no way to call back every one of the little winged things and send them into the flames. Andreae (one of those authors who can't resist reading their own prose, their old prose, when they come upon it) read the title page and the last page and the scene he loved the best, the one where Christian is induced by the wicked or reckless page to waken Venus before her time. He read from there to the end, when the brothers board their ships, the sign of Cancer painted upon the crimson sails, to go out into the world and make it new.

Did he think that his book had helped to bring about the ruin all around? Was he sorry? He was also one of those authors who believe their works do bring about things, and indeed he was sorry, he was. And yet surely, surely they should have known, he thought, those who had read it; they should have seen Andreae's smile, seen through him and his book. Look: just below the title and the false date he'd put on it (1459!) there was the motto *Arcana publicata vilescunt, et gratiam prophanata amissunt. Ergo: ne Margaritas objice porcis, seu Asino substernere rosas.* Secrets told to all are spoiled, things made common have no power; therefore do not throw pearls before swine, nor proffer roses to an ass.

It's true: it said that, and it says that still.

~

After his very interesting journeys René Descartes returned to Paris. Just at that time placards were appearing everywhere in the city to announce the appearance there of the Brothers of the Rose-Cross. *We are making a visible and invisible stay in this city through the grace of the Most High. We show and teach, without books or marks, how to speak all languages and how to draw men away from error and death.* Or perhaps there weren't any placards, maybe people only heard rumors that there were placards, or had been placards, and what they said or warned. *From invisible we will become visible, and from visible, invisible.* Were they witches, were they promising powers only granted to the Devil's followers—invisibility, flight, purses never emptied, eloquence to draw all men to them so that they would forsake the church and the prophets? René's friend Marin Mersenne was among those who denounced all such appeals, empty or wicked or both. But it was well known that Descartes had in Germany gone looking for the Rosicrucian brothers and returning as he did just now, when those brothers were said to be circulating invisibly among the people—Father Mersenne feared for him. So René, rather than hide or return to his solitude, went around town, showed himself, visited his friends, took their hands. In this way he demonstrated that he was visible, and therefore not a Rosicrucian. QED. In any case no Rosicrucians appeared to change the course of things or work wonders; the panic passed. Descartes resumed his meditations: a method for deciding what we can know with absolute certainty; how to strip thought of words entirely; how pure mind can know mindless matter.

A long time afterward—Frederick was dead by then, of the plague, in some German town, following another army—René Descartes came to know Elizabeth of Bohemia (as she continued to be called) at her little court in exile in the Hague; he became attached to her daughter, yet another Elizabeth, and dedicated his *Principles of Philosophy* to her. When she went to take the waters at Spa, he wrote to her that to get any benefit from them she should free her mind from all sorts of sad thoughts and even from serious reflections because those who look long on the green of the forest, the colors of a flower, the flight of a bird, can beguile themselves into not thinking, or thinking of nothing. "Which is not wasting time but using it well."

Once, Descartes met Comenius, still dragging over Europe his store of manuscripts and plans for a Polity of Universal Wisdom. The two thinkers had little to say to each other. For Comenius, Descartes was himself the *laceratio scientiarum*, the wound suffered by Knowledge. For Descartes, Comenius was the past. His Universal Language (*Panglottia*), Universal Dawning (*Panaugia*), Universal Education (*Pampaedia*), Universal Reform (*Panorthosia*) were actually no bigger than the paper they were written on. What he praised the older man for was the little primer he had written, the *Orbis pictus sensualium* or picture book of the physical world. But everyone loved the *Orbis pictus*; it really *was* universal; for a century and more boys and girls would learn language from it, in classrooms from Russia to the Massachusetts Bay, following along with the book's pupil and his Master (who's sometimes pictured in the Frontispiece as a Pilgrim with hat and staff) as they went along the forking paths and climbed the mountains of the real world.

Come, boy! Learn to be wise.
What doth this mean, to be wise?
To understand rightly, to do rightly,
and to speak out rightly, all that is necessary.
But before all things, thou oughtest to learn the plain sounds,
of which man's speech consisteth;
which living creatures know how to make,
and thy tongue knoweth how to imitate,
and thy hand can picture out.
Afterward we will go into the world,
and we will view all things.

Come, let us learn the words. Afterward we will go into the world, and view all things. Pierce Moffett alone in Baroque Rome walked the maze of streets, and went in and out of buildings built in the centuries of its triumph. The **Fountain of the Four Rivers** represents the Ganges, the Danube, the Plata, and the Nile, who hides her eternally hidden head. The **Obelisk** is a later addition. The right foot of the statue of the **Magdalene** has been polished smooth by the kisses of the devout. Pushing aside the heavy leather curtain, we enter the **Basilica.** Scarcely distinguishable in the shadows is **Giotto**'s mosaic of the *Navicella,* Peter's fishing boat. The **Santa Scala** is linked with the stairs to Pilate's palace that Jesus went up. The **papal chapel** at the top into which only the pope can enter. We can discern through the screen a (covered) painting of the Virgin made by no one, or by itself (**archeipoieton**).

Non est in toto sanctior orbe locus, no more sacred spot in all the world. Pierce wrote in his red journal:

> *Old women and children and nuns on their knees and aged men with whiskery jowls and canes trying to get up these steps one at a time, steep and narrow too, and I was at last overcome, why do we have to do this to ourselves, why do we spend our treasure and our time and our tears like this, why does it have to be so? A place into which you can't go, but only peer, led to by stairs you crawl up on your knees. Ah no, no. When the Labyrinth of the World* comes disguised as *the Paradise of the Heart, that's when it becomes terrible.*

His last morning in the city, Pierce woke late, the desk at the *pensione* had forgotten his wake-up call or he hadn't made himself clear; then it was a long way across the crowded and complex city to the Stazione Termini, and the cab, one of those that had always seemed so fleet, so crazily speedy in the circling streets, was held back as though in some thick substance or gum and unable to make lights, get across intersections, through indifferent and clotted crowds. When Pierce at last got out, thrusting into the hairy outstretched hand the remains of his tens of thousands of lire, he found that he wasn't exactly in front of the station, and began walking, circling the great building. Like half the city it was scaffolded, clothed in great blue billowing plastic sails; the way around it narrowed to muddy paths, duckboards, then debouched into open areas without fingerboards or any help.

Somehow he found his way within. Vast dark dome like the Pantheon's. Crowds eddying around the great central clock, gilded and eagle-topped. Gentle loudspeaker giving admonitions and advice, whose echoes canceled each other out. And the signs and notices in an unfamiliar font, something European and proprietary, he couldn't read it though he could guess at meanings. He guessed he could sit and wait. He turned, orientating. A man coming toward him stooped to pick up something from the floor, examined it, dropped it again, his lips moving slightly in private speech. It was his father.

"Axel."

"Pierce. Oh wonderful. Wonderful. This is what I hoped. Just what I hoped and prayed for."

"Axel."

"Wonderful wonderful and again wonderful," Axel said. Pierce supposed he was drunk. "Here. Here in the Eternal City. They say Rome fell. Rome never fell. That thug Mussolini tried to pretend he had resurrected it. But its spirit. Its *spirit*."

"Axel," Pierce could only say. Axel went on talking, seeming to be unaware of the scandalous impossibility of this, which was all that Pierce could think of. "How do you come to be here?"

"Well, it was the Chief," Axel said. "He's right around. He went to the pissoir, I believe. Oh, Pierce. Rome."

"What do you mean? The Chief? Is he here?"

"He brought me. A birthday present. Because you see we're doing so well. You know it was always my dream. Oh son."

"What do you mean, doing well?"

"Pierce, the most remarkable thing. The boys found something. You know, fishing around in their buildings there. Well, you know they bring me these things, pretty things, some of them quite valuable. Oh but this. This."

"Axel, are you okay?"

"It's all all right now. From now on."

"Axel."

"You see, you didn't have to go at all," Axel said. He was white and obviously ill, unshaven gray bristles on his cheeks. "Oh you did the right thing, setting out, and you've learned so much. Yes. But you don't have to go on farther. Because it's found. All along it was right there in Brooklyn."

"Axel, no."

"Right there all along. Down there at the very bottom." He put his hand in one blazer pocket, then the other, rooting around with a face that made Pierce's heart fill with terror.

"Axel!"

"See," Axel said. "See?" The thing in Axel's pocket began to come forth, it was large or small or bright or dark but it shouldn't be here or anywhere, and of any place not in his father's hand. Spirit forces filled the air; their horripilating hands were on him. Pierce cried aloud again as the thing was shown him, the thing at last, and then he woke in his bed in his *pensione* hearing his own ghastly moan.

No, he took no cab; after his first night in Rome when one had apparently pitied him he never snared another. He wouldn't learn till he came back to the Eternal City years later that taxis weren't really allowed to stop when hailed but only when called, that's what the phones at taxi ranks are for. In a stiff rain he trundled his bags aboard the Number 64 bus, which was hurrying away from St. Peter's to the far city gates, as he was himself.

The Stazione Termini, which was not at all the place he had dreamed of, unlike it in every respect but most unlike it in being real, its stubbed cigarettes and ads and the smell of coffee bars and engines. No odors in dreams.

He shuddered, ghost mice up his spine, remembering. Axel. *You didn't have to go.*

He had his Eurailpass, somewhat greasy and weary, less from being much used than from being so often sought for, make sure it's not lost. The morning *direttissimo* to Bologna, then Venice, Vienna, then north and west to Prague. The way Bruno might have gone if he'd really escaped; heading for Rudolf's city by way of Venice, where he had once had friends, the bookseller Ciotto had actually defended him as best he could before the Venetian Inquisition. He would have skirted imperial Vienna, though, maybe going instead by way of Budweis and Pilsen, seeking for Giordanisti among the Budweisers and Pilsners; and on to kindly Prague.

He studied the guidebook, measured with thumb and finger the thickness of pages through which he must make passage. In Venice he might be able to go into Ca' Mocenigo, the palazzo on the Grand Canal where Bruno first came after returning to Italy from his adventures in the north, summoned there to train a young man of the Mocenigo family in memory arts, and other arts too, a weird young man who thereupon turned him over to the Inquisition. But of course it would likely be *chiuso*. He knew the word for *closed* in four languages now.

He turned pages. Could it be that Prague's most popular brand of gas, with stations in many places, was Golem gas? Hadn't such enterprises perished with socialism? And could it be that on a hill above the high castle (how could there be a hill above the high castle?) there was a maze, as this guidebook said, and in the maze a suite of distorting mirrors, and a vast painted panorama of armies fighting for the bridge below during the Thirty Years' War? That's what it said.

A maze, armies, mirrors, a bridge.

The once-vast **imperial collections** in Prague are now largely dispersed, and those seeking the paintings of **Hofnaegl**, **Spranger**, **DeVries**, the

> famed collections of **medals**, **stones**, and **maps**, to say nothing of the **automata**, weird **mandrake roots** in the shape of persons, **portraits** done in fruit or meats or books or kitchenware, **nose saddles, carved cherrystones,** etc., etc. will have to go elsewhere. After the Battle of **White Mountain** the victorious Maximilian of Bavaria is said to have carried away fifteen hundred cartloads of plunder from Rudolf's city, and the Saxon armies continued the spoliation later in the war. The Swedes took whatever of worth remained, including several of those surreal portraits; Queen Christina received an itemized list of the appropriated valuables in 1648, just as the long war was at last ending. The Number 22 tram will take you to the **battlefield**, not a mountain at all but a low chalk hill amid pleasant suburbs (five crowns.)

It was Kraft's story that whatever it was that came to be in Prague city in the reign of Rudolf, whatever was concealed in Oswald Kroll's black trunk that the emperor and Prince Rozmberk both chased after, whatever drew the fated couple thither in 1618, it must have been later lost or carried off by captains and camp followers in the awful depredations of thirty years of war. Whether you were Protestant or Catholic you evenhandedly looted church and castle, took whatever of value you could carry, pyxes and chalices, reliquaries, jeweled caskets, vestments sewn with gold thread, until they grew too heavy or the plague or the fever weakened you and you dropped the stuff by the side of the road or were killed for it. And this thing too, perhaps, probably; it was just one more among the countless refugees, it was disguised as something else, it changed ignorant hands over and over, was bought and sold, suffered, died, and was buried. Gone. The best we could do now was learn its name.

But he had sent a telegram to Boney from there to tell him that he had found it himself, his own anyway, and was bringing it home.

He was lying, though. Pierce with a dream-sure certainty just then came to know it. It hadn't been taken away from there, and Kraft hadn't found it there either.

It was never lost. It had been overlooked in those days, missed by the unwise, untouched by the wise, its presence unsuspected by the victors, kept secret by the defeated. Hidden in plain sight, from then on. But it was there. Nowhere else it could be but there. Pierce was sure.

And there it would still be, now, there in the Golden City that it created around itself, Pierce's own Golden City as it was everyone's; the best city, toward which we all strive and which we never reach, because it is the city only of the past and of the future, where the labyrinth of the world is exactly coextensive with the paradise of the heart, and how then could it ever be traveled to? In this time, this week, from this terminus?

He had always known the secret of those stories in which heroes set out in search of precious hidden things; everybody knows it. The journey is itself what brings the jewel or the stone or the treasure or the prize into being; the act of seeking is the condition by which the thing sought comes to be. In fact the search isn't different from the thing sought. Which is why you go, why you must. He knew. Everybody knows.

Except that it wasn't so. Or rather it was so in other instances—in every other instance, maybe—but not in this one. It was just the opposite. The stone was there, it had been there all along, infinitely precious and sturdy, and he wanted it and needed it more than anything—oh yes, he did, that was clear now, as it should have been from the start. There it was, eternally, right there, and the only way to keep it in existence was not to seek it.

He laughed, and laughed again, and those passing by—Italians, Greeks, Hungarians, Austrians—turned as they passed to see if they could tell what he laughed at. After a while another express came in and was announced, its passengers summoned by far seraphic voices flitting beneath the glass and iron sky. Pierce sat still on the bench, trying now and then to lift himself up and move himself toward the gates, and failing—or perhaps succeeding in staying put. He laughed, wet to his shins with foreign rain. More trains came in during that afternoon, and set off to Milano, Napoli, Firenze, Praha, Budapest, Istanbul; still he sat, fat bag between his legs, and nothing could move him to get up and go.

7

When he was at work on his first novel—it was called *The Court of Silk and Blood,* about the fearsome Catherine de Médicis and the massacre of St. Bartholomew's Eve—Fellowes Kraft began to understand for the first time certain things that Dr. Pons had set out to teach him long before in the house on the hill. For the book he had written—not this book in particular or anything that was done or said within it, but the fact of it, its coming into existence—was just like the appalling universe that man described.

Except for brief moments of ontological doubt such as anyone could have, Kraft had always known that the physical world—this earth and its universe of stars, its gravity and mass and elements, its living and dying stuff—was the base layer of reality. What we *think* about it is mere evanescence and spindrift; what we *hope* dies with each day; we impose our inexistent notions and grids upon it, but earth and the flesh abide.

According to Dr. Pons, though, it was actually just the opposite. To him, physical matter had no real existence at all; it wasn't different from human, or divine, ignorance. It was an illusion, in fact a hoax. The slightest and smallest human emotion felt by the inward incarcerated soul is more real than any aspect of materiality. And more real in turn than all those emotions, all tears and laughter and love and hate, are the conceptions of the mind—Beauty, Truth, Order, Wisdom—which give to materiality whatever form and worth it has. Most real of all is the world beyond nature and even Mind: the realm Without, utterly out of reach, the realm of the Fullness and God.

What Kraft learned, in his first joyous labors of imagination, was that, different as Dr. Pons's inverted universe might be from what is in fact the case, it is necessarily very much like the world inside a work of fiction.

All the myriad material things that we, in our universe, touch and use and love and hate and depend on—our food, our flesh, our breath; cities and towns, roads and houses, dogs, stars, stones and roses—in a book these things have no true reality at all. They're just nouns. But emotions are quite real; there are tears of things, and they are really shed, and real laughter laughed. Of course. And in a book intellectual order is the most real of all, the governing, sustaining reality—the Logos, the tale issuing from its absent, its hidden Author.

They, those pretend people in their factitious world, they owe their embodiment, their circumstance of being caught in unreal souls and bodies, to an upheaval that happened before the beginning of space and time (*their* space and time): a dissatisfaction, a troubling of the Pleroma of a single soul's primal economy, a soul startled into awareness by a girlish or a boyish question: if things were different from the way they are, what would they be like?

More, even more: the most precious and only truly real thing within each of the conscious beings who had been made to inhabit Kraft's little world (well, not the hylic mob, the mere names, the spear carriers and extras) was their share of the original undivided consciousness from which they sprang—that is, his own. Into which, when their work is done, they are gathered again at last: when their false world is closed up as a book that is read.

He had laughed aloud in the midnight to think it, wherever he was then (a Paris garret, a rickety table, a kerosene stove), filled with a kind of hilarious pity for them in their pickle. Which was somehow more strait, and more pitiful, because so many of them had once lived in the world Kraft and his fellow humans lived in, out here. Catherine de Médici. Bruno. Nostradamus. Peter Ramus.

In subsequent years and subsequent books he had sometimes wondered if he might somehow send them a message, one of them or some of them; awaken them to their own condition, to this peculiar reversal of what we out here, most of us anyway, call reality most of the time. To speak into the ears of one soul at least the commandment, the suggestion, the hope of waking.

Like Dr. Pons leaning down to him, the tassel on his fez aswing and his hand by his mouth to call: *wake up*.

Of course most of the time authors are busily *not* noticing these things, and trying to keep readers from noticing them too, just as Ialdabaoth and his gods and demons are supposed to be busily at work to keep *us* from ever noticing their impositions and frauds. But if his, Kraft's, people could just for once get it. If they could awaken from that dream, the Red King's dream; awaken even from the dream of awakening: arise, and go into the limitless common day, into the spring and the rain and the beating of their hearts. Was that possible?

Yes; yes of course it was. But only in fiction.

Day had reached noon in the Faraways. Kraft thought he would have a whisky soon, not a great drink with ice but only a dram, enough to cover the bottom of a cut-glass tumbler and refract the light. Four Roses. He ought to look into the refrigerator too, get himself something to eat, but at that thought his stomach turned, it actually did, one of those old figures that if you live long enough, or too long, you find aren't figures at all.

He drank the whisky, though: more beautiful and encouraging in the glass than in his mouth or heart. Oh well.

The telephone rang.

"Old friend," Boney Rasmussen said, sounding almost as far away as he really was, in his big house a couple of miles and more from Kraft's. "I wondered if you were up for a game of chess tonight."

"Ah well."

"I'd be glad to come to your place." Kraft had nearly ceased to drive. His vanishing competence or what he believed to be its vanishing had begun striking fear into his heart at odd moments, causing him to brake suddenly on the road, nearly causing thereby the awful collisions he envisioned.

"*Mon empereur*," Kraft said. "I have a question."

"Anything."

"A question. Not a request."

"All right," Boney said. "Shoot."

"Suppose I were very suddenly to make an exit. I mean drop dead. I'm afraid I haven't prepared very well for this eventuality."

"No need to hasten things," Boney said after a funny pause. "Of course we must get all your ducks in a row."

"Ah yes. Ah yes. The very largest duck of course comes first, and that we have really firmly in place."

"You mean the books, the copyrights."

"Yes. They'll be yours. I mean the foundation's. And this house."

"Maybe I should come over," Boney said. "It's actually a beautiful evening."

"There are masses of things. I have kept diaries. I have covered paper with writing, more with typing. I wouldn't want just any-old-body going through it. Though boredom would no doubt keep person or persons from going far."

Boney was silent for a long moment. The thoughts of age are long, long thoughts.

"You could," he said at last, "destroy it yourself. Whatever of it you thought was too—too . . ."

"Somehow I can't do that," Kraft said. "It would be a little like putting an end to my own messy and overstuffed consciousness. I have profound horror of suicide."

More silence.

"Of course they're valueless. They're just *mine*. I'm like a bum on a park bench, his clothes stuffed with newspapers to keep him warm."

"Is any of it," Boney asked, "recent?"

"Oh, some." He raised his eyes to the ceiling, just as though Boney could see him do so. "Some. And there are things, too."

"Things, yes."

"A loathsome rummage sale. What to do. Is it a comfort to think we will carry our secrets to the grave, simply because others can't find them in the litter?"

"Old friend," Boney said. "Your house is not as large as mine. Or as full of this and that. I have a few years' collecting on you."

"Let me ask this. If I were to make over this house and its contents to you, to the foundation, of course I mean. Then would it be all right if I just left everything here as it is? I'd trust you to find all that was worth finding, and discard the rest."

"I don't know that you need to make this determination now," Boney said. "Though of course."

"Yes."

"If you needed to feel it was all."

"Yes."

"In case."

"Yes." He let all that was unsaid flow back and forth over the wire, a ghost conversation he (and Boney too no doubt) could almost hear. Then he said: "I will take a rain check on the game, dear friend. I have a date with a hot-water bottle. I feel better already, though."

"I'm very glad."

"Will you call again tomorrow?"

"I will. Don't worry about any of it."

After a time Kraft arose—it had begun to seem a small surprise each time nowadays, that he had another getting up still in him. He gathered together the letters he had been reading, and inserted them again into the envelopes from which they had come. Then the pile of yellow typing paper, its top sheet already growing pale from the sun through his study window. No one knew of its existence yet but he.

Dr. Pons had once, among his other tales, told him the story of the Shekhinah.

The rabbis say that the Shekhinah is the earthly dwelling place of the Glory of God. It is a fragment or sliver of godhood, left over from that primal disaster when God somehow contracted or removed himself from a space in his own heart, a hollow, which eventually became the universe. Though terminally cold and dark (before God's separated and self-conscious Aeons or Sephiroth began to work within it) it contained, as it had to, having once been God, something of divinity. That something is the Shekhinah, which the alchemists call the Stone that transforms matter to spirit. And it's still here. It could be, Dr. Pons thought, very small; small and big mean nothing when we talk about divinity. It could maybe be held in the hand. And it might be anywhere, not enthroned most likely, not honored; for it is the *lapis exulis,* the gem of lost home, and gutters and ash heaps are as likely a place for it as any. When he was a boy walking those streets Kraft used to keep an eye out for it, going up the town and back again; looking for its telltale gleam in vacant lots, kicking cans that might conceal it. Once he kicked a can that contained a nest of yellow jackets, and was badly stung.

It was very wrong of him to have teased Boney Rasmussen as he had, and sent him enigmatic telegrams from Abroad. He had never found anything on his travels that could extend Boney's protracted life, or warm his heart. But he had, one night in Czechoslovakia in the spring of 1968, found the stone of transformation, its powers intact, not superannuated or even asleep, not a story or a fable, lying in plain sight in the vacant lot of the present.

March 1968. Somewhere the journal for that year still lay, stuffed with the postcards he liked to collect on his travels, not new garishly colored ones but old-fashioned sepia-toned ones, which had always made him feel superannuated himself: as though he could not only see the colored present before him full of busy young people and shiny cars and advertising, but remember this old brown past too, the cars few and black, the trees ungrown or uncut. Like the one he got from a stand outside Franz Josef Bahnhof in Vienna, a picture of the very station he stood before, taken at the end of the empire, the horse cabs and taxis outside, the wide street clean and cobbled. From there the Vindobona Express departed at the difficult hour of eight in the morning, reaching the Czech border at Gmund two hours later.

It was a fast new train, the coaches smelly and low, where they had been smelly and high roofed before, thirty years and a year before, when he had last looked out at these scenes. He had entered a land in dissolution then, and everyone knew it: the Nazi gangs flush with German pay and German successes were starting fights in the streets, beating Jews, assassinating ministers; they had colored with their menace his book about Prague, the Emperor Rudolf, werewolves and golems. Everyone wondered if the nation could survive. So much worse was waiting for them too, so much worse than he could have thought of, than anyone could.

Most of the trains they passed were still steam driven, even in 1968, puffing their pipes as they went by on the parallel track. A former world still present. In fertile south Bohemia, all black mud and greening trees, sun-glitter danced over the broad pools built long ago by monks to breed carp to eat on Fridays, fish long-lived enough to be still there to remember, maybe. They went by Tabor, fortress town of the Hussite wars, the first religious wars in Europe since the Christians beat the pagans, but with many more to follow quickly after. All that the Hussites had wanted was a Bible in their own language, communion in both kinds, bread and wine, and the church's admission that though scripture could never be wrong, the church leadership could be. Their bravery raised wild hopes; people came to Bohemia from all over Europe—Wyclifites, Waldensians, proto-Quakers. And Adamites too, living naked in the woods and dancing around their fires and coupling indiscriminately: they believed, outrageously, that God entire was within each of them. *Let out your prisoner,* the women cried to the men as they tore their last rag of garment away, *give me your soul, and take mine!* They had to be killed like the beasts they were, even the Hussite preachers agreed with that; but they would not be forgotten.

Up in those very woods that he could see, maybe: which were very like the woods of his home, where there were the same little white churches rising above hilltop villages, and log cabins where the city people came in the summer. Adamites too in the greening valleys of the Faraways; so he heard. Safe maybe though now.

In midafternoon they slid down the long tunnel under the city to the central station, the big arches and glass: the train stations of Europe were the most lighthearted and heavenly of the works of the Iron Age; why had we never had these in our country, no, only windswept jetties or clanging Nibelung undergrounds. This station had been crowded with foreigners and journalists and spies too no doubt when he had got off the same train in 1937, for Tomáš Masaryk had just died, and still lay in state in the magic castle above the town. People were waiting in a long, an endless line to pass by his bier, to say farewell. A half a million people, Kraft had been told. The only wholly wise and good leader Kraft could think of, then or now; the only one immune to the twin European diseases of that time, rabid nationalism and anti-Semitism, and yet not a Communist either, not a utopian at all: only a just man. *Good men still live,* a Czech will say when something unexpectedly righteous is done to or for him. They were saying it now, today, for Dubcek.

With a feelable blow of shock he found that the beautiful huge trees that had always surrounded Wenceslaus Square had been ruthlessly cut down, pointlessly too, destruction easier than construction in socialist progress. God what a sin. He stood staring, appalled, until he felt his coat sleeve plucked, and a young man—not a hustler, surely; apparently not a black marketeer, either, looking for jeans or bucks, but not seemingly official, who could he be?—looked up at him with an air of affront and welcome.

His guide, who had been watching for him on the platform, and whom he had stridden past unregarding.

Prague was restless, almost atremble in that early spring, like a March tree about to put out buds. Public places were crowded with people, young people talking and smoking and hugging each other. Kraft's guide, a young student assigned him as a courtesy or for some less openhanded reason by the Writers' Union, seemed almost to have a fever; his eyes were bright and he quivered inside his leather coat from something other than cold.

He was first put in a taxi, an old Russian Volga—could that really be a picture of Tomáš Masaryk stuck on the dashboard? He didn't dare ask—and taken to his hotel. It was a wonderful Baroque building that he thought he remembered: but surely it had not been a hotel thirty years ago. No, a nunnery. Where were the nuns? His guide made a gesture like shooing chickens. All sent away, long ago, 1950. Reactionary elements. But now: now they were returning, they were being, what was word.

Rehabilitated?

New time, the boy said smiling. Now all old things come back again. And now what would he like to see? The Charles Bridge? The Jewish Quarter?

No, he knew those places well.

Eat? Writers' Union restaurant best in the city. Meet many writers. All new.

No, he didn't want to eat, and yes, certainly, he wanted to meet writers, but not there, or not yet, if that wouldn't be interpreted as an insult? For some reason he knew he could be frank with this unlovely lean young man, tense and somehow twisted, like a hank of wire, smoking more or less continuously and tapping his black pointed shoes. He would, though, like a drink—an easy and apparently welcome request, though he was taken a long way to fill it, to parts of town that seemed to unfold as though right out of Kraft's own jogged memory. The bars and the caves—*spelunka*—were the very ones he remembered, oh yes remembered well; in his guidebook (still with him here in the Faraways!) he had used to mark with a tiny, innocent star the places where he had *got lucky* as the boys now said, girls too for all he knew. They went into Slavie, the café on the corner opposite the National Theater, a long L-shaped room, a fog of smoke and talk. His guide translated what he heard. Rumors of a Soviet army massing just over the border in the GDR.

"And what new book do you work on now?" his guide asked. Move on, or away, from that subject.

"Oh none," Kraft said. "I would say I have no more to write. None that I think worth writing."

The boy studied him smiling, as though trying to guess how his guest would like him to react.

"I mean they're all not true, you know," Kraft said. "Not a word of any of them. All made up, you know? Even the parts that are true aren't true. And finally you get tired, and just don't want to play anymore."

The lad laughed, still eyeing him, pretty sure Kraft meant this blasphemy as a joke. And what could his weary abnegation mean here, where descriptions of actuality had for so long been made up, and the only hope lay in the imaginary? He felt a pang of shame, but really it was true what he'd said, there was no help for it, he had lived too long, through too many fictions, he couldn't feature multiplying them anymore.

The lad was not to be shaken. Next day he took Kraft up to the Hradcany Castle, climbing climbing up the palace district like Pilgrim on his way to the Celestial City. The steps to the castle were crowded too, not with the prostitutes and young men with collars turned up and shacks where red kerosene lamps were lit and Gypsy children plucked at your sleeve—all that was gone, cleaned away by socialism; instead there were more talkers, young and old, studying newspapers mistrustfully or gathered around transistor radios. His guide wasn't forthcoming about what might be happening, a government employee himself after all, but amid his shrugs and terse replies his eyes looked at his American in hope and supplication.

He took Kraft through the castle, beneath the astonishing vaulting ribbed like celery stalks and exfoliating in unfollowable complexity, the stairs up which armed knights once rode their horses, clattering and slipping. It was hard to get the boy to slow down; there was so much Kraft wanted to see, though less on display than when he had been here years before. When another huge army, he thought, had been massed in Germany, watching and waiting.

They climbed the spiral stair to the room in the palace where in 1618 representatives of the Holy Roman emperor met with the Bohemian Protestant nobles who had determined to break with the empire. When the emperor's people made threats and demands, the Bohemians threw them one by one from the window—that window, there, his guide pointed to it. The high cold room was crowded today with Czechs old and young, looking around hungrily, touching the table where the meeting had happened, the window's deep embrasure.

Taking Kraft back down through the castle district to his lodging at the Infantines, the young man made a sudden decision, pulled at the sleeve of Kraft's overcoat, and led him at a quick pace another way, smiling but unwilling to give away his surprise, and he led Kraft to the square where the candybox Loreto church stands next to a Capuchin convent (all the nuns and priests gone from them too, scattered), and across to a gloomy palace he didn't remember. A ministry of some sort now. Palace guards in blue caps and rifles at the wide gates to the courtyard, looking uncomfortable, for a little crowd had gathered there, peering into the courtyard within.

His guide pointed to a window above, overlooking the courtyard. Others pointed too. It was the window of what had been the apartment of Jan Masaryk, Tomáš's son, the one from which he had fallen to his death—pushed, yes certainly, pushed, the young man made violent motions as he spoke—the night after the Communist coup in the spring of 1948.

Kraft looked from the window to the courtyard pavement to the window again. The guide's face shone with something like expectation. This very month, this day maybe, twenty years before.

But Kraft knew that Jan Masaryk had only been the latest, and the poor officials of 1618 not the first, of an age-old series of such ejections in Bohemia. Change here seemed to require a man or men hustled out a high window, looking down shrieking in terror, fingers clinging to the jambs.

Defenestration. Kraft looked up with the others. It was as though the sources of certain events lay not in their antecedent causes but in mirror or shadow events that lay far in the past or in the future; as though by chance a secret lever on a clockwork could be pressed that made it go after being long still, or as though a wind blowing up in one age could tear leaves from trees and bring down steeples in another.

He thought—looking now out the window of his cell in the converted convent, the illusory castle alight and apparently afloat high up—you have to be on their side, you have to be. On their way into the actual future, still surrounded by brutal utopians. He thought: if I knew the secret laws by which history worked, I could reveal them, whisper them in the ears of this people in their peril, and they would know what to do, and what not to do. But the secret laws can't be known, and if known can't be told. You can only pretend to know them.

Yes! A simple clarity that had escaped him or not visited him in 1937, when he had needed it, was now his, as though an egg he'd thought was marble had now cracked, and a fledgling emerged.

You get power over history, he saw, by uncovering and learning its laws, formulating them, teaching them to others, who get thereby a share of the power you have. You form up your followers into an army, which can impose these irrefutable laws on Time's body; you have earned the power, by your grasp of History's Laws, to eliminate or hide away anything that confounds or flouts them. It is thus that in any age the Archons rule; the rule of the Archons in Heaven being contiguous with that of their epigones on earth.

So the way to defeat power is to propose new laws, laws conceived in the secrecy of the heart and enacted by the will's fiat: laws of desire and hope, which are not fixed but endlessly mutable, and unimposable on anyone else. They are the laws of another history of the world, one's own.

And didn't he, Fellowes Kraft, know very well how to build such a history? He did. He did it for a living. He had the tools and ingredients, and he knew how you used them: with heart's need you mixed pretend conversations, purported facts out of books, likely seeming actions, the light of other days.

The Archons who made the world, and whose shadows continue to rule in it, would have us believe that its laws are immutable, eternal, self-generated, necessary. Perhaps they themselves believe it to be so. Very well: then we confound them by a counterknowing: we know that in fact we have ourselves conceived the laws that make the world as it is, and can change them if we will.

When St. Patrick, servant and missionary of the great archontic church of Rome, which had formulated all the immutable laws of God, asked the Druids of Ireland who it was that made the world, they answered him that the Druids had made it.

Build a new world in the face of power, and make it go; show them how easy it is. His own could of course only be a fiction; so was theirs; but his would appear humbly between covers, unarmed, acknowledged to be false: that was the difference.

O my God, he thought, overcome momentarily with a familiar giddiness, an anticipatory exhaustion. He had come all this way paid to find fabulous treasure or at least the rumor of it, and what had he discovered instead but another novel.

Like a cold old man fallen absurdly in love. He knew the signs well enough, he had only thought that he was never to feel them again.

~

The next morning there was a bus filled with more happy yakking Czechs (was the nation on holiday or had they just thrown over their make-work jobs and gone out to the country?) to take him up into the mountains to Carlsbad, which was now Karlovy Vary, the Czechs having won the war of place names while losing all the others, so far, so far. Then up to Jáchymov, Joachimsthal when he had gone up there in 1937, in a jouncing truck with two young men—what were their names? He could not remember. Jewish. He remembered that.

It seemed suddenly foolish to have promised Boney he would go there, and dangerous too. He felt certain he would have an accident inside, lose his way or his guide, be unable to return.

Spring was still far off, up in the mountains; the resort was open though, open year round apparently, for the workers assigned vacations here in shifts in every season, and to keep the staff employed, insofar as they were employed. Kraft's room in a beaux arts hotel was huge and cold, the bed a hilly landscape clothed in mysterious stuff repellent to the touch.

He wandered around the stone gaieties of Carlsbad. Single words arose unwilled within him, each seeming capable of generating the new book all by itself. Salvation. Puzzlement. Aflame. A marriage. Urgent. A rose. Naked. Embers. He lay sleepless in the big bed nightlong, invaded by notions, his heart a great switching yard where train cars were shunted from every part of his soul, linked one to one to one in combinations he could not have conceived before and now could never forget.

Before he set out next day—unwashed and sleepless but feeling as though he had fed for hours on rich and satisfying food (he knew this sensation too, it would not last, there were dreadful fasts awaiting him)—he sent a telegram to Boney Rasmussen in the Faraway Hills:

MON EMPEREUR HAVE WHAT I PROMISED YOU PACKED
W/TROUBLES IN OLD KIT BAG SMILE SMILE SMILE SANDY

His guide awaited him in the lobby, sunk in one of the swollen armchairs that were the height of Soviet-style *luxe,* digging his toe into the unspeakable carpet. He wore the same shiny shoes and leather coat. It was the first of March, bright calm cold expectant morning; the mountains rose not so high as they had once seemed. And the deep and famous caverns at the end of the journey, where he would find at last nothing but what he himself would put there.

Kraft at his desk in the Faraway Hills put the typescript back into the box from which the blank paper it was typed on had at first come, a box of goldenrod draft paper, Sphinx brand. A book that even if he finished it would be too long for anyone to read, and would still have to be read twice to be understood. There it would lie, hidden like the purloined letter in plain sight, and Boney would come and search the little house and eventually find it, for Boney was going to live forever just because of his natural unkillable constitution, that was the funny part; he would find it, the thing that Kraft had found, the Stone at the end of the journey. Unfinished, unmade, as all of them are and must be.

For a moment he wept.

All his life he had searched for the words of power that would go beyond mere description, explanation, catalog, to effect transformation. He was modest; he had aspired to that language, that *gematria,* but had never really believed it might be his. Well, it was the other way around. He had aspired to what he already possessed; but he could never have what he despised as common.

Thought can't really encompass the world at all, *pace* Bruno's unresting daemon. It can't limn the world exactly or represent it adequately. Language, thought, conception, can't even cross the gap between the soul and the world; it may even constitute that unbridgeable gap. All that language can do is to transform.

Give me the base stuff of the world, sadness and nightmare and things tortured in the black smithy of history, and I will turn it all to gold, sophic, wonderful, gold that can't be spent. It was easy: all the old alchemists said it was. It was simply not as great an art as those unachievable others: as encompassment, as true representation. Transformation was what language could do. It was what language could do best. It was all that it could do.

He bent and rested his cheek against the cool bare brow of his Remington.

The power of transformation, which he and everyone had sought as the goal. It had of course been all along right in his own backyard, a magic small and white, but as necessary to the heart (to his heart, but not only to his) as its own beating.

O get up, he urged himself, walk to town. Keep moving, he ordered himself, an Arctic traveler facing a long dark night. Which he did face, *una eterna nox dormienda,* as Catullus had it, one everlasting night's sleep. Boney had been quite taken with that chilling little phrase.

He rose and breathed, looked at the clock. There was a high-school boy he paid to truck him around, take him shopping, rake his lawn or mow it in season. Hauls my ashes too, he joked or choked to no listener, old flaccid satyr. Anyway the boy had apparently forgotten today, youth forgets, no matter.

He put on a straw hat and took a stick from an urn of them by the door; the choice would once have occupied a minute or two of pleasurable fussing, no more now the games that you liked to play.

He got no farther than the garden. Stood in its midst astonished at how late the year had grown, had autumn come early? No, it was September; there was nothing unlikely in the leaves fallen amid the wild asters and the larkspur, the last daisies drooping, their leaves aged and eaten. Pitiful how it had gone unattended. Some sort of vine with star-shaped leaves was clambering over the rhododendrons, he hadn't even noticed it, but now it had blushed deep red and he saw it.

It was in this season that his mother had died, not so many years back that he could not still be filled with pointless grief on hot colored brambly days like this. She hadn't told him how ill she was, of course, she who hardly distinguished between illness and being alive. But then she decided to check herself into a hospital, and after a quick consultation with a doctor had elected to have a prolonged and risky surgery, get at this once and for all or die under the knife—he was sure that was how she had conceived of it, not even having a firm opinion as to which she would prefer. The operation had gone badly, complications, she had neither been killed nor cured, only lingered in awful discomfort and longing while more dreadful things were done to her.

He had gone back and forth to the city over hills and valleys caught in the glamor of golden stasis, September, this time of hastening transformation that always seems so perfect and changeless. Sat by her long hours as she lay suffering, and learned at last how you could believe, how you could be grateful for being able to believe, that really truly there was someone inside the integuments of suffering flesh, someone who could never be touched, never hurt, who only waited patiently in bondage to be freed.

And now that time was come again, once again. Unfolding tirelessly and willingly as it always had, always would. The older he grew and the faster the seasons came around the more permanent and inescapable they seemed, even though in fact he hurtled through them toward escape, his own escape.

He wasn't afraid of dying, never had been. He was uncomfortably, childishly afraid of being dead, in his grave, gone down into the underworld. Maybe because of living so long in that basement apartment. No afterlife had ever been convincing to him except that commonwealth beneath the earth, Pluto's realm, and none had ever seemed quite so dreadful either. It was going to be like that, it was; at any rate he *feared* it was going to be like that, which came to the same thing; after he was truly dead he did not expect to fear that or anything.

What he thought was that when Hermes came for him, to guide him down into the dark land (oh he could see his kind uncaring face), he would try to beguile him. That god had a special fondness for writers, wordsmiths as the papers called them; so Kraft thought he would ask him to listen, before they departed for that gate, to a story he had written in his honor. And if the god did not remember his own history, which probably a god never forgot, he might work on Hermes the trick Hermes had once worked on hundred-eyed Argus, to escape his vigilance: tell him a tale so involving, so long, so tedious finally, that his eyes would close, and he would sleep, well before the end was reached.

Which Kraft was not going to get to anyway.

He didn't grieve for himself, as good as a ghost already; he grieved for those others, men and women of flesh and blood, real people still caught in the machineries of history, whom he had toiled to release, and now must abandon.

Rabbi David ben-Loew, the Great Rabbi of Prague, who made or didn't make the golem, often repeated the saying of Rabbi Tarphon, that we are not required to complete the work, but neither are we free to desist from it. He meant the work of saving the fragments of divinity, sparks of life lost in the dark world of suffering matter, so that God could be healed. We redeem them by our prayers and our religious duties, the rabbis said. Dr. Pons had said that it was by Knowing. Dr. Pons said Knowing was salvation. But though knowing might be salvation, it was not release, it was harder than not knowing, it was only a more intense, a clearer suffering.

He wiped the tears from his face, with his own kerchief, his own. Better to labor than to sleep. We who have spent ourselves in the labor of making the Stone, or saving it from the dark matrix wherein it has been caught: we call the work a game, a walk in the woods, a play, a *ludus*, a *ludibrium*, a joke: and that is because the only way to make the Stone is by the action of the Stone. In other words by means of that lesser art, transformation: his own art, wherein he had spent himself. So at the end of life we turn homeward, weary, and with the work far from finished, but our own task anyway is done. And surely, surely turning homeward will not be climbing *down into*, but *up out of*: up out of a dark mine into the ordinary air, the surface of the earth, where we can wash and rest. He would believe it to be so, if he could.

A cloud, harmless, covered the sun, and Fellowes Kraft saw that far down at the end of his drive an unfamiliar big car was turning in. Not the high school boy's old Rambler, nor Boney's Buick. An Oldsmobile, an 88.

Am I not done now? he asked, of someone, of all. I can't finish. Is there really more yet to tell?

8

"It was in that autumn that he died then?" Pierce asked.

"No," said Rosie Rasmussen. "He got pretty sick, I guess. He spent some time in and out of the hospital. But he didn't die."

"He didn't."

"No. In fact I think I remember that he actually got quite a bit more work done that winter."

"You think so?"

"I mean I think Boney said so, but I don't remember all that well; it didn't seem so important to keep track of it. Why are you talking so softly?"

Pierce shifted the phone to the left side and bent into the corner of the little booth. "The phone here isn't actually supposed to be used except for emergencies," he said. "Not for like long conversations."

"Oh." There was a pause, suggestive of puzzlement, perhaps preparatory to asking where "here" was, but then she only said, "So why did you want to know?"

He couldn't yet say why, or what he was looking for in Kraft's last days. He had come within sight of the end of Kraft's typescript and felt as though he had caught up with him, had reached the point Kraft himself had reached when he ran out of certainties, and now the two of them stood together on the brink of branching possibilities, facing decisions: which now Pierce alone could make.

"You know Beau knew him in that year," Rosie said.

"Beau Brachman?"

"Yes. Beau came to the county just about then. He used to go visit at Kraft's a lot."

"Why? I mean what would he want there?"

"I don't know. This is before I came back. I was living in Bloomington then."

Beau Brachman thought the world is made from stories. He had told Pierce that, and surely not Pierce alone. All stories, he said, are one story. Or maybe he had said: one story is all stories.

In Pierce's cottage in the Faraway Hills, on a winter morning, the last day Beau had been seen in the Faraways. One story. You're not required to finish it, Beau said. But you're not supposed to give up on it, either. And so Pierce had set out.

"You still there?" Rosie asked.

"It's just not like his others," Pierce said. "It's different."

"Just because of the time when he wrote it, maybe," she said. "You know. In those years. Everything was becoming different. After being the same for so long."

"Yes," Pierce said. "For a while it seemed like that."

"Every day you woke up and something was different from the way it had been when you went to sleep. I remember."

"Yes."

"Hair. Go to bed and wake up and every man you meet has sideburns down his cheeks."

"I remember."

"Go to bed married," she said. "Wake up free."

"So you don't know," Pierce said, "how close he came to finishing."

"Nope."

"Nope?"

"Well, I guess it depends," she said, "on how long it was supposed to be."

"For a longer book, of course, he would have had to start sooner." Silence. "I'll just keep going," Pierce said. "I'm not far now."

"Call me when you get there. Wherever you are."

He hung up the instrument but for a time didn't leave the little cranny, small as a confessional, where it had been installed. There was a pencil stub, hideously chewed, there on the ledge, and a white wall never soiled with graffiti or the numbers of lovers. He thought what might be appropriate to scrawl. *Credo quia absurdum. Inter faeces et urinam nascimur. Call VAt 69—the Pope's phone number.*

In his cell again he sat at the plain desk, where the photocopy of Kraft's book lay, beside the gray slab of his computer. The computer was a Zenith; the "Z" in the name on the lid was the same lightning-bolt zag as on the great radio and record player they had listened to in Kentucky, whereon Sam had played his Caruso records, his Gershwin rhapsody. Two slider tabs on either side unlocked it, and it opened then like a box, the lower half being the keyboard and the works, the other half the glass tablet or screen whereon the work was shown. It was called a laptop, though wearisome to hold in a lap, even one as broad as his. Before him, on the keyboard half, were two small trapdoors, each made to hold a square flat "disk" of magically encoded information: on the left side, the instruction set by which the machine would learn and act; on the right side, the disks containing Kraft's book, which Pierce was retyping from Rosie's photocopy and rewriting as he went.

He turned it on. No daemon of Bruno's or Dee's as potent as this; when this one was born, this one and its million fellows, then the world began anew. So those who loved them and served them—and were served by them—were just then claiming. As it awoke it spelled out on the screen a question for him, a question he had set it to ask: *how can I help you?*

He directed it, with a few cryptic keystrokes, to call from its right-hand pocket the last of the twenty-five files he had made of Kraft's book, named in order by the letters of the alphabet. Thank the great stillness here: he was nearly done copying it all. The one that collected itself now upon the screen before him was called *y.doc*. In bright daylight the screen was dim and the letters and words hard to perceive, but now at evening it was a clear pool, book, lamp, and thought in one.

The book itself, Kraft's original, had turned out to be less complete even than Pierce remembered it being. As the pages had silted up Kraft had seemingly begun making the worst of fictional errors, or ceased correcting them: all those things that alienate readers and annoy critics, like the introduction of new major characters at late stages of the story, unpacked and sent out on new adventures while the old main characters sit lifeless somewhere offstage, or stumble to keep up. New plot movements, departing from the main branch of the story for so long that they *become* the main branch without our, the readers', agreement or assent. All of it inducing that sense of reckless haste or—worse—droning inconsequence that sooner or later causes us—us, the only reason for any of it, the sole feelers of its feelings, sole knowers of its secrets—to sigh, or groan in impatience, or maybe even end (with a clap) the story the writer seems only to want to keep on beginning.

At the bottom of the pile it began to turn into alternative versions, partial chapters, stuff that seemed to be maybe even from some other book entirely as the plot ran down or ran away. Pages started off hopefully with a standard coupling (*Meanwhile in another city*) only to be abandoned after a few sentences, or contained only a single paragraph of thought or explanation left floating alone on a blank sea. Then finally it just stopped. It actually stopped in midsentence—as Philip Sidney's *Arcadia* did, and Thucydides, and the *Chemical Wedding*, and Dante's *De eloquentia vulgaris*, for that matter, good company for an abandoned book, if it was abandoned. It actually seemed to Pierce, as he worked over it, not that the book was failing, running out of gas, but that a progressive disease was eating it up, and might go on doing so despite Pierce's efforts, corrupting it pastwards from the conclusion, which was already gone.

gone, gone to hide her head where no one knows, until someday somewhere

That was all the last page said. Which was maybe a sort of foreshadowing or unkept promise, and stories can end with those, but this one wasn't even the end of the matter of the story, for some of the events actually occurred later in time than this moment, though told of earlier, and if it were true, it would make those earlier parts untrue, roads not taken and impossible now to take.

Well. Beginnings are easy. Everybody knows. So are continuings. It's endings that are hard. Not only hard to think up, but maybe hard to assent to: the closer you get to the tugging of the final knots, the more reluctance you might feel, Kraft might have felt, after all his labor, decades long in a sense, since this was the culmination and closing of a series as well as of a volume. And the end of his own span approaching.

So maybe he just couldn't bring himself to end it, even if he knew how, and knew he must. All right then: the computer's winking cursor stood on the last line, at the last character, and Pierce's finger hovered over the point key, yet unwilling to press it, not even the conditional three times, certainly not the final single full stop. Of course if he did, if he "entered" it, he needed only to press another key and make it disappear; for it *was not yet,* that was the strange and unsettling thing about it here on this machine, none of it was *yet* in a way, all of it was still malleable, he could send a tide of change backward through it all with another key press or two. If he chose he could, with a few key taps, reduce it all to a simple list of words in alphabetical order.

But all novels are like that. This one only revealed to be so because of this new immaterial or unstable mode it was cast in. For readers, time in a novel goes only one way: the past told of in the turned pages is fixed, and the future inexistent till read. But actually the writer, like God, stands outside of time, and can begin his creation at any moment in it. All the past and all the future are present in his conception at once, nothing fixed until all of it's fixed. Then he keeps this secret from the reader, as God might keep his secret from us: that the world is as though written, and erasable, and rewritable. Not once but more than once: time and again.

Which isn't so, of course: which isn't so. Only in here.

He said or thought *Oh*. He felt a flight of little laughing *putti* tumble through the air of his cell and vanish. *Oh I see.*

For a long time he only sat, and no one observing him—no observer looking into that cell from outside, if such an observer there were or could be—would have supposed that Pierce saw anything more than the same words he had been looking at before. Then slowly he put out his hand, turned it, and looked at his watch, and then at the glow of the garden outside. The bells rang for Vespers, the close of day. He stood; then after a time he sat again. He took and turned over, faceup, the facedown pages of Kraft's book. And began again to read.

The abbey where Pierce read and thought was a recent foundation; its church was a great strong Romanesque one, as simple and lasting as the hill it stood on, but not old. It reminded Pierce of the welcoming and comforting structures of stone and timbers built in the wild places by the government just a few decades before, when labor was cheap and hopes were high, the lodges and the nature centers of state parks, the riparian works and dams, places Pierce had loved to come upon as boy when his cousins and he went on travels in summer to other, more American places than the one they lived in. Like those rough but thoughtfully crafted places too were the oak pews of the abbey church, the pale flagged floors, the ironwork hinges and candle stands. In high plain niches were statues, but only the required few, the family figures of Mary and Joseph on either side of the stage where their Son's passion and transformation were daily enacted. They and all the other pictures and devotional objects were on this evening blind and obscure, wrapped for the last weeks of Lent in their purple shrouds.

It was Compline, nine o'clock at night. In the bell tower, the bells swung and their carriages rocked, sometimes carrying the bells around in a complete circle, the circle children think they might make if they push their swings out far enough. At this hour Christ prayed in the garden, on the Mount of Olives. Around him his apostles slept and dreamed of what? *If this cup may not pass away from Me except I drink it, then not My will but Thine be done.* A problematic scene for trinitarians, Pierce thought. Jesus seemed to grow less sure of himself the nearer the agony came. Just a frightened human after all. What have I done.

Pierce was not, at this night hour, in the dim blank-windowed church at prayers with the brothers. He was seated again in the confessional-like telephone cubby. When the bells ceased he lifted the handset and after a moment's pause dialed a number, not Rosalind Rasmussen's this time. He told the operator that he wanted to reverse the charges. And when the phone was lifted and answered there, he heard the operator ask, *Will you accept the charges?*

"Yes. I'll accept the charges."

"Hi," Pierce said then.

"Hey. It's you."

"It's me."

"I thought you wouldn't call. That you couldn't. Except emergencies."

"Well."

"It's not an emergency?"

"No. No emergency."

Silence. She had a way—always had—of leaving phone conversations, going silent, having nothing to say it might be, or pondering or distracted. Unafraid that her interlocutor might think she'd gone, or was mum from hostility or impatience.

"So I had a little breakthrough," he said at last. She didn't respond, and after a while he said, "I was wrong about it. The book. I had, well, an insight. I think. Today."

"Good. How is it there?"

"It's okay."

"Just okay?"

"I don't know if I can make it. The whole two weeks."

"What."

"Prayer. Bells, every three hours. At every meal we listen to tapes, about meditation. This murmuring."

"Doesn't sound so bad."

"I kind of dread it. I shrink from it. I may be having an allergic reaction to Catholicism. After all."

She laughed. Pierce could hear cries and hilarity in the deep far-off, where she was.

"Like hives," he said. "I didn't expect it. How are the girls?"

"Jeez, Pierce, they're great. They're so great. You know I went to the doctor yesterday . . ."

"Yes and what . . ."

"And he remembered back when they were toddlers and I went to him for a physical and he asked was I getting any exercise. You remember? And I said well gee no not really, and then I said well actually I do. I lift weights. Yeah. Their names are Vita and Mary."

As though cued, Pierce heard the two children racing by, Doppler effect of their cries approaching and receding.

"They're still up?" Pierce said. "It's like nine o'clock."

"Courtney got them in bed but they wouldn't sleep. When I got back from work they'd just nodded off and the car woke them up. Courtney says."

More distant happy shrieking from her world. She wasn't going to tell him more about that visit to the doctor. "How's Axel?" he asked.

"He's okay. He misses you. When you're gone he walks around as though he's trying not to make noise, you know? And he's got this face. The Ghost Butler. Trying to help and not be there at the same time."

"Oh gee."

"He scares the girls. He tries so hard."

"I'll be back soon."

"No," she said firmly. "You stick. No running home. You do this job. It's what we agreed. Peace and quiet for free. A . . . what do they call it? Recourse? Defeat?"

"Retreat." A room in the Retreat House, plain meals, counseling (optional) and silence. Give whatever you feel you can. A mountaintop in the wooded hills. Perfect, he'd thought, for the job he had to do, the last hard push on Kraft's book, get it to its ending, his house a little loud and crowded, his office at school too. "I don't know. I just don't know."

"Well."

"Can I speak to the girls?" Condemned man asks for a little pity.

"Um sure," she said. "If they will."

He heard her call out: *Kids, it's Daddy*. And his heart filled. He heard a confused thunder, thump of feet, and one was shouting in his ear, Vita, joke-chiding him not very intelligibly even as her sister took the phone from her and spoke carefully.

"Daddy?"

He could see clearly the big instrument held to her ear, her hand around it, the missing teeth in her smile.

"Hi, girls. Yes it's me."

"What are the monks doing, Daddy? Are they making jam?"

"Maybe, hon, but it's kind of late. Do you want me to bring you some jam?"

"Are they scary?"

"Nah." The one pictured on the labels of their proprietary jam jars sort of was, cowled and faceless, stirring his witch's brew: Pierce had showed the girls before he left. The name of their order could be a little unsettling too, it just occurred to him.

"You said you couldn't talk."

"I can. *They* can't."

"I hope you have a nice time, Daddy."

"Thanks, Mary."

Vita yelling her encouragement too, from too far away.

"Yeah, thanks to you, Vita, too. I love you both."

Pierce's wife, whose name was called Roo, took back the phone.

"That was nice," he said.

"Yeah. Now get back to work," she said. "You wuss."

III
CARCER

1

When Pierce returned from Europe to the Faraway Hills it was March, almost a year's trip around the sun since he had first moved there from New York City. He had no home here now, though, as he had had then; no job, no car, no reason to be here instead of elsewhere. He came by bus, of course, all the way to Blackbury Jambs, where the two rivers—the Blackbury and the Shadow—meet in a Y: a fertile valley one way, a rocky tumbled woodland the other.

Leaving his bags where he had unshipped them, at the little store where the bus stopped, he walked out River Street to the bridge over the Shadow. He passed the Blackbury Jambs Free Library, and the Donut Hole. He remembered many things. He thought that wherever he went, for however long, the places of this town and its outlying regions and its rivers would be for him a Memory Palace, or maybe a Stations of the Cross (*Jesus Falls for the Third Time*). But actually that wouldn't be so, it only seemed so then.

Across the bridge, he turned down the river road toward Bluto's Automotive, as Rosie Rasmussen had instructed him to do, for Gene the manager kept a few old cars for rent cheap, Gene's Rent-a-Ride. Then in a large old and smelly but not necessarily unsafe sedan (a Firebird) he went back the way he had come and out along the roads to Littleville. All along the road forsythia was springing from what had seemed to be anonymous shaggy hedges, twiggy and snow covered when last he had seen them. No one passed him, no one came up behind. He found himself driving even more slowly than he was wont to do, as though in a funeral procession of one. He looked around himself to see what was changed, and what was still the same; but it was (we all know it) the observer who had changed, and stayed the same.

He reached the Winterhalter gateposts, and turned in there. Up on the rise was the big custard-colored house with its chimneys and gables, and here the road to go downward to the small model of it, servants' quarters or guesthouse, where he had lived. His poor old car, already sunken like a beached boat in new grass. Astonishing: the green fuses of what must be a hundred, a thousand daffodils had come out before the house and over the lawn, whose existence he hadn't suspected. Never suspected. He felt he would weep. More astonishing: the door stood ajar.

In the first hard freeze of the winter, the gimcrack jury-rigged water system that had supplied the bungalow from a well on the hill had frozen up, and Pierce had abandoned the house, draining the pipes and mopping out the toilet as best he could, carrying away what counted with him as valuables and leaving the rest; both banished and in flight. He wrote a letter to the Winterhalters in Florida, to tell them he wouldn't be watching over their house as he had promised to do, failing them as they had failed him (*Pierce, it's not your damn fault,* Rosie Rasmussen said).

He pushed open the door with his fingertips, and it swung inward gently, accommodatingly. He remembered that he had dreamed of doing this once, but not what had happened next. In actuality this door had often not latched properly when he shut it behind him, and apparently hadn't even when he had shut it behind him for good. It had stood open, then, for months perhaps. He stepped within cautiously, prepared to meet a new tenant, squatter or beast.

No one. The place smelled of cold, dust, mildew, his sadness. How could he have thought to live here, then or now.

You remember how it was laid out: the front door opening right into a little living room; the kitchen on one side and, through an arch on the other side, a dining room that he had made into an office. A flagged and screened porch in back, yes. A bathroom, and beyond it the bedroom, the bedroom Rose Ryder had called Invisible. You went into the Invisible Bedroom through that closed door, the door that he could see from the office where he stood.

None of the books had changed their places or disappeared, though they looked weary and bored. Piles of his papers. For a moment he couldn't think what they contained, only that he feared them. His typewriter slept on the desk, a sheet of paper still rolled within it, and he went and tapped the key that rolled it forward, just to see. And the machine, still connected, awoke and responded: the paper chucked forward two steps. There were only three words on it.

I am going

What had he meant to say? I am going mad. I am going to sleep. I am going to awaken. I am going home. Back. Farther. To learn better. To be brave. To lose. To die.

No way now to know what a man of that kind, in that kind of trouble, might have been about to say or think. Unless the sentence was in fact complete.

He tugged open a file drawer, and drew back with a shudder: in a shredded mass of his notes and facts a mouse family was living, pink infants wriggling blindly, four five six.

He sat down on the daybed there, its clothes still disordered from the last night he had spent in this house, when he had been forbidden the wide bed in the far room. He put his hands to his face and at last wept for real.

Love, Charis had said to him. That's just love, Pierce, real love.

His rag-and-bone shop. What if there was nowhere for him to go from here, nothing to do but lie down with what he had done here, to her and to himself. Yeats, or his angel visitant, said that after death there comes a long time—long for some—called the Siftings, when the soul sorts through its last life on earth, sits unpicking the garment, undoing what was done in hope and error and desire.

Ah well. He said *Ah well, ah well.* And he grew conscious of the approach of a car outside, and stood.

No, she was in Indiana, or in Peru, she had said, at the work of converting Peruvians or Hoosiers to her crabbed little faith. Or she'd given it all up, gone on her way, her way dividing eternally from his.

When he dared look out the window he saw a long gold-colored Cadillac that he recognized, just coming to a stop before his door. From it after a moment there came with some little effort a man he also knew: his landlord, Mr. Winterhalter.

Almost before Pierce could assemble himself and select an attitude, the man was in the house, rapping his knuckles in a merely symbolic way on the open door and calling out *Hello hello.* Then he was standing in the office archway.

"Well," he said. "The return of the native."

It was impossible: the last time Pierce had seen this man he was a shrunken wreck, hardly able to breathe, on his way south evidently for the last time. Now in a fur-collared coat and gleaming dentures he was hale, thrusting a mitt toward Pierce in a gesture that was at once conciliatory and hostile.

Pierce took the hand, unable not to, tried to crush back as he was crushed.

"We're just back this week," Mr. Winterhalter said.

"I just came to look in and," Pierce said at the same time.

"Yes, yes," said Mr. Winterhalter. "So you couldn't manage here."

"It couldn't be managed," Pierce said, and clasped his hands behind him.

"Now now," said Mr. Winterhalter. "Anyway our place didn't burn down without you. All is well." He clasped his own hands behind his back, but lifted and pointed with a grizzled chin. "We've decided not to ask you for the rent for those two months."

"I'm leaving," Pierce said. "I've just come in to look around, start to pack."

"You've got a lease. It runs till next year."

"It's impossible to live here," Pierce said. He was afraid for a moment that he might weep again. "Impossible."

"Now now," Mr. Winterhalter said again, and clapped Pierce on the shoulder in a buck-up gesture he could not have made in the fall; he seemed to have added inches to his stature. He was again the man from whom Pierce had rented the place in the summer, hale then too, stumpy and barrel chested, a pistol-shaped hose nozzle in his hand.

Rose Ryder with him then. Coming in the day to rent the house they had broken into in the night one year before, though they didn't know at that instant that it was the same house; not at that instant.

"Impossible," he said. "Really."

Mr. Winterhalter had turned away and was examining the room. "You're quite the reader," he said. "Lots of quiet here for reflection."

"Listen," Pierce said.

"My brother's something of a woodworker. Maybe we can knock up some bookshelves for you."

"No, listen." He buttoned his coat, and picked up his bookbag, thrust some papers into it that he didn't want as though he wanted them very much, had come only for them and was now gone, out of here.

"I'll go over the water system with you again. It was some little thing you did. Or didn't do." What operation had he had, what pills had been given him? His burnished face glowed like a cartoon sun. "Anyway it's a long time till then. It's nice now. Days are getting longer, you notice? Warmer. Pretty soon you'll be wanting these windows open." He unzipped his own coat. "I'm back. The winter's over."

"I've got to go," said Pierce.

"Tell me you'll think about it," Mr. Winterhalter said. "We don't want to be hasty. A lease is, as you know, a legal document." He had stepped into the bathroom, and Pierce thought he meant to throw open the bedroom door, but instead he turned the porcelain handles of the hot and cold faucets at the sink. Water came out of them, stopped; they coughed and gagged, their tracheae trembling noisily; then more water, brownish, then clear. Mr. Winterhalter held out a hand to them and one to Pierce, grinning as though to say, Come, drink and wash, it's all right.

Not thinking where he would go, wanting only to leave Littleville behind and not turn yet toward Stonykill and Arcady—where he imagined Rosie ensconced amid Boney's books and papers, awaiting him and his tale—Pierce turned off and up Hopeful Hill toward the other side of the Faraways. He found himself then at the Shadowland crossroads, with nowhere to turn but back toward the Jambs or up the Shadow River road and Mount Whirligig. As though he played snakes and ladders here, or some such game without exits, only returns.

Halfway toward the turn to The Woods he came upon the driveway of the little cabin Rose had lived in the summer before. The windows (he glimpsed as he went by; not for anything would he stop, he might have to do it all again if he did) were still covered in gray plywood, sheets he had himself put up.

But not much farther was the road down to the Faraway Lodge. There, he thought, he could visit. And just as he came within sight of it, and of Brent Spofford's Ram parked in the lot, the car he drove expired.

"So how are they doing, those two?" Val the bartender and owner asked when he'd told her of his run-in with his landlord. They stood in the sun on the Lodge's porch. Brent Spofford was examining the ancient and probably dry-rotted beams that supported the sagging roof, with an eye to giving Val a price for repairs. "I hear one's been sick."

"The man or the wife?" Pierce asked.

Val looked at him as though either he knew something astonishing, something that it was inconceivable she didn't know herself, or he was a complete idiot. "There's no wife," she said. "Just the two of them."

"The two," Pierce said.

"Mort, and. Mort. I forget the other brother's name." She chucked the Kent she had smoked to the filter. "He used to be a chef, one of the big fancy places around here. I think he's the one who's not doing well."

"No, it's the other brother," Spofford said. "The one that's not sick is not the chef."

"The other brother?" Pierce said.

"They're inseparable," Val said.

"Oh God," Pierce said, who had not separated them. "Identical?" he asked.

"Jeez, I don't know. They are a lot alike. But opposite, sort of, you know?"

"Complementary," said Pierce. "Oh Lord."

What is it, what accounts for the delight we feel when the world with a grin and a tug on the strings reverses the figure, delivers the punch line, a delight so pure it can even color our chagrin and make it hilarious too? Of course sometimes our souls are wrung and harrowed by a *peripeteia,* appalling knowledge given all in a moment, but—it's the difference between the joyous plunge of a roller coaster and a bad fall downhill—just as often not. More often, even, in lucky worlds. Pierce lifted his face to Heaven, and laughed aloud.

What was so funny, they wanted to know.

"Nothing. Nothing. I knew all that. All along. Sure."

So maybe, he thought, I really won't have to live there; maybe they can't make me. *You're all nothing but a pack of cards.* He laughed and laughed, and Val shook her head at him.

She and Spofford walked with Pierce down to inspect his stopped car, which he had been unable to get started, hadn't dared try too hard to cajole or insist with turning of the key and pumping of the gas, the battery seemed a little. The Firebird lay sullen and unapologetic on the soft shoulder. Val kicked the tire, more punitively than diagnostically, Pierce thought. "Christ," she said.

"Vapor lock," Spofford said when Pierce described the sudden ceasing of the engine. "Can't get fuel through the line." It was exactly the last car Spofford's father had bought for himself, and still drove down there in Tampa as far as Spofford knew: a car so deficient in every real virtue that you could only think of it as a deliberate trick played by the maker on sheeplike Americans, who fell for it too. Huge and clumsy, yet with almost no room inside; absurd streamlining and speed lines; fabulously expensive but starting to fall apart as soon as delivered. He had watched his father, proud yet not really gratified, get behind the wheel, and had felt pity and anger, shame too. "Start it up now and it'll be all right. Even odds."

"I've got to get something of my own," Pierce said. "I guess I'll start looking in the papers. Or the lots."

"Well," Spofford said. "There's one other option. It's sort of taking a chance, but it could work out for you. Has, for people I know."

Pierce waited.

"There's a guy in Fair Prospect who's a dealer, out of the business now, retired I guess, but he still's got a license and he makes a little on the side. What he does is, he takes you to these auctions that car dealers go to, where a hundred cars, two hundred, get sold in a day. Only licensed dealers can bid. You look over the cars, and give him your choice, and a top price you'll pay. He bids. You give him a hundred, hundred fifty in cash on the side."

"Huh."

"You can't beat the prices.

"Well, sure."

Val lit a cigarette. "Are you talking about Barney Corvino?" she asked. "Jeez, I don't think he's doing it anymore. Ugh, that's a sad story. Sad." She waved away their inquiries. "He doesn't do much. Last I heard."

"Worth a call," Spofford said.

Just as Spofford promised, the Firebird started again after its rest, and now Pierce had had a drink, and a chat, catching up with the local gossip, and there was no longer any way to put off what he must do next.

She was digging in the earth around the foundations of Arcady, wearing a pair of huge bright yellow gloves like a clown's, and overalls over a raveling sweater. She ran toward the unknown car when she saw who it was inside, pulling off the gloves and waving. He was inordinately glad to see her, his heart soared in fact, with only a touch of guilt, which seemed small after all. He got out of the car with some difficulty—the door was bent somehow and ground horribly as he pushed it open with his foot—and then she was in his arms exulting. Why so glad?

"You talked to Spofford?" she asked.

"Yes. At the Faraway Lodge."

"The Faraway Lodge!" she cried in cheerful indignation. "What the hell's he doing *there?*"

"Getting advice. He said."

"Advice! Well, maybe he needs it."

He'd never seen her thus, as though incandescent, radiant. Who is it that's always called *radiant?* He made a guess, and she began to laugh, as though spilling over with goodwill or delight, and so did he.

"I thought you were going to wait," he said. "For a long while. Maybe travel. Maybe see the world. Walk in the woods."

"I walked in the woods. I can't explain. It's a big surprise to me."

"I knew he was going to ask. Hadn't he already, before?"

"Yeah. Well. That wasn't what surprised me." And they laughed uproariously together.

"When?" he asked.

"We thought June," she said, and they laughed again together, at the great and glorious absurdity. "And you're telling me he never said a word to you?"

"No word."

"So, what did you talk about?"

"Cars."

"For heaven's sake."

"June, huh," he said.

"You'll come?"

"Rosie," he said, as though the answer was so obvious he refused the question. And for a moment she only stood and glowed. Then she took his arm.

"You're back," she said. "Come talk. Tell me everything."

She led him toward the house, the door, and he remembered many things: not a list of items (Boney, summer, grief, winter, Rosie's daughter, night, drink, Rosie's bed) but a taste, a garment warm and binding; a thing both his and not his but all of a piece. Inside renovations were going on: not the same place at all, pleasingly.

"So what happened? What came of it all?"

"It came," he said, "to nothing."

"Oh." She sat down behind Boney's big desk—he'd always think of it as Boney's, and no doubt so would she—and put her hands together as in prayer. "I guess that's all right."

"Yes?"

"I guess I'm sort of glad."

"Glad?"

"Well, you know. What would I have done. If you'd come home with the Holy Grail."

At that moment Pierce, seeing or feeling something indistinct behind him, turned to see Rosie's daughter, Sam, standing in the doorway. He would have greeted her, but her attention seemed not pointed his way.

"And what about the stuff *you* were looking for?" Rosie asked. "What you needed for yourself."

"I found it," Pierce said. "But I left it there."

Sam wore a knit dress striped in rainbow colors, red to orange to yellow to green to blue to purple; and when the dress ended, the colors began again on her tights.

"So no book?"

"No. There never really was one."

"Oh." She scrutinized him, as though to see if she should extend some hope, or pity, or consolation. Then she said: "Did you have enough money?"

"I've got lots left," Pierce said. "You have to tell me what you want me to do with it."

"Keep it," Rosie said. "It was a grant. Nonreturnable."

"But . . ."

"It would cause endless accounting problems if you gave it back. Believe me."

Sam had clasped her hands together behind her back, and put one foot out to rest it on the heel, which made the S-curve of her torso more pronounced. Pierce recognized it as a common human pose, more common in girl children than in others. Still she had not chosen to turn his way. He thought she'd grown a lot.

"She's grown a lot," he said to Rosie.

"Who has?"

"Sam. How's she feel about all this?"

They both looked to the door, but Sam was gone.

"You know what she said to me, when I told her?" Rosie said. "She said it was good because Spofford'd be here in case she needed him. I asked if she thought she might need him, and she said well there was the time he had brought me to the Woods, that night when Beau was there."

"Yes." Winter dark. Sam taken away from the Powerhouse and brought here again where she belonged. Could all that have really happened, really truly, the month he had last been here in this land?

"And she said," Rosie said, and seemed to laugh and cry a little at once, "she said she was glad, because he got me there just in the nickel-dime. That's what she said. In the nickel-dime."

She stood in her rainbow dress again at the top of the stair when Pierce went out the door, and he waved to her, and stood for a moment to see what she would say, but she only stood and smiled. He went out into the day.

So, he thought, and said: "So."

So he would not ever do what Frank Walker Barr had charged him to do: to take up, in a book, the questions people ask, that history might answer. His own question had been *Why is everything the way it is, and not some different way instead?* Which he had meant to answer by showing that everything *is* a different way instead. And then, in that laboratory, those pages, gather the evidence for his proposition, or in that sealed courtroom make the case for it in contrast to the case against it, bring it forth even *shaped* by the case against it; build the case over slow time, so slow it would seem to build itself, gathering like storm clouds or battle, forming always in the direction of a conclusion. *It's so.* Or *It's not so.*

Why had he imagined he could do that. He didn't have the thought to make the language that would draw a new thing, like wire, out of the future:

or he didn't have the language to embody the thought, same thing. The only marvel was how long he had believed otherwise, without even understanding that he did.

Because he was not, actually, all that smart. He really knew next to nothing about European history or Hellenistic religion, he read no modern or ancient languages with any real comprehension, had no way to judge if what he projected was what had happened, or like what had happened, or something else entirely different. How could he have spent so much time on a thing so inchoate, cutting off its blooming endless heads until he just couldn't anymore, and so going away with nothing?

You could say, of course—anyway Fellowes Kraft might, in jest or not—that the book had become impossible only because the world was ceasing to be different: that the possibility of difference was once again leaking or running away, and that his apprehension of the possibility of a magical renaissance had itself been a sign that it wouldn't last much longer. For magic—great magic, world-making magic—vanishes from the world at exactly the same rate as it is perceived to be there: a rising and a falling line on a graph, and right where they meet the world trembles uncertainly for a moment, and then goes on alone.

Which is why Prospero has to drown his book and break his staff: when the world has gone on, you must live in it without magic. Or there will, at last and in the end, be no world for you to live in.

You could say that. But he wasn't going to say that. His lips were sealed. He would, from now on forever, be a true Rosicrucian, and keep his mouth shut. *Silentium post clamores.*

Whistling—when had he last whistled?—he went back to the pretend car he had been given. When he was seated he spent a moment counting, mentally, his money; then he backed out of Arcady and drove to the Jambs and out to Route 6 toward Cascadia, where the trucks and the travelers pass and repass, to look for a place to stop and stay.

From the room he was given at the Morpheus Arms Motel, which was just as he had expected it to be, he called the number of the car dealer that Spofford had given him.

"Corvino," said the phone. It was a woman's voice, and was one of those voices on the phone that sound somehow sadly far-off when they first speak, making you almost shy to go on.

"Hi. Is Barney there?"

"He's not available."

"Ah. Well. I had a question for him."

"Call back."

"It's kind of hard for me to phone," Pierce said. "Can I leave a message?"

"Sure."

"I understand he sometimes can get cars, or a car, by, well on an individual basis, from the auctions . . ."

"He's not doing that anymore."

"Oh." Impasse. "Well."

"Who told you about this?"

"Brent Spofford, actually. I guess he's a friend of Barney's?"

A pause, unreadable.

"Well, no," she said. "I'm not sure they've even met." Something in her tone had altered, maybe (Pierce thought) for the better. "You know Spofford?"

"For years."

More pause.

"So what were you looking to get?"

"I hadn't decided. Mostly small and cheap."

A derisive snort. "Spofford told you the deal?"

"Well, he said . . ."

"Two hundred cash, no check. And a cashier's check when you get the car."

"Sure. Of course."

"We'd have to leave early. The next auction is Saturday, up around Nickel Lake, you familiar with that area?"

"Um no." Before she could give directions, he said: "Wouldn't you have to ask Barney about this?"

"What?"

"You said he wasn't doing it anymore."

"He's not doing it. I am."

"Oh."

"I'm his daughter. I've worked for him."

"Oh."

"Problem? I have a dealer's license."

"No. No problem at all."

She said nothing more for a moment, for so long in fact that he thought she might have left the phone, gone away for some urgent thing.

"Okay," she said then. "Tell me where you'll be. I'll come. We'll go up in your vehicle."

You can only know you have reached the springing of a Y when you look back from on ahead; then it's apparent that what seemed to be the important junctures weren't, they were simply the plain way continuing, but ways you bypassed without even noticing (saying *Yes* or maybe *No* unhesitatingly) were in fact the way you might well have gone, but didn't.

"Yes," he said. "All right."

"I'm Kelley," she said. "Kelley Corvino."

"Pierce Moffett," he said unconvincingly (it always seemed so, to his ears). "My um vehicle is a little unreliable. Vapor lock."

"I'll take a chance," she said. "Where do I meet you?"

"I'm, right now I'm at the Morpheus Arms Motel, on the Cascadia road."

"Oh jeez," she said.

"Yeah," he said. "I need a home too."

"I'll be there," she said.

She was his own age, he thought; actually she'd turn out to be some years younger, but the lines of her face were deep cut, and her throat incised too with finer lines. The hand she held out to him was knuckly and strong.

"Roo," she said.

"*Rue?*" he said. "You're called Rue?" He seemed to remember a different name, but not what it had been.

"What's the matter? You know some other girl with that name?"

"Oh yes," he said. "More than one. Many more. Almost all, in fact."

She seemed to decide he was making a joke not worth investigating. "It's a nickname," she said. "I've had a lot of names." She looked into the room, took in the unmade bed, the still-packed bags. "You're ready?"

"Yes."

"Got your money?"

"Yes."

She turned away to where the cars stood, each before its owner's door. She didn't seem to fill her faded workpants, but you couldn't tell, they weren't designed to reveal, or conceal either. He found himself fixed by her face, trying to place her. She seemed to belong to none of the three sexes he lived among, these being men, women who drew him, and women who didn't.

"The Firebird yours?"

"Yes. I mean I'm driving it. It's a rental."

She nodded, regarding it with a certain caustic knowingness, a face he would come to learn she wore when looking at all old cars and certain other classes of things, but he didn't know that yet, and supposed that he'd made an obvious wrong choice at Gene's, and should have known better. "Okay. We gotta go. You want to take the short way? I can show you. Save half an hour."

"I tell you what," Pierce said. "Why don't you drive."

He held out to her the Firebird's key on its ring. How attuned we are to the faces of our kind. Something happened in Roo Corvino's mobile features, something slight, too slight to interpret but not too slight to catch, a kind of relenting or unlocking, he would have had no word for it even if he'd been wholly conscious of perceiving it; distant cousin of a smile, the troubling or calming of some deep water.

"Okay," she said.

And they set out.

Nickel Lake is in the north of the county, a round deep pool like the mirror taken from a compact that you might set into papier-mâché hills for your HO locomotive to pass and repass, or into the wintry Bethlehem beneath your Christmas tree for miniature skaters to pose on. That's what Pierce had imagined on first hearing the name. In fact it was a dun waste of water glimpsed now and then through the burgeoning sumac and other roadside trees, and around its marge a spread of roadhouses, low motels, auto graveyards, and bike shops. On the far side were summer places and a beach, where last July he (and Rose Ryder) had watched fireworks. He told her this, though no more.

"We had a place over there once," Roo said to him. "Burned down."

She told him her history, and it was patent and severe. Her father, handsome devil, hot-rodder, soldier, then car salesman; her mother some years older, divorcée, their romance a scandal, burning hotly. Years go by, a couple of kids, the dealership, a big new house in Labrador, that development east of the Jambs? Pierce knew of it. Her father was one of those guys who are sure that everything they have is the best there is, and everything they know can't be beat: my fishing rod, my power saw, my gas mileage, my wife, my club sandwich, enjoying himself daylong with a profound and seemingly unalloyed enjoyment, and always ready to tell you with a smile how you too can get the best of everything.

She said that women like guys like that. Pierce thought he'd never heard the type described before, and wasn't certain he recognized it. Oh yeah: women love it when men know exactly what they want. Especially if what they want is you.

"Lucky man."

"Well. He always had a lot of affairs. Long ones, short ones. It was sort of well known. My mother kept finding out, and kicking him out, and taking him back. Because she knew that underneath he always wanted her most. Then one year no more."

"She couldn't take it."

"That wasn't it. She fell in love. A guy lots younger. And she left. In a day. The one thing he wanted most and was gladdest he had. She never came back; she never looked back."

"And when was this?"

"I was ten. So it was me and my younger brother and him. I loved the guy too, but I couldn't stand him. I was fairly messed up by him, about a lot of things. By her too. You can imagine."

He wondered if he could. He didn't know that much about the world, this one, and knew he ought to keep his eyes and ears open.

"Then."

"When I was eighteen I left. Didn't say why or where. One day they woke up and no me."

"Where'd you go?"

"West. It was 1967. It was easy to get lost. People were nice. Even I could get along. I was never coming back."

"You live there with him now."

"Yeah. Well. He's pretty sick. He drank a lot there, after his women went. Still does. I don't know if that did it, but anyway. He'd fought with my brother by then and he left—I never see him, which hurts. I don't know, maybe he's still mad at me too. So, big empty house. The deal was I'd get my own room, my own entrance, no questions." She seemed to sense this left a lot unexplained. "I work when I want, not when I don't want. I cook, he cleans. Sometimes. It's a good deal."

She said the last sentence as though it were a different one, and maybe because she knew it showed, she rubbed her forefinger rapidly under her nose, throw off pursuit. Pierce thought he already knew more of her than he did of most his acquaintanceship, and wondered at it.

"So you," she said. "How about you?"

He opened his mouth to say Well, but just then she saw the tower made of zigzag girders, surmounted by a '56 Impala, that marked the auto auction grounds; she turned in, and business began.

The cars were lined up in groups large and small, in categories probably, though none Pierce perceived, by seller maybe or the cars' provenance. In the center of the field was a sort of shed with wide doors at either end, through which the cars were driven, to be bid upon. Roo saw people she knew loitering there, and walked away, leaving Pierce with an injunction to look around, see what he liked.

He looked around, though taking no steps, at the day and the earth. The plants that flourish in waste places, like slum children, have their spring too and their springing. The little one that smells, astonishingly, like pineapple when it's stepped on. American earth. It seemed to him that he had actually not been away: not that he hadn't traveled, but as though he had undertaken and undergone a long journey without moving very far, or at all. Like an old melodrama where the fleeing heroine crosses terrible terrains by running a treadmill, staying center stage while the scenery unrolls beside her.

So let's see. He began to review the cars he stood beside, which were not American as it happened, small Foxes and Beetles. He opened their doors, sat in them and smelled their insides, looked out their windows. He happened upon the hood release of a brown Rabbit, and with a dim memory of disaster he pulled it, and then went to look at the engine, which sat mum in its well.

"There's a nice '71 Python over there," she said, suddenly beside him. "Nice clean car."

"I was thinking of something smaller. I like this."

"A Rabbit? You do stick shift?"

"I've had instruction." In Rose Ryder's Asp convertible. *Don't worry,* she'd said. *After a while it becomes automatic.* Where was it now, the red Asp, shed probably like the resurrecting snake's skin, left by the side of the road. Kelley Corvino had been speaking for a moment before he heard. "What?"

"I said I don't know a lot about foreign cars, to tell you the truth."

"Front wheel drive," said Pierce. "Good for winter driving." Where had he heard that?

"Like a Cadillac," she said. "You do a lot of winter driving?"

He was about to let the hood fall when she stopped him. "Something you should know," she said. "This car's probably been in an accident."

"How do you know?"

"It's been repainted."

"You can tell that?"

"It's kind of obvious. And see?" She pointed down to a place on the frame where the warm brown color (what had initially drawn his eye, in fact) feathered away on the body. "Spray," she said. "Factory color doesn't look like that."

"Oh."

"Might be nothing. But it might have been rolled. You don't want a car that's been rolled."

"Huh."

"Never know what got shook up. Hey, Frank."

A passing male in a NABCO cap and windbreaker turned her way.

"You think this car's been rolled?" she asked.

Frank shrugged noncommittally, put his meaty hands on the fender, and gazed within, as Pierce and Roo did; he eyed the roof, and averred that it didn't look creased; shrugged again, and moved off.

"You want it?" Roo said.

At some time in this day he apparently would have to say yes. There was no test driving, she'd said; most people came here knowing what they wanted, and the cars were all certified as driveable. For a moment he wondered where he was, how he had come to be here; then he said: "What do you think it'll go for?"

"Well, I wouldn't go over, say, a thousand. If you want it."

"Okay," he said. "Stop at a thousand." He thought about his money, not his at all, and how little there would be now for anything else, and for the only time that day his heart contracted in anxiety. He followed Roo back to the shed, to sit in the bleachers while she bid. One by one the cars proceeded through the space and were bought or rejected; some were greeted with murmurs of appreciation or a scattering of mocking laughter, but Pierce couldn't see why; not because of their ludicrous excess of color or tail fin. At length the little Rabbit was brought in, and in moments she'd approached his limit, and he felt his heartbeat. Eight hundred and fifty, and silence; the light stroke of the hammer.

"Good deal," she said, filling out the papers. "Lucky."

She got the keys, and he held out his hand for them.

"No you got to drive the Firebird," she said. "This one's unregistered. You can't drive an unregistered car, no plates, no sticker, but I can." She bent close to him, eyebrows lifted, the way a schoolmarm listens for the small voice of a kindergartner. "Okay?"

"Yes," he said. "Sure, of course. Makes sense."

He saw to it that she left the parking lot first, sure that he would never find his way back the way they'd come, and embarrassed to ask. It hadn't been more than a couple of turns, left or maybe right.

Evening, and the chartreuse sky darkening; the gray road striped with yellow. Following her, going where she in the little brown car went. Only long after did she confess to him that that was in fact the first time she'd ever bought a car for anybody in that way at that auction, though indeed she did have a license and had gone once, twice, with her father in former years.

Why did you then, that day?

Well? Why'd you trust me to?

Why had he? He would claim it to be a part of what he regarded as his natural optimism, a reliance that things would work out okay, probably, the odds anyway well in your favor; his sunny disposition, or trustfulness. And she said—because she knew by then—that it wasn't so, that when he walked off the end of the dock that way it was his own kind of nihilism, daring the world to get him, almost willing it to: she'd been clocking instances for years, she said.

But anyway the Rabbit had hummed along for years too by then, skipping amid all the Foxes and Bobcats and Lynxes and Rams, with him and then with him and her safe within, until the day the front seat fell down right through the rusted floor when he got in to drive, the engine still willing even then, strong lapine heart unstilled.

2

Barney Corvino's dealership was not far down 6A from the Morpheus Arms, and Pierce sitting in his overcoat at a mossy picnic table that stood behind his wing could watch the traffic come and go, the old cars drive in there and the new ones out. Too far for his sight to resolve a person, Roo say, at work giving test drives, if she did that. The sheltering sycamores over his head had been saplings when the place opened not long after Pierce was born, it was long-lived for a Tourist Cabins and now showing its age; when summer came the gold-green shadows that the old trees cast on his bed, and the leaves' susurration through his open window, would keep him paying the rent there. That, and his continuing paralysis, or stasis, which had seemed so dreadful to him and now seemed not so dreadful: healing, maybe, he thought, or at least now not unfamiliar; just his own old self, a trait rather than a disease, a trait he could have inherited. *My get up and go got up and went,* Winnie used to say about herself.

Winnie had always taken his side in this, and of course he had always taken Winnie's side too, her role of chaste inaction and apartness. No surprise; it was she and Pierce alone, and then the rest of them all together. That she was only a sort of half mother to her brother Sam's kids, unwilling to take power fully among them, might account for the ironized way she would make gestures toward raising them, offering antique rules of behavior or morality in a voice that withdrew them at the same moment: *Children never let your angry passions rise / Those little nails were never meant to tear each other's eyes.* You didn't know whether she was siding with you or taking you to task. She had had no official power to act there or anywhere, and couldn't teach her son how to take that power either, or to accept it for himself, there or anywhere; she only taught him the wry jokes to make—the kind she made, apparently at herself and her ineffectuality but really at all who had been fooled into acting in the world. She applauded all his meager accomplishments, without questioning why they were so meager; when periodically he returned from that world of strife and action to her room upstairs beside her brother's, having failed in one attempt or another—predictably, comically, lovably, failed again—she'd say *Oh well,* resigning all other possibilities, at once sad and gay. *Oh well.*

That appeared to be a tallish blondish woman slamming with a great heave-to the door of a huge sedan in the dealership's parking lot. If he had a pair of binoculars he might be able to resolve the figure. Did she have a little dog on a leash? Why would that be? He bent forward, as though to bring himself a little closer to the scene, and at that moment felt a touch on his back, so that he leapt, startled.

"Hey," said Roo. "How you doing?"

"Um. Good. Quite well. You guv me a start, as they say down where I come from."

She sat beside him, hands in the pockets of a sheepskin coat. "Yeah? Where's that?"

"Kentucky."

"You don't sound like a southerner. Or a hillbilly."

"Good. Are you not working today?"

She shrugged. "You?"

"Well, you know. I loaf for a living," Pierce said.

She laughed. Her teeth were astonishingly crooked, a great gap in the middle, and others crowding the row like spectators at a streefight. They sat there in the last of the spring sun for a time, and talked on general topics, each ready at any moment to back away if an impasse was reached and politely take leave. But that didn't quite happen, and evening came, and they still sat. She learned that Pierce had taught college once upon a time, and did no more; that he'd set out to write a book, and had given it up; that he was in a dispute with his former landlord about a lease and that his belongings languished in the old place; that he was living at the Morpheus Arms on a grant from the Rasmussen Foundation that he hadn't quite earned, and was without a further plan. She passed no judgment on this career, even while making it plain that it seemed to her a waste of some uncommon resources.

"So? You've kicked around," he retorted. "Never anything long. Right?"

"I worked as a lineman for a whole year," she said. "In Idaho. I'll never forget the procedures. I could recite them now."

"You mean a telephone person? Shimmying up those poles?"

"Well, a cherry picker, actually, mostly. But yes. The hard hat. The tool belt. You know."

"So did that alter your social life? Being a hard hat?"

"Well. You know there's men—I don't think a big number—that have a thing about a woman in a tool belt. Don't ask me why."

"Really."

"When I say, 'Don't ask me why,' that doesn't mean I've got no idea."

"Aha. Yes." He could see her, in fact, and didn't need an explanation: her narrow wide-set hips in creased jeans, brown arms, wristwatch, the heavy belt.

When it was too dark and too cold to sit at the table, they rose together, and almost as though they'd had a date to do so, they went (in the little chartreuse Bobcat she was driving that day) to the Sandbox, a cousin establishment to the Morpheus Arms, where she chose a dark corner far from the bar and the pool table. A hangout for the guys from the dealership just down the road, it appeared, and maybe others she might not want to run into, but still the place she chose to be; where Pierce (this was what he remembered on entering the dim sweet-sour-smelling place) had heard or seen Rose Ryder speak in tongues as a country western band played and brayed. Or he'd thought she had. It seemed certain to him now that she had not, which made less difference than he felt it ought to.

"I fell in with bad magicians," he told Roo, when she wanted to know the story.

"Oh really."

"They claimed to have power over death. That if you believed in them you wouldn't die. You might look dead and rot in the grave but somehow you'd get up again alive and well when the time came."

"In Heaven."

"No. Not somewhere else. Here. Right here. In the Faraways, say; only the Faraways made better just for you. And then never die again."

"Sounds good."

"It was terrifying."

She studied him. "Are you afraid of death?"

"I don't know that I am. I mean it doesn't frighten me to think about it. Or name it anyway."

"But these people frightened you by talking about it."

"Yes." He felt the dread or danger again; it was a beast that accompanied him, rousing now and then at a soul-noise it heard. And as it roused he knew also and certainly what he had not known before this iteration—that he would not ever understand the reasons for it, his dread, not if he lived to a hundred, and that in this unknowing lay the way he would at last be done with it: he would forget it, as the worst dream is forgotten, the awful force of its logic in dreamland finally canceled by its illogic in this land. Only the story of it left. "And you?" he said. "Are you?"

"I'm sort of afraid. More like tense, sometimes. It seems like it'll be a kind of test—you know, a big final. Everything points to it. You want to get it right."

"How would you do that?"

"Probably not a lot you can do *then.* At that moment. Especially if you like get hit by a truck. It would be the things you'd done all along."

"Like a final grade."

"But one you give yourself. I mean nobody's taking attendance. I don't think."

"And then?" Pierce asked.

"Then?"

"Afterward."

She turned her bottle's end against the napkin on which it rested, which caused the paper to fold neatly around the bottle in a rose shape: it was a habit he himself had. "Here's what I think. Well, *think*'s too much to say. I feel like if there is some part of you—of me—that goes on after, then it has to somehow in life get up enough velocity to get off, right then. At that moment. To get away."

"Escape velocity," Pierce said.

"And you get that by what you do in life. You build it up." She drank. "That's all."

Later she brought him back to the motel and stayed at the wheel, motor running, while he got out, which seemed to be a clear enough signal, but just as he gestured goodbye—*So hey, okay*—she offered to borrow a truck to carry away from the house in Littleville his belongings. Next day or whenever. He accepted. The larger furniture he thought could take its chances with the Winterhalters for a while; he wanted only to take away the life he had led, in case they grew vindictive, held it all hostage, put new locks on the doors, forbade it to him. When she called on the appointed day to get directions, he asked her please not to actually come into the house if that was okay; he made sure to drive over first, and when the little panel truck appeared, rolling like a bear down the rutted driveway, he had already put into boxes and bags all the books, the papers, the clothes and household goods, unavailing regrets, mysteries, bonds, tools, greatcoats, galoshes, grammarye, medicines, shames, hooks and eyes. It had all shrunk or shriveled into a list of nouns, inanimate, abstract, but he was still knee-deep in it. So much, so much.

"I asked you to just wait."

She stood leaning in the jamb looking in. "Smells in here," she said.

"I'll be ready in a second. I'll just toss this last stuff in. You don't need to help or."

She had picked an old Polaroid camera out of a box, chuckled over it. "Man," she said, but he didn't respond. It went back in its box, with other less patent things, a fancy carved black picture frame, empty, an open bottle of green liqueur. Who keeps such stuff?

"What in holy hell is that?" she said mildly, ready to be amused by the collapsing scenery of his past, as squalid and as interesting as anybody's, and at Pierce's discomfiture amid it.

"It's a mask."

"It's a horsie. No, a donkey."

"Yes."

"You're leaving it?"

"Not only that."

"It looks like some kid made it."

"Yes."

"Is that the book?" She meant the masses of paper he was stuffing in a padded bag, one in which Winnie in Florida had mailed him a birthday sweater. "So called?"

"Some of it."

When it was all out, he shut the little house's door, and then went back to shut it again when it opened behind him, tempting him to re-enter. The deathless daffodils were now almost out in the yard, braving the cold. On the crest of the pale lawns, up on the big house's verandah above, there appeared the two Winterhalters, the erect and the stooped, one's hand lifted as though to say Hello, or Halt.

They trucked the cartons and bags and an ancient duffel and the lamps and rattling boxes of kitchenware down to a warehouse at the end of a muddy lane in Stonykill, put it all behind a wooden door like a stable's and padlocked it. Later Pierce lost the ticket and forgot the name of this place, and later still, the storage bills not reaching him at his changing addresses, the stuff was all thrown out and ended up in a landfill beneath tons of other similar but different things for future archaeologists to find. Now and then in aftertimes Pierce would suddenly remember some item, book or charm or trinket, that he had once owned, but by then the world (his) was accumulating new things, not only material things, at such a rate that he could hardly remember *them* from morning to evening, much less the artifacts of a past age that no longer had a substantial claim on actuality at all.

It was a cold, retarded spring in the county, bitter and dispiriting rain in April and a thick snow in the first week of May that fell on the unfolding, near-full-grown leaves and the tulips and lilacs, breaking many limbs with its sodden embarrassed weight. We all felt chastened and hurt, as though it were our fault, or as though we were the object of it. Then it melted and the damage done was covered in green again, and everyone felt less in the wrong: that's what Roo said.

She wore a gray man's fedora on those cold days, or on colder nights a blue watchcap pulled down low, her chapped lips still sometimes helplessly atremble. Her long narrow beak pointed into the world's wind and her green eyes narrowed often, as though she stood at a helm, or first in a line of explorers, searching for the way ahead. When she went to work at the dealership, she liked a pair of wool bell-bottom pants that might or might not have been real sailors' wear in some navy of the world, tall morocco-leather boots, and a patchwork jester's jacket of many-colored silks that was the closest she came to finery—he would preserve a snapshot (inward, virtual) of her throwing on this garment, the quick and practiced way she did it, the way everyone pulls on clothes, with mind elsewhere pulls straight the sleeves, tugs the collar loose; and he preserved it because it was the first time he saw in her a human universal, which afterward she would embody; and that was a sign, and one he knew how to read.

She forbade him to call the Corvino house, and instead she met him at the Sandbox or came to the motel on no fixed schedule, driving up in a variety of trade-ins from the dealership. She would break in on him, press him to bestir himself, but then when he had gone along and they went journeying together and he behaved in some way to which she objected, or (more often) he took some stance or expressed some view she thought offensive or inadequate or dumb, she might suddenly and firmly draw away, arms crossed and eyes smoldering, or turn dull, truculent, and unwilling to be pleased, as though it had been he who had done the importuning in the first place, and now she had had it with his presence. He found their incompatibility soothing.

When they'd been seeing each other for a month he knew more of her life and opinions, her deals good and bad, than he'd ever known of Rose Ryder's. And he'd told her more of his: all of it true too. They talked about their parents; they figured out it was in the same year of their lives that their parents had parted, but where she had stayed at home with her father, he'd been taken by his mother to a far place and a family strange to him. He told her why this had happened, though it was something he hadn't known then, and how when he was grown up he'd come to know his father again, as a different person, the person he had probably somehow been all along, though a person the child could not have comprehended, any more than he could have known why he was sent away.

"You loved him." She seemed to know this. "You see him now?"

"Well. You know. He's a chore. But he's all alone. He needs somebody to listen to him talk."

"Yeah," she said. "Yes." Barney, glad-hander, bullshitter, genial kidder with a core of irremediable bitterness that he perhaps didn't even know about, that could hurt you badly if you weren't careful—she returned his banter but she'd stopped listening to him, a lesson long ago learned. "A guy," she said. "You don't have to listen."

"I'm a guy."

She grinned at him, her snaggletooth smile. "You are so not a guy."

They talked about their old spouses and lovers, with circumspection—each of them guarding, for different reasons, the border of a land neither had as yet received a visa to reach—but they talked about their ghost children too, and without shame: his with Julie Rosengarten, aborted before that was legal even, long ago; her own two. One the child of her husband of six months who, after she split from him and all his pomps and works, had come around to her place one night, found her alone, and coerced her into bed.

"He was a Catholic," she said. "I didn't tell him about getting pregnant that night. And what happened after. I wanted to, though. Just so he'd know."

He logged both these things: that she'd wanted to, that she hadn't. It was past midnight in the Morpheus Arms.

"So if you divorced," Pierce said, "I guess he wasn't a good Catholic."

"He wasn't a good anything," Roo said. "Not a thing about him was good."

"You were never Catholic," he said. "Right?"

"I'm not anything," Roo said. "No magic helpers. It just never came up, when I was a kid, and it's too late now."

She lifted herself on her elbows in the lumpy bungalow bed, reaching across him for his smokes. This the only circumstance in which she smoked, and soon she'd cease. Her pale body: like a worn tool, he thought, every part of it showing clearly what it had been long used for, the thickened pads of her elbows, strong tendons behind her knees to pull and foreshorten her legs, and around her neck to turn and point her head. She looked like she'd last forever.

"Actually I've liked the Catholics I've known," she said, holding the unlit cigarette. "There was a big family that lived near us, like six kids. They were *generous*. In a way that was—I guess new or different to me. Inclusive. You know?"

"Really."

"They took me to church and stuff. Family dinners. I slept over a lot. Then sneaking out too. A lot of laughs."

"Uh huh."

"Maybe it was just because it was a big family, and I was a singleton. The little ones used to line up for baths at night by age, or size. It was sweet. But that's not all. I think what I liked, or wanted, was something about their being Catholics."

"Yes?"

"Because Catholics," she said, "have mercy. That's a good thing. They have that."

"Well," Pierce said, astonished and ashamed, ashamed for his old church, old in its countless sins and its un-mercy. "Well, yes. That's what they say." Tears had bloomed in her eyes when she said it: *mercy*. He didn't yet know how easily it happened with her, at the suppressed motions of the soul within her.

"Because justice," she said. "You can demand justice, but there's an end to justice, when everybody gets their fair share. But there's no end to mercy."

She looked around her at the room, the sad-clown painting askew on the wall, the gas heater, the chenille bedspread sliding to the floor. Him.

"I've got to go," she said.

"Don't," he said. "Stay."

The first time they'd shared this bed—after a couple of drinks at the Sandbox, and well after they'd first begun to consort often—she had seemed unsettlingly cagey. She kept breaking off, or slipping away, to change the radio, or fool with the heat; and she kept talking—not about what was going on right there between them, but about other things, general remarks, questions about life, his life, his thoughts. *So tell me.* He wondered if it were some kind of test, see if he could keep up his concentration, or his attention to her. He was about to ask if maybe she'd rather just stop, and talk, but just then a sort of smothered fire within her seemed to burst softly, and she pressed hard into him; she ceased to say words, only sounds, sounds that seemed, somehow, like further admissions, hard to make at first and then more willingly made.

"It's late," she said, and lay back again on the pillows.

It was late, a night deep in May by now. It was still that time in a love affair (neither of them called it that or thought those words in any hollow of their hearts) when it's hard to sleep together, something always seeming to remain undone or to be continued or gone on with, that wakes you after an hour or two of sleep, to find the other's awake too in the hollow of the bed's deep inescapable center; or that never lets you shut your eyes at all, till dawn's approach at last calms everything. Maybe sometimes too a sense of fighting off something that approaches, or at least preparing to fight. Fight or flight.

"So what was it about?" she asked him.

"What was what about?"

"Your book."

"It was," Pierce said after a moment's thought, "a historical novel."

"Oh yeah? About what period?"

"About ten years ago."

She laughed a low laugh, her tummy rolling beneath his hand.

"You remember," he said. "You were there. You were actually here then."

"I don't remember that much," she said. "And I wasn't here."

"But you came back."

"Family's all you got," she said, and he pondered why—it wasn't wisdom that seemed to apply to her, or to him. So many people said it: when did it become true for them? Would it ever for him? "Anyway there isn't any back."

"That's what my book was about. How if you change the way ahead, the way behind changes too."

"Seems kind of obvious," she said.

It seemed so when she said it; it was obvious, or at least a commonplace. More than one history of the world; one for each of us. A bright moment arriving when you choose a new way into the future, which illuminates a new past, the backward way, at the same time. Everybody knows. It had been true all along.

"Because, you know," she said. "You can't step in the same river twice. You ever hear that?"

"Nope," he said, pressing her now meaningfully downward to supine, enough talk. "News to me."

3

She had always willed her way forward: and if that was so, then what was the name of the thing that was the opposite of it, the force or quality or power that had brought her back again? It was something *like* will, just as forged and handmade; something not easier anyway. It was only people who had never done it that could say running away was easy; people used to say to her that going back was hard, but they couldn't tell her what the hard parts really were, or how you did them. Running away, you hurt yourself by what you did; going back, it was what had been done to you that hurt. It was like the difference between falling hard and getting up again: which is worse? She found out that what she must do in going back (and it *was* hard) was that you had to come to believe that the world you had left behind and all its contents really had existed, and moreover that you yourself brought it and all the obscure pain of it into being by doing that—by believing that it really had been *the case* (as Pierce said)—and thus you were somehow then responsible for it too, which hurt you all over again. But only by thus bringing the past into existence could you ever really turn all the way around again, and go on from there. It was so. Actually it was what everybody knew: and as soon as you learned it for yourself, you knew that too, that everybody else knew what you had just learned.

The farthest place she had reached when she went, the place she had to begin to start back from, was Cloud City. To remember how she left Cloud City was to create the things that happened to bring her to Cloud City in the first place—it was to go forward backward, to go down the mountain, losing on the way down all the things you knew, in order to regain the things you had forgotten on the way up. You had to put yourself back on the path, just past sunset, at the same hour when you first saw Cloud City up on the bluff, itself still in the light though you no longer were: the Watchtower seeming to be silvered in mercury, as real and insubstantial as that (*quicksilver*) and the white wings and hyperbolic sails of the City too, colored by sunset just in the way the white clouds in the west were colored, rare shades that had no names she knew. How she had got there, on the path upward to the bluff, was the first thing that turning back would reveal, maybe, the names or faces of the one or ones who'd brought her there.

There were such places then, places you found your way to and couldn't have imagined before you reached them, places that other people knew of and could lead you to if you said *yes,* places coming into being as you approached and then vanishing again as you went away. That's what it seemed like. Even some that were a million years old—mountain hot springs where in winter the naked people soaked for days, their long hair jeweled with droplets and steaming in the cold, their pale bodies distorted and fishlike down in the water and wiggling in glee—she thought even such places as that might not still exist, or couldn't any longer be found, and Cloud City had been made of nearly nothing.

What was his name, that tall stork of a guy in his homemade haircut and his supply of old dress shirts, the one who had thought up Cloud City and seen it built, only to stop thinking about it when it was still unfinished? A last name for a first name like Watson or Hoving or Everett but none of those. He shook her hand once, gripping hard, smiling and screwing her arm around as though the handshake could produce something from her. Then she'd seen him hovering here and there in the City as though he should be standing on one leg, or he'd be meditating in a group but a whole trembling head higher than the others. It was Beau (*his* name she would not forget, no matter how far backward she went from there), Beau who told her that it was he, Wilson or Evans, who had conceived a city made of tents under tension, that the wires and couplings and the fabrics all existed to do this, and the sun would heat the interiors and a hundred flaps and diaphragms would vent and cool it; a city that could be rolled up and carried away to be built elsewhere, maybe over the ruins of those made of stone and steel when they failed and died. And they had experimented with a thousand shapes for their tents, the older ones still standing as the newer and bigger ones went up. All were white, not for no reason, and the light of day within them was sourceless, bright, cool, the building an idea on the point of evanescence, only the colored carpets, sun catchers, clay water pots, hanging strings of coral peppers, and dirty-faced naked children who were contained in it solid and actual. Watching one put up, all the laughing laboring people pulling gently at the wires, the fabric taughtening into curves that math described: like a barn raising in Heaven.

It was already different, though, when she left there to go down into the plains with Beau: the City people had stopped thinking about earth and air and the properties of polyesters and the physics of stretch, because a change of heart or mind had come over many of those living there, one of those waves of sudden weird conviction that in those days could sweep over families like theirs, as someone among them or arriving among them declared a revelation, or a revival, or a long-buried new-arisen truth. At Cloud City they were mostly spending their days asleep and their nights awake, outside, looking upward, awaiting those they called the Old Ones, mild good wise beings from the stars, or the skies anyway, who were supposedly now willing to draw closer to those who perceived their existence and strove to know them in spirit. That was what the Watchtower was for, to gather and focus the spirits of the city dwellers to be projected outward in love toward those waiting great-eyed ones (some of the Cloud City family could see their faces in meditation) to bring their ships down to the wide dusty floor of the mesa, a place left empty for their landing. Beau with his faint eternal smile had watched the people and spoken to them and listened to them with a kind of attention she had never seen anyone give anyone else, at once open and untouched; and he said (not just to her) that they were right, in a way, about these Old Ones who came from elsewhere, but what they didn't know, and would be a long time learning this way, was that they were themselves those Old Ones whom they awaited; they were looking in the wrong direction, out not in.

So they walked away from Cloud City, she remembered the way down now, Beau and some others and herself, following another tale that Beau had come to possess. They went down into the dry plains, and there they met the dark small people who had come on foot hundreds of miles from their homes far to the south, as they did every year just at this time—this journey, this hunt they were set out on, was the bearer and the continuer of their lives, not a thing they did to find sustenance or goods but that which brought into existence all sustenance and all goods. The ten or dozen people from Cloud City, Beau and Roo and others who had learned of their quest and come to meet them and learn from them, were permitted to accompany them on their hunt, which was a hunt for a person, a person infinitely beloved, who must be shot and killed—they had bows, decorated in feathers and yarns, and arrows remarkably long. The prey they sought turned out to be small indistinct growing things sheltering amid the rocks and cactus, and whenever found it was pierced with the long arrows and held aloft amid cries and mourning, though the hunters' dark faces never seemed to change.

Through that night by a fire of gray greasewood they shared the flesh of the person they had killed, which was the worst thing Roo had ever tasted, not a thing to be consumed at all, and she couldn't continue with the rest of them, and never could tell if what she knew ever after had been imparted to her by the being they had all partaken of that night or was something she would have come to know anyway. Beau had said that we, we here, are the Old Ones that were awaited in Cloud City, and she knew then what it meant to say that, though she might not ever be able to say what she knew—that she was indeed old, the result of a process ages long; that her body was *hers*, a thing infinitely complex and valuable, made of the rarest and most delicate materials and parts, that she would have to bear it and tend to it and keep it from harm every day of her long, maybe endless life. Wonder and weariness. She laid it on the desert floor by the fire, wrapped it gently like a mummy in her sleeping bag, fended off the enormous stars from entering too far into it.

All of that—all that knowing, those stars, that search, those roads—was feelably gone now, persisting in her tissues if at all in amounts almost too small to perceive, by no matter what tests, just trace elements. Maybe because of an association with tracer bullets, Roo thought of *trace elements* as brief stardust streaks across or within the matrix or mass they were detected in, evanescing as soon as caught, without effect. She had only ever been an observer of those people and places, those tribes and crowds and families she made her way into; as willing as she had been to seek them and lucky as she was in finding them, she hadn't ever really quite been able or been allowed to join or become enfolded with them. Why? They were no less wanderers than she was, she was an ox for work, she had insights into their ways that she knew they could use if they'd listen. But she remained outside, and always walked away, and when she was long gone she felt sometimes with weird conviction that she had caused that world of wonders to cease to be because she could not be part of it, and now it was lost to everyone.

Anyway she went on, and her onwards came more and more to resemble her backwards, because that was when she parted from Beau and those who went with him. Because Beau, the only one she would have stayed with, was unclaimable—not all the nights she had spent by his side had let her into him, he would stop at her frontiers, always, or gently stop her at his own—and it was so painful and disorienting that she thought she had better find out if it was because of something that was in her or something in Beau or something in all men, something that wouldn't couple with whatever it was in her, as though she were threaded wrong, or they were. She went into town, went into the city, found a job and then another job, recovering those things (cities, towns, jobs) and taking them on again as she had done on her way away in the first place. Figuring out how to live, pulling a way to live out of the future, careful not to hope, careful not to trick herself into thinking she could see far or know much about what was coming next. She got good at a few things she would later have to unlearn. She got married, and divorced, and pregnant—those weren't among the few things, though the few things maybe led her there, the worst hole or burrow without exit she'd ever find herself in, she *found herself* as though finding a zombie twin, inert and helpless. The rage she'd learned was aimed at herself, at that self, as much as it was at the morons and hardheads and inert unmovable men she'd lived among in those days—for now she had a *those-days* that could be counted again, counted in rented rooms and thirdhand cars that she could name, their wheels turning backward to link one to the previous one (*ah, the Nova; oh right, the Barracuda*) until in them she passed back eastward again, creating the world in that direction as she went. And as she did so she could almost (never entirely) remember how she had first gone west, on those same roads. How she'd shut the door on her life in the Faraways, or the life of her house at any rate—it didn't seem to her that it was her life, nor had it been hers for a long time; she couldn't have said when it ceased to be hers, it ought to have been easy to identify it with the year her mother was caught by love and left, but when Roo told herself the story that way, it seemed not to be a story about herself; all she knew was that the onward-pointing life she had afterward occupied with Barney led down an ever-narrowing tunnel or gullet, like those tight spots she now and then willingly and stupidly (*oh well okay*) entered into in dreams, eventually to be stuck irremediably and suffocating till she woke asweat, heart racing. Anyway it was some sensation like that which impelled her outward and west (the note she left Barney said east, but that was a lie, the only lie she told). She hadn't understood then all that had gone into her decision, but she definitely applied a lot of good sense to the doing of it. She had money saved, all her own. There were plenty of rides to choose from around the house, always three or four cars in the driveway, some splendid and glossy and others more odd and declassé, trade-ins that Barney had an interest in—she suddenly remembered (but not until she hit Route 6 on her way back, when she got within a few miles of the dealership) the very one she had left in, the scabbiest and least valued of those available on that June day, crimped rocker panel, babyshit color, Japanese in the days when that meant cheaply made and impossible to fix when broken—most of the intersecting roads she'd taken thereafter had sprung from garages where grinning mechanics without even a set of metric wrenches had stared into the ridiculous mysteries of its innards, while she sat in the bitter sun smoking a Lucky and awaiting the offer that she got used to arriving at just that juncture, an offer from somebody to go somewhere.

So then she had them all, and in the tale she reached the time when she arrived back in the Faraways and the town of Cascadia, which seemed to awake from sleep as she went through it, confused and unready for her, building after building and road after road, till she stopped her last car in the driveway in front of her father's house in Labrador, thinking that she remembered the house as oriented the other way on its lot, as though it had been flopped somehow meantime, like a photograph, but her feet seemed to be unconfused and to know it was okay, and she was already used to it this way by the time she reached the unlocked door, pushed it open, and called to her father.

Pierce had told her how people once thought of the world as made of Ys, that you are constantly choosing one or another branch, the obvious and easy one or the less clear and harder one, but Roo thought it was really the reverse or upside down of that (as she had lived it, anyway): the ways didn't part from one another but led to one another, like the thousand little streams coming down Mount Randa: each one joining another, which joins another till they reach a stream, or a Y's stem, wide enough to contain them all, which will be the only way the drop of yourself can go or could have gone. When she came home to the Faraways she learned (almost the first day she was back) that Beau was there too, had come to live in the county, the town up the road from the town where she was born. But near as he was, glad as she was, amazed as she was at whatever it was in the world or the heavens that had contrived to bring him so close (the same forces that had brought her back the way she had come to find him there), he was as far from her as ever; farther, because she wouldn't endure those people who gathered around him and depended on him. She said cruel things to them, told them the truths they ought to have known and didn't, and Beau sent her away, or didn't welcome her there, which was the same thing. And in the last winter, at the drought's end, as though the plotted curves of the two of them rising and falling in opposite directions had only happened to cross as they, or the worlds that bore them, moved apart ineluctably, he was gone again. She wouldn't join with those others who wanted her to mourn with them, wouldn't share her grief. She kept hers for herself. Beau had taught her—she knew it before he said it, but that didn't mean she hadn't learned it from him—that if you divided love it wasn't like dividing money, or food, which came out less for each portion you made. It didn't; the act of dividing it did not cause it to lessen, actually it grew, it doubled with every division and everyone got more. She knew it, and she knew that Beau not only knew it but could do it, which not many people could, not she certainly: she wondered if the original allotment she had been given was so small that it could never be divided, and so grow larger. A little hard uncracked nut inside her: that's what she felt as she came and went to and from Barney's house, and learned to sell cars, which was what was left for her to do, and one day in spring came home to catch the phone ringing: somebody needing a car.

4

The foundation's abundance was gone, and Pierce had to look for a job, and quick.

"Well, you're not good for much," Roo said. "Can't tend bar or wait tables. You'd be sunk."

He wouldn't nod agreement, but couldn't deny it. "Teaching," he said. "Substitute teaching."

"You sign up," she said. "Then you wait for a day here, a day there. You'd be a newbie, the last person they'd call. And school's over in a couple of weeks."

He had bought the newspapers, sat with her at the Donut Hole and went through the ads. She watched him with interest, chair tipped back. She wore the coat of all colors.

"They're hiring at Novelty Plastics," she said. "I hear. Down in Cascadia."

"Sure," he said.

"Well?"

He looked up to see that she was really asking.

"I can't, really," he said. "I mean it's not exactly what I."

"It's what people do," she said. "Work."

He shook out the inky sheets. How easily, not even aware, he had bypassed so many common hells. He had not even had to get up to go to work in the morning for over a year. And before that he was a college teacher, not really employment in any arduous sense, it was simply the extension of student days by other means: the same long vacations, the same short hours. Now he stood at a brink for sure, though, no way to go forward or sideways, down or up.

Here was their ad, in fact, his eye just then fell on it. Novelty Plastics. Hiring all departments.

"Is it," he asked, "hard?"

She regarded him with a weird compassion. "It's a job," she said. "It's not hard to *do*. If it was hard the people who do it wouldn't be doing it. You have to do it a lot, though. You know. All day. Or night."

He shook the paper. "So how much does it pay?"

"I guess minimum and up. It's an open shop, as far as I know."

He wasn't sure what an open shop was. It sounded like it ought to be good, but he had the impression that maybe it wasn't. "It would only be for a while," he said. "I have to get a CV together. Send it out."

"Sure," she said. "A couple of months."

His soul shrank. Not so long surely. A couple of months.

"That's if you get hired," she said.

"What," he said. "There's a lengthy application process?"

"No. But they don't like to hire your type."

"My type."

"Oh, you know. Fuzzy-faced wiseacres. Educated gents. They think you won't stay. That you're only there out of desperation, and something else will turn up for you." She crossed her arms. "They see that."

How did she know these things? He thought she was vamping, but he had no way to tell. "Fuzzy-faced intellectuals," he said. "Narrow-chested cack-handed . . ."

"What handed?"

"Soft-handed yellow-bellied . . ."

"You definitely need to lose the face hair," she said. "And get a haircut."

"Weak-kneed," he said. "Wet-eyed. Double-domed."

"You want a haircut?" she asked. "I'm pretty good."

He looked at her without speaking for so long that at last she goggled at him, hey? Well? But he was thinking of a haircut he had himself given, once up along the Shadow River, and a pair of gilt-handled long-beaked scissors, and the sound they made, snip snip.

"Tell me something," he said. "Why do you keep on being so nice to me?"

"You're not worth it?"

"I'm not sure I am. And anyway."

"Are you asking what I'm expecting back?"

"No." He tried to appear offended. "I didn't mean that."

"Just doing my job," she said softly.

She chose clothes for him too, that wouldn't give him away, a hooded sweatshirt that was the oldest piece of clothing he owned, cheap new sneakers he had bought once thinking he might take up running for his health, a billed cap she brought him that said NABCO on it—she snorted when he asked what that meant.

Thus dressed and lamb-shorn, he went with her in a car of hers, a long livid Cougar this time, to American Novelty Plastics, which was one of the few enterprises still housed in an old factory complex, almost a small brick city, that crested the foaming yellow falls of the Blackbury River at Cascadia. He'd never been so far inside such a place before. The parking lot was crowded with cars as similar and as varied as the workers within must be. They drove in and out of the corridors of brick looking for the personnel office.

"There," she said.

"What do I tell them about what I've done before? Do they check references?"

"They don't care what you did before. Tell 'em you just moved here from, I don't know. And you worked at, what, something not anything like this."

She parked the car where it could be seen from the office; her plan was to make Pierce look like he had big car payments to make, maybe an expensive wife too. Ties you down, she said.

"I'll wait here," she said.

"Okay." Rusted railroad tracks ran around the building, long unused, he thought, where depressed-looking weeds grew. A sign on the wall, made decades ago, said NO ROOM FOR MAN ON CAR. He opened his door but for a moment he couldn't get out.

"Here," she said. She took a plain gold ring from her right hand and worked it onto the third finger of his left. *Pronubis* was the name of that finger, if anyone—Pierce thought—wanted to know.

"Okay," she said.

He got out. Geraniums, not real ones, grew in flowerpots at the windows of Personnel, and the door said, WELCOME. But this was the bottom, this bleak yard, that chain-link fence. He had come to the bottom: how strange to recognize it. Everything, everything once begun or seen in prospect or expected now foregone, lost, tossed, torn away. And no rest either. He supposed it was possible, it was probably likely, that he was going to just live on at the Morpheus Arms, and work here, if he was allowed, in this place, from now on. So many did.

The bottom. Why then was his heart so quiet, his sight so sharp; what was this new cold clear air he breathed? He glanced back to toss an insouciant wave to the Cougar, and saw her stern faced, a warning and encouraging thumb held up.

Pierce worked at American Novelty Plastics for six months, not two, mostly in packing and shipping but sometimes in assembly, putting together toys and gimcrack "gifts" and things that were apparently parts of other things that he couldn't guess the nature of, their unintelligibility a dull ache in his mind for the time he spent handling them; nobody else cared to speculate on what they might be and seemed surprised at his curiosity.

Roo had been right that management wasn't interested in his past. The people on the line were cautious in asking personal questions too, less from indifference than from delicacy; he might not want to say much, neither might some of them. The few facts they got from him right off were enough to classify him, even get him a nickname (Cowboy, from the smokes he rolled himself at breaks, no other reason; that was the joke). A few facts about themselves enough for them too, it seemed, repeated over and over.

She had been wrong about the hair, though, not keeping up lately maybe. That moment had come when hair was getting shorter on those who had first grown it defiantly long, and beginning to grow out on the heads of those whom they had once defied, rednecks and crackers and truckers and tattooed ex-servicemen: for they had a defiance of their own to express. For the rest of the century it would be so.

What was hardest about it wasn't the work, or the isolation he'd expected to feel among people too different from himself, or the hours of boredom; all of that was actually okay; the hardest thing was how at some time in the past the many-paned windows of the plant, as tall as a cathedral's or a palace's, had been boarded up on the inside and the daylight replaced by banks of fluorescents, the outside air by conditioned air. He came in from sunstreaked moist summer mornings and stamped his time card and till late afternoon, sky fading to green or clouds forgathered, he knew nothing of the day. Did they mind, those around him? It seemed impossible to ask, and he never heard; better than not working, surely. Something else that others bore continually without (it seemed) complaint, that he hadn't ever borne. He remembered the miners in Kentucky, remembered hearing how in winter they went down before dawn into the darkness and unvarying cold, and didn't come out till darkness had come in the upper world as well: how hurt he had been for them, how afraid for himself.

He didn't miss a day's work, or only one or two, days when he couldn't get out of bed, lay struggling with something that held him: or not struggling.

Roo once came to him as he lay there at the Morpheus Arms, neither struggling nor resting from struggle, because she'd called Novelty and they said he hadn't come in to work. And a man living alone in a motel room who hasn't come in to work needs to be visited.

"You sick?"

"I don't think so." He climbed back into the bed he'd left to open the door to her. The sleazy blanket made of chemical waste must not be touched; he slipped under the sheet with care, wiggled his toes in the warm bed's bottom.

"I can call a doctor."

"He wouldn't come."

"You go to him. New thing."

"I'm all right."

For a long time she looked at him, and he tried to hold her look, to be placid and resistant.

"I could beat you up," she said. "I could go buy you a bottle."

"I'm all right."

There was the longest pause then, the pause between two people that starts as absence or emptiness but that fills as it goes on with thick stuff, stifling or tickling, so that it might result in an explosion of laughter or a gasp for breath if it isn't ended. Who was going to end it?

"I need to know what you want from me," she said at last, her voice reaching him through the cotton batting. "I don't mean just right now. Maybe I can't give it and maybe I won't *want* to give it but I won't know if you won't tell me."

"Nothing, nothing. Really. I'm okay."

"Nothing." She crossed her arms. She was dressed in heels and capris, for work at the dealership. "Nothing gets you nothing."

"I know. Nothing will come of nothing."

Another pause, or the same one, not yet dissipated. Then she turned and took the two steps to the door and was gone.

He found his tobacco on the bedside table, rolled a cigarette, and lit it, though there was already a horrid brown blister on the chemical blanket where he had dropped an ash.

He heard her car depart.

He was afraid, is what it was. He knew she wouldn't like to know that he was afraid, and he would try hard to keep it from her, but he was; more than anything he was afraid of her, afraid of her certainty that he had choices to make, things to ask of life, a deal to strike. Of course it was impossible to claim that no, he was quite sure there were no choices to be made, not for him, that it was his particular condition or job to have to await what became of him, and see what it was when it arrived. That sounded ridiculous, but it was so; he believed in choice no more than he believed in fate. The best he could hope for was that he would recognize his own story as it unfolded, the path of it as it came to be beneath his feet, and could follow it.

But if there was no more path, what then? How did you hew one, what huge appetite did it take, what certainty of need or desire? What *did* he want from her? Why did she say she needed to know? She'd spurn him if he couldn't answer, that seemed clear. Would that be bad? How the hell did he know? He seemed to have no warrant for such a person as her in his story at all, and how could he tell her that? She'd only tell him to make a new story, as if that was easy. Easy as pie.

He had never made his general happiness, the furtherance of his goals or the fulfilling of his needs, a condition of his love for anyone, certainly not any of the women he had been with. He had tried to find and supply what *they* needed; hadn't asked anything for himself but that they not go, not tire of him, not discard him. He'd never learned—who could have told him, if he didn't simply know?—that one thing you can do to keep her by you, given a general good disposition toward you, is to give her something to do for you: something that, maybe, would take a lifetime. That way she'd remain, maybe. And the thing you asked for would be done for you, too, to some degree, in some way, which would be heartening and lovely even if it wasn't always or entirely successful. *I need your help*. He felt like a robot or a brain in a jar, working his way by deduction toward these unfamiliar common human things.

What, then, could he ask for? What did he want or need? How long was the acceptable wait till you finally declared, if you could? What would the negotiations be like, and how long would they go on, how often be repeated? He might want to just say *Give me something to want and I'll want it for your sake,* but of course that would precisely not do, so he had to think, in his bed in the Morpheus Arms, the bedclothes drawn up to his chin.

After a time—it was long, or short—he heard a big car roar into the parking lot and brake with a pissed-off squeal before his unit, and he waited motionless in alarm and hope for his door to be flung open again.

On Midsummer Day, Rosie and Spofford were married at Arcady. Pierce and Roo went down in the Rabbit. She claimed not to be a friend of theirs or even to know them at all, to know nothing of their circumstances and lives anyway, though it seemed to Pierce that she knew more than she ever said about everything that went on around her, at least in certain strata about which he (for instance) truly knew nothing; she had firmly decided not to go with him, then said she had nothing to wear, and finally came anyway, in a white lace dress and cowboy boots, more visible than she supposed herself ever to be.

"Never been here before," she said as the drive approached. "Big."

Their car was one of many; there was even a boy to point you to a parking place. A Rasmussen wedding could not be small, or hidden; Rosie Rasmussen had tried in every way to make it small, and wherever she pressed it down or trimmed it off it sprang out elsewhere; finally she called her mother in and gave it over to her, and did as she was told. Which for some reason allowed her mother to regard her for the first time as an adult, and enjoy her company, and laugh with her and dispute and approve, as though they were any two people, any two friends with a history. Her mother, rosy cheeked and tireless, seemed drawn back from limbo, at whose gray doors Rosie had last parted from her. She could see now (from the windows of the study, where she and Spofford waited to appear, like actors in the wings) her mother making her way amid people she knew long ago, who greeted her with what appeared to be the same pleased surprise.

Out on those lawns guests were disposed in artless groups, sitting on the grass or the stone seats; wandering musicians entertained (actually these were a few former members of the Orphics, a recently disbanded band; they now called themselves the Rude Mechanicals, and played a variety of instruments). Not far off, sheep munched grass and gave voice, happy that it was hot and green and blue again, as we all were. At length the musicians gathered us all into a great circle on the lawn where once Boney Rasmussen had played croquet, where Pierce had first met Rosie. In those days, he had believed that there were two of her, or that she and another were one. It's the simplest lesson a stranger can be asked to learn, the plainest puzzle to solve, and yet it can for a long while or a little while become inescapable, create all by itself a forest where no man is his own. Anyway now he knew. With Roo he walked in amid the circle—there were actually two circles, an inner and an outer, moving somewhat in contrary directions, as though for a dance, that old dance called *labirinto*—and he saw many he now knew, and many he never would. Rosie had seemingly invited the county, and then some. The last time Pierce had seen so many of them together this way, laughing, milling, celebratory, they were all masked and pretending to be who they were not. Val escorted her mother, tiny and bright eyed. Allan Butterman, the lawyer, was talking with—Roo pointed to him—Barney Corvino.

"Do you want to introduce me?"

"No. Maybe. Later."

At length there came out from the house a child, in white, white flowers in her hair, her feet bare; she carried a bowl or vessel with care. With steady, grave confidence she came into our dance, and from her bowl she took and scattered white petals on the path, or rather she made a path of petals for the two who came after her to walk.

"It's her daughter," Pierce said to Roo. Surprising tears stood suddenly in his eyes.

"Not his, though."

"No. But I think she was a big reason for this."

"Sure," Roo said, and pondered how it was that now children brought about marriages, when it had always been the other way around. Sam's eyes fell on them, but her smile was general, for herself as object of our attention, and for the couple too—he and she, not in white but wearing bright coats and chaplets and holding hands, as though they were taking a stroll in a long-past or just-past age. The former Orphics played Mendelssohn on zither and ocarina.

When they were among us, Rhea Rasmussen separated from the circle, as though just then remembering her duties, and came to Rosie and Spofford and took their hands; she spoke to them words we couldn't hear, meant for them alone, so that we went on talking among ourselves for a moment, murmurs of appreciation touched with light laughter here and there. Then Rhea stepped back, holding the two of them in place before her; we were stilled; Sam with her now empty bowl beside them lifted her face in rapt attention to them and what they might do next, lifting a leg absently to scratch where a bug bit.

The vows that Rosie and Spofford took at Rhea's promptings were the standard ones engraved on every heart there, a relief (Roo whispered to Pierce) that they hadn't made up their own. To have and to hold, to honor and cherish, in sickness and in health, till Death (even he, old friend, among the wedding guests, Pierce for the first time truly took notice of him there) did them part. When they kissed, and all was accomplished, some applauded, as for a performance, and others murmured in awe or delight, as at an accomplishment. Our circles dissolved, and shyly or boldly one by one friends and family came up to embrace them. Roo, gripping Pierce's hand too tightly, turned away with him, a fixed smile on her face.

"I get so embarrassed," she said when they were apart. "All those things they say that they've said before. I mean *she's* said them, anyway. I don't think you get to say them a second time."

"It's always the first time," Pierce said. "Every time. By definition." Roo looked at him in disgust or contempt, and he perceived that perhaps his brand of irony or doublespeak was no good anymore, and he ought now to put it aside, if he could. But still he returned her look in mock surprise. "What," he said. "You don't believe in marriage?"

"I didn't say marriage. Marriage is long, anyway should be. Weddings are short."

"So you're no romantic," he said, as though he'd just learned this.

"Romance is I guess a nice way to start off. But everybody says it doesn't last."

"Everybody says?"

"As you ought to know by now," she said, rifling a steady look at him, "I've never had one work out. In fact you could pretty much say I've never had one at all. Not with all the parts."

He wouldn't look away from her, though her own face seemed to be daring him to do so. "Well, I can tell you," he said, "'cause you wouldn't know, that it's the romance that does last. It's all that's left after everything else is gone. Including her. Or him I guess. That's the problem."

"Then I'm a lucky gal," she said, and walked away.

Pierce, after a moment of chagrin or discontent (Why was she like that? Was the obvious answer as unlikely as it seemed to him? Was he supposed to know, or know better?), turned toward the long tables whereon the food and drink were laid. He encountered Val going that way too, unsteady on the grass in tall shoes, seeming a little out of place altogether in the sun and air, like an upholstered chair, swathed as she was in figured fabrics and hung with chains and (Pierce noted in wonder) a pair of tiny mother-of-pearl opera glasses.

"Hi, Val." He took her arm, and felt leaned upon for real.

"So they went and did it," said Val.

"Yep."

"Tied the knot."

Pierce nodded in solemn agreement, though it seemed to him not so much a knot tied as one untied, a great Celtic knot, one of those mazy ones that though apparently undisentanglable are seen at last to be made out of simple symmetries, a tug at one end would return it to its primal state as an undifferentiated thread or string or braided belt with both a beginning and an end, though both had been hidden in the design.

They were the first at the long table whereon open bottles were displayed, and stacks of plastic wineglasses, which Pierce from a distance had taken as real, as they had been at Boney's memorial, held here too.

"Who will be next," she said, as though pondering an awful force that was mowing down the innocent or the fated. She hadn't ever; neither had he; she never would, he (she knew, from his ambiguous natal chart, still in her files) either would at last, or never would. Barren, anyway, that much was for sure. "Was that Barney Corvino's daughter I saw you come with?"

"Yes, it was."

"Sad story," she said.

They looked together back to the lawn, where Rosie and Spofford were making slow progress through their well-wishers, taking the hands of elders, laughing and embracing friends they perhaps had not earlier noticed among the guests, too busy with their ritual and one another.

"You know," Pierce said, lifting a glass. "This is a beautiful place we live in."

"Yes, it is." They both looked to the shade of the tall oaks and maples, and to the pale hills beyond. "The Land of Heart's Desire."

"Of course no place is that," Pierce said. "Not really. But still."

"Actually," Val said, "it really was. Once. But of course that was before *you* got here." She shouldered him gently, to show she was kidding. Pierce left her to refill and meet her neighbors (and clients, as some of them were) and made his way to where the well-wishers clustered around the wedded pair, waiting their turn. He stood by an elderly man, in a straw fedora and seersucker suit, whom he felt he had seen somewhere, and in this connection, too—maybe only because he reminded him strongly of Boney Rasmussen. He was talking to the Blackbury Jambs librarian, today without her glasses.

"Yes," the gent was saying. "The fierce vexations of a dream."

"Yes," said the woman. "And in the end—what does Robin say? 'Jack shall have Jill, and naught shall go ill.'"

"So he says," replied the elder. "So all the confusions of the night are straightened out. But—as I always pointed out to my students—there's an interesting exception."

A teacher, Pierce thought: and an unexpected envy arose within him. How much fun that had been: to tell people what they didn't know, things that weren't even maybe so important, but that caused that sudden light to arise in their eyes, effulgence of an inward connection just then made. A small sound made too, sometimes, a sort of call or coo that was made on no other occasion. Meaning.

"What exception?" the librarian asked.

"Well, you'll remember that Robin anoints the eyes of Lysander and Demetrius, who both love Hermia, and Cupid's flower causes the both of them to love Helena instead."

"Yes."

"And when Oberon is setting things to rights, he anoints Lysander's eyes with the new herb, and wipes away the effect of the love drug. So that when he wakes, he loves his Hermia again."

"Yes."

"But Robin doesn't anoint Demetrius. When *he* wakes, he still loves Helena, not Hermia as he did before. For him the spell's not broken. And since this makes up two couples, the fairies leave it that way. So Demetrius went to sleep, was put under a love spell, and never wakes up."

"Well, good. It should happen to us all."

They both laughed loudly, heads nodding together, as though they'd pulled the trick themselves. It was their turn then, and Pierce was surprised to see tears in Rosie's eyes as she took the old man's gnarled claw and listened to the words he spoke for her alone.

Pierce approached them next. He too was embraced with sudden gratitude, and tears appeared in her wide eyes for him too; Rosie seemed like a shipwreck survivor come to shore, glad for every human touch. Spofford more manly, each of them pounding the other's back as though to eject a bone from the throat. Pierce thought he smelled in Spofford's beard or collar a sweet herbal smoke.

He was the last in their receiving line, and they took him by each arm and drew him to sit with them at a long table beneath the oaks. They talked there of many things. Pierce felt the sun on his back, and thought he should not have worn black, all he had, though, in suitings. At a silence he asked, his heart contracting in his breast, if Rosie had heard from Mike, and what, and how he.

"Gone," she said. "Still gone." For a month or more as winter went on he hadn't called or come for his turn with Sam; neither he nor anyone speaking for him had appeared at the new custody hearings that Allan Butterman had arranged at last, his claims therefore evaporating as her own had done that day when she had sat for an hour in the wrong room in the Cascadia courthouse, and Sam had been taken from her. He was gone from the county, it appeared, gone from this area, gone entirely.

"I got a call then from Indiana or Iowa or I forget where," she said. "He wanted to tell me he was there, and that he was still here, I mean that he was still, you know. But then nothing more since then. I don't think anything's changed."

Pierce nodded. It seemed not to trouble her to be asked, in fact she put a hand on his black sleeve, as though she knew that it was harder for him to ask than for her to answer, and why. He thought—he had not thought of it since the midwinter, it had come at a time when so much else had thereupon tumbled over on him—how he had on a dark morning given to Rose Ryder two hundred of Fellowes Kraft's dollars, his share of money found in Kraft's house, in a book, where else; two hundred dollars of getaway money, to replace the money she'd paid to the Powerhouse to train her in their theurgies. What if she still had it, what if a time came when. Those bills were oddly large, he remembered, dating from some earlier currency era, and maybe could no longer be spent. Pierce felt the inescapability of all that he and she and all of us everywhere had done, still going on somehow. Inescapable and unreleasable things, altered though at every iteration, past and present like a boy and his mother holding hands and swinging in wide circles, first one standing his ground and impelling the other around and then the other impelling the first, and at the same time both moving forward, across the lawn, across into the future, neither able to go without bringing the other. If that's what he'd meant or known about the way the world goes, then maybe Roo wouldn't have said it was obvious, that everybody knew. Or it was the most obvious thing of all.

He saw Roo now turn back toward him. She lifted her hand from far off. All three of them returned her slight salute.

"How's that Rabbit working out for you?" Spofford said to him. He seemed fully, almost insolently at ease in his atemporal finery, as though he had been married countless times, as though he'd done nothing else ever.

"Good. It's good."

"Nice little vehicle." He had that smile Pierce knew, as though he was playing a not really unkind but unsettling joke, as though he knew something to Pierce's credit that Pierce didn't know.

"Yes."

"Good winter car. Sturdy. Front wheel drive."

"So you're going on with the sheep?" Pierce said, defensive swerve. "How many have they become?"

"Varies," said Spofford.

"You'll sit up there on your hillside, telling your tale."

Roo had come up, and stood silent before the two, listening to the end of their exchange.

"I've got no tale to tell." He stood, and shaded his eyes with a great hand to look into the distance; then to Roo.

"Oh yes," Pierce said. "Oh yes. 'Telling your tale' means counting your sheep. In an older English. 'And every shepherd tells his tale, Under the hawthorn in the dale.'"

"Where does he get this stuff?" Spofford asked Roo.

"Congratulations," she said, and gave startled Spofford a long and ardent hug.

It was time then for cake, and toasts, some of which were long and maudlin, some tongue-tied and earnest. Rosie's angular mother (with her new old husband at her side—he looked splendidly at ease here where he had never been before) told us of Rosie's childhood in this place and in this county, and tears glittered in her eyes. "That was long ago," she said. Last toast was that elderly gent in the seersucker, who turned out to be a cousin, a Rasmussen, the eldest of the clan, and Pierce remembered him then, here among the mourners a year ago—could it be only one, one year? He lifted his glass higher than the others, so high it seemed not a glass of wine but a torch or an aegis, held up for all of us to see: and he spoke in a ringing voice, audible all around, yet not loud.

"*Be* . . . as thou wast *wont* to be," he said. "*See* . . . as thou wast *wont* to see. Dian's bud o'er Cupid's flower. Hath such force and *blessed* power."

Many nodded, as at wisdom, which this sounded like it surely should be; some laughed indulgently; those who had only half heard lifted their glasses anyway. Pierce thought of his own eyes, unanointed or unwashed as yet, maybe probably, and a troubled dissatisfaction with himself and everything he knew and didn't know arose in him. Rosie, though, knew she didn't understand what had been said, and decided she would go ask, but on her way to do that she got distracted, and after a time sat down on a white chair with pale champagne in her hand. Everyone just for a moment had left her, or turned their backs to her. She drank her drink, golden fresh and cold, as though poured in Heaven, or the sky, and thought of a thing that had happened to her almost twenty years before. She remembered it not for the first time since then, nor at all fully, for it was one of those we don't need to fully open to remember, we only need to pat its cover and glance at its frontispiece and there it all is as always, though changed in import maybe.

It was how once when she was a kid, when she still—for just a while longer—lived in this county with her mother and father, and was sent to play at a big farmhouse with a girl she hadn't known before, whom she found she didn't like after spending the day with her in her big bare yard and barn. At last she decided she'd had enough; she'd earlier determined that if she took a dirt road or path through a wood beyond the house, she'd eventually come out on a road she knew, and could walk home. With the other child's cold imprecation following her, she went into the wood, and the way was clear; she expected that in only a little time, not half an hour, the open land on the far side would appear. But in a while, when the way back had grown occluded by trees, the path she followed dwindled away to a track, became less clear (as the other child had warned her it would, trying to keep Rosie with her); she seemed to see its continuation ahead amid the lichened stones and wood plants, but when she struck out to reach it, it somehow snuck away—what had seemed a weed-and-sapling-bordered path was only weeds and saplings when you got there, or seemed to have got there. But it couldn't be far anyway through this middle part before the track picked up again to lead out on the other side, if she just pressed on straight ahead. She went on a long time. She put her foot into a swampy spot and wet her sneaker and sock, which seemed like a bad sign, and the wood did seem to be gazing on her or looking away from her with that unsettling indifference that accumulates in wild places as marks of human habitation get left behind, but Rosie wasn't scared—she was only growing aware that in a while she might start getting scared—and at that point the woods, as though relenting unwillingly, really did thin in the distance, and show sky and space ahead. Then the path reappeared, as she certainly knew it would; she wouldn't have to wander for hours lost in the trees and undergrowth or, worse, have to turn back and face that mean and needy girl again. The track became a path and then a real road, divided into two wheel ruts and a grassy hump between, and she could see where it went out through an arch of trees. She came out. She wasn't at the paved road, as she expected, but at the edge of a ragged field, across which she guessed the road must run. A small field. On one side of it a frame farmhouse, on the other a gray barn. A truck in the drive that led to both. A doll's baby carriage in the drive too. All these things were at once intensely familiar and entirely foreign, foreign because of the impossibility of their occurring here, at the path's far end. The mean girl in her striped shirt appeared, and looked Rosie's way, squinting and uncertain.

Later on she'd read in books how people who are lost wander in circles, and could explain to her mother or whoever she might tell about this (she told no one) that she had proved or illustrated it. But then on that day she didn't think that. She thought (she *knew*) that she had kept straight on, and that therefore the farmyard and barn and house (reversed as in a mirror by her coming at them backward) were actually not the same ones she'd left behind;

she had in fact gone through to where the same things occurred in a different place, and that was the place she now was. She almost turned, to go back the long straight way she was sure she had come, but just then her mother's car appeared too in the drive, come to collect her (as her mother put it), and that evening at supper Rosie was told that they, she and her mother and her father, were moving away from this place and this state, going west to live—told by the two of them leaning close to her and smiling their nicest smiles, touching her shoulders and taking turns to speak softly to her—and so it seemed to her that the path she had taken into the mirror world would just continue, as the backward worlds in mirrors do or must though we can't see them.

Look now, though. She had finally found that path's extension: had gone straight on far enough to have come around again to the unreversed world, and this was it.

Far off she saw Sam, sitting alone on an iron bench. The car salesman's daughter sat down beside her.

Where anyway was that farmhouse, would she recognize it now? That girl, who stood at both ends of the path, in and out again, the same hostile anguish in both her faces? As old now as herself, and gone on as far. A joyous pity struck her, for that girl (Margie!) and for herself. Only one world after all, here where it had always been, like it or not. She had thought a summer ago that she and the county and everybody in it lay under a spell, and somehow it was hers to break it, but she'd come finally to see that of course she never had been, and neither had they or anyone and that's how spells are broken.

"That's a pretty dress," Roo said.

Sam smoothed it with her hand. "We have the same."

"Sort of. I think it's called eyelet lace." She smoothed hers too.

"I have seizures," Sam said.

"I'm sorry to hear that," Roo said. "Do you have them a lot?"

"I had the last one," Sam said. "The last."

"Good." They looked at one another for a moment in quiet stillness. "It's nice for your mom, getting married," Roo said.

"I made them a song," Sam said. "Do you want me to sing it?"

"Yes," Roo said. "Definitely."

"I made the tune," Sam said. "But God made the words."

"Okay."

She began to sing, and the tune was long and lilting, without shape or repeat, an endless melody; Roo guessed it was never the same twice. The words God had made up were not for human ears, apparently, or not for other humans, for they were only Sam's voice put forth in a single vowel or call, shaped by the melody and the movement of her mouth and slim throat—Roo could see it move as she sang. Pierce and Val and Rosie and Spofford heard it too, and Rosie took Spofford's hand, laughing, as though she'd had the gift before, maybe in another form though not different.

Sitting beside Sam, on her left hand as Roo was on her right, was the last of the great crowd of small brothers and sisters Sam had once known well, inhabitants of her old house; he was a girl as well as a boy, he was the mean one who laughed and smiled and whispered in her ear to tickle her until she made him stop. Stop! And for the first time, on this afternoon, he did: he stopped, and he began to go away. He wasn't angry and he surely wasn't sorry, he just went away. And since for Sam whatever departed from her into the past seemed (would seem, always, all her life) not to have gone outward or into the distance or even behind, but to have gone *in*—to have been swallowed by her, or passed away in the direction of her innermost inside (which seemed to her endless or bottomless, containing all of her own self and all of everything that had gone before her as well)—then he remained a part of her, though he was no longer *with* her, and soon wouldn't be remembered by her at all. The last.

Sam couldn't know all of that; nor could she know that the song without words that she sang was the last breath to be breathed, the last spirit exhalation of the previous age, or the first of the new, same thing. What I tell you three times is true: it was the *Hieros gamos* achieved in her own small person, and thus achieved for everyone; it was the final reconciliation, too, of Wanting and Having, Having and Giving, kind Wisdom and hard Knowledge, if only for the space of one afternoon in one faraway county. Never mind; in her singing and our listening was completed the *renovatio* and atonement we all needed, whether or not we knew we had longed for it and sought for it, or would ever recognize we had it. It was the Great Instauration of everything that had all along been the case, the last part of the work set out for all of us to do, never to be finished, as it never has been nor ever will be.

5

After that things would roll forward swiftly and without further contradiction or hesitation, though no one could actually tell the difference. Before long one of Pierce's letters of application got a response; and when a couple of further letters had been exchanged, and a brief visit made, he received an offer of a teaching position at a private school for boys called Downside Academy.

"It would mean leaving," Pierce said. "Leaving here. The Faraways."

She laughed. "Well, that's possible to do," she said. "The roads lead out. As well as in. I," she said, as though imparting a secret, "have been out before."

Here wasn't all he meant, of course, and she knew that too, and he knew she knew. He read the letter again, as though it were hard to understand, needed study; rubbed the paper, felt its watermark.

"How's the pay?"

"It's not good. No. But they give you a little apartment. You have to manage a dorm or something."

"Oh."

"If you're single. If you're married you get a house. Or a House. It's full of kids too."

"You like kids?" she asked.

"Well. I have experience with them."

"You do?"

"Yes. I was one. For some years, actually."

"So go," she said with sudden force. "Go."

That night she lay still but sleepless in his bed. He had never known, among all the women he had lain beside, one who could lie so still, faceup on her pillow like a funerary sculpture, and yet project such a ferocious wakefulness. He tried to match her stillness, and his thoughts were addling into nonsense when she spoke.

"So do you get health insurance?"

"I don't know."

"You didn't ask?"

"No."

Deeper stillness, baleful.

"Pay scale?" she said into the dark. "Like is there a way of figuring raises?"

"I don't know."

"You didn't ask."

"Um no."

"Don't care?"

"Um well."

"What did you talk about? If it wasn't this stuff."

"Latin. Could I teach Latin."

Her scorn was so deep that at last it lifted him to his elbow to look into the mystery of her face. "Listen," he said. "If you know so much about this, about about. Life. All the questions to ask. Then why are you, why. You yourself. I mean."

She didn't move or speak for a long time. He had no way to take back what he'd said.

"You mean," she said, "why should I talk. Because I haven't got shit."

"No. Come on."

But it was so. He could see it even in her still body and the eyes that looked into the dark vacuity of the room; he could almost hear her thinking it. Like him she had somehow come to nothing. She had gone away and not come back, not anyway to the crossroads where she had turned aside; but nothing had become of her out there either, nothing that stuck or stayed. She lived in a room in her father's house, but that didn't mean she'd returned to him, or to it, not really. She had no job but selling cars part-time, which she usually got out of doing, preferring to sweep the floors and file; but she never looked at want ads, not as seriously even as himself.

"Just because," she said, "you know how to get to the future. Just because you know it's real. Doesn't mean you think it can happen to you."

He had the illusion—maybe the soft passing of great trucks at regular intervals, like falling surf—that his cabin was beside the sea.

"But how can you know that it is, or could be, or anyway," he started to say, meaning futures, their metaphysical or ontological unreality all he really knew about them; but she too now rose on an elbow and put her face pugnaciously close to his.

"You're a dope," she said. "What made you such a dope?"

The way she said it made it seem not a mere rhetorical question, insult or upbraiding, and staring at her, searching for a comeback, Pierce for the first time in his life wondered if indeed there were a reason why he was such a dope, one reason, and if it could be known, and if so how, and if known at last, could be wrestled with, dragon or worm or slug at the base of his being, and defeated, or ousted. Would just knowing be enough? Probably not. Necessary, maybe, but not sufficient, and inaccessible to him anyway, right now and always so far, if not forever.

She had watched and waited for his answer for long enough, and turned back to her pillow beside his. She crossed her arms as though she were standing upright and confronting something, him forgotten.

"Any future that gets too close to me better watch out," she said. "If it knows what's good for it."

He laughed then, at this, and after a moment and a sidelong glance at him, so did she. "Shit you know," she said. "I have a really bad attitude."

"Yes," he said thoughtfully. "I like that in a woman." And he and she laughed more together.

Later though, very late, he rolled over toward her in the melancholy bed, and—as though she had not slept at all—she turned immediately to him and put her long arms around him and clung with the single-minded silence of someone who can't swim clinging to someone who has come to pull her out, clinging so fiercely that they might both drown if they don't both make shore together.

After Downside's letter had sat beneath the ashtray on his pressboard dresser for a week, he suddenly (*Oh well*) wrote to accept. For some time he didn't tell Roo, for reasons he couldn't say, even to the other side of his self, the one that didn't show; that he thought didn't show. When he did tell her, she only regarded him for a long time without speaking.

"So when are you quitting at Novelty?" she said then.

"Oh God," he said.

"If you quit they have to give you your vacation pay. A week's worth. Ten days. Maybe you should take a vacation. Before you start this job."

"Sure," he said. "Take a jaunt to a tourist spot. Get a motel."

For a moment he perceived her head, like Oz in the movie, as though engulfed in affronted flames, and expected an awful curse. It might actually be nice to get away, he thought then, run and hide someplace right now, if there were someplace.

"Okay, well," she said. She left with a curt goodbye.

When she came back a couple of days later, she said, "I got an invite." She held out a typewritten letter, airmail stationery. "I'm going to Utopia. Maybe you'd like to come."

"To Utopia. That's *Noplace,* you know."

"It's real," she said. "Really Utopia. The best place. I've wanted to go there for years."

"Me too," Pierce said. "Years. So does everybody."

"Well, it can't be for everybody," she said.

"No?" said Pierce.

"That's what ruins it."

"Ah," said Pierce.

"The masses," she said. "Then you get the Big Brother thing."

"Plus ungood," said Pierce.

"You'll see," she said. "If you want to come."

"You know how to get there? I thought there was a lot of uncertainty about that."

"I do," she said. She took a thick book from her bag. "I've got a guidebook. See?"

A book, another book. A map, directions, commands. But this was a new paperback, and bright with color, and it said *Let's go!* in happy letters, and she proffered it with guileless delight, and the world right then unfolded and laid out the land that the book described, brightly colored and as real as real.

You got to Utopia by flying there; it lay in another direction he had never traveled far in, on the wry neck of the continent, very near the peaks of Darien.

"I can't go to the tropics," he said, even as they drove to the airport. "I hate beaches. I have beachophobia."

"What!"

"I get burned," he said. "I lie on the bare shingle staring at the sun. Me and a hundred naked others, each on his towel square. It's like going to existential hell. And the pointless sea repeating itself."

"Oh for heaven's sake." She wore sunglasses already, in the wintry light. "You don't just lie there. And you don't try to *read.* I bet you try to read."

He didn't admit this.

"Hard books. Small print." She changed lanes, the airport turn ahead. "No. No no. You've got to get up, and walk."

The capital of Utopia was, surely still is, called the City of Eternal Spring. Not its name, but what its name is called. To reach it they would fly to Florida first, and cross the state in a rented car, and fly again from the Gulf Coast. She'd found out it was the cheapest way.

So on the way they stopped in that small and largely bypassed resort town where Pierce's mother and Doris, her partner of many years, kept a small motel.

"You're going where?" his mother said in bewilderment. "You're doing what?" Having been asleep till late, she stood in the kitchen of her small house and office in her rayon negligee (could this be one of those that she'd had when he was a boy? Or was she still able to find and buy them somewhere?) and looked at their swollen backpacks—Pierce's borrowed—and at him, and at Roo. "You hate the beach," she said.

"It's not just beach," Roo said. "It's mountains."

"Jungle," said Pierce.

"Rain forest," said Roo. She put her arm around his shoulder, as though she were the taller of them. "He can do it."

That night, though, she stayed far from him in their double bed in their cabin, which he had insisted on paying for—the same cabin he had once suffered in, you remember—as though a sword had been laid between them. Next day she bade goodbye to Winnie cheerfully, almost euphorically, as Winnie did too back to her, and on the road again, silent beside her in the rent-a-car, Pierce understood in amazement that he, or he and Roo, had started an emotion in his mother, the first new one he had witnessed in decades, and it was jealousy.

The little City of Eternal Spring (high enough in the mountains, near enough to the equator, that its useless thermometers stood every day at room temperature) was plain, nearly paradigmatic: a grid of streets, some named for heroes and the dates of victories and the rest numbered; a brown and white population neither rich nor poor, churches neither grand nor squalid, the one cathedral humbly made of wood. Pierce and Roo took buses here and there, sitting amid placid people and their babies. How still they sat. A peace began to descend on Pierce, and Roo took his hand. Later he would doubt that he had, in the weeks they spent in that nation then and afterward, ever seen a child crying.

Some thirty years before, a brief and nearly bloodless revolution had toppled a corrupt oligarchy. A Cincinnatus from the countryside had come to power; he disbanded the army, reformed the electoral system, set up national welfare and health care. They wanted him to be president for life but he told them No no you must have political parties, and candidates, and you must vote; and then at the end of his term he went back to his ranch, and they did what he had told them to do, and now election days are joyous celebrations, and everyone votes.

"It's true," Pierce said. "All true."

"I know," Roo said. "All true. Not even the police have guns. I told you."

They went on a bus out of the City of Eternal Spring into the country. The people of the country were woodworkers, famous for what they made of the hundred different woods of the forest. Their houses, even humble ones where chickens scratched the dirt, had great paneled carved doors that would last a century. After going a long way downward they changed in a sultry plaza for a smaller hand-painted bus and went upward again, rising toward another mountain (there were three mountains pictured on the great seal of the nation, two tall peaks like a wide green M with the third between them, like Randa, Merrow, and Whirligig in the land from which they had come). The bus lurched, straining like a fat man to climb steep dirt roads increasingly narrow, its holy pictures and beaded valances and rosaries swaying side to side. People got on and others got off. "It's on ahead," said Roo.

Up on the mountain that they climbed, at the end of the tortuous track, was where she had been invited to come. There, a body of American pacifists, Christian farmers, had come long ago fleeing the draft that wanted to take their sons, and there they had established, on the eternal cool green meadows of the mountain's heights, the new nation's first and now its largest commercial dairy. Pierce thought of them arriving here, self-exiled, in a small nation just disarmed, to make milk.

"We walk from here," said Roo, studying a travel-stained typed paper she had carried from the States, her directions; they'd come to her from an entomologist, an old friend or boyfriend, Pierce gathered, who with a dozen other researchers from around the world lived and worked here too, as though in Eden, naming the animals: bugs in particular, of which there were countless kinds. He'd invited Roo; Pierce didn't know if he had also been expected. There were scorpions around too, Roo said; scorpions galore.

"This way saves a lot of time," she said. "The bus goes all the way around the mountain. We can go straight up. There's a path—see?"

They weren't the only ones setting out on it, there were mothers with bundles and children and a man with a machete slung at his waist in a worked leather scabbard, like a knight's sword. Pierce lifted the backpack, slung it over his shoulders as she'd shown him, and pulled the waistband tight. That was the secret, she'd said. You can carry a lot of weight, if you balance it right.

A lot of weight. Almost immediately sweat tickled on his brow. The path wound upward, and one by one those who walked with them came to their houses, small farms and cabins, and waved farewell. Roo asked the way, said the name of the dairy and the research station, and they nodded and pointed ahead. The path entered the forest and narrowed, as though making up its mind what it must do, and then decided to ascend straight upward, seeming to disappear. Take small steps, she called back to Pierce. You don't have to lope, she said. You don't have to stride. Just make a little progress, a little steady progress.

And they came at length over a crest, and into green meadows, right amid the clouds: clouds actually stood on the next higher crest, and the next crest beyond that couldn't be seen at all under its broad hat of white. Black and white cows lifted their heads to see them, and one by one returned to cropping the emerald grasses. A flight of parakeets occurred, red and yellow. A tall, vanishingly thin man was walking toward them, white shirt ballooning, gibbon's arm raised in welcome, what a coincidence.

They three walked together, Roo and her friend in reminiscence. To Pierce it seemed not like visiting the tropics but like returning to the land his fairy ancestors had come from. The lowing cows, belled and horned, were called home at evening, winding slowly o'er the lea. Little lanes led through the dewy grass and along the tangled hedges from house to house, and from their open Dutch doors he and Roo would be hailed in cheerful English, but rainbows, single, double, triple, came and went continually over the breasted fields as the big clouds and their small children passed over just above their heads, and warm showers wet their faces for a moment. Underfoot grew a million small flowers in candy colors, just like the flowers that color the edges of the forest floor in woodland cartoons—they were called, Roo said, *impatience.*

Why impatience? She didn't know. They seemed patient enough to him; the whole place seemed imbued with a holy patience, the brindled cows at evening, the changeless weather—there weren't even silos, because the green sprang yearlong. But at night Roo's weedy entomologist friend—Pierce's too already, unjealous as a saint or a house pet—hung a white sheet on his cabin wall, and shone a black light on it, and from the surrounding night there came will-lessly in the things he studied, in all their multitudes: bugs just like twigs a half a foot long, great beetles like warhorses caparisoned in heraldry, tiny sparks and atomies, moths with trailing raiment green and gold. He told them about the army ants that, on a biological cycle not yet understood, would appear suddenly in billions on the horizon and march like an army of Wallenstein's through fields, through houses even, eating everything in their unswerving path—meats, clothes, green lizards, unfortunate infants; then gone till next time. And he told them to shake out their shoes in the morning.

"Because of the scorpions," said Roo.

They walked up higher, toward the cloudy-headed heights; they sat in a glade—he hadn't before ever found himself in a glade, he didn't think, but here was one for sure—on a fallen log and listened to the insects seethe. Royal blue butterflies of impossible luster visited Oz like blooms, stamen and pistil, comically obscene.

"It's real," Roo said. "It's all real."

"It is."

As they held hands and looked around themselves like the First Boy and Girl, a pair of slow mammals appeared from out of the forest, cat sized, great eyed, with tall tails erect, a boy and a girl, maybe; what were they called? Coatimundi, Pierce remembered or imagined.

"So do you ever," Roo in time said, "really think about kids?"

"In what respect?"

"Well, for instance. Having kids. Being a parent."

"You think about that?"

"Yes."

"It's something you want."

She didn't answer; it wasn't a question; hers to him remained in the air unanswered.

"Well," he said. "I have a son."

She didn't say anything for a time, neither did she move, though she removed her hand from his. "You have a son?"

"I had one. Not a real one. An imaginary son."

Nothing.

"His name," Pierce said, looking down or out but not at her, "was Robbie."

"Robbie."

"Yes."

He knew that he was about to tell her that Robbie, who had not long ago been more real to him than almost every corporeal person he knew, was only twelve, or maybe thirteen, though big for his age in some respects, and of all that happened between them and after. It was as though he could see himself from afar sitting there beside Roo on the fallen log, as though he were at once the poor stupid mortal he in fact was and at the same time a laughing god watching him, watching him dig himself deeper. He told her. It took a while.

"Oh my God that is so strange," she said softly. She had raised her hand to her mouth, as though she saw a wound she hadn't known he bore. "That is so creepy."

He took his own hand, looked at his feet.

"And you just made him up? Just like that?"

He couldn't say that he had made him up, because it was so clear to him that Robbie had arrived, unsummoned; wished for, yes, though not in such a form, not foreseen or imaginable even. Would he have to say *Yes I made him up* in order for him to be able to pass away and not have been? He tried to think of a way to say that it hadn't really been his idea, somehow; that yes he had welcomed Robbie and elaborated his presence—added facts and flesh and a gaze to him, whatever he was—had been glad, so glad he'd come; but that still he hadn't thought him up, had only and suddenly found him to be there, complete, as though on his doorstep. Which he knew mitigated nothing.

"It seemed," he said, "to solve a problem. That's what it felt like. It solved a problem, at last. I was glad."

"But the stuff you did." She swallowed. "I mean are you, is that something you."

"No," he said. "I never did. Never before. Not even when I was a kid. Never. I never even thought of it." He said nothing more for a long time, and she said nothing, only looked at the forest floor, the beasts and bugs.

"I don't know," he said at last, "where he came from. I really don't. I don't know why."

"Was it," Roo said carefully, as though afraid to guess wrong, "like a dream? Like dreaming? Or like pretending?"

"I," said Pierce. It was like dreaming in being given, and unchosen; not like a dream in its willfulness. "Like sort of a dream."

"Well." She touched his arm, and then in a moment withdrew her hand again, as though she found him too hot. "You know how they say everyone in a dream, all the people, are you. You yourself turned around, or put outside of you for you to see."

"Yes."

"And," she said, thinking. "And here's a son and a father. And didn't you want your father's love? I mean wasn't it taken away from you? Like you told me."

"I," Pierce said. "I." Something huge was gathering in the forest around him, and now built toward him, or it arose greatly and swiftly within him, in the forest within.

"So this Robbie," Roo said, "came to get love from his father. Right? You said. And you could give him that. And what you gave, you could get. Sort of in a way. If you're both."

"Both."

"Well, yes, sure. You were him as much as you were you."

"Ah. Ah, ah. Ah."

"Pierce? You okay?"

The sounds Pierce had begun all suddenly to make were startling, outlandish. *Ah, ah ah. Ah ah.* He threw his face into his hands as though to contain them; they seemed summoned from somewhere she hadn't known sound could issue from in a person, and she touched him again.

Tears shed in Eden. It went on a long time, he trying to cease, mop up, then bursting again as though whelmed in grief. It *was* grief, astonishing and right, grief ungrieved till now, witheld for no good reason but ignorance. You were him as much as you. What amazed him most just then, as he wept, was that he could not ever, never ever, have thought of it himself, when it was so obvious to her: she took that old crabbed page from him, turned it over and right side up, and he could read it immediately. Later on what amazed him most was that he had to climb such a mountain to hear it said.

"But," he said. "But then why that, why *that*."

"Yeah, well, that's what's sad," she said. "That you could only think of that. Of that one way."

He tugged his shirttail from his pants to daub his eyes. "He wasn't real," Pierce said. "He really wasn't. And now he's gone."

"He's gone?"

"Gone." Still he didn't dare look at her, still he clung to his own hand and then his knees. "So anyway now you know," he said. "About me."

"Yes," she said. "I guess now I know."

"I had to say."

"Yes."

"Yes."

Unsilence of the glade.

"There's more," he said.

To travel down from that green mountaintop was to pass through one climatic zone and then another, the air growing hotter, the vegetation changing, until they reached the sea, the unstilled Pacific. He swam with her and he lay beside her under the netting of their bed, for some nights in a stillness and isolation that finally neither could stand, then making cautious plain love while the bugs gathered on the net and watched. He walked, as she taught him to do, walked for miles behind her and beside her along the tiger-striped coconut walks, or over the beast-shaped rock heaps that lay in the surf just off the endless empty swathe of sand; he studied her and thought about her, he found himself waiting for something she would do or say, without knowing what it was, thinking maybe it had already been said and he had missed it; he recounted his own story to himself, seeking for the premonition or foreshadowing that would point him toward what he must say or do. Why was this so hard? Coleridge had written (yes he'd brought a big thick *Biographia literaria,* small print, hard thoughts) that "the common end of all *narrative,* nay of *all* poems, is to convert a *series* into a *whole*: to make those events, which in a real or imagined History move on in a strait Line, assume to our Understandings a *Circular* motion—the snake with its Tail in its Mouth." And a poet is a maker, and a *poeia* is a made world, and in his own world or history, real or imagined, he perceived no such figure, long and hard as he had tried, much as he desired to.

And if not that story, what? If he had reached deep enough into the sun-erased pages of the *Biographia* he held, he would maybe have noticed where Coleridge mentions the distinction made in alchemy between the *automatica* (things that are changed by a power in themselves) and the *allomatica* (things that are only changed by the action of something—which in alchemy is almost always some*one*—else). *Automatica* can change, and change back, but only the *allomatica* change by changing what in turn changes them: a spiral rather than a circle, going on and not returning. But he didn't get that far.

"So tell me," he said. "If somebody sometime wanted to ask you to marry them, do you think that having had such a bad time before would . . ."

"No."

"No?"

"No. Like they say: that was then, this is now."

She had in her hand a bottle of soda, and on it was a picture of Betty Boop, looking like an old flame of his, or every old flame of his, as she always would, and her name in this country was Lulú.

"So if," he said.

"Watch it," she said. "It says in all the books that you're not supposed to propose when you're on vacation."

"All the books?"

"You're having fun, you're free of everything, feeling romantic. You can fool yourself. You could make a big mistake."

"Thanks for the warning. I'll take no steps without consulting you. But I wasn't proposing."

"What were you doing?"

"Wondering."

"As usual."

"As usual."

Anyway it *was* there, of course, it had been there "all along," that prolepsis, foreshadowing, figure, destiny he felt he needed: the three of them (of course it was three) at the Full Moon party, rising naked together before him from the waters of the Blackberry, the endless river: *a dark, a light, a rosé*. And one of them her. There they are still, unchanged except in meaning, or rather with their meaning not yet unfolded, a *complicans* of which his life thereafter was to be the *explicans*. Pierce no longer remembered seeing them, right there at the beginning, nor did he understand what it had meant, if it really had a meaning beyond or within the fact of its having been. So his very last solemn wish went forever ungranted, unspoken in fact, though not the less urgent for that: his wish that he might, please, be allowed to do what he must, and to know it too. But no, he had to choose it for himself, by himself, in ignorance and incertitude, and then do it. And eventually, but just in time, he did.

6

Three years later, Pierce sat down in the office of the dean of studies at a community college in a northeastern city, to be interviewed for a teaching job.

The dean was struck by the shape of his résumé, as anyone considering hiring him would have to be: how he had quit or been let go from Barnabas College, where he'd been tenure track, then vanished (the résumé described work on a book, but there was no book) and some time later surfaced as a second-tier private-school dogsbody, teaching history and English and running the chess club and the debate team. Pierce, hands clasped in his lap, knew what this looked like, and knew better than to account for it. Never complain, never explain.

"Downside Academy," said the Dean. He was a boulder-shaped black man in a tight three-piece suit and stiff collar, tight too, gray bristles on his big cheeks. "I'm not real familiar with this institution. Is it large?"

"Small," said Pierce.

"Downside?"

"Downside." It had been a fine, even an evocative name for years, but now the trustees were rethinking. "It's about fifty years old."

The unsmiling dean continued to regard the name, as though it would grow transparent, and allow him to see the place itself behind it. "You had a house there."

"I was a housemaster, yes," Pierce said, and felt a wave of pointless embarrassment.

"You're married?"

"Yes. Three years."

"Your wife teaches too?"

"No. No, oh no. She's. She's going to be studying to be a nurse. She's actually been accepted at a school here in the city. That's one reason this position would be. Well." He stopped this line, his own convenience not the important consideration here. He crossed his legs.

"It's good you're continuing again in your vocation," the dean said. "I think you will find the students here to be different from those you might have had in the past, at other institutions. Some of them will not be as prepared as even the upper students at your private school were. On the other hand they'll bring to your classes a wealth of other experiences, life experiences. And you'll find them eager to get from you all that they can use in their own lives. Unlike some young people in other institutions, most of our students—and not all of them are young—they mostly know why they're here, they know what they want from this place, and they are ready to work to get it. They are remarkable people, many of them."

Pierce nodded. He was leaning forward, all ears. He thought he could descry what the dean meant, and what those students might be like, and in what sense his own case was theirs. He found himself moved by them, never having met any of them, and by the round man before him, by his tender gravity, his careful pomposity, and how he might have come by them, after what experiences, like his students'. Moved too by what he, Pierce, was being charged with: his old vocation.

"Frank Walker Barr," said the dean, returning to pore over Pierce's slim résumé. "There's a name."

"Yes."

"You did your thesis with him."

"Yes." No, not exactly, but Barr was certainly not going to come forward to deny it. Not any longer.

"He was never found," said the dean.

"No. Never found."

Years had passed by then since Barr had disappeared into the *sahará* south of Cairo while on expedition with two other scholars. Never found: no rumor, no body, no story. He had (maybe, probably) walked out at night from the lodge where the party had stopped. The Valley of the Kings, the American papers said, but it was actually a nameless place to the south of that, near the ancient location of the island sanctuary of Philae.

"Remarkable."

"Yes."

"A great scholar."

"Yes."

Isis, still worshipped at Philae, said a writer at the end of the fifth century

CE. It was Isis who "by roses and prayer" returned Lucius Apuleius from his asinine to his human shape when he was visited at last by a vision of her. *Her vestiment was of fine silke yeelding divers colors, sometimes yellow, sometime rosie, sometime flamy, sometime (which troubled my spirit sore) darke and obscure, covered with a blacke robe whereas here and there the stars glimpsed.* (It's Adlington's translation.) *And she disdayned not with her divine voyce to utter these words to me: Behold Lucius I am come, thy weepings and prayers hath moved me to succour thee.*

The desert sky is nothing like ours—Barr had used to say this to the students in his History of History seminars, Pierce among them—and as soon as you stand beneath it you know, he said, how certain you can be that the stars are gods, and near us.

I am she that is the naturall mother of all things, mistresse and governesse of all the Elements, the initiall progeny of worlds, cheife of powers divine, Queene of heaven, the principall of all the Gods celestiall, the light of the goddesses: at my wille the planets of the ayre, the wholesome winds of the Seas, and the silences of Hell be disposed. Leave off thy weeping and lamentation, put away thy sorrow; behold the healthfull day which is ordained by my providence; therefore be ready to attend my commandment.

Dawn winds rising as night turned pale.

Barr had written, in the draft of his last unfinished book, about how a lifelong student of myth, its cross-cultural transmission, its continual transformations, can feel at times like a parent watching children act out a story for their own pleasure: the way the plot is liable to be softened or hardened or curtailed or reversed, the boring or unintelligible parts flashed through with a gesture and the amusing parts repeated and expanded, characters swapped among actors so that one actor may end up battling with himself as another person, the whole transmuting suddenly into a different but similar tale, and never ending at all. "Any such student, as any parent, can tell you of the tedium these constant developments inspire, even as they assert again and again the endless willingness of the human imagination to play, the eternal primacy of the hand over the clay, the teller over the tale."

"Let us consider all this," the dean said at the end of the day, "and get back to you. Real soon, I think."

Roo had put up with Downside as long as she could, which was less long than Pierce, his general immobility her constant grief and burden. She'd knocked around the big once-fine old house that they managed feeling as though stuck daylong in the hour between rising and going to work: washing and tidying and readying and finding this and that, the whole place smelling eternally of morning, of unwashed boys and their belongings and their food and drink and their sneakers and unmade beds—the boys, too young anyway to be so far from home, and some of them very far from home, in effect exiled, following her on her rounds to ask pointless questions or tell tales about sports or homework or home, just to be near someone motherlike or mother-shaped, she thought: once, one sitting beside her on the sagging couch had simply bent his little cropped head and laid it in her lap without a word. It was the need that got her, when there didn't really seem to be a need for there to be a need. Why did they get sent so far from home?

Meanwhile Barney far away got worse and worse without her. Something debilitating drained him of his cheer, and when it was diagnosed as cancer (prostate) he at first summoned his considerable will to protect and sustain what was left of his wonderful life, but by then the odds had tipped out of his favor; the cancer metastasized; weekends Roo packed a bag and left the house to Pierce while she went with her father through that, his needs the reverse of the needs of her growing boys, but just as demanding. Barney somehow did fine day to day, anyway as long as she came often, to notice new things that ought to be seen to, and to get him out to doctors. Roo soon learned that, like the dead Egyptians Pierce told her about, the only way you made it all right through this passage was if you had a guide and a mentor, somebody to fight for you and negotiate for you at every station. That was Roo. Her only sustenance was what she learned, about what to do and how to do it, learning more every day from men and women who knew, the doctors and nurses and the social workers, they were all called *caregivers* now.

"You should see," she told Pierce on returning late. "You should listen to them talk to these old men." She meant the nurses, shift after shift. Barney was in a VA hospital by then, mostly men, mostly but not all old. At their kitchen table Pierce gave her coffee, which she had come to need at all hours of the day and night though it seemed to have no effect on her. "They have this—I don't even know what to call it. Humility. The good ones do, not all."

"Humility."

"I mean that they just keep on seeing these guys as people, no matter how far off they go; even when somebody stops responding, stops talking, seeing, eating, *thinking*. I mean they're realistic, they know what's happening, they try to be very truthful and observant, but they don't write them off, not ever."

"Uh huh."

"They talk to them. Hi, how are you today. Somebody just this side of a cadaver. One nurse told me: I know he's not in there anymore, but he's still right around here somewhere. He can hear. He minds if I don't say hi."

"Uh huh."

"How do they. That humility. It's what you have to have. Never thinking you know when somebody's life ought to be written off. It must be so hard. You could pretend, but it's not like being a used-car salesman. It would be hell to go to that job every day and pretend. You just couldn't. Your heart would die."

Pierce listened, pondering the limits of his own humility, his own humanity. He'd never liked Barney, and he wanted to stay as far from Barney's yellow canines and domineering intimacies as he could get. But his own father. Himself. *If you do not know how to die never trouble yourself,* Montaigne said. *Nature will fully and sufficiently instruct you; she will do all that part for you; take you no care for it.* Maybe not, not these days.

When Barney had at last made it over (his cropped head, too, laid upon her lap) Roo told Pierce she wanted to go to school and study nursing. "It's a future I can see," she said to Pierce. "But also it's really the first one I think I can get to."

"Okay. I'll help."

"It's actually a good job. A good career. Steady."

"Yes."

"It's gonna cost, though. You have to trust me."

"I trust you," he said.

After a further interview, Pierce was hired by the community college.

"It was a tough decision," the dean said. "I hope you don't mind my saying that. I myself was a definite yes vote. I thought we could overlook some of the gaps in your CV." He leafed through the file he held. "You know we never got a letter from the dean of Barnabas College. A Dr. Santobosco?"

"Really."

"No matter. You impressed me, Pierce, and not only with the accomplishments. You can't always go on those alone. You have to go with what you see."

"I hope," Pierce said, "to live up to your expectations. I certainly will try to. You have my promise." And he meant this, with all his heart, as he had meant so little in his life; almost, indeed, couldn't get through the saying of it for a hot lump that rose in his throat. He got to his feet, and shook the dean's great fat warm hand.

"First we'll go down and look at your office," said the dean, taking a big ring of keys from his pocket. "You'll be sharing with Mrs. Liu, whom you've met, she's Elements of Communication."

"Yes."

They went down through the plain halls of a standard utilitarian building, the dean greeting students with a raised hand as though in blessing.

"In here."

A battered gray desk, near another similar but different one; steel shelves and a gooseneck lamp; and a wide window.

No he hadn't been an alcoholic, or insane, nor had he burned down his life smoking in bed, or thrown it away by mistake like a winning lottery ticket, but he was as grateful as if he had done a thing like that, and been saved, for no reason. *Lucius thou art at length come to the port and haven of rest and mercy:* thus said many-colored Isis to Lucius the Golden Ass, not an ass anymore at last. *Neither did thy noble linage, thy dignity, thy doctrine, or any thing prevale, but that thou hast endured so many servil pleasures, by a little folly of thy youthfulnes, whereby thou hast had a sinister reward for thy unprosperous curiositie; but howsoever, the blindness of Fortune tormented thee in divers dangers: so it is, that now unawares to her, thou art come to this present felicitie: let Fortune go, and fume with fury in another place.*

"Welcome to our family," the dean said.

So Pierce and his wife became urban pioneers in that city, which was a real city in a real conurbation and not just a hallucinatory compound of fears and longings, omphalos of a smoky underworld—say it was Holyoke, or Bridgeport, or Albany. It was a city that had got rich very quickly about the middle of the nineteenth century and then slowly got poor again. When it was rich, and the rich didn't mind living near the factories and mills and canals that supported them, the city had built splendid neighborhoods of huge houses, houses that now nobody wanted, for most of those who could afford to live in them wanted to live farther away. Even Roo and Pierce—moved as they were by the big echoey rooms with parquet floors, the curved bay-window glass, the massy radiators and tubs that the desperate salesmen pointed out—in the end couldn't feature managing so much.

But then they found, beyond those proud sad streets and their great trees, in the direction of the (former) farmlands, one of those little suburbs that about 1910 developers were arranging out at the end of the trolley lines, places designed to be the best of town and country. Once surrounded by rose-burdened walls, entered through rough ivy-clad brick gateways (gone when he and she drove through in the Rabbit), it was surrounded now by a shabby nameless precinct of the city, and overlooked by a medical building done in raw concrete (they would see its minatory red cross in their bedroom window in the leafless winter). But it still clustered around its own little rocky sunken parkland and duck pond, and the Tudor red-brick and Queen Anne shingled houses were nearly all still there, some clad in vinyl siding, some with fiberglass carports or chain-link fences. Several of them were for sale.

The one they got, where they still are, was at the end of Peep o' Morn Way, right on the Glen (as the parkland was called). It was absurdly narrow and tall; two stories faced on the street, and another went down behind as the house fell off a steep ledge into its little garden and backyard down in the Glen. Oh it was cute. Tall trees watched over it and its neighbors; its paneled door sheltered shy behind an arched trellis and a fence; a little gate opened in the fence by the house's side, and a winding wooden stair went down and around the house until it reached the backyard far below. Down there they could glimpse, as they stood by the gate, a wooden bench, and pots and potting tools, and a pair of old gardening gloves.

It was probably the gloves that sold it.

It was large for them, three stories large, though each story was no more than two or three rooms deep or wide; they had no plans to fill it further when they bought it. No *firm* plans, though looking back Pierce can see himself propelled by an unspoken urgency toward propagation. Roo had always told him she couldn't imagine growing old all alone, and he came to know that what Roo could not imagine she would not allow to befall her: she would instead bring into being what she could imagine.

7

On the fourth anniversary of their marriage, Roo won an office pool at the dealership in Cascadia that the salesmen had put her name into, a sort of memorial to her or to Barney. The prize, to Pierce's horror, was a pair of tickets to Rome and four days–three nights in a chain hotel to which Barney's dealership was somehow connected.

"Uh-uh," he said to her.

"What?"

"I don't want to go back to the old Old World," Pierce said. "Besides, I'm not sure it still exists to return to."

"Let's not be silly," Roo said with something like patient indulgence. "*I* am not returning anywhere. I've never been, and I think it would be a good and great thing to see what you've seen."

"You don't want to see what I've seen."

"You'd be good to go with. You could explain it all to me. The churches, the pictures. The meaning of it all." It had surprised Roo that, on the odd occasions (other people's weddings or christenings, chance, curiosity) when they found themselves in a Catholic church, Pierce was able to decode the surreal images in plaster and stained glass, the woman with the toothed wheel, the man in brown with the lily, the man who wasn't Jesus bound to a pillar and pierced with darts, the effulgent bird and crown, the random letters, INRI, XP, JMJ. "Couldn't you?"

"I suppose I could. A lot of it."

"We'd come home different," she said. "I mean by a different way. Barney used to say—I don't know where he got this—that the Roman legions when they went somewhere to conquer something always came back by a different way. That's how they mapped the world." She did that herself, in the states of the New World, accumulating knowledge. She liked houses that were planned so that you could go from room to room in a circle to return to where you started, rather than having to retrace your steps. She never wanted to retrace her steps. Pierce seemed to himself to be one who never did anything else.

He was right, though, that the City, however Eternal, was not there to return to. The place to which they arrived, after passing eastward through the night and raising the sun over the Middle Sea, was not the place he had been before, only resembling it in certain sly ways, places with the same names and histories but otherwise different. It was midsummer, and the streets and squares were filled with crowds of people young and old but mostly young, and from all over the world, laughing girls with bare brown midriffs and crowds of boys behind them, passing from place to place, standing six deep to toss coins into the Trevi Fountain, clustered beneath Bernini dolphins and playing guitars and flutes and radios for one another in the transfiguring sun.

But it wasn't just that, the crowds and sun, it was the place itself, which had somehow shrunk or contracted into a small brightly colored place, a toy-town, all its funny old monuments and historic sites open and the people passing in and out. Places it had taken him so long to find, places he had never found, turned out to be mere steps from one another, clustered together like a theme park, no longer containing the past, just a pleasant setting for the present to occur in. Where were the endless dark avenues he had trod in confusion, the puzzles of entwined streets impossible to escape from? Where were the shuttered prisons and palaces he had come upon by chance, so far from one another?

"Oh, hey," Roo said. "Look at the elephant!"

It was in a little piazza no more than a New York block from the Pantheon; he must have walked around it again and again without ever stepping through this little passage, or that one, or the other one. For a long time he stood before it, watched Roo walk up to pat it. She laughed at the little beast, more Dumbo than Jumbo in size, and the absurd great weight of the figured obelisk it bore on its back.

"What's it say?" Roo said to him, pointing to the tablet beneath the elephant, the writing that explained it all, in a dead language. "What's it mean?"

Pierce opened his mouth, shut it again. As though in a Rose Bowl parade or carnival or mass demonstration, he observed a set of explanations proceeding to the forefront of his mind from the deep old interior: a line of floats and figures great and small, in groups and singly, mounted and afoot, led by the elephant they stood before. Hooded sodalities bore the *Crux ansata* and papyrus rolls brought from the fall of Constantinople, Colonna and Botticelli the great folio of the *Hypnerotomachia Poliphili*, open to the page where the elephant is shown. There came theriomorphic deities of Egypt, made into parables by Baroque symbologists, Hermes with finger to his lips bearing a smaragdine tablet, rendered with hieroglyphics that supposedly said *As above, so below* but actually didn't. Athanasius Kircher, the Jesuit who studied the Egyptian picture language, including the symbols cut into this very obelisk, and proved they were the unsayable terms of a mystic philosophy. Sir Flinders Petrie and the Invisible College in its winged car, Pope Alexander and Io, queen of Egypt, the *crater* of Mercurius, the *arcana* of the Masons carried by apron-wearing men in drip-dry shirts and fezzes. Walking alone, the gloomy Huguenot figure of Isaac Casaubon who showed that Hermes Trismegistus wasn't really Egyptian at all. All moving forward, and then moving past, moving on. The Monas, in Father Kircher's version, that collected a Cobra, a Scarab, the Ptolemaic planetary nest, and more into John Dee's bare bony symbol. The same symbol cut in a ring. His cousins on a ragged hill in Kentucky marked with it. Charis feeding him snowy coke from her poison ring, asking why people think Gypsies can tell fortunes. Julie Rosengarten in a New York slum apartment lifting her hand to him, the nails painted with symbols, Sun, Eye, Rose, Heart, saying, *It makes a lot of sense.* Rose Ryder moving her finger over a wineglass rim and raising a faint eerie wail.

"I don't know," he said. "I can't say."

He did tell her that the church before which the elephant stood was called Santa Maria sopra Minerva—a church of Mary over a temple of Minerva, and before that a temple of Isis too. He said that in the Dominican priory opposite, Giordano Bruno had been tried and condemned to death when at last the Dominican inquisitors stopped trying to get him to renounce what he believed he knew. He tried to tell her something of what Bruno believed: infinities, transmigrations, relativities. He told her what Bruno had been heard to say when the judges pronounced sentence on him: *I think you are more afraid to hand down this sentence than I am to receive it.*

"What did he mean?"

"I don't know." They walked out of the square. The Dominican priory looked like an office building, though perhaps it was church offices. Blue glow of fluorescent bulbs. A blind just then drawn. "It may be he was saying that if the church officials felt they had to kill a philosopher investigating the nature of things in order to keep their power, then it couldn't last as an institution. Someday it would lose. And someday after that it would just dry up and blow away. And he thought they knew it."

"Did it?"

"Yes. It did. A hundred years later it had no power to kill people anymore. And it has less now."

"So he was right?"

"No. If real power could be annihilated by wisdom or shame it would have been, long ago. But look at the Soviet Union today. Still there."

They wandered on. The empires were gone, here where tourists trod.

"Did they really kill him?" Roo asked.

"In public. Here in Rome. At a place called the Campo dei Fiori."

"Oh? And where's that?"

"Well, I guess it can't be far," he said. A strange burble of laughter arose in his breast or throat. "I guess. Right around here somewhere."

"Have you been there?"

"No."

"Okay," she said. "First off, I've got to go buy some things. I need some tampons. I don't want to go any farther without some. Dumb I didn't get them before."

"Okay."

"There was a whatchacallit, a *farmacia,* a few streets back that way." She turned, her outstretched hand moving like a clock's, and pointed. "That way. I'll go back and get stuff, and meet you."

"Okay."

"So what's the place again we're going?"

"Campo dei Fiori."

She pulled out the map from her bag, and together they found the little square. "Yeah," she said, "see, it's a triangle from here. So you go on and I'll go back and we'll meet there."

"Okay."

"Okay?"

"Okay."

She started to put the map back in her bag—she had glanced at it once that morning to orient herself, then refolded it and put it away, and they had just wandered together—but instead she withdrew it and gave it to Pierce. Then she was gone.

Pierce looked around himself to see where he stood relative to the map. He found the intersection of streets where he was, and could trace with a finger the way to the Campo dei Fiori.

Okay. He set out.

Within minutes he was not where he had thought to be. He walked to the next corner, and it was not the street he expected (or now, rather, hoped and prayed) it would be. He looked from the map to the world, the world to the map, making no connections. He turned the map this way and that, trying to match it to his own stance and the way he faced, but could not. He walked another block. The sun stood at midheaven, no help there. He had no way to choose a way.

He was lost.

He could perceive no reason at all to go one way rather than another. It might be that if he chose a way it would immediately lead him to a place he recognized, where he could make a clear choice: but within himself there was no reason. It was Roo who had made the city intelligible, because it was clear to her; he had only shared in the order she perceived; without her it disintegrated in a moment, he couldn't hold it together.

The thought that he might not find her again at all, or for hours, and have to endure her scorn and her bafflement, was terrible. But what was more remarkable (he still hadn't moved, the chattering young people and burdened tourists passing around him like a tumbling brook around a stone, a *pasticceria* on one side of him and a store selling religious goods on the other) was the thought, also just unfolding within him, that perhaps after all he was a profoundly limited person. Not just inattentive, or feckless, or forgetful, but actually incomplete. Someone who did not know, and could not by effort truly discern, where he stood in space, or where the things and places around him were in relation to one another. He could learn from experience and habit how to perambulate the places he lived in, and this could sometimes give the appearance that he, like others, had a map of the surrounding space in his brain. But he didn't. He clearly didn't. He was missing it, a part or organ others had, as someone might be missing an eye and be unable to perceive distance.

He turned one way, then the other, and started walking. He walked slowly but not attentively, for he had given up trying to know what to do or where next to go. After a time he stopped again, with a choice of ways to make. The street was named *Vietato l'affisione* (it said so on the corner building's side, where as he well knew Roman street names are posted, but the crossing street seemed to be named the same, *Vietato l'affisione,* Old Affliction Street?). He thought of all the times he had stood just as he stood now, ashamed of his bafflement among his fellows, or so ensorcelled he couldn't even notice his fellows. There was a place in the city of Conurbana where two streets crossed, on one corner a photographer's shop, on the corresponding far corner a store selling children's clothing. There he had stood trying to find a way back to Rose Ryder's apartment. There he still stood.

"Hey." A hand was put upon him. "Wake up."

"Oh Jesus," he said. "Oh hi. Hi."

"Doing good," Roo said.

He looked from Roo, slipping her arm in his, to where she pointed, a fingerboard he hadn't seen labeled Campo dei Fiori. They went that way. They passed again the *pasticceria,* the store selling crosses and incense. He tried to tell her what he had learned, alone on the streets, without her; what he knew now.

"I know," she said. "I know what you mean. It happens to me in dreams. Go someplace, you can never get back again to where you were. You can't remember where things are. Or they're not there anymore."

"Yes. But not in dreams."

"Just concentrate," she said. She stopped him, and took his shoulders, looking in his eyes. "From here, which way's the hotel? I mean which compass point? You know."

He looked at her and could see reflected in her face his own blank one.

"So never mind," she said, releasing him. "Ask when you don't know. Ask for help. If you need help, you ask. That's all."

"Well."

"Men are so bad at that. Everybody says."

"*You* never ask. I've never seen you ask."

"I always know."

"Oh. Okay." He wouldn't tell her how often—suddenly a long parade of incidents, all similar, tumbled backward from this moment to some far-off original—how often he had asked the way, of strangers and loungers and busy shopmen and a hundred others, and listened to them and watched them point, and stood beside them trying to sight along their fingers to see if he could see what they saw, and learned not much, and went a block or a mile or a turning and asked again. He had told no one, not even himself, how bad it was.

It was very bad. He walked holding Roo's hot hand and it was as though with each step he was changing from vegetable to animal, or opaque to transparent, growing more clear about how bad it was. It wasn't some trivial flaw or amusing tic, a stutter or a missing digit; no, it went all the way down into what he was and what had become of him, all that he had and all that he lacked, all that he knew and didn't know, all that he had imagined to be possible and all that he had failed to see was not. It was the reason he was here, and also the reason why he was not elsewhere. He couldn't tell if he felt cursed or liberated by knowing, only that he knew, and knew for sure. He thought that if Roo or someone like her were to be able to inhabit his sensorium they would see the problem too—well of *course,* given *this,* no wonder.

No wonder he had never known what was to become of him, or been able to choose one way ahead over another, or imagine the future to be inhabitable. *Because space is time.* The flaw in his knowledge of space was not different from his bafflement in time. How have I come to be here? he would ask, of a place, a street, a dilemma, a context. Where was I that I could have reached here from there? Which way should I now choose? Or he could not think even to ask. What do you want from the world, and how do you plan to work your way toward it? His uncle Sam had asked him that, and other people, kind or impatient, had as well. Where do you want to be in ten years, Frank Walker Barr had wanted to know when Pierce was in school. Not a question he could address, either then or later, much as he would have liked to, shamed as he was that he could not, and with no good reason to be so unable. But there *was* a reason. There was. Not yet an explanation. Not yet, if ever, a cure, or a fix. *What makes you such a dope?* If he knew, could he cease to be one?

"Look. Here. See?"

The Campo dei Fiori was a small narrow square, seemingly unchanged since the Renaissance—no baroque facades or churches, just tall houses in shades of ochre and orange, and the flower sellers' tables, as they must have been then.

"It means *field of flowers,*" Pierce said. "Or *place of flowers,* I guess maybe."

"Bloomfield," Roo said. Her hands were in her jeans pockets.

"When I read about it first," Pierce said, almost unwilling to take steps there, "I thought it meant a flowery field, like a meadow. I could see it. Tall grasses and flowers, and a platform and a stake."

"He was burned at the stake? I always thought that was a kind of joke."

"No joke."

The long square was filled with loiterers, the lights coming on in cafés, music from radios and guitars colliding. There was a fountain, not running now, a long narrow trough, and at its end a statue: a man in a flowing robe and hood. It was strangely hard to grasp that of course it could be no one but he, his jaw set in defiance, his hawk's eye on the future, in the Dominican habit he never wore again after he left Italy for the great world.

"That's what he looked like?" Roo looked upward into the hooded face.

"Nobody knows what he looked like. There's only one picture, maybe not even contemporary." Yet somehow this false craggy hero with only a virtual interior made it certain to Pierce for the first time that the man had, in fact, lived and died.

The monument was dated 1869. There was an inscription in Italian, and around the statue's base were scenes in bas-relief of Bruno's life (teaching his heresies, defying the Inquisition, being burned), and also a set of medallion heads whose significance Pierce couldn't at first work out. He expected Galileo, but couldn't find him. After some study he discerned that one of them was Peter Ramus. Ramus! Bruno's nemesis, the iconoclast, neo-Aristotelian, inventor of the outline. So these faces weren't Copernicans but victims of religious bigotry: yes, here was Servetus, killed by Calvin; and Hus, the Bohemian ur-Protestant. Tommaso Campanella, another Dominican, magician, utopian, who got out of the Inquisition's prisons just in time to die. Ramus, Pierce recalled, was murdered on St. Bartholomew's Night for being a Huguenot. How annoyed Bruno must be, to share a plinth with him.

Two young people at Bruno's feet, spooning (living young people, not bronze), looked up at Pierce when he laughed, or wept. *Che?*

"Bruno," Pierce said, pointing up. "Giordano Bruno."

Ah yes. They nodded, looking to each other for more, getting nothing. They looked up at Bruno above them as Pierce might at a statue of Millard Fillmore in a public park. Just then Roo came up beside him, and she bore a trio of red roses, just bought at one of the flower-sellers' stalls around them burdened with poppies and roses, oxeye daises, lilies and blue lupines. She put them in Pierce's hands. Swallowing in embarrassment and grief, with the incurious eyes of the hylic youth in their beauty upon him, he laid them at the statue's base, and stepped away. He took Roo's hand, amazed to see her eyes had filled.

"There," she said.

The next afternoon they went up through the Castel St. Angelo, as Pierce had done alone: Hadrian's empty tomb, the catacombs and tunnels now as harmless as a funhouse, laughing children in plastic sandals racing up the newly cleaned and plastered spaces lit with bright strip lighting, laughing at the underground dungeons and at the tub made for the fat pope, who was hoisted with that block and tackle to take his bath, no really; and up and out into the sunlight, all Rome around. There was an alfresco bar there, at the very top, fully furnished with bored waiters, Campari ashtrays, wooden tables under grapevines, and all other things. The *prigione storiche,* though, were gone: Pierce circled the tower twice to find the entrance he remembered, but time had closed it and hidden the door. There wasn't even a sign.

"Maybe it was someplace else," Roo said.

"No. It was here. I can't understand." He had told her how he had visited that cell, the cell that might or might not have been Bruno's, the stone bed, the high narrow window, the strip of sky. "It couldn't be anywhere else."

They had come around again to the same place, the arched way back downward, the tables of wine and coffee drinkers who pointed out at far places in the city beyond.

"I'm sorry," Roo said, and took his arm, sad for him: but his own heart actually lightened, as though a window had opened within him, light airs allowed in, and old things out. Oh well, he thought: oh well.

"We'll ask," Roo said. "We'll go back and start over."

"No. They've probably been renovated out of existence. Probably somebody found out they were really just storerooms after all. Revision."

They sat instead, and ordered wine. The sky was clear green and gold, stained with dark contrails. Of course he knew that they were there somewhere, the row of dark doors, one of them his, and he felt sure he knew now why he wouldn't and couldn't find them, why no more than in dreams could he go back to a place he had once been, start over, and find the right way ahead. But it was all right. The world is only a cruel maze if you think you ought to be able to find a way from where you have been to where you want to be. He knew nothing of the sort; where he had been was the unvisitable Then, and this was the never-before-imagined Now. So maybe he was, and had always been, if he had only known it, a lucky man.

8

In an April of the following decade, Rosie Rasmussen drove over to Cliff's, going the back way over a hump of the Faraway Hills from her office in the Rasmussen Conference Center. Unafraid of spring mud in her new car or truck (it was a little of both, and called a Sport-Utility Vehicle) she went down an old road officially closed, bouncing and splashing hilariously through a slough at the bottom, and stopping to hear what she hadn't yet heard this year: peepers in their hundreds.

Upward again, and the roads improving as she rose, till the still-bare woods gave way a little and there were houses, many new ones, some huge ones, on new-made lots. A dozen years before no one lived out here but Cliff; pretty soon now it would be a neighborhood, the school bus would have to come. In some of the new driveways there was a Sport-Utility Vehicle like hers.

Cliff's place was still part of the woods more than it was part of the world. The entrance, marked only by a yellow mailbox on the other side of the road, was as easy to miss as a woodchuck's burrow; you turned in and went down a rutted way through a tunnel of trees more than a dozen years taller than they had been that first time she came, to a fairy-tale glade, where Cliff's house was. Cliff had made the house, with Spofford and others too to help sometimes, and it had seemed raw and just hewn when she had first seen it (Spofford was bringing her then, to have her heart healed or looked into): made of bare beams and boards, a row of old storm windows not all alike making up a front wall, the scragged necks of trees that had been roughly executed in the yard. Now it was different: the never-painted wooden heap looked ancient and gray, archaeological even, a lost galleon at the bottom of the sea. Not forbidding anymore. Maybe because she'd come so often since then; maybe because her heart had healed.

Cliff was working on the engine of his truck, an oily rag on the fender where tools rested. He looked up to see Rosie drive in and roll to a stop. He too, she thought: fifteen years ago his hair was as white as it was today, and almost as long, but back then it was shocking, wrong, like his pink pale skin and colorless eyes. Now he was only, or might seem only, an old man gone white with years.

"Hi, Rosie."

"Hi, Cliff."

"Just let me clean up."

"Don't hurry."

He smiled. It's what he told her: don't hurry. What he had told her so often, as though he knew she had a lot of time, when she didn't feel she did: no time at all.

When Spofford first brought her here, Cliff hadn't been at home. It was the Fourth of July, emblematic summer day; it was the day of the night Boney died, leaving Rosie (though Rosie wouldn't know it for some time) in charge of his house and his family foundation and all the business he had refused to finish. So that day nothing of what Spofford said Cliff could do was done to her.

Once, when Spofford was at his lowest, coldest, saddest, Cliff had bent over him, placed his mouth against Spofford's breast and made a sudden loud noise. A noise like a shout or a bark. *Hey! Wake up!* And Spofford had felt the whole of his being shaken, and startled tears had rushed to his eyes.

She too, when he had done the same to her: like one of those machines they start a stopped heart with. He had done it only twice.

He made her tea, which she didn't really need but which she thought he had his own reasons for wanting to occupy himself with. His house smelled of the fires that had burned all winter in his tall stove—his wife, Cliff called the stove, because of its matronly hourglass figure maybe, and its merry warmth. He asked Rosie about herself, about Sam.

"Sam's away," she said. "Did I tell you where she's going?"

"No."

"The Antarctic," Rosie said gravely. "Can you imagine?"

"That far."

"It's a university research trip she was selected for. Two months. She ought to be there by now."

Cliff took no notice, but she knew he listened.

"So, Cliff," she said softly. "Do you ever think of that night."

"That night."

"When Beau and you and I went to The Woods." She took the cup he gave her, and put her hand around its warm body. "That night in winter. When Sam was there."

He sat before her, sliding onto his stool with that wasteless motion, and bending toward her as though she had not asked for a memory or a story but offered to tell one.

She didn't need to, of course. Cliff knew it. How Sam's father, Mike Mucho, had joined a supposed Christian group, the Powerhouse, and they'd helped him to get legal custody of Sam. How then on a night in December Beau Brachman had gathered them, she and Spofford and Val and Cliff, like a SWAT team or band of brothers, and they had gone up to The Woods where the Christian group was squatting, and Cliff and Beau went in, and in a while they came back out, with Sam. And never after had that group or Mike complained or tried to get her back or sued to recover her. Why? No one could tell her that either. Mike went away to the Midwest where he'd come from, just a trip, he'd said, and then to California, where eventually he'd married a Christian wife; he'd sent long letters to Sam telling her stories about God and prayer that she liked at first and then grew bored with, then angry at: like a tiresome old aunt who keeps sending you babyish clothes or cheap jewelry long after you've got too old for it, because she can't really imagine you.

He loves you, though, Rosie would say.

He doesn't love me, Sam said simply, a fact. How can you love somebody you don't know?

Rosie had never decided if Sam had really ever been in danger from those people; it might be (she thought later, not then) that they were well intentioned and kind enough in their way, but only narrow and self-deluded, their conceptions driving them to cruelties they couldn't even perceive or count as cruelties. Maybe. But what she remembered—it was all that she could remember now with any of the intensity she'd felt then—was how Sam was returned from dark to light, danger to safety, like a lost child in a fairy tale rescued from an ogre who had imprisoned her and meant to eat her. It seemed at that moment, that winter night, as she took Sam in her arms, that the world ceased rocking in its socket and settled down to turn equably again.

Even the weather. Hadn't a drought, one that had lasted for months, ended the very next day—well, it might have been a week later—in a series of vast and heartening snowstorms all over this sector of earth? Heartening, exhilarating, alarming finally as the ploughed snow piled over Sam's head and nearly over her own, as it had when she was a kid herself; she watched Sam incorporate it all, the felt physics of frozen water, bluejay on the seed-speckled snow-clad pine, unforgettable even if you never exactly remembered it either.

The time she had spent there with them in The Woods, too. She'd had a seizure there, before Beau and Cliff and Rosie had arrived. Rosie used to ask her, with care, then and later: Sam, what happened? Do you remember? Do you remember being there? And she always said she forgot, or wouldn't say what she remembered.

The two profoundest words there are: *remember* and her brother *forget.*

"She's okay then," Cliff said, as though that were his answer to her question.

"She's good."

"Beau," he said. "Beau asked me that night to go up there with him. He said it meant everything."

"He told me that too. But not why."

Beau also told her, that night, that she wouldn't see him again, but not why, or where he would go, and thereafter no one had heard of him again, or if they heard of him, what they heard was that somebody else had heard of him, or seen him. But he never came back.

"Where is he? Don't you wonder? Don't you want to know?"

"If he wanted me to know, I'd know," Cliff said. But he didn't try to show in his face that this made it all better. "You know some people think he'll come back, maybe after a long time; that things will come back around, and so will he. Sometime. But some other people think the world is made differently; that it doesn't go around in circles or in spirals, that it splits."

"It splits." Rosie was content to listen to these things, not questioning or even doubting them, as she never had when Beau talked about them. She only thought they didn't have anything directly to do with her, or the world she inhabited: they were like travelers' tales, tales of lands from which the tellers had come, to where they were going.

"It's like a Y," Cliff said. From a cluster of pencils and pens in a cracked mug he took out a black wooden pen with a chisel point affixed, a Speedball: Rosie had one like it. And a paper from a pile of scraps. "If the world is like a Y, then you can never go back. He can never come back." He dipped the pen in a bottle of India ink, and drew the letter on the paper: where the pen's point struck the paper flush, it drew a wide vertical bar, the upright, and then another wide bar, the left-hand way, the pen pulled toward him to intersect with the upright's top. And last the right-hand way, the edge of the pen point sliding upward from the intersection, leaving only a slim trail.

Y

He turned it to face her. "If the world without Beau in it goes the big way, and he took the narrower way, then he only gets farther away the farther on we go."

Rosie studied it, the great brace or crotched tree he'd drawn. She thought: if it were drawn by a left-handed man, the left way would be the narrow one. And she thought of The Woods, and the night. Suppose it was we who had left the main way then, and he'd gone on. Without us. "Is that what you think?"

"No," Cliff said. "I don't think there's one big Y in the road, where the world turns off. Parts company. No. I think there's a Y every single moment we're alive."

"Did Beau think so?"

"I don't know," Cliff said. "He and I. We start from different places. It's why we could work together, sometimes. Sometimes not."

"Different places how."

"Beau knew—he thought, he believed, he saw—that everything begins in spirit. He thought reality was spirit, and the physical things and events of life were illusions, imagination. Like dreams. And he wanted us to wake up. He knew he couldn't just shake us awake: for one thing he knew he was dreaming too, most of the time. What he thought he could do, what could be done, is go down into dreams, the dreams we share, the dreams we call the world, and alter them. Or he could teach us how to alter them ourselves. He said that he could be leaven, like Paul in the Bible says we can be."

"And then."

"And then, if we could do that, we'd know they were dreams. All hopes and fears, power, pain, but also all gods. Ghosts. Earth, nations, space and time. It's not that they don't exist; they exist *as dreams,* and people are bound by them. They exist as much as anything can. But none of them is *final,* even if everybody shares them."

"And you don't think that?"

"I know what he means. I listened. I heard." He looked around himself, and ran his hand over the surface of his table, smooth and varicolored wood and not quite level, like a plain or a body's back. "I think I'm from here," he said. "I think this is so, this is actual. I think that all we do and can do and will do arises from it. I just think we don't know all of what *it* is. We learn. We learn by doing what we think we can't, and when we can, we share, and so we find out more of what *it* is, or can be."

"So spirit's made of this too," Rosie said. "Made here. Home-made."

"I think so."

"But not Beau."

"No."

"Do you think," Rosie said, "he could dream a place for himself to go off into and be lost? Lost to us, I mean."

"Maybe. Not something I know."

"You used to say"—Spofford used to quote it to her, so that it became her truth too over time, to be used with a thousand meanings—"you used to say that life is dreams, checked by physics."

His great broad smile at once shy and cocksure.

"Beau I guess wouldn't say that."

"No," Cliff said. "But Beau's not here, and I am." He took away from her the cup he had given her. "Do you want to do some work?"

At the post office in Stonykill Rosie emptied the Rasmussen Foundation's big box, a slurry of stuff, it never stopped coming, glossy announcements and posters and news of other conferences elsewhere, in other centers here and abroad, a great circuit or intellectual circus entertaining itself. Among the stuff was a letter for her, though, in a hand she knew: not a postcard but a real letter.

Mom—I've got some bad news, bad for me anyway but not bad bad. I tried to get away with something and it didn't work, and now I'm in trouble. Here's what happened. I didn't tell the captain of this boat, ship I mean, or the director of the program, that I'm taking seizure medication. I know I should have, I know it was the right thing to do, but you know sometimes I get tired of telling people, sometimes I want to just not, and be like everybody. Don't tell me there's no "everybody." I know. I just want to be like everybody. You don't know the feeling, but you don't need to know. Anyway I got separated from the damn pills, and I couldn't go searching for them, and what do you know, after five years okay, that very night I get hit with a biggie. Wet the bed and all. I still might have got away with it except that my bunkmate was awake and saw it and freaked. O God they were mad. Ranting at me for concealing a serious medical condition, breach of trust, impossible for me to go on with them.

No oh no. Oh poor babe.

So there I was like the Ancient Mariner and I've got to go. We had to turn back so I could be put ashore. I thought they were going to leave me on an ice flow or floe. At least we were only a day out of Rio Grande on Tierra del Fuego, where by the way the phones aren't working this week. There's a plane out tomorrow to LA, I'll get Dad to get me there maybe. Mom I'm so hurt and ashamed. I wanted so badly to be there. I get why they said what they said but I wanted to be there and I wanted them to take a chance, and they wouldn't. So I'll call. I'm coming home.

Life is dreams, checked by physics: and physics made or ruled biology, and so also our brains and the flaws in them, and also the medicines that sometimes fixed them, which were dreamed up by other brains, their dreaming limited by physics too, which they therefore had to learn. And they did learn, and kept dreaming, and so did Sam, and only stopped where she had to. For now. Because maybe physics has no end, no end we know, any more than dreaming does.

Oh my dear, oh my dear dear.

But she was coming home anyway. The thought filled Rosie with an expectant hunger, a wondrous craving to see and touch her again. Almost scary to want something—no, someone—that much, but more wonderful than scary: wonderful that you could so much want to have what you actually had. The thought of Sam called down into her heart as Cliff's yell had done long ago when it was asleep or cold: woke it, and started quick tears in her eyes, as though it was, itself, their source.

She drove out through Stonykill and took the turn now marked with a new sign that pointed discreetly but plainly to the Rasmussen Humanities Conference Center up the tree-lined way.

It was the smartest thing Rosie had done as executive director of the Rasmussen Foundation, and she was still proud of it, and it still made her heart clutch in panic sometimes when she thought back on it, of the nerve it had taken, the chance of screwing up. Allan Butterman, in the course of some dealings he had with the state university, had first noted the possibility and alerted Rosie to it, but it was she who'd done the work, gone back and forth to the university to meet deans and alums and the president, a fearsome woman whom Rosie could actually call *not so bad* in the end to Allan when the deal was done and the press release sent out. So "Arcady," which was the name a nineteenth-century Rasmussen had given to his new shingle-style fairy castle in the Faraway Hills, was now the university's Rasmussen Humanities Conference Center, and the university was responsible for it, for its plumbing and its boiler and its pretty multicolored slate roofs, for the professors and scholars who came and went there in season, like migrating owls or hawks. Rosie was greeter and facilitator and majordomo, and ran the foundation's business from an office under the eaves in what had been the attic before the splendid renovation. Fellowes Kraft's little villa too had been included in the deal, also now renovated and rearranged and repainted, new windows punched in the old walls and new floors laid. From there and from this great house the proprietary ghosts had vanished gratefully, like old ulcers healed or old errands run at last; their only reality had been their persistence. And every workday evening Rosie pulled a plastic hood over her computer and went home to her own handmade house at the verge of an old orchard up on the slopes of Mount Randa, to the man she still called by his last name (Spofford) and not his first, which would have been odd if she had changed her own name to his on that June day when they swapped rings and those vows at once so profound and so unenforceable, but she hadn't, she was Rosalind Rasmussen, as she had been when she first learned she had a name.

The first conference at the Rasmussen Humanities Center that Rosie oversaw when the renovations were done was entitled "Wisdom and Knowledge:

Gendered Hypostases in Western Religious Discourse." How scholars were to spend days in discussion of a topic even whose name she could not understand was a mystery to her, but she was new to the game, and she'd learn.

There were three scholars bound for that conference who met at the Conurbana airport, coming from three different cities. They were a large round one, a tall lean one, and a very old one; two were acquainted, the third they knew only by reputation. They each were to be greeted there by someone from the conference center, but each had neglected to notify the organizers of their arrival time, and now, finding themselves together and alone, they decided they would take the initiative and rent a car and drive themselves the fifty miles (it couldn't be more) to the center. It was Rosie Rasmussen's constant grief, the way these academics would get up to things like this. The car was a Caprice, and the large round one took the back, the other two the front. Bloom, Wink, Quispel.

"Since the Renaissance we have believed that man is making up these stories, that we ourselves are the authors of the tales we live within. That's the ultimate arrogance of power, the arrogance of the gods: for all the gods believe themselves self-created." That was the tall thin one at the wheel speaking. Old Route Six wound through winter fields, and night fell.

"Man is projecting his own illusions on the patient screen of eternity. This solution is so simple that it can't be true," said the very aged one. He rubbed the frosted window with the back of his gloved hand.

"All thought is necessarily sexual," said the large one in the back. "Except in the case of those few great souls who can liberate themselves, and bear the terms of freedom."

"And this is done by . . . ?" asked the driver.

"This is done," said the man in back, "by remembering."

Night had fallen when they reached the turnoff to Blackbury Jambs, and there they misread the brief instructions they had, brief because it was thought they wouldn't need them. They wandered into the village, and asked at the Donut Hole—just closing its doors—where the conference center was, and received directions; went up the Shadow River road, all wrong, past the closed cabins and camps, through Shadowland and past the Here U Are Grocery, the three of them silent now and wondering: but at length they came to a tall lightless sign. *The Woods Center,* they made out in their headlights, and turned up that way.

The Woods Center for Psychotherapy had long been closed by then. No buyer had been found for the great pile, full of defects obvious and subtle. Once that pseudo-Christian cult the Powerhouse had gone so far as to make deposits and sign binders but in the end had failed to meet the stiff conditions that the owner (the Rasmussen Foundation) had set for a purchase, God not choosing that way for them. There could have been no mistaking the fact that the place was shut up, and yet the scholars were drawn to park their little car and get out—the two in front, anyway, the third in back looking on with anxious care. They went up the path of wrinkled ice, arms outstretched for balance, to the great central portal. From there, doors led into each wing. The tall scholar went to one door and pushed on it; it was locked; the other scholar went to the other door, and it, incredibly, was not locked, not even latched, and it swung open at his touch. A strange desire or fear entered him. He called down into the darkness, the other beside him now and also looking in. There wasn't any answer.

How long they waited there they would not remember clearly (when at length they got to the Rasmussen Humanities Center at Arcady, and had company around them and drinks in their hands before the fire in Boney's old study). Laughing at themselves, perturbed and exalted, they told their tale once again. *A charisma,* said the oldest of them. None of the three said that it was a light burning in a window of the large lounge on the main floor that had drawn them on, a light that had been burning a long time, and was now seemingly going out; but it was not a light you could name to others, even if you had seen or known it yourself.

Pierce Moffett missed that first conference, though its subject was one he would have been glad to hear about. A paper was read there in the freshly painted music room entitled "*Sophia prunikos* and Snoopie Sophie: Gnostic Persistence in Popular Culture." But he and Roo were not in the Faraways then, or in the country: they had returned together to the little Utopia on the green mountaintops, to adopt a girl child.

9

All Pierce and Roo's great efforts to produce a child of their own had failed. She thought that it was the old abortions, those refused children, that were the cause, though doctors couldn't locate any harm she'd suffered; she imagined that no baby soul was willing to take a chance on her again. And since there was no organic reason to be found, it did seem some deep reluctance on the part of their children to materialize: they seemed to hover just beyond the physical, just not paying attention maybe, or maybe trying their best to turn that way and set out but failing, just as their parents were failing, despite the recipes they followed, ancient and modern. It was profoundly frustrating and saddening, to Roo, thus to Pierce.

So it was a good thing—and Pierce spending his working retreat among the barren celibates of an abbey could see how good a thing, when he thought of his daughters waiting at home—that Roo was the kind who could set out on the way to finding a child for herself by other means, and begin to compile the files of agencies, and type up at night the notes she had made in the day, and call phone numbers and go to the agencies and state with great firmness what she wanted, what she was prepared to do, and what she needed therefore to know. It was a process as arduous and vivifying and scary and uncomfortable, and just as long, as any pregnancy, and the outcome just as doubtful.

Until at length they came down out of the skies, holding hands, to Cloud-Cuckoo-Land again.

The little country had a social welfare system it was proud of, especially the efforts it made on behalf of mothers and children, and in front of the modern building where Pierce and Roo went first to be greeted and (once again) interviewed and given forms to fill out, there was a great statue of a mother and child. The rules for foreigners adopting the country's abandoned or orphaned children were strict: whenever Pierce and Roo were asked for some further information, or made to vow some vow, or supply some required proof of their intentions or their identities, they were made to think of how many wrong things might happen; had happened no doubt in the past, not so long ago.

They were taken from there to a city orphanage to meet Maria, their prospective girl child. Her mother had died in giving birth to her, their guide said (black hair in a severe bun but her arms soft and plump). Toxemia, Roo said, you can never tell who'll develop it. Roo had admitted to Pierce that it was easier that the child was orphaned rather than abandoned or given up: she wouldn't at least feel guilty about stealing a mother's child, who might one day. Though she did feel kind of guilty, she said, that she felt that way. They drove through the grid of streets and out to the suburbs; their guide, in an English that she pronounced with a ferocious effort at correctness, told them other stories, of how the country's children came to be given up: the common panoply of human griefs and wrongs, poverty and drink and desperation and incompetence. So the country had changed, or wasn't just what they had thought it was before. That's what Pierce said. "Well, of course they've still got *troubles*," Roo said. "They always did. All the usual ones. There's nowhere people don't. And this isn't nowhere."

"Just not extra ones."

"Yes."

"War. Tyranny. Displaced persons."

"Yes. That's all."

The place they were taken to—one of many to which the national placement agency was connected—was a Catholic orphanage, but as plain and white and simple as though run by Quakers; nuns in white smocks with only a workmanlike suggestion of a veil. They were given over to one, who took them inside. Soccer practice in the courtyard; the children stopped to watch them go by. In the nursery, Disney characters painted hopefully on the walls, the preternaturally quiet children of the country in a miscellany of chairs and cribs.

"Why is she crying?" Roo asked in undertone.

"Who?"

"The nun."

She was: a tear and then another formed in her eye and hung on her fat cheek; she looked devastated. "Maria," she said, with a kind of sob, and picked out and lifted to them the child who would, or might, be theirs.

All infants, almost all, can do what this one did when Pierce and Roo looked down at her and she up at them with her great eyes: the thing they do to new mothers, but can also do to strangers, to flinty maiden aunts, to the crusty bandit or miser in stories who unwraps the mysterious blanket, looks inside. If they couldn't do it—most of the time anyway—we wouldn't be here.

"Ask her why she's crying," Roo said sidewise to Pierce, who shook himself from Maria's eyes to see that yes, the nun was still brimming, unspeaking but uncomforted, and regarding them.

"*Estas lagrimas,*" Pierce said to her, guessing, and pointing to his eye. "*Que esta es?*"

She looked at them a moment as though in wild hope or fear, and turned away, and went out, and then in a moment she came back from the adjoining ward and in her arms she held another baby, wrapped in the same blue and white blanket, with the same huge eyes full of what surely *seemed* to be wonder and love and happy expectant need, that's the trick of it, and she brought this baby before them, and placed it in Pierce's lap, right next to the one in Roo's lap, Maria.

"Jesusa," she said.

Any two babies can look very much alike. Roo and Pierce both thought that thought, for a moment. Very much alike. The nun wept quietly, her hands clasped before her.

"I never *thought* of two," Roo said to Pierce. "I didn't imagine. I never once thought of two. Did you?"

"No. Never." He had not, in any practical way, been able to think of one; had dreamed and imagined, had seen himself in some conceivable future holding the hand of a small black-eyed girl—as though in a movie, himself and her, on their way to, oh, school or the candy store—but he knew this wasn't *thinking of* the way Roo meant it.

They sat with coffees in a *soda,* back downtown now. The place was open to the street like a stage set with the fourth wall missing. Ancient cars of kinds no longer made in the land they had come from, Studebakers, DeSotos, went by slowly; Utopia is a country of slow drivers. The table they sat at—had been sitting at a long time, stunned and silent mostly—was red, white, and blue enamel, with the word PEPSI written on it in swirling blue letters, a message from his youth.

"I don't know what to do," Roo said, devastated. "I can't think. I can't take one and leave the other. I can't."

"No?"

She looked at him as though suspecting he could, and shocked by the suspicion. "No. No, I don't think I. I *couldn't*."

They sat silent. He thought of Jesusa appearing in her towel or wrapper. Was that even real?

"Maybe it was just a terrible dumb idea," she said. "To come here to this country and dig around for what we want, not knowing anything. How could that go right." She stared at empty futurity. "We should just go home."

There are some silences and stillnesses that we remember afterward with greater vividness than acts: as though even after a long time, after years, our souls can still flow out of us and into them. As Pierce's did then.

"No," he said then. "We won't go home."

"Pierce."

"We'll take them both."

She clapped her hand to her brow, staring down at the coffee spill on the enameled table. "Pierce. Don't say that. You don't have to. You're a good guy, I know you want this for me, I know it. But don't be stupid. Don't."

"No," he said. "Not for you. For me. It's what I want. I want this to happen, I want to take both of them home. It's the only way, and it's what I want."

"No."

"Yes."

"Pierce," Roo said. She had grown still, ceased to comb her hair with her fingers and slap the table; was only regarding him. "Think about it. What it's going to be like. This is years and years of commitment. All your life. Two, not one but two, and it may be that even *one* you could be sorry about, and think later you'd made a mistake, in a way you never could if it was your own, you see? Have you ever thought about that?"

He hadn't, really; she could see that in his silence; and in his silence she could see him understand that she *had* thought about it, which she had never plainly said before.

"I mean can you see what this is going to take? Can you? I mean just the *money*."

"No, Roo," Pierce said softly. "No, I can't see."

"Can't?" she said.

"I can't, no. I can't really imagine. You're right. I never have been able to imagine the future, or see what's going to come of what I do, or of what anybody does. I can't do it. I don't know why. I try to work it out, practically, but I never really can."

"Yes."

"You know."

She said nothing, but of course she knew it was so, had always known, and from now on (he thought) she would know he knew too.

"So I can't tell what this will be," he said, "or what it really means, no. But it's what I want. I know that. And if you'll do it with me, then I'll do everything I need to do, whatever it is. But just step by step. Just step by step."

The *soda* was filling up with men and women, men in white figured shirts, women with children.

"Really?"

"Yes. I want to do this."

"I don't know how you can say that without knowing."

"Well, I'm saying it. And you don't know everything anyway."

She wouldn't smile; he wished she would, and he refused to think that she didn't smile because she truly saw all that lay ahead, for him and her and them.

"Both," she said at length. "Oh my God."

He waited.

"We could go back there, at least," she said. "Arrange another visit. We could ask, ask what, what . . ."

"Okay," he said. "Okay then. Come on." For a brief moment the *soda* around him, the poster for Emu cigarettes and the coffee machine and the Pepsi tables and the street outside lurched or sank as though preparing to vanish, but that was only because of his own rising to his feet, his own lifting of himself by his legs and arms, which changed his Point of View and the world with it. Relativity. It all settled again peaceably in an instant, and he felt in his pocket for taxi fare.

Maybe it was only because Roo had been so well prepared for the future she had previously cast for herself that the different future she was offered had unsettled her so badly. Pierce thought this later, when not having the two of them was inconceivable. She wept in the taxi, she shook her head to shake him off when he asked why, but shook her head too when he offered to turn back.

Strong and clear, though, and fearfully gentle to take one and then the other in her arms, then to do what had to be done. *Come on,* she said to him, and he did. It meant starting all over again, as she had known and he hadn't, because the forms, stamps, seals, permissions, visas, authentications, oaths couldn't simply be copied exactly, alike as they would need to be; they were identical yet unique, as Jesusa and Maria were. And there would be a journey home alone for one of them, Pierce the one, and back again, as the unbearable days and weeks slid away.

But then on the airplane together, going home bringing them both, looking down at them as they looked up or slept or woke; bigger already than they had been when the four of them had first met.

"What'll we do," Roo said, leaning over close to him, "about their names?"

She'd asked before. "I don't know," Pierce said.

"Their names are their *names*. New ones would be so . . . fake."

"But."

"Well, I mean you know. Maria, okay. But together with Jesusa?"

"I know. Why are we whispering?"

"You can't just change one name; that would be terrible."

He thought it would be too, and thought maybe he knew why. "Well, we'll change both. Maria can be Mary. Mary, Mary, sweet as any name could be."

"Okay and?"

"Jesusa. Jesus. Hm. Well, he said I am the way the truth and the life. Via Veritas Vita. How about one of those? An epithet."

"I thought an epithet was a cussword."

"No no."

"Say them again?"

"Via. Veritas. Vita."

"Vita," Roo said. "I might actually have a relative by that name."

"Vita," Pierce said. "Life."

It's what I want, he'd said in the *soda.* He felt again, with huge, calm pride, himself saying it, as though it had been the first time in his life he ever had, and in the deepest way it was: the very first time. And he had felt his soul thereupon coming back to him, double.

"This isn't going to be easy," Roo said, and that too she'd said before.

It wasn't easy, though sometimes it was delight, the unspeakable delight that's in hymns and songs, *the valley of love and delight.* Sometimes it was atrociously hard, hard as a rock face he climbed toward a retreating summit, he'd had no idea. Once, with two babes asleep in his arms, a working wife asleep in the couch's crook, he watched on TV in pity and fellow feeling a climber, defeater of K2 or some such peak, who told how he was once benighted in the midst of scaling a sheer wall, and he had a little sling hammock he could string up on his pitons and sleep there in a crevice, like a bug on a window blind. And all night he hung there? Yes. It was cold and lonely, he said. Often he cried. Then in the dawn light he went on.

Stressed out, they said to one another, to the other parents they inevitably came to know, who marveled at their fortitude, two at once. *Stressed out,* as though they were metal members of some machine at the limits of its endurance, heating up with torque and tension, about to fail. Only now and then in the midst of uproars and disasters to be granted a blessing by the cold moon as he stepped outside his door, a charisma of blessing, a pause anyway for an eternal moment.

With so many things to do each day that must be done without fail—a circumstance he had never been in before, except for his own transmuting dreamworld imperatives and curses—Pierce found that not only could he not foresee real futures, he couldn't remember the present; he was, very likely had always been, absentminded to an almost pathological degree. He had lived mostly alone, and his disremembering had not come much to the attention of others, and so he always supposed that he *could* pay attention and keep his business straight if he really needed to; the problem, however, was apparently a part of the great flaw he had discovered on the streets of Rome: it was beyond the reach of his will, and though it could be mitigated, still he would forget his children at day care, leave their dinners in the grocery cart when he went to cash the check that he then found he had forgotten to bring. He would leave the children themselves in stores or public places, wander off, and then, when in horror he remembered them, be unable to find his way back—but that was only in dreams, all fathers have those.

He was proud when he seemed to be mastering the basic arithmetic of a life lived with schedules, a mortgage, twin children, and a couple of aged cars, but Roo was meanwhile doing higher algebra with the same quantities; he felt himself to be in the doghouse, often for reasons he couldn't entirely discern. I'm not a saint, he thought angrily, at the sink after a round of impatient reproaches, and all in a moment—glass and towel in his hand—he thought that though he surely wasn't a saint he was, or maybe could be, or had been, a hero, and if that was so, then he knew where and with whom he stood.

He laughed out loud. She turned, babe in arms, to shoot a baleful or warning look at him from the door, thinking maybe she was mocked, but he shook his head, no nothing, go go, doctor's waiting.

The third person of the trinity, last in the sequence or story. She who came after the Mother, who bore the hero, and the Beloved, whom he sought with pure heart and willing sword. (He'd just been reading about her in an old book of Barr's, *Time's Body*, where Barr in fact dismissed the triune figure as synthetic.) She was the Crone, the one who buries and bears away. Also appearing as the Ill-Favored Lady, who humiliates and challenges the hero and charges him with interpreting her commands and unriddling her harsh riddles, to labor under her sanctions until liberated. He makes no complaint, nothing he can't bear, but it's not just about bearing, suffering, patience: it's about the creation of a new self, one without grievance, longing, regret over the self's old hurts.

So with her the hero enters into a new stage of life, the last. And the goal would be to win a death: so to behave as to have a right to die.

He had put down neither dishrag nor polished glass. The house was all still around him, just for this hour, and for a long time he only stood; the water babbled softly from the faucet. It was so: anyway it made sense, which is the same thing, as far as some matters go, matters like this one. He had been young, and now was not; he had been given daughters into his care, his four-eyed *anima*, and the Crone to obey, to learn from. To learn at last both how to act and how to yield; how to be both agent and patient, and be changed himself by working to change another; how to grow old, how to die.

"Oh that is such bullshit," Roo said to him, not unkindly, when on a later night Pierce (in purely abstract or mythopoeic terms, nothing personal) described this tripartite scheme to her. She pulled her flannel nightie on over her head, got into bed with her wool socks on. "You don't believe that stuff."

Bullshit it exactly was. Roo beside him was no avatar; she was of this earth; more than anyone he knew she belonged nowhere else, on no other plane. Which was strange, because she had felt herself kept out of this world for so long, and finally had to break in, and find a way to stay. Just as he had needed to be chastened and cajoled down or up into it, into here where everybody, everything, was. One world, where they could both only be: which she had had to break into, which he had tried so hard and so futilely to break out of.

All the while, that world went on ceasing to be what it had been and becoming instead what it was to be. It had been winter back when Pierce first went to Europe, all those old states under snow; the worldwide spring that had seemed to sprout universally in his own twenty-sixth or Up Passage Year had by then already turned back and blasted by a cold wind from the east that then just went on blowing. *Prague in Winter,* said the *New York Times Magazine* one Sunday in 1979 after Pierce returned, having not however gone there, and the big pages showed the snow thick on the palaces and the statues he hadn't seen, the people in the cobbled streets bent into the wind and the weather. It was the deep cold in the bones that was meant too, the despair as things got only worse, the hunkering down to survive, to not waste energy; the resolve to wait and hope, or to forget hope; the temptation to eat the dog, and maybe the neighbor too. *Unicuique suum* in the jailer states of socialism.

Winter; spring. Barr had written, in the old book that in another winter Pierce was rereading *in memoriam,* that human culture turns centrally on the transformation of biological and physical facts into *systems of opposition.* Higher, lower; pure, impure; male, female; alive, dead; dark, light; youth, age; night, day; earth, heaven. In the economy of meaning these were the counters; the world is maintained as it is in the keeping apart of these pairs, and shocked into change by the combining or dissolving of them. *There are certain scholars (J. Kaye, 1945, e.g.) who posit a principle in history that might be called the Law of Conservation of Meaning, by analogy with the principle in physics regarding the conservation of matter. There is, this principle holds, a certain fixed amount of meaning existing in a society's life; when it is subtracted or leaches out in one place, it merely outcrops in another; what religion loses, science or art or nationalism gains; when selfless acts of civil heroism are emptied of meaning by an age of cynicism or analytical criticism or social despair, then the lost meaning will be found in selfless acts of nihilism, or in the worship of the dandy or the hermit. And just as none is ever lost, so no new meaning is ever created; what seem to be brand-new vessels of meaning—in various ages alchemy, or psychiatry, or socialism—are only catchments for meaning that has evaporated elsewhere unnoticed.*

And in 1989, the old ironbound empire rusted away, all in a few months; it had lost meaning even for those who most depended on its continuance, who couldn't bring themselves to call out the armies to defend it, and went to prison or exile or into the arms of their former victims with stunned expressions, you saw them every night on television, as one by one the sets were struck behind them, their cosmos rolled up as a scroll to reveal reality behind, shabby, scabby, blinking, like the prisoners let out from their dungeons in *Fidelio,* but right there where it had been all along. The elation of hearing human voices speaking, not in the accents of revolution or revenge but of plain humanity, civility, sense, as though you were truly face to face with them. Surely it was only because we here had not been paying attention that it seemed so sudden, whole regimes evanescing overnight and in the streets commonsensical smiling men and women young and old saying obvious things to cameras, surrounded by tens and hundreds of thousands of others.

So it happened: a new age really did begin, just as Pierce had once been tempted to promise in a book, no matter that he could actually have neither imagined nor foreseen it. And it began in Prague, there where it must, golden city, everyone's best city, city of the past and future become the present at last: just as if they had found and brought forth the stone of transformation, had known all along where it had been kept, as we all do. Václav Havel and his fellows met and spoke and argued and smoked like steam trains in their favorite *spelunkas* and then they held their forums in the Realistic Theater. Some theaters are more realistic than others. Or they met to make their plans and imagine an as yet nonexistent civil society in the basement of another theater, the Magic Lantern. The magic lantern was first described in 1646 by Athanasius Kircher, who succeeded Kepler as mathematician in chief to the Hapsburg court, and who decoded or thought he had decoded the hieroglyphs of Egypt. The magic lantern is pictured in his book *Ars magna lucis et umbrae,* the Great Art of Light and Dark, and in his illustration of the invention (p.768), the slide that is projected against a wall for some reason shows a soul suffering in Purgatory, raising his arms to ask for prayers, the prayers that will free him.

Light, darkness. In that autumn, in a Prague shop window, a poster appeared, showing a big number 89, and on it the word Autumn; arrows were drawn around it to show how it could be turned right around, and 89 would become 68, and on it when it was upended was the word Spring.

And then Mary and Vita were seven years old, and asleep in their small beds, and Pierce Moffett was preparing his midterms in Shakespeare and in world history, and Rosie Rasmussen called to give him a job.

10

Endings are hard. Everybody knows. It's probably because in our own beginningless endless Y-shaped lives things so rarely seem to end truly and properly—they end, but not with *The End*—that we love and need stories: rushing toward their sweet conclusions as though they rushed toward us, our eyes damp and breasts warm with guilty gratification, or grinning in delight and laughing at ourselves, and at them too, at the impossible endings; we read and we watch and we say in our hearts, *This couldn't happen,* and we also say, *But here it is, happening.*

When in his abbey cell he had set out on Kraft's typescript, Pierce thought it was going to turn out to be like a work out of the former age of the world, one of those vast ones like *The Faerie Queene* or *The Canterbury Tales,* which are unfinished but not therefore necessarily incomplete, their completion actually hovering perceptibly around them like a connect-the-dots puzzle half connected, or like the ghost limb that amputees feel, only not amputated but never grown. And he thought that maybe if Kraft could himself have ended it, it might have been in that way, so that what he had left undone would be clear.

But no, it wasn't like any of those works. That was obvious to him now, now having reached the end of it again, again. It wasn't like any work of the former age. Nor was it a work of the first age, like one of those endlessly cycling epics that Barr used to talk about, with simply no reason to end. Rather it seemed to be trying to become a work of the age now beginning, the age to come, which it and other works like it (not only in prose or on paper) would bring into being, of which the new age would at length be seen to consist: works that don't cycle or promise completion as the old stories or tales did, nor that move as ours do by the one-way coital rhythms of initiation, arousal, climax, and inanition, but which produce other rhythms, moving by repetition, reversal, mirror image, echo, inversion: vicissitudes of transformation that can begin at any point, and are never brought to an end at all, but just close, like day.

At the close of an August day a lot of years before, in Kraft's own study in his house in Stonykill in the Faraway Hills, Pierce had first read these pages Kraft had piled up in his last year or two and put into a copy-paper box. He had wept to discover in them a country he had once lived in, a country too far ever to reach again, even walking backward forever. And he had asked then, asked of no one, why he must live always in two worlds, a world outside himself that was real but never his own, and another within, one that was his, but where he could not stay. This old question. Rosie Rasmussen was out in Kraft's garden that day, he could see her from the window of that small room where he sat: she and Samantha her daughter, gathering flowers from Kraft's overgrown garden.

But there is only one world. Was, is, will be: a world without end. Kraft's book was finished; Kraft had finished it. It was without end but it was finished.

He left his cell, the face-down pile of papers and the glowing engine, and went through the silent halls to the little cubby where the phone was. He dialed Rosalind Rasmussen's number.

"Hello?"

Dim sleepy possibly alarmed voice. Pierce thought of or felt another time he'd awakened her by phone, far later than this: Brent Spofford beside her then, as he probably was now.

"Hi, Rosie. Sorry if it's late. It's Pierce."

"Oh. No. It's fine. I fell asleep in front of the TV."

A silence. He sensed her rubbing sleep from her eyes and brain. "So."

"So."

"How's it going?"

"Well, interesting. Rosie, it's finished."

"Oh. Wow. You've got it all copied? You're done with it?"

"I mean it's finished," Pierce said. "Kraft didn't leave it unfinished. It's a finished work."

"But you said it was a mess."

"I know. I didn't understand it."

"Well." Pause for thought, or yawn. "If you didn't, is anybody else going to?"

"I don't know. I don't know if it's *successful.* I don't know if it's good. But I know he finished it."

"There were lots of things left unresolved. In the story."

"Yes."

A soft silence like an erasing wave.

"So we can publish it now?" she asked.

"Well, *it's* finished," he said. "But now I'm not."

"What do you mean?"

"Now that I understand it," he said, "I have to go back and take out a lot of my improvements."

"Oh really? That might make it worse."

"Well. Maybe."

"Why did he write it that way? If it takes so long to understand."

"Mercy," Pierce said. "I think."

"Mercy?"

Mercy. Kraft knew that endings, all endings, trap characters in completions, and he wanted not to bind them but to free them. Not merely to end their stories in freedom, in the way that stories often do end, as several even of Kraft's own earlier books had ended—a door opens, dawn breaks, the road unrolls ahead, The End—but never to end them at all.

Mercy. Because there is an end to justice and to fairness, when everything is paid out, and all accounts are settled: but there's no end to mercy.

"You okay?"

"Yes. Yes. So. I'll bring you this."

"Okay."

"A couple more weeks. Spring break is over soon, I have to go home, go to work. But I'll keep at this."

"Okay. Come over when you want. Bring the family. What's-their-names."

"Vita and Mary."

"We'll have a day. The daffodils will be out up on Mount Randa. They're kind of famous. We can walk up to the Welkin Monument."

"Oh yes."

"You've been there?"

"I've never seen it. I've gone up the mountain. I never got that far."

"Hurd Hope Welkin," she said. "The Educated Shoemaker. The monument's really something. A surprise, when you finally get there. I won't tell you."

"Rosie," Pierce said. "I want to thank you."

"For what? You haven't even got the check yet."

"For making me do this. To find the way to finish it. I never would have, and it would have followed me to the other side, undone."

"The other side?" Rosie asked drily.

"Anyway, thanks," Pierce said. "It was just in the nickel-dime."

On the various occasions he had walked the halls of the Retreat House, going to and from the abbey church and the refectory, Pierce had passed the door of the retreat master's office, and noticed, when the door was open, the immobile figure of a white-haired monk within. The door said Welcome. Pierce had not responded; one of the things he had ascertained about visits here before he signed up was that the monks asked nothing of retreatants except reverence and silence—beyond that, your experience was your own. He had spoken to no one, and no one had spoken to him. Returning from the phone now, though, he paused there, surprised to find the office open for business, and in that moment the brother within saw him there, and raised his eyebrows and smiled. Rather than spurn the evident invitation in his look, too late to merely amble on, Pierce entered.

"Would you like to sit?" the man said. No tonsure nowadays; an ordinary businessman's haircut. He was older than Pierce had at first thought; maybe very old. "You might shut the door."

Pierce sat.

"I'm Brother Lewis."

"Pierce Moffett."

"Have you come with the CFM group?"

"No. I'm a singleton."

"Ah." Brother Lewis had a soft, unblinking gaze, and his head hung a little forward on the skinny bent neck that emerged from his robe's wide folds, so he looked a little like a kindly vulture. "You're making a personal retreat?"

"In a way. I mean yes, that's how I'd describe it."

"Are there any particular concerns you're thinking about?"

"I don't think there are any I can discuss, really."

"Are you a practicing Catholic? I only ask for information's sake."

"Actually no." He should by now be feeling very uncomfortable, but he didn't. An odd sweetness was within him. "I was raised Catholic but don't practice now much. At all."

Brother Lewis had not ceased to gaze upon him compassionately. The Trappists were known for the welcome they extended to all forms of religious rapture, and invited Zen monks and Sufis to speak; at their silent meals Rumi as well as Julian of Norwich and Böhme were read aloud. "But you haven't ceased seeking," he said.

"I don't know," Pierce said. "I'm not sure I know what that means. I know that I don't consider myself to be a believer. I don't think I believe in God. If I'm a seeker then what I've sought—or anyway what I've been gladdest to find—is evidence that God doesn't probably exist."

Brother Lewis blinked slowly. "Well, you can't mean that you can conceive of no creator of the universe."

No answer.

"I mean how does all this come to be? Just chance?"

"I don't know," Pierce said. "I don't know anything about how the universe came to be."

Brother Lewis closed his hands together before him with great slow care, and for a moment Pierce thought he might pray. But he still only looked at Pierce, maybe a shade more interrogatively.

"It's when I seem to myself to find some clear reason—in biology, or history, or psychology, or language—for *why* a religious belief, or a notion about God, might be pervasive, or convincing to people, even though it's really insupportable, or even dumb—that's when I feel I've hit the truth. That I'm on the path. Mostly."

This felt like a great relief to say, here, and Pierce even fetched a sigh when he had done. Brother Lewis nodded, then propped his cheek on his fist, which seemed a very unmonklike, or lay, gesture.

"Has it occurred to you that this might be work toward God as well?" he asked.

Pierce said nothing.

"I mean the discreating of false creations about God? Refuting false statements, rumors you might say, skeptically? It is, in fact, a way toward God, or it can be. Many mystics have understood this. Saint Thomas himself said that it is proper and right to say that God is *not*: not good, not big, not wise, not loving. Because these things limit God to the definitions of those words. And God is beyond all definitions."

"The *via negativa,*" Pierce said.

"You've heard of it." Brother Lewis said this indulgently, as you might to someone who had tossed out *extravehicular activity* or *death row* or *cast away.* So that Pierce made no nod in return. "I wonder if you have thought how hard a way it is, though. Very lonely, for a long time, as God loses his familiarity. *Not loving, not good.* Maybe you know."

No answer.

"In our spiritual practice," Brother Lewis said, "we sometimes are filled with sensations, of love, of goodness, of sweetness. Of *rightness.* All problems seem resolved, all matters clear. Tears of joy. God's love for you. And a spiritual director might say to you then, well you're very fortunate to have these moments, and you should be grateful for them. But the goal lies farther on, and has little to do with any of this. And when it's reached there will be nothing at all to say."

No answer. Either (Pierce thought) this is so, and I have gone partway without knowing it, and will never truly rest till I go on, or I'm not doing anything like the thing these guys do, whatever exactly that is, and never have.

God.

"Well, tell me," Brother Lewis said, and crossed one leg over the other, which made his beads rattle, "tell me a little of yourself. Your circumstances."

"Ah. Well. I'm, a teacher. History and literature. In a community college. And."

"Are you married?"

"Yes. I have two daughters. Adopted."

Brother Lewis seemed neither to approve nor disapprove.

"I am actually my wife's second husband," Pierce said. "She was married once before. Very briefly and unfortunately."

"Oh?" Brother Lewis's attention was caught. His vulture's head bent closer to Pierce. "So you weren't married in the church."

"Well, no. She's divorced, and . . ."

"You aren't then truly married. You're living in sin."

Hard to tell if Brother Lewis was shocked, but it was evident he was certain.

"Um," Pierce said, and lifted his hands in a miniature got-me-there gesture.

"You can't continue to live with her," Brother Lewis said. "You can urge her to return to her former husband, to whom, of course, she's still married. I don't need to quote Scripture to you. In any case you are doing her a great wrong."

"Ah well," Pierce said.

"I'm obliged to say this."

"Ah. Well."

Before Pierce could address the matter, Brother Lewis, one knee clasped in his hands, looked upward, thinking; and he said:

"You could of course go on living with her, but as brother and sister. That would be acceptable. But it might not be easy."

"No," Pierce said. "Maybe not."

"This is where prayer comes in," Brother Lewis said.

Pierce made no answer. The sweetness he had at first perceived in Brother Lewis, that stilled fear and revulsion, hadn't ceased flowing, but Pierce wondered if maybe it was coming not from the monk but from himself, the layman. He almost laughed aloud, as though the flow of it outward were ticklish. Brother Lewis put his long strange old hand over Pierce's where it lay.

"You'll be in my prayers," he said. "Be certain of that."

After a certain time, as it was meant to do when it had had no command from him, Pierce's Zenith computer shut its eye and went to sleep. Pierce returning from Brother Lewis's room looked at the blankness of it, not sleepy himself. He regarded his bed, his chair, his open bag not yet and never to be unpacked. A pint of Scotch beneath the extra jammies. His watch told him it was near nine, or Compline. He drank from his bottle, shuddering. Then he took his coat, checked for his keys and wallet, went out into the hall, closing his door softly behind him, not knowing where he would go but unwilling suddenly to sit or lie. All silent; distant sounds of washing up in the refectory. Brother Lewis's door now shut.

The ironbound door to the outside was huge. The night was clear and cold. Orion, though tumbling over slightly now, was still aloft. Pierce saluted him: Hey, big guy. You'll be gone soon. Gone to sleep in the nether waters, while Scorpio rises every night and the year grows, from leaf to flower and flower to fruit. All the same as always.

He got in his car, the number two car; the capacious new wagon had been left for Roo and the kids; this one irremediably filthy, cookie crumbs and worse down in every crevice too deep for any vacuum.

The long drive down the mountain was easy and broad, and completely dark; no habitations but the monks' for miles. Not until the road leveled and debouched onto a state highway did the world begin again.

And the flesh. And the devil. Pierce taking a left onto the highway came almost immediately on a neon-lit roadhouse: the Paradise Lounge. On its sign a palm tree and a pineapple, a pair of conga drums, and a female figure as iconic as an African sculpture, all breast and behind, but with a cheerful smile and Barbie ponytail. The Paradise Lounge offered Exotic Dancers.

Surely this place hadn't been here at the mountain's foot when he arrived. But surely it looked different in daylight. He turned in, and parked his car in a row of mostly pickups and older sedans, and sat for a moment hearing faint drumbeats and wondering if he actually meant to go in.

He had, always had had, a squeamish and sheltered boy's fear of squalor and affront, and never had liked joining his sexual feelings with those of other men in public places; maybe he didn't like thinking that his were like, even interchangeable with, theirs. So he hadn't often gone into places like this even when he'd lived in the city and they were common.

He went in.

They—places like this—had changed, it seemed, or maybe the country edition or version was different. The Paradise Lounge was a long low room with a bar at one end and a raised platform like a fashion-show runway, around which men sat as at a banquet, with their drinks, looking up, bathed in a pinkish light. He was asked for a five-dollar cover charge by a polite but large man, who then offered him the place with a hand. All yours. Smells of smoke and sweet liquor, or something. On the runway a naked woman moved with a kind of acrobatic lasciviousness to characterless rock. Entirely naked, even to her shoes, which he thought always remained. A silver stud in her navel the only manmade thing upon her. Her pubic hair removed. She seemed very young, and shockingly beautiful, nothing he had expected.

He ordered a beer from another woman, clothed, who approached him, smiling in welcome. For a time he only watched, standing at a narrow counter that ran around the room's perimeter, meant for the shy, it seemed, and now and then lifted the bottle to his lips. A vast emotion filled him that he couldn't identify. He observed that there were precise rules for what went on between customer and girl. She came on her circuit before each of them, but if you put down a bill on the counter for her, she stayed a while longer before you, made her motions for you, as the rest waited; she came close with her nakedness, brought it calculated inches from your face, front and rear; smiling and answering if you spoke, bending over you and offering her breasts like fruit, even draping over you her hair. No one else spoke, and no one, not the object of her attention nor any of the other men, called out any of the coarse exhortations Pierce supposed he might have expected: on some faces there was a beatific grin, on others a perfect sweet mammalian blank. And no one touched. No one—not at this hour on this day anyway—so much as lifted a hand from the brown bottle it held. The rules and the reasons were otherwise. But what were the reasons? Why pay to be offered and at the same time forbidden? No, something different or other than that.

A small dark man in a wool shirt and gimme hat vacated a seat at the runway, and Pierce took it. Now he too looked upward into the body of the woman displayed, or would when she came to him. He took from his wallet a wrinkled bill—how much? It seemed, strangely, that a single would do; it was all that others had put down.

Edenic. Maybe what he felt was awe. It was so shameless as to precede shame, to precede Eros even, like playing doctor, which the bare pubes also suggested. Show me yours. He and all of them swallowing down the sight of her so utterly offered. Pierce's brain, spinning along somewhat independently of his full soul, tried to think of that word, a vowel-less Sanskrit word, that Barr in one of his books said meant the entirety of nature, expressed in the revelation of female nakedness to awestruck males.

The eye is the mouth of the heart. What they were all shown here wasn't temptation followed by privation; no. What they saw fed them, he just didn't know how.

Here she was before him, his turn.

"How are you?" he asked.

"I'm real good," she said gently. "I want to know how you are."

"I'm forty-nine years old," he said, astonishing himself.

"Well. You thinking of quitting?"

She turned before him, squatting and extending gracefully. It was possible to study, in her actuality, those soft spreadings and minute tremblings that were absent from the glossy near-naked women whose images were ubiquitous now on television and in magazines, their flesh honed, machined, like something put on over flesh rather than flesh itself. Smoothed with unguents and depilated this body was, but there was no denying (why would he be tempted to deny?) that this was flesh.

"I do," he said. "Sometimes I do."

"Betcha you won't," she said, turning. "Not for years yet."

Her hair fell over him, odorous and fine. Her dark eyes on his, most unashamed of all. He felt a wave of gratitude and immense privilege, like great good luck. "You're so nice," he said. No tax on asininity here.

"I'm not nice," she said. "I'm bad."

"No," he said. "Nice."

She gazed at him from beneath her black brows, and, smiling, shook her head minutely, what's to be done with this guy; meanwhile she had begun to move away from him, his meter on empty.

"When you get to Hell," she said, "mention my name. You'll get a good deal."

"I'll remember that," he said.

"No, you won't," she said.

She was done, pretty soon after that, with her set or stint, and after a few vacant moments another woman began hers, inserting into a boom box on the stage her own special recorded selections, little different to Pierce's ear. She wore cowboy boots, a hat, and a rudimentary vest, but these last were soon discarded; the ecdysiastic art was reduced here to a gesture or two. Softer and less defined than the earlier dark pale woman, her parts smaller and more secret, she reminded Pierce of the first woman he had been naked with, how he had felt faintly embarrassed for her, so undressed, which had not caused him to cease his attentions to her; no more than to this one, striking poses over them in her boots, soft thighs quivering a little. Beyond her at the stage's edge a third woman sat waiting on a stool, bare legs crossed, cigarette in hand, a sort of vampiric or devil-doll one, but really no different, just another young woman. Pierce folded his hands before him. Since there was no end to it, only repetition, there was no reason to leave at any time, and no reason to stay longer than now. He thought of waiting till his original friend came around again, and it occurred to him that it was after all possible to spend a lot of money here. At last he was lifted up as by some external hand, and propelled toward the door. He passed the first woman, sitting at the bar, drinking with chums, now minimally clothed; she lifted her dark brows and trilled her fingers at him, so long. *And when thou descendest to Hell, where thou shalt see me shine in that subterrene place, shining (as thou seest me now) in the darkness of Acheron, and raigning in the deep profundity of Styx, thou shalt worship me, as one that hath been favourable to thee.*

He felt oddly triumphant, faintly atremble, erect generally but not specifically. He was as though rinsed in something, something delightful and right yet equally unfamiliar. He wondered if this was what the ancient Gnostic worshippers felt in their chaste naked prelapsarian orgies: that by this nakedness the rules, the iron rules of the Archons who made the world, could be broken, shuffled off, and the world and the self experienced, if only for that moment, as though the rules didn't exist. Not just the social or cultural rules that any outlaw can flout but rules a lot deeper than that: species-specific rules of courting, mating and bonding, male and female, competition and procreation, the million-year-old mammalian rules that *can't* be broken, that underlie endlessly mutating human culture and all society, tight or loose.

That was what Rose Ryder wanted, he thought. To be carried, by the breaking of the rules, by the making of other rules absurd in their strictness, to that limit beyond which everything could be forgotten, every physical constraint and fear; there to be naked and enwrapped, filled and hungry, at once and endlessly, beyond will, beyond pleasure, beyond even the limits of the flesh that bore it. He hadn't had her wild mad courage, but what he had sought in her for himself, and not only in her, what he had bent his heart and strength toward in all the multiplying beds and hearts and cunts in all his former life, what he had so often traded whatever he had for, without any deal, it was the same—not to overpower or win or have or achieve or succeed or know or even love but to *escape,* to reach escape velocity, flee through the only cleft or crack (!) that was open in the closed universe he found himself in.

But no, of course it was foolish, there wasn't any escape, there hadn't ever been an escape, for there was nothing to escape *from.* All human journeys, all flights and fleeings, can only be inward, farther into the world, no matter which way they point or where they lead, to whatever heavens or hells: because there just isn't anywhere else. That's all.

He stopped, in the cold spring air of the parking lot, with his car keys in his hand, in the chartreuse light of the Paradise Lounge girl.

And yet there is a realm outside.

There is a realm outside.

It wasn't a thought or a notion arising in his heart or head, it was as though presented to or inserted within him, something that wasn't of or from himself at all. He had never felt even the possibility of it before, and yet he knew it now with absolute plain certainty. It wasn't even a surprise.

There is an enveloping realm, beyond everything that is and everything that might be or can be imagined to be. It was so.

Not Heaven, where the Logos lives, where everything is made of meaning, or better say, where meanings are the only things. *That* realm, of any, is deep deep within. But beyond the realms of meaning; beyond even any possible author of all this, if there was one, which there was not; outside or beyond even Bruno's infinities, outside of which there could be nothing; outside all possibility, lay the realm in which all is contained.

It was so. He knew it, without any wonderment; he knew it by its total usefulness.

It answered.

It provided all that was needed for this world to be, but it touched nothing here. It made nothing, altered nothing, wanted nothing, asked nothing, urged nothing; the fact of its existence beyond existence had nothing to do with what went on here, didn't shine through it as through a dome of many-colored glass. No. This world shone with its own light, and its light is all the light there is.

It *made no difference* to the world, it didn't even know of our world's existence. All knowledge went only outward, toward it. The only part of it that could ever be in this neighborhood of ours was the knowledge that it existed. And yet that made all the difference.

Pierce knew: and now that he knew, nothing was ever going to be the same again. Here at this place, existence divided in two, before and after, though nothing, not an atom, had changed because of it, nor would.

Here at this parking lot, in this electric light, this spring night. The dancers' music returned into his ear, and he realized that for some time he had not been hearing it or anything. He looked down at the car keys he still held in his hand, three thick keys with their own golden or silver sheen, the tips of their teeth alight, so real and irrefutable. For an unmeasured time he had stood here with them in his hand.

How had he come to know this? Had he labored to learn it, without understanding that he was doing so, and here at last it was, or was it a gift, or just a random collision here of this soul with the secret? The knowledge was as infinite as the thing known, it was infinitesimal, it dwelt at the root of himself, not different from the root of being, and always had.

He opened his car door and folded himself within. The door of the Paradise opened and the music grew loud for a moment; men came in and went out; around him pickups were lustily revving their engines. He turned his lights on and drove out of the parking lot and upward again.

Well how do you like that, he thought, not shamed by his own inanity. How do you like that. In his rear-view mirror he saw the spot of light that was the Paradise grow smaller, and vanish into darkness around a curve of the road. He supposed he would soon forget this thing that he now knew, or rather he would cease to truly know it without forgetting that on this night he had for a moment been certain of it. He had begun to forget it already. He wished—he even prayed—that, now and then, it might come again to him, a whisper or a call in his ear, though he supposed it couldn't be compelled: once was more than he had known was possible, and was enough. He knew why there are things, endless things, and not nothing. And as though they had all forever been waiting for this, all leaning forward eagerly or impatiently and fixing on him, waiting to see if he would finally *get it,* those things now sank back, and let go, and letting go they went comfortably to sleep. It was all right. Pierce yawned hugely.

The never-closed gates of the abbey came before him and he drove in, dousing his lights so as not to disturb, or alert, the housemaster or porter, and rolled to a stop. He thought of his bed, his desk, the work on his desk, the unfinished finished thing. All the same as always. He felt entirely whole, as he had never quite felt before, and at the same time no different at all. He wondered if he could ever tell anything of this to his wife. He thought of going to knock on Brother Lewis's door, just to tell him not to worry, it was all okay. Would Brother Lewis understand? Maybe they could sit a while together, in silence: for there was finally nothing to say.

Down at the Paradise, things did get a little wilder and not so Edenic as the night met the morning. The stolid Mexican migrant workers who had quietly filled the seats when Pierce was there were gone, asleep in their dorms even as Pierce was asleep in his, and another bunch had come in, louder and richer and wanting more, getting it too. Women came along with some of them, shrinking back or shrieking, in delight or maybe defensively. Guys climbed to the runway and some, wide eyed and bleating, were ready to show themselves along with the girls, who managed them with skill and wisdom, gave them their money's worth too, the bouncers drawing close just in case and a sharklike police cruiser drifting slowly past without stopping. Orion set, or seemed to in the turning of the world. Dawn was green and calm when the abbey bells rang for Prime, and the men there arose to pray: the first hour of day, the hour at which the manna fell on the Hebrews in the desert, when Christ was brought before Pilate, who asked him *What is truth?* At this hour too, Christ sat down, back in his body after his Resurrection, to eat fish and honey with his disciples. In the silent Retreat House refectory Pierce sat down before his own breakfast, a more lavish meal surely than the monks were given, retreatants not expected to attain the same levels of abnegation as the *parfaits*. But then he decided that he would go to Mass instead, as he had not done since coming here. He would receive Communion. Then he would gather up his papers and his disks, clean and close his room, and go home.

11

In the Free Library on River Street in Blackbury Jambs, they will give you if you ask for it a small brochure or pamphlet, published some time ago, about the life and work of Hurd Hope Welkin, "the Educated Shoemaker." In the .900s on the lower floor, they have several of his once-popular natural history books, such as *The Daughters of Air and Water* (about clouds) and *Ancient as the Sky* (geological formations). In an alcove of the main reading room is the well-known last photograph (a Santa with fluffy beard and laughing crow's-feet) next to a framed letter of commendation from Louis Agassiz.

He was never really a shoemaker, as he's often described; he owned a small specialty boot manufactory down the Blackbury River from the Jambs, a business he inherited from his father, who really had started as a cobbler. He was self-educated, though; he never went to high school, and taught himself botany and biology and ornithology when those were branches of knowledge that could be mastered one by one, and he did come late in life to be nominated for membership in several learned societies, and (the pamphlet will tell you) campaigned to have scientific journals exempted from international postage and pass freely around the world. The pamphlet lists the four species of local wildflower he discovered and named, and has somewhat muddy reproductions of his own drawings of them. There's a picture of the big plain house on West Plain Road that burned down in 1924; he lived alone there all of his life after his parents' death (a double suicide, but the pamphlet doesn't mention that) and died on the lawn in a kitchen chair on a warm spring afternoon in 1911, *aetat* seventy-five, no age he had ever expected to reach—so he once said.

Down in the basement archives of the library are other documents, which you can consult if you can convince the librarian you have good reason to look at them, though no one has asked lately. Here are the pamphlets Welkin wrote in support of many causes, and letters to and from him over many decades, and copies of his journal *The Hylozoist,* all filed in red cases. And here too is the remarkable manuscript account of his combat over many years with a number of demons or devils who pestered him and pursued him in youth: how he suffered, and struggled; how he freed himself at last from their dominion.

There was talk after his death that his papers should go to some more august repository than the local library, which pleasant and spacious as it was for a town such as it served tended to be damp, being right next to the river; many of its older books smelled of it, faintly, shamefully. Welkin himself had made no arrangement for the disposition of his stuff. In the end it went to the library by default, no one caring to make an appeal for it to any other body or institution, maybe because it would have meant accounting for or explaining that manuscript book.

Rosie Rasmussen had read it, or read some of it, in revulsion and pity, the day she was given a complete tour of the library, from basement to dome, and a survey of its holdings. It was one of those times when Rosie went out (she felt) in disguise among her neighbors, to listen to their needs and hopes, and ask questions (when she could think of questions), and try to think of ways to help. During the time that she'd been doing this—she'd been director of the Rasmussen Foundation then for a dozen years—she had got better at it, the Zorro disguise became familiar to her and the phrases that promised to advance causes without exactly promising to pay last month's bills came more readily and with less shame. And yet now and then she would be told some extraordinary story, or have an age-old seam of need or hurt opened to her that she'd never known about, or *had* known about for years but had never understood or put together—and she would think how big the world is, all folded up though it is and so secret.

That was how she felt before Welkin's book, which the librarian lifted out of its archive box and put on the table before her. It was all handwritten, in a tiny perfectly legible hand, legible except for the paragraphs and pages of symbols meaningless to her. There were many illustrations done in what seemed to be colored pencils. The pages were sewn together with strong red thread, shoemaker's thread maybe, and there was a leather wrapper on which his name had been burned with a tool of some kind, and more symbols. No one, the librarian said, had ever recognized any of the symbols; they were his alone. Rosie turned the pages, awed by the care and thought the young man—only twenty-four—had lavished on the thing, thinking of him laboring over it, choosing among his tools, coloring carefully these demon faces, thinking. Every page had faint guidelines laid down in red ink to keep the pictures and the text squared up.

The saddest and most fearful thing in it, Rosie thought, though she'd read only a few pages, was how proud he seemed to be of what he'd done: how strong a demon battler he'd been, how he kept them at bay and hurt and harried them. How, in the end, he won, or said he had. It was almost hard to think about.

But it was time then for her to go meet the artist who claimed to be able to restore the long boarded-up pictures (of Dante, Shakespeare, Homer, and Longfellow) that filled the dome above. So Rosie closed the book, and the librarian replaced it in its box; Rosie would never look into it again.

Pins, common steel ones with colored glass heads; the smoke of burned bay leaves and certain other fumigations; abjurings and yells spoken at varying speeds; and the written *signaculae.* These, though, could very quickly be emptied of their power, thus forcing him to discover others all in a moment, which fortunately he could usually do. They knew this, in Hell, as they knew and feared his other weapons; in their great conclaves they complained to their chiefs of his depredations and the harms they had all suffered at his hands. (He made a picture of them all gathered there in Hell, just as he had witnessed it, and surrounded the picture with images of the pins, the leaves, the words, the marks, to make them suffer the more.)

They disguised themselves in ingenious ways, as animals and objects (he knew that one of the lamp mantels in the drawing room, which when lit glowed and sizzled just like all the others, was in fact a devil named Flot, but for a long time he pretended not to know). Not all of them intended him harm, not all seemed to concern themselves with him, but he felt always that he was at threat, in a way that none of the folk around him seemed to him to be: as though *they* all lived out of harm's way in Faraway County and he alone lived in some dangerous city neighborhood, Five Points, Robber's Roost, the loiterers and evildoers and unregenerates eyeing him and grinning.

Sometimes they caused him harm. Sometimes they were able to kill his birds and chase away his helpers. In the greatest and most sorrowful defeat he suffered, they killed his parents. But they could not touch him, not deeply, not mortally.

Nor did they know that he had learned how to reach the lands beyond death without himself having to die. He traversed the hilly uplands that were Heaven, and found his parents there, weak and vanishing sometimes, distracted, unintelligible, like the gibbering ghosts of Homer's underworld, but sometimes in good fettle and able to return his embraces and answer his questions. Why, if there are so many dead, did he see only the two of them here, and mere glimpses of others? They answered softly, maybe even without speaking, but he thought he heard them say that the land is vast, actually endless, room enough for multitudes. And why when he came here did he feel so oppressed and watchful, and when he was in the underworld feel so alert, so powerful, so delighted even? They didn't know, they were only sure that they would not.

Yes, when he was in Hell, invisible to his enemies, he seemed to himself to be huge and ruthless. He overheard there the devils plan how they would invite him to join their fellowship, because he was so strong an opponent they could not defeat him; then when certain ambassadors came to him in his house, he, knowing their mission, was able to imprison them in a number of bottles specially prepared, and there they stayed, unable to get out. All the while they inveigled him he had kept his eyes fixed on his mother's picture of a holy angel, star on her forehead, who guides a little child across a rickety bridge over a chasm. In such ways he imprisoned some thousands of devils in his green and brown bottles when he was at his busiest. For the frontispiece of his book, he drew a portrait of himself, showing his weapons, his beloved starling, the Cross, his bottles, and a legend: *Scourge of the Devils.*

When later on he read Swedenborg, he understood in what place he had wandered so long as a youth, for Swedenborg taught that the world beyond death has the shape of the human body: head and heart and limbs and all other members. That, then, is where he had been journeying all along, right here where he now was—inside his skin and flesh. He could laugh by then, and he laughed aloud in pity and wonder for all that he had suffered in here, in the body-shaped world, which is at once in the midmost of everything and is its outermost as well.

The later, unbound pages that are now included with the Welkin manuscript were apparently written when Welkin in later life rediscovered what he called the "Battle Book." The handwriting of these later pages is that of a different man entirely: a swift, fair-sized script, careless of margins and written on sheets of varying sizes.

In the "Battle Book" itself, there is a Welkin drawing of Horace Osterwald, in which he appears as an opponent, murderer, and front for demons; the portrait is carefully enmeshed in powerful signs, including a drawing of a beef heart pierced with tatting needles. But there is also, among the unbound pages, a photograph of him, dating from the 1870s perhaps: a lean man with a wide white moustache, a gaze of compassionate, calm inquiry (or is that simply the nineteenth-century photography face, the features composed for a long exposure?). He sits in a wicker peacock chair and holds in his lap a great curled labial shell.

Hurd Hope Welkin's parents provided in their will for a guardian for their son for life. Horace Osterwald was a church deacon and former schoolmaster, and it was he who first interested Welkin in the wonders of the created world: animals and insects, rocks and flowers. He set him to collecting and classifying, naming and sorting—perhaps to calm his spirits with work that was exacting, time-consuming, and boring, or to reveal to him that these were creatures with their own insides and not the hiding places of demon enemies or both.

Actually the demons were—Welkin knew—still there, but they had become less compelling, or attractive; he began to feel their attention slip away from him, and it seemed to him that they turned instead toward the things he studied, the things that he placed beneath his lenses, copied in colored inks: as though they hungered painfully for what they couldn't have, the sealed and well-made solidity that any leaf, any quartz crystal or hair root possesses. So he ceased to fear them, or hate them, and when we cease to fear them, or to love or hate them in fear, they lose their interest in us, and go away.

"Whether it were the attentions of that good man," he wrote of Osterwald, "who was for so long my only friend, that effected my release from the self-cast spells I labored under, or merely that (as has been often noted in cases of *dementia praecox*) the mania passed away by a natural physiological reduction, I do not know. But even now, in my old age, when I take up our albums of pressed specimens or the curious stones he liked to bring me, I can feel a sort of thrill through me that is the old madness, still lying like a long-healed lesion in my being. One of those stones was taken from the stomach of a deer, and Horace Osterwald called it a *mad-stone,* and said that it had the natural power to keep melancholy at bay. I no longer believe, if I was ever tempted to do, that it keeps me safe, but I still have it, in my pocket, for Horace was very clear that it would help me whether I believed in it or not."

From stones and plants Welkin at Horace's urgings moved on to more fearsome things, to the weather and the animal world, with their apparent free will and their malevolence or benevolence. With them it wasn't enough merely to classify and sort, because thunder clearly spoke in words to him and foxes really looked out from their eyes into his, and this conviction took time and care to overcome: not to *you,* son, Horace would say to him, taking his hand; not at *you.* Last of all he faced those wise apes or primates his fellow townspeople, whose hostile or needful souls, clothed in the figments of their flesh and their dress, he had always shrunk from.

Then when he could do that he was empty, or the world was: still, and possessed only by itself. He could ever after name the summer day on which, at dinner, he had looked up from his soup and realized that not for one moment in this day, from dawn to blue-green evening, had he feared, or sought to see, or growled at, a demon in hiding, and what was more wonderful, hadn't even noticed he had not. He put down his spoon, and with Horace he knelt on the floor and prayed. *The sorrows of death compassed me, and the pains of Hell gat hold upon me,* he said. *Return unto thy rest, O my soul, for the Lord hath dealt bountifully with thee. For thou hast delivered my soul from death, mine eyes from tears, and my feet from falling; I will walk before the Lord in the land of the living.*

He was asked later by one who knew of his experiences if he didn't regret so much of his youth spent in unrealities, and he said he felt no regret, only gratitude that he had left them behind. Maybe there's always a regret, though, that the once-possessed know, along with their thanksgiving: to feel the wild beings they have shared themselves with, the vivid powers making free within them, depart, and leave them nothing but themselves.

And his poor parents: whom no one could reassure him had not died from fear of his ungodly intractability, and grief at their own impotence to help him. He never altered the bedroom they had shared on the second floor of the West Plain Road house, and he never after entered it either.

When he was thirty years old he read Darwin's *On the Origin of Species by Means of Natural Selection,* which Horace Osterwald had long steered him away from, fearing it would threaten his religious certainties, and thus his mental health: the terror of blind, meaningless, mechanical evolution. And for a long time after he read it, Welkin watched and waited, like a man who has taken something he thinks might be poison, for the dire effects to appear. There were effects, but he couldn't at first determine what precisely they were; anyway they weren't fearful. Darwin's arguments themselves were to his mind entirely and utterly convincing; it was as though he'd known them all along, as though so far from exciting his madness they described with great beauty and hopeful clarity the world he had recently awakened into.

On a certain spring day he was botanizing on Mount Randa, the very day he discovered a theretofore unknown subspecies of *Silene virginica*, and—though he had not been pondering Darwin or his scheme for days—he understood, suddenly and yet without surprise, that what Darwin had done was to relieve God of the awful burden of making the world: of shaping every leaf and snail shell, squeezing out every litter of kittens and every pupating butterfly, building every snowstorm; relieved him both of the labor and the guilt. He had chosen an assistant to do that work, and the assistant was Chance. Indeed he probably had no choice; nothing else would do.

Chance.

Welkin wrote that at that moment there came over the world around him—he could see all the Faraways from where he stood—"a loud yet still gentle noise," and a darkening, then a brightening, as comes when we stand up too fast. But light and sound were not what they were; he could not say after what they were, except to call them, together, Love, though he said he knew that made no sense, and his soul entered a new land. He saw that he had formerly, and without knowing it, thought of God as simply the greatest of the demons: a powerful perhaps good being, but working just as demons did, working in the world, working working his designs upon us, which it was our duty to discover, if only we could; his meanings, laid deep with every fashioned thing.

But it wasn't so. There were no meanings, no workman, no designs. The world had no designs upon us. God's Love walked in Eden in the cool of the evening, our Friend, his infinite heart empty and cool, even as Hurd Hope Welkin's was just then. Together they walked down the mountain.

It was after that that Welkin began talking and writing to others; he taught natural history in his books, and God's love in Sunday school, which he was allowed to do after years had passed and he had done no one harm and seemed as sane as the next man. Hurd Hope Welkin had climbed out of the demon world and into uncreated creation, a world whose only reason for being was being—that is, no reason, no blessed reason—and found, at the end of his journey, that he was returned into the human community. For him there had been no other way but this long way around to reach it, just as Dante could not climb the holy mountain he at first set out upon without going the long way around, right through the universe. "I saw my fellows in the town hall and in the markets and I saw them in the Church at Divine Service," Welkin wrote. "They said to me, Come sit, and I did sit. I joined with them in praise and thanksgiving, not soul to soul, but now only face to face: which was to me, after all my wanderings, a great Relief."

12

And that's the last chapter of the history of the world: in which we create, through the workings of the imagination, a world that is uncreated: that is the work of no author. A world that imagination cannot thereafter alter, not in its deepest workings and its laws, but only envision in new ways; where our elder brothers and sisters, the things, suffer our childish logomantic games with them and wait for us to grow up, and know better; where we do grow up, and do know better.

I know, Hurd Hope Welkin wrote in his "Little Sermons on Several Subjects," *I know now there is truly no Up, no Down; there is no Right, no Wrong, no Male, no Female, no Jew, no Gentile; there is not Light, nor Darkness, not Higher, nor Lower; there is not* is, *there is not* is not; *there is not Life, not Death. But there surely is suffering, and joy; pain, and surcease of pain. And from these come again all the others: for men must work and women must weep, and if we are to relieve the one and console the other we must have cunning and wisdom. For this the Serpent gives us to eat of the tree of Knowledge, and we do eat, and then we turn to our labors.*

Pierce and Roo, Mary and Vita, Sam and Rosie Rasmussen, Brent Spofford, Val, Axel Moffett, all awoke within minutes of one another to find that the morning was not sunny as it had been the day before but that April silver-gray that pales and lightens the saturated greens and the violets and casts an unplaceable shine or glitter over what's looked at, or just away from what's looked at, like a secret smile.

While Roo fed the girls Pierce carried a mug of coffee up to his father's room on the third floor; if he was left to himself he might putter and daydream for a long while, and today was a day to get going.

"Axel?"

"Come in, come in. *Entrez.*"

When the door opened, though, he seemed startled to see his son. Pierce wondered whom he expected: it could be one of a number of people lately; people only Axel could see had been visiting. Axel was still in his ancient gray pajamas, which gave Roo the creeps, like cerements: as though one of her patients had moved into her own house, in an upstairs room, and taken to walking around. Sometimes through the house; sometimes in the middle of the night. Just what I need to come home to, she'd said or shouted at Pierce one bad night. Another sick old man.

And yet it was also Roo who, when Axel had called in despair a year before, had said or shouted in fury that of *course* Pierce had to take him in, of *course* there wasn't any damn thing he could do otherwise, didn't he see that, what was he going to do, tell him *no?* Pierce with his hand over the phone, caught between her rageful certainty and Axel's faraway tears. The building in Brooklyn was gone, taken by the bank. The Chief dead, the Renovators dispersed, bills Axel had no idea were accumulating falling suddenly due; judgments, liens, seizures. When? Almost a year had passed since then, Axel said. Axel had been on the street. *Nothing,* he kept saying. *Nothing. Nothing.*

"So I talked to the doctor yesterday," Pierce said. "She got the reports back on the tests and everything. Do you want to go talk to her? I can make an appointment."

"It's senility, isn't it," Axel said. "Second childhood. Sans eyes sans teeth sans taste sans everything. Mewling and puking, plucking at the coverlets."

"No," Pierce said. "Or not exactly."

"You can say it, son," Axel said with great compassion. "You can say it to me. Don't be afraid."

"Well," Pierce said. "If senility means Alzheimer's disease, you apparently don't have that."

"Ah." He seemed uncomforted.

"There are some other possibilities. You might have Lewy's bodies."

"What?"

"Lewy's bodies. It's a form of brain damage or disease." What the doctor had called it was *dementia with Lewy's bodies.* "The 'bodies' are these deposits of some kind in the brain."

"Help me, Doctor, I've got Lewy's bodies," Axel said. "And he's got mine." And he made a show of laughing gamely.

"Anyway, it's not Alzheimer's. Though apparently Dr. Alzheimer and Dr. Lewy knew each other. They were chums."

"And what," Axel asked, "is the prognosis?"

"Well. *If* you actually have it, more things like the things that have happened to you. Hallucinations. Sleepwalking. Vivid dreams. Paranoia."

Axel gave a great shuddering, self-pitying sigh. And Pierce remembered Brooklyn for a moment.

"I have not had hallucinations," he said. "I am haunted. But by the real. The quite, quite real."

"The girls," Pierce said softly, "want you to tell them again about the time you got hit by a train."

Axel's great white head turned on him, eyes full of affront. "Train?"

"They said you said—oh never mind."

Day grew brighter.

"Is it," Axel asked, "progressive?"

Pierce said nothing.

"Oh God, Pierce. You'll have to lock me in my room. I might commit some hideous crime. And not know."

Pierce made reassuring noises, but Axel rose up distracted, nearly upsetting his cup. He gripped the bedpost and stared.

"Oh Pierce," he said. "I'm so tired. I long to die."

"Oh you don't either."

"I to my grave, where peace and rest await me. I do, sometimes I do."

"*Some*times! Sometimes *I* do."

"Thou thy earthly task has done," Axel said. "Home art gone, and met thy maker."

"Home art gone," Pierce said, "and *ta'en thy wages*. Is how it goes."

"Golden lads and girls," said Axel. "Oh God." He was weeping, head high now. He wept a little almost every day, and Pierce had begun to weep with him, which astonished them both. Much of the rest of the day he was cheerful; he was, he said, himself.

"Can you get dressed? I mean, *will* you get dressed? We want to get going on this expedition."

"This what?"

"Journey. Trip. To the Faraway Hills."

"Oh leave me behind. Leave me, leave me."

"No," Pierce said, softly but definitively. "No, no. No."

"He says he can't tell sometimes whether time is passing, or rather how *much* time is passing," Pierce said to Roo at the breakfast table. "He thinks sometimes it's days since I went up to see him. That after I've gone it's hours till I come back, when it's been minutes. Not *believes.* Just doesn't know."

"Tell him to pray," Roo said. She was doing Vita's hair.

"Well, gee."

"No, I mean it. He remembers all these prayers. The Hail Mary. The Our Father. The Whatever. They aren't going to go. So tell him he should pray, and keep count, and that way he'll know how much time is going by. Keep aholt of it."

He looked at her: hair clip in her teeth, Vita's dark fell of hair in her hands.

"Okay," he said.

"Just another day," Pierce said, loading his car, the Festina wagon. "Another day of living and striving in the fields of the actual and the possible."

Striving is from strife, he thought, like living from life. Wiving from wife. He called out to his children and his father. Let's get on our way. Way is from Via, and Via is Vita; we think so, because we are the beasts who know we are on the way, that we've come from somewhere and are going somewhere else, and it might be somewhere good and it might be bad, we don't know.

"Beep the horn," said Vita. "Bye-bye house."

"Bye-bye."

"Bye-bye."

Great animals had used to roam the roads they took toward the Faraways, but they were mostly gone now, the last of them weary and slow and liable to be seen on the side of the road, hood erect or an orange sticker blinding their mirror: Cougars, Mustangs, Stingrays, Barracudas, Eagles, Lynxes. The new cars had neither beast names nor number names nor names of glamorously speedy things like Corvettes and Javelins and Corsairs; their names were meaningless syllables, which were maybe the cars' own real secret names in the land they came from, Carland: that's what Pierce told the girls. Camry. Jetta. Jolly. Corolla. His own Festina, which he was sure wasn't Latin.

Crows rose from the greening fields, or messed with dead things by the roadside, prancing and picking delicately. "God bless you, crows!" the girls called out, as their mother would too sometimes to the dusky tribe, the crow being her Totem Animal, because of her name, Corvino. "Have a nice day!" they called back to the retreating crows. "And we really mean it!"

Names. Vita and Mary, reciting their own origin story, recounted their mother's name, and how it, therefore they, came to be.

"Because her mother's name was *Rose*," said Mary, "and her father's name was *Kelley*," cried Vita, "and so she was named *Roseann Kelley Corvino*," they said together, and they laughed, as they always did at this point in the story, hearty stage laughter. How Grandpa Corvino later came to be known as Barney and how the "Roseann" turned into "Roo" or was dropped were later chapters they sometimes wanted their mother to recount. But now they stopped listening and played rhyming games, rhythmic rapid hand-patting in a pattern too quick and complex for Pierce to follow, left hands to right hands, right hands to right hands, hands to knees and hands together, never missing.

Mama mama lyin' in bed
Called for the doctor and the doctor said
Let's get the rhythm of the hand
Let's get the rhythm of the head knock knock
Let's get the rhythm of the haaawt dog
Let's get the rhythm of the haaawt dog

"Who's been teaching your children these ribald rhymes?" Axel asked.

"What's that mean?" Roo said. "'Ribbled?'"

"He means dirty," Pierce said. "Erotic. Full of double entendres."

"Are you kidding?" Roo said. "That one's on *Sesame Street*."

"It's a doctor joke," Pierce said. "Everybody knows."

The girls repeated that one a while—the last line had a rudimentary or vestigial hip swing or grind to go with it, *Sesame Street* or no—and then embarked on another, more complicated one: smiling even in their deep concentration at the jokes, but sometimes breaking rhythm to laugh, and then beginning again.

Miss Sophie had a steamboat
The steamboat had a bell
The steamboat went to Heaven
Miss Sophie went to

Hello operator
Please give me number nine
And if you disconnect me
I'll cut off your

Behind the frigerator
There was a piece of glass
Miss Sophie sat upon it
And cut her little

"Well?" Pierce said.

"Oh can it, Pierce."

Ask me no more questions
I'll tell you no more lies
The boys are in the bathroom
Zipping up their

Flies are in the parlor
Bees are in the park
Miss Sophie and her boyfriend
Are kissing in the d-a-r-k dark dark dark

It occurred to Pierce that you might be able to date some parts of the rhyme by internal evidence: that operator, like the one in Bondieu, gone now forever. But more of it was universal, eternal, coded wisdom older than the old gods. Life on earth. Oh dark dark dark.

The dark is like a movie
A movie's like a show
A show is like tee-veehee
And that's not all I know.

"There's the exit," Roo said.

~

They left the old turnpike, entered Skylands, and crossed the Jenny Jump Mountains; they skirted the Land of Make Believe without stopping, despite the children's pleas. At a certain point they crossed out of that state, and in not too long a time found themselves on the eastern bank of a wide southwest-flowing river.

"The Blackberry River?" asked the girls, but no it wasn't quite; Pierce told them how it got its name, from a certain Lord Blackbury, to whom the king long ago gave a grant of land, in what was then called Ferroway County. Long, long ago.

"Is that true?" they said.

"It's true," he said.

They crossed the bridge at Fair Prospect, and since now they had been on the road some hours, they had to stop, and there ahead, as it had always been, just where those who have turned toward the Faraways are meant to stop, was the village store by the side of the road. Pierce told the story of how he had first come to stop here, when his bus had failed; he imitated how it had tried to climb the last hill like the Little Engine that Could, only it couldn't, and here had stopped.

"Daddy, is that true?"

"You took a *bus?*"

They all exited from the Festina, small to tall, and dispersed.

The soda machine like a long red sarcophagus was, of course, no longer there; from the dark, cold waters within it Pierce had on that August afternoon chosen a Coke, and opened it on the rusted fang by the slot where you put in the quarter that it cost. Instead, a huge glowing repository gaudy as a jukebox offered drinks twice the size for four times the money. At the register, though, stood the same rack of cigarettes he remembered, many brands the same, and he picked out his brand, the ones he'd always smoked when he didn't roll his own, back in the days long ago when he smoked. The oblong pack in satiny cellophane, the smokes within yielding to his thumbpress. But it was too small: it felt absurdly little in his hand, as though it had shrunk with distance, or stayed the same as he went on, same thing. For a long time he held it as the incurious clerk observed him: turning and turning it, intrigued by the impossibility.

"The cigarettes?" asked the clerk, finger on his register.

"No, no," he said. "I don't smoke."

"Never too late to start."

"Ha ha." Camel, pyramids, sandy waste. And where would you go if you found yourself lost in this desert? Why, you'd go around to the city on the back. He returned the pack to its place.

Outside he sat down at the picnic table that was still there, going gray like himself, to wait for his women to finish in the bathroom. A great maple shaded it, its leaves begun but not done, veined damp and tender like the wings of newborn insects. Full, plush, and heavy when he'd first sat here. A little breeze had on that day stirred the leaves, and his hair. And out from that side road, beyond that now-shuttered house, had come Spofford and his sheep. Pierce sipped the Coke, and thought of those elaborately contrived fictions popular (or at least intriguing, to some) in the days he had first left the city to come here: stories that, though maybe vastly long, are shown at the end to have taken place all in a night's or a day's or even just a single moment's imagining, at the end of which the world of the beginning picks up again: the drink that was on the way to being drunk is drunk, the cigarette that was being lit is lit and the match shaken out. No time at all, thank God, has passed, except in the realm of thought, or desire: all ways (but one, for the now-chastened hero) lie still open.

"Let's go," said Roo beside him.

Now Vita and Mary were carried past the scenes of Pierce's life and Roo's life here, before their own existence. See that motel? Daddy lived there. Daddy, you lived in a *motel?* And see that place that sells cars? Mommy sold cars there; well, she helped to sell cars, with her father, Grandpa Barney. Mom, you sold *cars?* The road had been widened, the strip repopulated with the new franchises, the dealership sold Yugos and Nissans. Barney had said once that he wanted to be buried on the lot, where the test-driven cars could ride over him every day, but he lay in a cemetery, a small brass plaque at his head noting that he was a veteran of the U.S. Army, his rank and unit: like Sam Oliphant's far away.

Everything had grown smaller. Pierce caught himself thinking he was glad to have come back before it all became too small to enter, but when they actually came close to them, doors and roads and gates let them pass the same as ever. Relativity. See down that road? See that big yellow house?

Daddy used to live there; not *there,* but down that way, no, let's not go down, let's go on.

At Arcady, the Rasmussen Humanities Center, Roo parked in the new parking lot that covered a swathe of meadow where once Spofford had kept his sheep. Spofford and his truck had turned in just ahead of them, coming from the other way.

"No more sheep?" Pierce said to him, taking his hand and then falling into an embrace. "Your Totem Animal."

"Too much damn trouble. It was all I could think about, even when I put 'em on the table. The damn trouble they were." He was grinning, turning to Pierce's girls to be introduced. And Rosie was suddenly there, in the doorway of Arcady, unchanged, it seemed, not gone gray as he and Spofford were rapidly doing, bright shawl around her shoulders, and beside her a young woman Pierce didn't know, a woman who seemed to be both here and not here, graciously present, secretly absent. *Self-possessed,* he might say.

"God, Pierce!"

"Hi, Rosie, hi. Rosie, you remember Kelley Corvino, my wife. My father, Axel Moffett. And our girls, Mary and Vita, no Vita and Mary."

Roo raised a cool hand to Rosie, and put forward the girls, who in earlier years would have hung back and hid behind her, but not now. Roo didn't know that Pierce and Rosie had once slept together, but then Pierce didn't know that Spofford and Roo had. Indeed they could hardly, any of them, exactly remember these things, only the bare names of them. Gone.

"And you all know my daughter, Samantha," Rosie said, and the young woman, dark brown curls and plumbless blue eyes, put out her hand to Pierce.

Rosie took Pierce and his package—the photocopied typescript, which she'd said he should chuck but which he found he couldn't, and the set of little plastic squares within which the book hid, at once changed and unchanged—down the hall to the office. *It* was all certainly changed, clean and bright; even the floors had been bleached and varnished so that they glowed like buttered toast.

"You haven't seen all this before," she said.

"No."

"Like it?"

"Um," he said, not knowing how to answer. In the office, the same fruitwood bookcases anyway, filled with software manuals and file cases of white plastic. There were posters and notices of lecture series, conferences, calls for papers.

"You'll like this one," she said. "You have to come. We're so proud."

The topic was "Civility and Civilization: Eastern Europe After." Of course in that month of that year you didn't need to ask after what, though the term might puzzle the future. Photographs of those who were coming to speak. Pierce pointed to one in awe.

"You could meet him," Rosie said. "I mean you were there, before."

"I was never there," Pierce said.

"Sure you were. You wrote me from there."

For a moment he wasn't sure himself. The face on the poster was dark, minatory, storm-cloudy, as the man surely was not. The same picture was on the cover of a book that lay on Rosie's desk. Pierce opened it and read.

> *Genuine conscience and genuine responsibility are always, in the end, explicable only as an expression of the silent assumption that we are observed "from above," that everything is visible, that nothing is forgotten, and so earthly time has no power to wipe away the sharp disappointments of earthly failure: our spirit knows it is not the only entity aware of these failures.*

What other statesman, what other politician, anywhere ever, would say such a thing: would ever speak of failure, of his own failure, as inevitable as anyone's. Pierce felt a stab of desire to have been there for real, in that city, in the days of the man's youth and his own; to have learned a harder and a better thing than he had learned during the same years in his own bland land. He couldn't know that Fellowes Kraft, author and traveler, actually *had* once seen him—touched him even, tickled his fat belly: for the elder Havel, his father, also named Václav, had one day late in the 1930s brought his baby son to the brand-new swimming pool at the Barrandov site south of Prague where the beautiful boys used to gather on summer days. Václav Havel Sr., builder and real-estate magnate, was himself the developer of the new district, responsible for the elegant cafés and brilliant terraces and the film studios where the future was coming to be. One of the young men, a film actor, had introduced Kraft to the smiling fellow and his baby, and the proud papa had talked away while Kraft could only say *Nerozumím, nerozumím,* I don't understand, I don't understand, one of the few Czech words he knew, one of the few he wouldn't forget.

There was more than one way up the mountain. One way started, or had once, not far from Pierce's little cabin by the Blackbury River, but the broader and more popular way, a long traverse plainly marked, began at a roadside cluster of picnic tables and featured a granite plinth surmounted by a symbolic shoemaker's last, the last that Hurd Hope Welkin had not stuck to. A plaque let into the plinth listed his attributes. They all got out from the cars that had brought them there, and paused for a minute; Rosie told them a little of what she had learned of him, his strange career, how the demons had got him and let him go, or been defeated.

While they lingered there Val arrived in the same red Beetle as ever, now pied brown with primer for a last hopeless paint job and thus looking more like a ladybug than ever; on the top of the antenna a plastic flower nodded, filthy and degraded, put there so Val could locate her little car among the big ones in parking lots. Val too unchanged, in a pair of vast painter's pants for a day in the open air.

"My God, these are yours?" she asked Pierce, looking down at Mary and Vita, who looked up at her transfixed, at the cig bobbing at her lips as she spoke, the ringed hands reaching for them, to finger them like exotic goods. "How old are you guys? What day's your birthday? No, lemme guess. November."

"We're not sure," said Roo, retrieving them. "They thought February."

"Aquarius! Sure. Like their grandpa." Val turned her great gaze to Axel, who was keeping to the periphery, and who now, catching her look, gave a startled twitch. Val approached him. "They won't think to introduce me, sir, so I'll do it myself. I'm Valerie. A cousin of that lady's, the redhead there." And she and the redhead laughed, for no reason Axel could discern.

Val looked around at them all then—Rosie, Sam, Pierce, Spofford, the children, Roo. "Who would have thought," she said, and the way she said it seemed to mean that *she* would have, and had, if she hadn't actually brought them here herself by her knowledge. Then they all set out and up the trail, toward where it vanished around a bend, Axel shading his eyes and pausing in alarm.

"A long way up?" he asked Val.

"Stick with me and we'll make it."

"A banner with a strange device," said Axel. "Excelsior."

Pierce farther on walked beside Spofford. "You know," Pierce said, "you said once that we ought to climb up here sometime."

"I did."

"Yes. In fact it was the first day I came here."

"Sure. Yes. No doubt." He remembered none of this. "And here we are, too."

"Yes. Here we are."

They wound upward, by ones and pairs, transiting the mountain's face by the path's rising switchbacks, where those ahead going up leftward were sometimes able to look down and see those below coming up rightward. Pierce found himself walking along beside Sam. He studied her to see if anything remained of her from before, when he, when she. She wouldn't remember, it was fatuous to ask, even to ascertain if she had indeed journeyed here from the past they had briefly shared. He asked instead about her studies.

"Your mother didn't seem real clear on what exactly you were researching."

"It's hard to explain. I'm just really starting. I mean this is lifelong."

They walked on companionably. The mountain was as unfamiliar, perhaps as much changed, as she was.

"When I first told my mom I was taking biology," Sam said then, "she told me she had a biology question I might find out the answer to, that she'd always wanted to know. And I said I would if I could. And the question was *Why is there sex?*"

"Huh."

She nodded, it's true.

"And did you find out?"

"In a way. I found out what sex does—what it's good for, you could say, but don't tell any of my teachers I said it that way. But I didn't find out why sex is the way this gets done, if there could be a different way or not. I don't think anybody absolutely knows."

"And what *does* sex do? What's it good for? You know." He was grinning uneasily, he could tell, but Sam's self-possession hadn't altered. Soon enough his own daughters.

"It's a way of increasing the genetic variety that evolution has to work with," Sam said. "If an organism just divides, or reproduces asexually, new genetic material can't get in to produce variation, so all variation has to come just from replication errors, genetic material making random mistakes."

"That's what makes for variation? Errors?"

"Right. It's amazing when you think about it, I was amazed. If your DNA never made mistakes in replicating cells, you'd never die, you could live forever, but your offspring would never be any different from you, you'd never evolve. So the same process of replication that eventually kills us as individuals is the reason why we're here at all."

"And sex doubles the mistakes, the variations, that get passed on."

"Yes, sort of. Sex is the way we've come to do it. Have to have babies."

Remember Man that you are immortal, and the cause of death is love. What Hermes said, Hermes Trismegistus. *Corpus Hermetica,* his genetic material passing down through the ages, generating errors, making unlikely babies as others coupled with him, Bruno and all of them.

"But I don't think that's what she meant," Sam said, looking ahead to where her mother toiled upward with tall Spofford. "I think she meant why are there, you know, boys and girls. Moms and dads, who do different things. If genetic variation has to increase, what's so good about *this* way? Actually the question more is, why are there men. I mean," she said, smiling sidewise brilliantly at him, "males."

"Yes," Pierce said. "I've wondered too."

"It's what I wrote my senior honors thesis on." She lifted her head, listening: a bird sang, stopped. "Well, not really. I wrote a thesis on territorial singing in sparrows. You know it's only males that sing."

"But females call the tune."

"Right," she said, and laughed. "Yes. I studied chipping sparrows. They're going nuts right now, you can hear them. . . . So the question is this, I didn't answer it or even try to answer it, but I thought about it—what's the advantage to putting all that energy into a song?"

"So what question *did* you answer? If it wasn't that."

"I studied inheritance and variation. Statistically. Not every female likes the same song. You can show that whatever attracts a female to a male's song, the same song will also attract her sisters. And a song similar to one she likes, but coming from another male, can lure her away for a quickie, you know? And if that male fathers children with her, his daughters will share their mother's predilection for that exact type of song, and his sons will inherit some of his ability to sing like that."

"And so taste shapes chance."

"And vice versa. And we get to be what we are." She stopped, listened again. Pierce didn't know the song of the chipping sparrow, and couldn't pick it out from the chorus. "They sing so hard," she said. "You just feel sorry for them that they have to. They can sing all night in spring. They sing in the morning even before they eat. These males. They have to."

"We don't mind," Pierce said.

She smiled. He thought of her child self. Everything had changed but that smile, sign of an inward knowledge she couldn't have had as a five-year-old, but the same now that she had grown, and really did know better, or really had reason to think she did.

"You know," he said, "there's a famous anthropologist who said that the biggest problem in any human society is finding something for the men to do."

"They should study emperor penguins," she said, and he didn't know whether she meant anthropologists should, or men, or societies. "I was going to Antarctica to study them, but I got sent home. Long story. But they're amazing. The male sits on the eggs the female lays. The females go away back to the sea; the males just sit. They sit all winter long, in Antarctica, in a circle for warmth. It's dark dark dark. They don't eat. They don't move. When the chicks are born the fathers have this stored fluid they throw up to feed them with. When the females come back in the spring, stomachs full of fish, the dads are almost dead."

"Variation," Pierce said. "A lesson to us all."

"Yes. And the females lead them to the sea."

"Amazing."

"Yes. So even if there have to be males and females, they don't always have to do the same male and female things." She was starting to go on faster than he could go, bored maybe with his pace, but she looked back to smile at him again, her clear eyes deep and witty. "And that's not all I know."

Pierce stopped there. White-painted boulders marked the way upward. He didn't remember anything now of that morning years ago, in the time of his madness, when he had climbed here toward the summit and not reached it: or rather what he remembered hadn't taken place here, not any longer. But something surely had taken his hand here, something, someone, an entity aware of all his failures, and spoken to him. *It is not of thy charge.* It had been the first day of winter. There was a dog who met him on the way. And for the first time he had seen where he stood, and that he might go on by turning around, by turning back: might find, on his own, an exit from the labyrinth of the heart, his heart, and a way out into the paradise of the world: the fragile, sorrowing, inadequate, endless paradise of the world, the only one he or anyone could ever know.

After a time a child took his hand. Roo and the girls had come up to him where he stood, and pulled him along with them. Roo sang to the girls as they all went up, an old song:

First there is a mountain
Then there is no mountain
Then there is.

Then they came out of the woods, and a high steep meadow was before them. A number of those great marbled boulders dropped by passing glaciers before the beginning of the world and called *eccentrics* squatted here and there amid the tender grasses, and shelves of metamorphosed rock poked out of the earth's skin like its broken bones, compound fractures. There was no path any longer, maybe because now it was evident where you must go to reach the top. A wind had come up, the mountaintop's.

"Old Mother West Wind," said Pierce.

"And the Little Breezes," said Vita, nodding in solemn certainty.

"What's that?" said Mary, always alert to danger, and she stopped her father and her sister.

"What?"

"That."

There was a sound that hadn't been there before, a varied, subtle sound, like wind in a cave, Pierce thought; or no it sounded not entirely natural, but not like a mechanical sound either, not a distant Cessna or far-off factory humming. And it was sweet.

Samantha and Roo up ahead reached the ridgeline, and saw something Pierce and the girls couldn't yet see, and they raised their arms and seemed to laugh or exult. The end, or the goal. Roo called to the girls, who left their father and ran up to where she stood. Pierce looked back, down the path, where Rosie and Spofford came along, and his own father last, holding his hand to his heart and studying the ground around him, looking, Pierce knew, for something to pick up: but there was nothing here, nothing to spy, every leaf or blossom like any other, none out of place. Pierce waited for him.

"Pierce. I wasn't sure what had become of you."

"Almost there," Pierce said, and took his arm. Axel straightened himself, noticing now the strange sounds emanating from on ahead: and in a gesture Pierce had never seen a human perform except on stage, he tossed up his hand and held it fanwise gracefully behind his ear.

"Yes," Pierce said. "I hear it."

Now the company went, one by two, over the ridge, and as Pierce and Axel too went up, there appeared to rise from below some sort of structure, unintelligible: a tall thing of weathered wood beams and iron cabling, erect in the flowered meadow. The strange sweet noises increased, and were clearly associated with it. From the ridge's edge which Pierce and his father, last of all, achieved, it could be seen entire: twice a man's height, no, higher; a shape familiar but so outsized it was ungraspable. Everyone else was gathered around it, or else approaching in awe or delight, and, as though in greeting or acknowledgment of them all, a big consonant sound was produced.

An instrument. Not cabled but strung; a hundred strings, not for hands to play.

"A harp," said Pierce, and his throat filled with sweetness. "An aeolian harp."

"O harp and altar, of the fury fused," said Axel. "Father Kircher's harp." They walked on down toward it, and it rose over them as they did so. Axel's granddaughters stood beneath it, their hands extended and their fingers spread, mouths open too, as though every part of them could hear if it listened. Only their brown eyes were abstracted, unseeing.

"Amazing, huh?" Rosie Rasmussen asked them. "I told you so."

How did it make such a perfect concord? They talked about it. The steel strings were tuned with turnbuckles to those intervals Pythagoras had discovered, sacred numbers of which the universe is made; chosen somehow so that any of them sounded together would agree, aleatory harmonies of the wind's wanderings, for the wind bloweth where it listeth. You knew what harmonies were possible because of how you strung the instrument, but not what harmonies you'd get.

"Well, didn't David hang up his harp on the end of his bed, to hear the wind blow through it in the night?"

"I don't know," said Pierce.

"Yes," said Axel. "Oh yes. David's harp."

"Imagine a stormy night here," Roo said, and Pierce remembered one, down the mountain from here, one stormy night; all possible concords, discords too, played all at once and loud as hell. He took her hand. Vita and Mary brought their fingers close and closer, feeling the buzz of the sensitive strings transmitted into them through the changeful air; looked up to their father and mother as though to ask, *Is it true?*

There was an inscription cut into the harp's base, beneath Hurd Hope Welkin's name and dates. Val came closer and bent to read:

> *Yea, the swallow hath found an house, and the sparrow a nest for herself, where she may lay her young: even thine altars, O Lord of hosts.*

They had come up as far as it was possible to go. They stood smiling at one another and listening to the wind play the great instrument all by itself, in the same movement by which it blew the light fine hair of Pierce's children. One by one, or two at once, they put their hands upon it to feel the vibrations, as much those of the earth below, it seemed, as of the silver air around. The hills of the Faraways lay around them, they themselves upon the heights of the highest; Spofford and Val pointed to Mount Whirligig to the west across the Shadow River valley, and what might have been the blue edge of Mount Merrow, over east beyond the Blackbury's wide bolt of silk carelessly unrolled. They sat, some of them, and Roo and Rosie opened bags in which they had brought food and drink, which they divided. It seemed to one or two of them that there was no reason now ever to go farther, or to go anywhere else at all, just as there is no reason for the small pilgrims or shepherds or lovers in a painting by Claude of a mountain, a temple, a sky, to do anything further than they are doing at that moment, and at the same time they knew that when they had rested there for long enough they would have to arise and start back down again along the path, into the spring and the rain that would soon begin to fall.

LAST AUTHOR'S NOTE

With *Endless Things*, the work I have always in my own mind called *Ægypt* is as complete as it will ever be, and consists now of four parts: *The Solitudes*, first published as *Ægypt* in 1987; *Love & Sleep*, 1994; *Dæmonomania*, 2000; and the present volume. It will be noted that exactly twenty years have passed between the publication of the first part and the publication of the last. This was not my plan. The conception and writing go back ten years farther.

The present volume has been largely finished for some years; references to emperor penguins, and to speculations about Jesus' lineage, predate the current ubiquity of these subjects.

I have tried to honor the many authors and works from which the historical, geographical, or philosophical underpinnings or overlays of *Ægypt* derive. To the many mentioned in earlier volumes should be added, for the special contents of this one, *Prague in Black and Gold* by Peter Demetz; *Giordano Bruno and Renaissance Science* by Hilary Gatti, which largely informed the dialogue between Bruno and his prison visitor, though all distortions deliberate or accidental concerning his theories are my own; *The Companion Guide to Rome* by Georgina Masson, from which the fictitious guidebook entries in this book are not taken; *The Maharal of Prague* by Yaakov Dovid Shulman; *Comenius* by Daniel Murphy. There are others I can't now remember. To all these authors, and to those named in earlier volumes, their predecessors and forebears persisting and vanished, the long chain from digital Now back to Thoth, I dedicate this series.

2

Poznávací zn. vozidla | Mezinárodní zn. vozidla
Tovární zn. vozidla | Barva vozidla

ŽÁDOST O ČESKOSLOVENSKÉ VÍZUM

Příjmení	Jméno	Den, měs. a rok narození	Muž Žena
CROWLEY	JOHN	1 DEC 1942	M

Stát narození	Místo narození	Stát bydliště	Místo bydliště
MAINE	PRESQUE ISLE	MASSACHUSETTS	TYRINGHAM 01264

Ulice bydliště	Státní příslušnost	Povolání
WEBSTER ROAD	USA	WRITER

Název zaměstnavatele	Sídlo zaměstnavatele
SELF	SAME

Místo pobytu v ČSSR - okres	Jméno navštívené osoby - instituce - hotelu v ČSSR
PRAGUE	

Účel cesty do ČSSR	Doba pobytu	Spolucestující děti do 15 let	Série a čís. cest. pasu
RESEARCH			A100 895

Razítko PK - ODJEZD

Razítko PK - PŘÍJEZD

John Crowley

Podpis

Upon arrival in the Czechoslovak Socialist Republic you are obliged to register with the Czechoslovak police authorities within 48 hours.

Please type or print in Roman letters all the … case of illegibility the application will not be considered.

John Crowley was born in the appropriately liminal town of Presque Isle, Maine, in 1942, his father then an officer in the U.S. Army Air Corps. He grew up in Vermont, northeastern Kentucky, and (for the longest stretch) Indiana, where he went to high school and college. He moved to New York City after college to make movies, and did find work in documentary films, an occupation he still pursues. He published his first novel (*The Deep*) in 1975, and his fourteenth volume of fiction (*Lord Byron's Novel: The Evening Land*) in 2005.

Since 1993 he has taught creative writing at Yale University. In 1992 he received the Award in Literature from the American Academy and Institute of Arts and Letters. He finds it more gratifying that almost all his work is still in print.